NOT PART OF THE PLAN

BLUE MOON #4

LUCY SCORE

Bloom books

Not Part of the Plan

Copyright © 2017 Lucy Score

Cover by Kari March

ISBN: 978-1-945631-06-1 (ebook)
ISBN: 978-1-7282-8265-7 (paperback)

Published by Bloom Books, an imprint of Sourcebooks
P.O. Box 4410, Naperville, Illinois 60567-4410
(630) 961-3900
sourcebooks.com

lucyscore.com

082322

*To Ginny and Harold
and Ila and Lloyd.
Your happily ever afters
are my inspiration.*

1

*N*ikolai Vulkov shifted his weight from foot to foot, his scuffed leather boots planted on the pretty farmhouse porch. Flowers in a rainbow of colors exploded out of planters and hanging pots, a testament to spring's celebratory arrival after an interminable winter.

Spring meant new beginnings. Not that Niko wanted one of those. He'd prefer to go back, back to a time when everything in his life held a little magic. He hoped like hell it was possible to go back because forward no longer held the appeal it once had.

The lowing of a cow in the pasture beyond the house drew him back to his purpose. He was probably making a huge mistake. *Definitely probably.* His lips quirked at the irony. World-traveling fashion photographer "The Wolf" was vacationing indefinitely in Blue Moon.

Oh, yeah. He was definitely losing his mind. Niko raised his hand and rapped lightly on the door before he could change his mind and get back in his rental car. A cacophony of crying, barking, and yelling erupted from within the neat-as-a-pin two-story.

"Mommy needs *some* hair, Meadow!" The front door was wrenched open by the woman he was here to see, Summer Pierce. At least, he thought it was Summer. His chic, lovely, always put-together friend was grimacing as a baby—or was she a toddler now? —yanked a fistful of corn silk tresses out of Summer's ponytail with chubby fingers. Summer's t-shirt had several stains in varying shades and degrees of dried-on-ness.

The hulking dog next to her, spotted black and white like the cow in the pasture, stood hip high, and when Valentina yawned, Niko guessed she could accidentally swallow one of the twins with ease.

Summer's pretty, bare face lit up when she processed his presence over the stimuli of sobbing child in her arms and another inside. "Oh, my God! Did I forget that you were coming?" she asked, her denim-blue eyes widening more when she spotted his duffle bag at his feet.

"I winged it. I should have called ahead," he said sheepishly.

Summer yanked her daughter's fist out of her hair again. "No! I'm just so happy to see you. And thrilled that I didn't forget. How long can you stay?"

Niko scratched the back of his head. "A while. If that's okay?"

He saw the spark of curiosity flash to life in her eyes and was relieved when her husband bellowed from the back of the house. "Who is it, babe?" The crying inside intensified, and another dog, a chubby beagle, slunk down the hallway casting wary glances over its shoulder.

"Poor Meatball," Summer clucked at the dog as he sidled his hefty body up next to her.

Summer shoved Meadow into Niko's arms and grabbed his bag. "I'm so happy to see you, by the way."

"I'm glad to be here." *At least, he hoped he would be.* The hopeful desperation that bloomed across Summer's face made him wonder if it wouldn't have been a better idea to have his life crisis on a sandy beach on the Mediterranean.

"Carter! We have reinforcements," Summer shouted as Meadow began to cry in his arms.

THE TWINS at fourteen months were teething again—molars this time. "It's only temporary," Summer insisted brightly as she lugged his bag upstairs. Niko, still carrying the now quiet Meadow, followed her over a baby gate at the top of the stairs and into the sunny bedroom at the front of the house.

Meadow, to his relief, seemed content to stare warily up at Niko with eyes the same brilliant blue as her mother's.

"The main bath is all yours," Summer said, placing his bag on the narrow desk under the window before flopping down on the patchwork quilt that covered the bed. She yawned. "I forgot how comfortable this mattress is," she sighed.

"So, how's life?" Niko asked, hiding his smile.

She yawned again. "Amazing. Like absolutely amazing. Also, exhausting."

Meadow must have taken offense to her mother's statement because she chose that moment to sneeze, sending a shower of slobber and snot all over Niko's button down.

"Crap. Four seconds in my house, and we've already ruined your very nice Tom Ford. Sorry about that. Fluids just fly constantly around here," Summer apologized.

"I figured that's how you got twins," Niko joked.

"Ha. There's a whole pile of clean burp rags across the hall," Summer said, directing him with an outstretched arm. "Missed you," she called after him when he ducked out the door.

In the nursery, Niko found the towering pile of cotton cloths in every shade of pink and blue. Meadow's little arms flapped like a baby bird when she spotted a stuffed giraffe in the closest crib. She made a squealy cry that sounded as if it might intensify into a shriek.

Panicked, he snatched the giraffe from the crib and shoved it into her grabby hands.

While Meadow amused herself by biting the giraffe in the face and cooing, Niko grabbed one of the clean-looking towels and scrubbed it across her face and then his shirt.

She frowned at him and let loose a stream of gibberish that sounded vaguely accusatory.

"Yeah, how about we let your Mom handle that?" Niko suggested.

"Mama?"

"Yeah, her."

"Mama," Meadow insisted, nodding enthusiastically.

Niko crossed the hall again and entered the bedroom. "Hey, Summer—"

A soft snore was the only response. Summer was curled on her side, face buried in the crisp white pillow, sound asleep.

"Mama!"

Niko shoved the giraffe back into Meadow's mouth and hustled out the door and down the stairs. In the foyer, he picked up the gift bag he'd brought with him and headed into the kitchen to find Carter.

"Dada!" Meadow squealed.

Carter took the little girl from him and jiggled her. "Hi, sweetheart," he said planting a loud kiss on her head.

"Hi, honey," Niko snickered.

They shook hands in manly fashion. "It's good to see you, man," Carter said. "Did we, ah, know you were coming?"

"Your wife, who passed out on the guest room bed in the thirty seconds I left her alone, asked me the same thing."

"We're not getting a whole lot of sleep this week," Carter said, carting Meadow to the fridge and reaching for two beers.

"Hang on," Niko insisted, handing over the canvas bag. "Maybe we should start with this."

One-handed, Carter fished the bottle from the bag.

"Bless your taste in alcohol," Carter sighed, gazing lovingly at the vodka. "Have I told you that I love you?"

"Never," Niko said, rescuing the bottle when Meadow made a sticky-fingered grab for it.

"Let me put this troublemaker in baby prison with her brother. Glasses are in there," Carter said, pointing to a glass-faced cabinet next to the pantry.

Niko poured two fingers each into rocks glasses while Carter deposited Meadow into an octagon of baby gates and pillows in the great room. He appreciated the design of the great room addition. Huge trusses held up the two-story cathedral ceiling, and sets of French doors that ran the length of both sides of the room flooded the space with light. The hulking flat screen, the one that had inspired him to upgrade his own TV in his apartment, was mounted above the stone fireplace.

The kitchen was just as well done. There were enough modern conveniences—like the oversized fridge and stainless apron sink deep enough to bathe a dog—to balance out the farmhouse charm in the white cabinetry and view from the windows.

"They should be good for at least two minutes," Carter announced, returning and grabbing a glass like it was anti-venom.

"Rough week?" Niko asked.

"Our daycare was closed all week. Disney trip for the

woman who runs it and her family. So we've been splitting shifts, which wouldn't be horrible if it weren't for molars." He sipped and sighed.

Niko swirled the vodka in his glass and shook his head. He couldn't imagine living Summer and Carter's life, but wasn't that part of the reason he was here? To see how the other half lived?

"What brings you to Blue Moon besides a desire to babysit?" Carter asked.

"Funny." A shriek from the great room echoed off the hardwood and granite. "Uh, are they okay?"

Carter shrugged. "Happy scream. We've got another minute before it gets ugly," he predicted. "How's your life these days? What's it like not being sticky all day and interrupted fifty times a minute?"

Niko worked up a smile. "It's, ah, great." Wasn't it? Didn't he have everything he'd always wanted? Carter didn't look like he was buying it. If there was anything Niko knew about his best friend's husband, it was that Carter Pierce knew bullshit when he saw it.

Thankfully, Niko was saved by the banging open of the kitchen's screen door. A harried redhead with pink cheeks, an overflowing tote bag, and a baby strapped to her chest rushed in, bringing with her the warm spring breeze.

"Oh, my God! I got so sucked into this ad revenue report that I lost track of time," Gia Pierce, Carter's sister-in-law, gasped, skirting the island and dumping the bag on the floor. Her fingers flew over the confines of the wrap that housed her tiny bundle. "I've got class at noon and a private session after that. You're still good with her until two, right?" she asked, handing the sleeping baby over to Carter.

"Beckett will be here for his shift to cover for me and Summer as soon as he gets out of his meeting so we can make sure the farm hasn't burned down and Thrive is still thriving," Carter recited, expertly tying himself into the wrap.

"There are fourteen diapers in there, and you better pray it'll be enough." Gia pointed at the bag. "Hey, Niko," she said, giving him her sunshine grin and skimming a kiss over his rough cheek. "I didn't know you were visiting!"

"Hey, Gia," he said, returning the kiss. "Gorgeous as always." He'd photographed her for Thrive's New Year Yoga piece the year before, and they'd hit it off. However, he couldn't imagine anyone not enjoying Gianna Pierce. She was strong, confident, and ridiculously flexible. She was also a disaster with details and constantly losing everything except her children. She and Carter's brother Beckett, Blue Moon's beloved mayor, ran herd on three kids, a dog, and a three-legged cat.

"Catch up later?" she demanded, plucking the glass out of his hand and sniffing.

"Sure. Vodka," he said, answering her unasked question.

She surprised him by taking a healthy swig and sighing. "That'll get me through class!

"How about dinner at the brewery tonight?" Carter suggested.

"Not cooking after the week we had? Hell. Yes." Gia said. Her green eyes widened. "Oh! Speaking of the brewery before I forget again..." she dug through the tote on the floor and pulled out a large manila envelope. "This was accidentally delivered to Thrive's office. It needs to go to the brewery. Can one of you sexy, strapping men drop it off with my sister? I think Emma's been waiting for it."

Gia's phone chimed interrupting her stream of consciousness. "Shit. That's my 'you're already late' notice. Dinner tonight!" She swooped in and pressed a quick kiss to her daughter's forehead. "Mommy loves you, Lydia."

When the door banged closed behind her, an ear-splitting scream sounded from the great room at the same time that a rank stench rose from the baby strapped to Carter's chest.

Carter wrinkled his nose. "Jesus, kid, what do they feed you?"

She answered by filling her diaper as if it were an Olympic sport.

"I'll take the screaming," Nikolai volunteered. Anything to stay away from that diaper. He knocked back the rest of his vodka, squared his shoulders, and marched into the great room.

"Coward!"

*N*ikolai used the temporary lull in screaming children to escape the Pierce house and run the package up to the brewery. Carter made him promise twice that he would give the brewery manager a head's up on a Pierce family dinner.

"The last time we showed up *en masse* unannounced, she made us eat in the bottling room," Carter had explained.

"Don't you own the place?" Niko had asked.

"We also sign her paychecks. But that doesn't make her less scary," Carter had warned him.

Niko took the warning and the envelope and headed out on foot following the dirt path behind the cheery red barn that cut across the property to the brewery. Meatball the beagle jogged along at his heels.

The rich bloom of spring was so different here from New York's careful, measured resurrection. The city had spent most of the wet winter blanketed in a soupy, gray slush that ruined shoes and kept moods foul. But here, under the upstate sunshine, spring was breathing life back into the fields and hills.

His photographer's mind captured and catalogued the way the light played over the lush green grasses caressed by the warm breeze. If he were shooting it, he'd have the model face away from him dancing through the field on an endless, sun-drenched adventure.

But he wasn't shooting. And if he was being honest with himself, this moment was the first he'd felt even remotely interested in picking up his camera in a long time. Boredom and lethargy had crept in behind the lens clouding his eye.

A flock of chickens darted out in front of him, and Meatball gave a half-hearted yip and waddled after them into the field. Niko's boots scuffed at the dirt, and he turned his face toward the sunshine.

Pierce Acres and the funky little town had a certain novel appeal as did spending some time with Summer. He'd worried at first that she wouldn't have room in her new life for him. But moving, marrying, and having twins hadn't dampened Summer's insistence that they remain friends. Between his sporadic visits to the farm, she made a point to come into the city to catch up with him nearly every month.

Friendship intact, he'd turned to her without thinking, without questioning, in his own time of confusion. Maybe a week or two of Blue Moon fresh air would be enough to snap him out of whatever funk he'd fallen into.

EMMALINE MERILL ROLLED her eyes behind the hostess stand at John Pierce Brews as the supplier on the other end of the phone blatantly lied and then attempted to tap dance her way into the runaround.

"Lynlee, let me stop you right there," Emma said briskly, flipping through the reservations on her tablet and taking note of the evening's larger parties. "I ordered your stunning peacock blue table linens not only because they exactly match the groom's eyes, but they are also a dead ringer for the bridesmaid's dresses. So no, swapping out peacock blue for the periwinkle ones you tried to sneak past me won't work. I have every confidence that you'll do whatever it takes to get me the linens I ordered by tomorrow morning."

When she hung up thirty seconds later, Emma was satisfied that Lynlee was scrambling to keep the promises she'd just made, and a man who might as well have had Bad Boy tattooed on his forehead was in her space staring at her.

He was tall enough to make her tilt her head back to take in the full picture. Artfully distressed jeans were worn low on narrow hips. Under his battered leather jacket, a slim fitting button down in slate gray hinted at a very taut stomach beneath. His boots, scuffed leather, probably cost more than the Tamara Mellon pumps she had tucked in her office for the evening.

His hair was thick and dark and carelessly tousled as if he'd just rolled out of someone's bed. A day's worth of scruff on his perfectly chiseled jaw played up the bad boy look. His dark eyes held darker promises, and there was just the faintest hint of a smile playing on his firm mouth. Aviator sunglasses were tucked into the opening of his shirt.

He had to have an accent, Emma decided. Gorgeous, badass men that looked like that had accents and made poor life choices.

"Can I help you?" she asked, trending on the cool side of polite. She didn't fall for bad boys anymore. She kept them at a safe distance where she could admire the way their jeans fit without becoming collateral damage.

"I'm looking for you," he said in a voice made to tempt women into dark corners.

Damn. No accent.

"Oh, really?" Emma kept her tone light. She knew the rules. *Don't give a playboy anything to play with.*

"If you're Emma, I am."

She crossed her arms, drumming her purple manicure on her upper arms. "What can I do for you, Mr....?"

"Vulkov," he offered. "Nikolai."

"Wolf?" Emma translated the Russian with an arched eyebrow. "How appropriate."

He grinned at her then, and the full wattage was dazzling. Emma felt her pulse kick up in reflexive appreciation for the fine male specimen before her.

"I like you, Emma." The way he said her name, like it was something that tempted him, irked her.

"I'm sure you like a lot of women, Mr. Wolf," she countered. "Now, if you'll get to your point, we can both get on with our days."

"Please, call me Niko," he corrected her, seeming to be in no hurry to get to the point.

Her brushoff appeared to have no effect on his attentiveness or his amusement. Emma was used to dumping a little cold water on men's egos now and then when necessary. However, this particular man appeared to be immune to it.

"Your sister asked me to deliver this to you, and Carter is requesting a dinner reservation for the 'whole family.'"

"Are you family?" she asked, the curiosity getting the better of her. He certainly had the tall, dark, and gorgeous thing going that the rest of the Pierce men did.

"Friend of," he said.

She wondered just whose friend he was and made a mental note to quiz Gia when she had a moment. Not that she was interested, just curious. Emma pursed her lips and opened the reservations again even though she already had them memorized. "I guess you can have the loft at 6:30," she decided.

He winced. "6:30 dinner on a Friday night?"

Emma felt her lips quirk. "City boy?"

"New York, born and raised. You?"

"L.A. most recently," she said, plugging in the reservation. "Blue Moon takes some time getting used to." She'd been here nearly a year and was still getting used to the town's quirks.

"I've visited before." And the way he said it made her think that Mr. Vulkov had seen enough of Blue Moon to be a little apprehensive about his stay.

"How long are you staying?" she asked, mostly out of politeness.

"As long as it takes." He shoved his hand through his hair, somehow making the new mess even sexier.

His answer was cryptic, and she left it at that. She didn't have the time or the inclination to play "getting to know you" with a bad boy stranger who looked like he was accustomed to women's attention.

"Excuse me, Emma?" A petite pixie of a woman with close-cropped dark hair, a tiny nose stud, and a John Pierce Brews t-shirt bustled up with the cordless phone.

"What's up, Lila?" Emma asked, grateful for the server's interruption.

"Rupert's on line two trying to call off again," Lila said with a dramatic eye roll. "He and Sunny broke up. Again."

Emma bared her teeth. "You can tell Rupert that he can either get his skinny, heartbroken ass in here or I'm hiring Sunny's new boyfriend to replace him."

Lila's big blue eyes got even bigger. "Seriously?"

"No! Gimmie." Emma held out a hand for the phone, prayed for patience, and gave Rupert a sympathetic greeting.

She didn't have a lot of time before opening, so she was

going to have to make it quick. In four minutes, she got to the bottom of Rupert and Sunny's fight, convinced him that not only would showing up for his shift give him a chance to apologize to Sunny but the tips he'd make could go toward a bouquet of apology flowers.

That had him sufficiently perked up enough to promise to be on time.

She hung up, giving it a fifty-fifty chance that the gangly perma-teen would actually show, and immediately launched into the next call that came from scorned girlfriend and dining room server, Sunshine.

Emma paced as she talked, helping Cheryl the bartender flip down barstools around the massive U-shaped bar made from reclaimed barn wood. She signed for a delivery and waved to Julio and Nan when they arrived to open the kitchen all while working on Sunny over the phone.

Girls were tougher to talk down than guys. But after eight minutes, Emma had Sunny convinced that the girl's best revenge for Rupert ditching their two-month anniversary date so he could pull an all-nighter playing a medieval zombie video game with his cousins would be to show up at work looking gorgeous and happy and ignore his very existence.

Emma disconnected after procuring Sunny's promise that she would indeed show up to "rub Rupert's face in her awesomeness" and then dialed Every Bloomin' Thing.

"Hi, Liz," she said, when the floral shop owner answered. "Is there any way you could make up a pretty spring bouquet and have it sent over to the brewery tonight? I'd love you forever."

"I just did up an arrangement of roses and lilies in yellow and pink. Will that do?" Liz asked.

"Does it look like a solid apology for skipping a date to slaughter zombies?"

"Oh, Rupert. When will you learn?" Liz sighed.

Blue Moon's grapevine had clearly been working overtime. Emma did her best to avoid it, even refused to accept the invitation to join the town's gossipy Facebook group.

"Yeah, these'll work," Liz decided. "I'll throw in a purple ribbon since that's Sunny's fave."

"You're my hero," Emma sighed. "Put them on my card, please."

"With all the business you've thrown my way the past year, this one's on me. I was coming in for dinner anyway," Liz told her.

"Then the first round of drinks is on me," Emma promised. She heard the tinkle of the front door bell on Liz's end, and Liz called out a greeting.

"Gotta go. Jax Pierce just stormed through my front door looking like he's in trouble with the wife."

"Mmm, tell him he's having dinner here tonight with the rest of the family so he'd better apologize fast," Emma warned.

"Will do," Liz said cheerfully. "I'll see you tonight."

Emma thanked her profusely and hung up. She glanced at her watch and muttered a string of curses under her breath. She was officially behind schedule.

She needed to talk specials with Julio and program them into the POS, double check that the keg room was in order, and count the bar drawer.

Inwardly cursing the lovesick antics of her team, Emma turned to drop the phone back in its cradle at the bar when she spotted Nikolai helping Cheryl flip the rest of the stools at the high-top tables.

She crossed her arms and watched, keeping a mask of disapproval in place. He moved with economical grace, hefting the stools as if they weighed no more than folding camp chairs. His shirt stretched tight over an expanse of chest and well-honed biceps, and the rolled-up sleeves allowed a peek at the ink on his arm.

From the looks of it, Cheryl was overjoyed with the help *and* the view. She fanned herself and winked at Emma behind Nikolai's back. *Not everyone could be immune to a gorgeous male as she was*, Emma thought with a sigh. But not everyone had learned the lessons she had.

She straightened her shoulders and cleared her throat. "I'm sure you have better things to do than help us open, Mr. Vulkov."

Her voice carried across the expanse of space. Nikolai flipped the last stool and sauntered toward her.

"Nikolai," he said again. "I didn't want to interrupt you while you were playing puppet master." He picked up the leather jacket he'd draped over the back of a stool. "And I didn't want to be rude and leave without saying good-bye."

"Good-bye," Emma said pointedly.

He laughed, low and husky, and pulled on his jacket. She smelled leather and spice and cursed him for being everything sexy.

"I can't wait to see if Rupert and Sunny work things out tonight," he told her.

"All I care about is my employees showing up on time for their shifts," Emma lied in irritation. She wasn't innocent enough to fall for the old "I'm so interested in you I'm actually listening" routine.

"Do you always lie to strangers?" Nikolai wondered with an arch look.

"Do you always overstay your welcome?" Emma shot back. *Damn. She was kind of enjoying the verbal sparring.*

"Only when I'm not ready to leave. I'll see you tonight, Emma." His parting smile set her blood humming. He was completely immune to her Ice Queen routine. She knew from experience that the men who were immune to it were generally too stupid or too wrapped up in what they wanted to care about crossing boundaries. But Nikolai Vulkov was different. He found the freeze off... entertaining.

"Please tell me he's single and in town looking for a wife," Cheryl demanded, joining Emma to watch Nikolai's fine form walk out the front door of the brewery.

"That kind of man is never looking for a wife," Emma sighed.

"What's his story?" Cheryl asked.

Emma shook her head. "No idea. He's a friend of the Pierces."

"That, my gawking gals, is none other than uber-famous photographer Nikolai Vulkov," Lila announced, joining them at the hostess stand. "He's Summer's BFF. They worked together in New York for years. He visits occasionally but showed up today at one unannounced on their doorstep with a bag and no end date for his visit. Usually he's seen escorting the sexiest of models around the city or Europe or wherever he's working, but he's been pulling a hermit the last few months."

Emma stared at Lila. "How in the world do you know all that when he got here only two hours ago? Do you have Summer and Carter's place bugged?"

Lila patted her arm. "I keep forgetting you're still relatively new here, Em. We know everything about everyone. That's just from Blue Moon's Facebook group, which you should totally join, and a little society column digging I did. Mooners are predicting he's facing some sort of life crisis and came here for perspective."

Emma's gaze returned to the entrance. A life crisis? Real life players didn't have life crises.

3

---

*D*inner was a circus. The Pierces and their progeny occupied the entire loft of the brewery, and Nikolai soon realized it wasn't necessarily an issue of space. Emma had tucked them away to protect Blue Moon from a chaotic dining experience and the Pierces from being interrupted every five seconds by Blue Moon.

Beckett, or Mr. Mayor as his brothers ribbingly called him, had been called downstairs three times before the appetizers arrived to deal with a little town business and shake a few hands. Each time, he took a different kid with him to make the rounds. Evan, technically both Beckett and Gia's stepson, was a mini mayor at thirteen with neatly combed hair and the uncanny ability to carry on conversations while wrangling his two little sisters. There was no "step" about the relationship between Evan and his parents that Nikolai could see.

And there was no awkwardness between the Pierce brothers and their mother's fiancé, Franklin Merill, the jovial restaurateur holding court at the head of the table. Phoebe Pierce juggled grandbabies that were passed their way and grinned as if there was nowhere in the world she'd rather be.

The youngest Pierce, Jax, appeared to be in the midst of a battle royale with his wife, the sarcastic and leggy Joey. Just by looking at them, Niko could tell the fight was more foreplay than fury.

Niko was wedged in between Joey and Summer at the long table. The upstairs of the brewery had all of the charm and architectural impressiveness of the first floor. The same scarred, pine floors from the first floor ran the length of the dining and bar area on the second. The massive timber rafters loomed above their heads reining in the sheer space and reminding all beneath that they were drinking and dining in one of the oldest structures in Blue Moon.

Old and new twined together within John Pierce Brews. Wood that could claim decades or centuries of previous lives gleamed under sexy industrial lighting. A small freight elevator ran all three levels of the barn from basement keg room to loft. The art was all local with pastoral prints and bucolic landscapes.

Niko had to hand it to them. The Pierces had an eye for design. And judging from the rumble of the crowd below, the population of Blue Moon appreciated it as well.

He sipped his saison and observed the energy around him. It would be a fun scene to shoot. The blur of action while freezing a smile, a laugh, in time. Here, perhaps, was what had pulled him back to Blue Moon. Summer had married into a real family. A large, loud one. But here, even an outsider could see the love that flowed fast and deep.

They ragged on each other in one breath and offered a helping hand in the next, each depending on the other. They formed their own community, a village, a family.

Niko shook himself from his reverie. He wasn't here to feel envious of the Pierces. He was here to remind himself how much he loved the life he'd already built. Consuming, exciting work, sleek, interesting women, and many of the finer things in life that a padded bank account could provide. He called the shots and had climbed the ladder high enough that he now chose his assignments.

And yet, suddenly it wasn't enough.

He thought about what an entertaining distraction Emma would be. He felt the corners of his lips lift. She ran hot and cold in a way that fascinated him. Orchestrating the happiness of her employees in one breath and then coolly shoving him out the door in the next, she was nothing short of intriguing. And it had been a long time since he'd found a woman that intrigued him.

He'd seen her when they'd arrived. Emma was dressed in the same slim pencil skirt and black sweater she wore earlier. But she'd exchanged her flats for impractical stilettos. He couldn't help but watch her as she shifted from task to task, greeting guests, hopping behind the bar, poking her head into the kitchen. She'd given him a cool nod before warming up her greeting for the rest of the family.

For whatever reason, Emma was insistent on putting him in his place, and that place was as far away from her as possible. He couldn't wait to find out why.

He felt the weight of a gaze on him and found Summer eyeing him expectantly as if she'd already asked him a question.

"What?"

She shrugged delicately, her shoulders moving beneath the silk of her blouse, and smiled. "Just wondering when you're going to come clean about what you're doing here."

"I'm visiting my overly suspicious friend and her family."

"Are you on the lam?" she asked conspiratorially over her wineglass. "Did you murder a model?"

"No," he said dryly.

"Get caught in bed with a married woman?"

He felt the energy of the space change and looked up to spot Emma standing within earshot. She held a plate of wings, and the chilly smile on her lips told him Summer was confirming what Emma had already believed about him.

And for the second time that day, he felt everything else lose a few shades of vibrancy as his attention focused solely on her. She leaned over him to slide the wings onto the table, and he caught the hints of citrus and vanilla on her skin. She'd pinned her wild curls back in a low twist, showing off a delicate bone structure and the sensual line of her neck. Her skin was a lovely ivory, and he couldn't tell if the flush on those high cheekbones was skillfully applied makeup or a natural glow.

She was enchanting, like some sort of magical fairy, yet she moved with the determined energy of a general marching into battle.

He brought himself back to the conversation that was currently giving Emma the wrong idea about him.

"The only married woman who's been in my bed is you when you passed out in it this afternoon," he reminded Summer loud enough that Emma would hear.

"Slept for two whole hours," she announced proudly. "I feel like a new woman. Also, remind me to get you a new pillow since I drooled all over yours."

She leaned over to pick up the pea-encrusted spoon Jonathan had flung to the floor. The baby's toothy smile meant he'd be pitching the spoon overboard again next chance he got.

Summer dumped a fistful of organic puffy treats on the table in front of Jonathan and expertly tossed the container to Carter who repeated the move for Meadow.

"Seriously, though," she began again. "You look sad. And

while that lonesome, Russian cowboy thing will probably get you a million dates, I get the feeling it's not just an act geared toward luring in the ladies."

Niko glanced up at Emma who made solid, smug eye contact with him before leaning down to put Evan and Aurora in headlocks.

"How are my favorite niece and nephew?" she asked as they both tried to wriggle free.

"Aren't you supposed to be so absorbed in motherhood you forget all about your big city friends?" Niko asked, changing the subject.

"No one could forget about you, Niko." Summer fluttered her eyelashes at him. He watched as Emma blew her father a kiss and headed back downstairs without another glance in his direction.

"If that's how you flirt, you're lucky you locked down Carter. You'd scare the guys off with that eye action," Niko teased.

"She doing her creepy eye flutter?" Carter asked, leaning in to snag a fried green bean from his wife's plate and dropping a kiss on her forehead.

"It's not creepy," Summer insisted. "It's highly effective." Summer hooked her fingers into the opening of her husband's Henley and pulled him down for a kiss.

Carter grinned down at her and winked before shifting his attention to Joey. "You hire any more help yet, Joey?"

The brunette's spine stiffened to the snapping point. Joey's hair, which was pulled back in a serviceable ponytail, quivered with rage.

"Oh, so now you're siccing your brother on me?" she demanded, jutting her chin out at Jax.

Jax raised his hands defensively. "Hang on to your bitch fest, Brunhilda."

The table "oohed."

"I didn't sic anyone on you. But maybe you should take the opinions of your partners into consideration instead of going into your vacuum of stubbornness."

Joey bared her teeth at her husband, and Niko sat back to enjoy the show. He knew from past visits that Joey ran the stable operations and new breeding program for Pierce Acres. She tended to be more than a little territorial about it.

"You think I'm not doing my job?" she demanded, daring someone to drop the accusation.

Jax wasn't one to back down from a fight. "I think mucking stalls is a waste of your god damn time," he snapped back.

"So you think that because Calypso, one of the finest pieces of horse flesh in the country, is ready to foal at any damn moment that I should cut back on my time in the stables?"

Carter waded bravely, or stupidly, into the fray. "Look, Joey." His tone was calm, even. "You are the most valuable piece of the stables operation, and if you're going to insist on spending your time dabbling in basic tasks, we'll bring someone in to help you run it. We'd all prefer for you to hire help, but if you want a manager, we'll bring in a manager. It's up to you."

For a second, Niko thought there might be bloodshed. But then Beckett put down a beer in front of Joey.

She hefted the glass and Niko knew women well enough to know she was contemplating dumping it on one of the Pierces. The table breathed a sigh of relief when she sipped instead. "If you have a problem with my performance—"

"Oh, for fuck's sake!" Jax threw up his hands. "Do you see what I deal with?"

"Joey," Carter sighed. "You're wasting your time handling

all of the shit that we could be paying someone else to do. And to get it all done, you're pulling twelve-hour days."

"I want things done right," she snarled, clenching her jaw.

Jax yanked her chair around so she was forced to face him. "Then train someone to do it exactly how you want it done. Be a god damn barn Nazi, and stop wasting your own time."

It felt like an old argument to Niko with lots of history on both sides. Summer and Gianna wisely pretended they were deaf to the discussion and focused on entertaining the kids with their grandparents.

"I'll help, Jo!" Aurora, Gianna's firecracker of a daughter with her halo of red curls, piped up. When he had arrived for dinner, she had proudly announced to Niko that she was almost a second grader.

"Thanks, Roar," Joey acknowledged the little redhead, some of her temper disappearing.

"She can shovel sh—"

Evan's comment was cut off when Beckett cuffed him affectionately in the back of the head.

"Ow!"

"Language," Gia said mildly.

"But Uncle Jax said f—" Aurora's defense of her brother was cut off when Evan clamped a hand over his sister's mouth.

"I'll explain double standards to you later," he hissed.

Franklin's laugh boomed out, and the tension that had settled over the table fizzled out.

Jax leaned in and whispered something in Joey's ear, and while the stiffness in her shoulders remained, Niko saw the corner of her mouth lift.

Emma returned with pitchers of water to top off the glasses. "See how we rate? Service from the manager. How's the crowd, Emmaline, my lovely?" Franklin said with a fatherly smile. Emma gave him a smacking kiss on the cheek and did the same to Phoebe.

"Under control, at least downstairs," she said, pointedly eyeing Joey. "How are my two favorite soon-to-be-newlyweds?"

Niko had learned that Franklin and Phoebe were finally tying the knot in a week, and he was invited. Their engagement had stretched out first to accommodate the weddings of each Pierce brother and then the building of their dream home on the farm. Now that construction was complete and four of their six combined children had been married off, it was time for them to tie the knot.

"We're thankful you let us crash your restaurant tonight so none of us had to cook." Phoebe's eyes twinkled behind her dark rimmed glasses.

"Happy to accommodate," Emma said, topping off their glasses and moving around the table. "Everyone having a good time?" she asked, her gaze landing on Nikolai before flitting away again.

They all answered in the affirmative.

"Good. Because I could have sworn I heard shouting, and I know you wouldn't want to ruin a paying customer's night with a family squabble," she said as she skillfully juggled water glasses and doled out guilt.

"Emma, you're still new here. A family feud in Blue Moon draws a crowd," Phoebe teased.

"Just try not to shed any blood. The stains are hard to get out of the linens," Emma said, leaning over Nikolai and reaching for his glass. He made the mistake of looking up at her and felt a swift, almost painful awareness rush his body when those gemstone green eyes met his. She felt it, too. He could tell by her white-knuckled grip on the pitcher.

Emma fumbled his glass, nearly upending it, and Niko closed his fingers over hers on the glass to steady it.

Yeah. There was something there, he thought. *Something worth exploring if he could get past the prickly exterior.*

Emma slid her hand free but didn't move away. And when she leaned in, the anticipation of what she would say had his blood thrumming. She was unpredictable, and he liked it.

But instead of moving her lips against his ear, she was whispering in Joey's.

"There's a girl downstairs who says she wants to see you," Emma said quietly.

Joey frowned. "Literally everyone I care to know is sitting around this table."

"She's young and very determined," Emma told her. She hesitated a moment and then added, "She looks hungry."

Joey tossed her napkin on the table and sighed. "Fine. Whatever. It's probably better than listening to these assholes browbeat me."

Jax gave his wife a winning smile, and Joey rolled her eyes at him. She made a move to get up from the table but stilled when she saw the girl waiting at the top of the stairs. Joey and Emma shared a look that Niko couldn't read. Some kind of feminine intuition was in play.

The girl was tall and lanky and looked barely old enough to drive. Her hair, somewhere on the border of blonde and brown, was tied back in a long braid. Her pale skin had a smattering of freckles over her nose and cheeks. She had solemn brown eyes.

Emma was right, Niko thought. She looked hungry and very determined. Joey got up and he saw the girl straighten her thin shoulders under the plaid shirt that had seen too many washings. She stalked toward Joey with a purposeful stride.

"Mrs. Pierce?" she offered her hand to Joey.

Joey took it, shook. "Mrs. Pierce is my husband's mother. Call me Joey."

The girl nodded showing no hint of a smile.

"I'd like to work for you at the stables," she announced briskly.

Joey turned back to the table and glared at the Pierces. "Which one of you dildos put her up to this?" she demanded.

"What's a dildo, Mama?" Aurora asked in an unsuccessful whisper.

"Aunt Joey will explain later," Gia said, shooting a dark look in Joey's direction.

The girl retook control of the conversation. "No one put me up to this," she insisted. "My name's Reva. I've had riding lessons before, and I like horses. I'm strong and a fast learner, and I'll do what you tell me. I'm always on time, and I have no life, so I'll work as many hours as you can give me except for school. I'll muck, I'll groom, I'll feed, I'll clean tack," she ticked the tasks off on her fingers, her pitch coming out in a rush.

"If you worked for me, and I told you one of these 'gentlemen' was banned from the barn, what would you do if he tried to weasel his way in?" Joey asked jerking a thumb at the Pierces.

"I'd chase him out with a pitchfork," Reva answered, showing no hint of humor.

Niko saw it in the girl's eyes, the pride, the hope, and that sliver of hungry desperation. *For the love of God, Joey,* he thought, *give the girl the job.*

"Fine. You start tomorrow. Be at the stables at seven," Joey said.

Elation and disbelief sparked to life in Reva's sad eyes.

"Seriously?"

"Yeah, seriously," Joey said, shaking her head as if she was already regretting it. "Now go away before I change my mind."

Reva surprised them all, and possibly herself, by throwing her scrawny arms around Joey before practically dancing down the stairs. Emma turned to follow her.

"Happy now?" Joey demanded, tossing a middle finger at Jax and Carter.

"That's the bad finger!" Aurora giggled. "What's a dildo?"

"Joey, you're scarring my kids," Beckett teased.

4

*N*iko rose and hustled after Emma. He caught her on the stairs between the Friday night happy hour crowd on the first floor and the family chaos on the second. "Hang on, Emma," he said, touching her arm lightly. She tugged away from his touch and nearly keeled headfirst down the stairs.

Niko's hands clamped on her arms to steady her.

"Holy shit," she breathed. "I would have broken my face."

"It's too nice a face for breaking. Why the hell are you wearing those shoes?" he demanded. "You're going to be on your feet for hours."

"I like to look professional," she said, frowning up at him. But this time she didn't try to pull away.

"This is Blue Moon. They'd think you'd look more professional in clogs or Birkenstocks."

"I like these better than clogs," she retorted. "And are you really keeping me from my plethora of managerial duties on a very busy Friday night so you can complain about my footwear?"

"A. No one said I was complaining. I like the view just fine. B. I'm taking up your time because I want to add something to my order."

"If you say my phone number, I will throw your ass down these stairs."

"Actually I was thinking dinner—"

"You're not my type," Emma announced it as though she'd said those very words a thousand times before.

"Actually, I meant Reva. You were right. The only time she looked away from Joey was to stare at the appetizers on the table. She's hungry."

Emma blinked. "You want to buy Reva dinner?"

"Yeah."

Her face softened marginally. "I already have the kitchen putting some sandwiches together for her," she confessed.

"Why, Emmaline," Niko teased her with her full name. "Patching up employee love lives *and* feeding mysterious strangers? If I didn't know better, I'd say you had a heart."

Her smile, grudging though it was, was worth his wait.

"If I didn't know better, Nikolai, I'd think maybe you weren't just a vapid player."

Niko laughed. "Go out with me. Just once, Emma. I'll take you to the nicest place in Blue Moon and let you insult me all night."

"A. This *is* the nicest place in Blue Moon. And B. I don't date masochists," Emma said, her tone haughty.

He studied her a moment, enjoying the energy that sparked between them and the light of challenge in those moss green eyes. "At least do me a favor," he cajoled.

She raised a perfectly sculpted eyebrow.

"Throw in a few pieces of apple pie with the sandwiches and put it on my bill."

"That I can do."

"Look at us getting along." Niko tempted his luck and leaned in a little closer.

She didn't back off. Instead, Emma leaned in to whisper in his ear. "Hands off, Big Bad Wolf. I'm no one's Red Riding Hood." And with those parting words, she ducked out of his grasp and sauntered down the stairs. There was a little extra sway to her hips that Niko hoped she put there just to torture him.

~

NIKO CLIMBED the stairs with a grin on his face. Emmaline Merill was a challenge, and that's exactly what he needed right now.

He spotted the now obviously made-up Joey and Jax locked in a passionate embrace outside the second-floor restrooms and averted his eyes. As many times as he'd shot romantic scenes, nothing ever exactly compared to the real thing. There was no Photoshop filter to mimic the look and feel of two people in love.

He returned to his seat and found his meal waiting for him.

"What was that all about?" Summer asked, bouncing Jonathan in her lap.

"What?" he asked, not bothering to cover his smirk.

"You bolting out of here after Emma." Summer tugged a strand of hair out of her son's grabby fingers. "I've never actually seen you run after a woman before."

"Maybe I never met one worth chasing." He picked up his beer and laughed. Summer's blue eyes were wide with shock. "Relax. I just wanted to ask her something."

"Did you ask her out?" Summer hissed.

"Only to annoy her," he grinned. "She turned me down."

"And does she have any clue that's like waving a cookie in front of Clementine?"

"Your metaphors are suffering since you moved here."

Summer snorted. "Tomorrow, I'll give you a cookie to wave in that goat's face, and you'll see exactly what I mean," she promised.

"Nothing like down on the farm fun," he quipped. "Now tell me everything you know about Emma."

Gia, who was delivering a freshly changed Lydia to Beckett, overheard him.

"You and Emma?" She leaned between them and snatched a French fry from Niko's plate.

"Thoughts?" Summer asked.

Gia nipped the fry in half. "As much fun as my sister would have with you, dear Niko, it's never gonna happen."

"Reeeally?" The way Summer drew out the word told Niko she was firmly in his corner. "I think you're underestimating the appeal of my Russian bad boy pal here. He's more than just a pretty face."

"That's the problem," Gia insisted as if he weren't there. "He's the exact opposite of her type. Sexy playboy who only does casual flings? She goes for golf playing, preppie guys with boring jobs. There's no way straight and narrow Emma is going to give up on her idea of Mr. Perfect for a steaming hot roll in the hay with Niko here."

Summer frowned, considering. "Care to put some action on it?"

Gia's grin was quick and sharp, a predator sensing easy prey. "Oh, hell yeah. One unit?"

"I'm feeling lucky. Let's make it two."

Gia whistled. "Someone's awfully confident in your flirting abilities, Niko," she teased.

"Oh, good. You remembered I'm still here."

They ignored him and, shuffling babies, shook on the bet.

"What's a unit?" he asked.

EMMA LET herself in the front door and pried off her shoes, sighing with relief. She could have changed out of them for closing. But Niko's criticism weighed heavily in favor of an extra hour of torture just to prove she could. Her sisters called her stubborn. Emma preferred to think of herself as strong-willed.

Her feet were tough and so was she, she thought, dumping her bag on the little foyer table she'd added to the cottage's décor.

Her self-imposed year-long trial period in Gia and Beckett's guesthouse coincided with the one she gave herself at the brewery. And she was officially sure it was time to start looking for a place of her own in this ditzy, sweet town.

Emma limped into the tiny kitchen where she poured herself a glass of Merlot. She'd been worried that the culture shock of leaving L.A. for Blue Moon would break her brain.

It had taken her some time to get used to the little town and its... quirks. But Blue Moon had won her over with its unapologetic weirdness, unpretentiousness, and pride in its oddity. Everyone was welcome here, enfolded into the culture without being asked to assimilate. In Blue Moon, you were good enough just because you existed.

That wasn't to say that it hadn't still been a difficult transition. In L.A., she'd go out for drinks with friends after closing. The night was just getting started. In Blue Moon, by the time the brewery's midnight closing rolled around, the rest of the sleepy town had been shut down for hours.

She took her wine to the window and stared out into the night. She was content here. Maybe a little lonely in the late nights, but that was to be expected. Yet, she couldn't quite shake the feeling that she was waiting for something. And the only thing she knew for certain was that she'd find it here.

She wasn't unhappy, Emma qualified. But she also wasn't the deliriously ecstatic woman Gia was.

She looked out at the main house that rose cool and white in the sliver of spring moonlight. Its gables and elegant trim cast a romantic spell. Within its walls, her sister loved and lived. *Is that what she wanted?* Emma asked herself. Was she ready to finally call someplace home, finally ready to start her life?

A vision of the devastatingly gorgeous face of Nikolai Vulkov rose in her mind's eye. That crooked, cocky smile, angular cheekbones and granite jaw. He was exquisite and other-worldly... and he obviously knew it. Emma wondered why, when he looked as he did, he chose a life behind the camera rather than in front of it.

She could only imagine the agents and brands that would quiver with anticipation at that face. Niko was like a joyride. Something dangerous and ill-advised that would make a woman's system sing until the adrenaline wore off and she had to face the consequences of a bad decision.

Niko was a bad idea, and she was wise enough now not to fall prey to a pretty face again. He was not the stable partner she was looking for. Of that she was sure. And it would be best for her to forget all about him.

With a sigh, Emma sank down on the couch. She pulled her tablet into her lap and dialed her night owl sister on the video chat app.

Eva's pretty face and disheveled hair filled the screen.

"Hello, fellow night dweller," Eva said by way of a greeting.

Emma's little sister wrote mysterious technical manuals for a living and moved around like a vagabond, but Emma managed to catch up with her once or twice a week. It was usually late at night when normal people were tucked safely into bed.

"So, how was your date this week?" Emma asked. The incurably optimistic Eva was always on the lookout for love.

"Ungh." Eva wrinkled her nose in distaste, inching her reading glasses higher. "He lives with his grandmother as a freeloader and mentioned we should go back to my place to have sex since 'Gram-Gram is a light sleeper.'" She shoved her hands through her mass of red hair that she hadn't bothered styling that day.

Emma choked on her wine. "So how was it?" she teased.

"Oh, my God. You're disgusting!"

"Where do you find these guys?"

Eva rested her chin on her hand. "This one I met in the convenience store. He picked up the iced coffee I'd ordered. I thought it was a mistake and a 'meet-cute', but looking back, I think he was trying to steal it."

"Eva," Emma sighed out her sister's name.

"Hey, at least I'm meeting guys. You live in Hot Guy Heaven and have yet to land a sexy farmer or a poetic candle maker. I know Beckett is fresh out of single brothers, but there's got to be some cousins in that family tree."

"For your information, I did meet someone today," Emma tossed back.

"Does he freeload off of his grandmother?"

Emma couldn't imagine Niko freeloading off of anyone. "Definitely not," she answered.

"Ill-fitting glass eye that falls out?" Eva asked.

"I'll make him blink extra hard next time I see him to make sure. You know the guy on the cologne commercial?"

Eva sighed dreamily. "The one who comes out of the water glistening like a Greek god, and he's wearing those sexy white briefs that you can almost see through?" She closed her eyes and let her mouth spread in a feline smile. "Chest like a linebacker? Biceps perfect for defending damsels in distress?"

Emma nodded. "That's the one. This guy is cologne commercial hot. I bet women walk into glass doors staring at him. I almost took a header down the stairs looking at him."

Eva squealed. "More information please!"

"He stops traffic when he walks in the room, and when he looks at you, your heart literally stops."

"He looked at you?"

"It would have been weird if he didn't look at me while he asked me out." Emma allowed herself to gloat just a teensy bit. "Technically, he demanded that I go out with him."

Eva pressed her hands to her flushed cheeks and then her face lost all its glee. "Why'd you say no?"

Damn. Emma hated being predictable. "Who says I said no?"

Eva rolled those emerald green eyes heavenward. "You *always* say no. What was wrong with Mr. Perfection?"

"He's got this whole 'dangerous, bad boy, player' thing going. Not my type."

"You're bad boy prejudiced," Eva accused.

"Shouldn't we all be?" Emma felt her defensiveness kick in. "This guy is an award-winning fashion photographer. He's probably got a new model on his arm every night of the week. He's the kind of man who would talk you into dropping your panties in a coat closet at a party, dole out orgasms like after dinner mints, and then never call you again."

"I don't think you're making the point you think you are,"

Eva interjected, wistfulness tingeing her tone. "I keep hoping I'm going to call you one day, and you'll have eloped with someone you met in a rainstorm with a flat tire."

Emma shook her head pityingly. "You are so weird."

"Subject change?" Eva offered.

"Definitely," Emma agreed. "When are you coming in for the wedding?

5
_____

On Saturday nights, Cheryl the bartender had fallen into a routine of kicking Emma out by ten or eleven if the brewery crowd was manageable. Emma didn't mind putting in the hours, but she also understood the value of not working fifty-hour weeks.

She'd watched her father struggle with the impossible work-life balance of a single parent. He'd had three young daughters and a restaurant to run. Growing up, she'd spent more hours at her father's restaurant than the family home.

To this day, every time she smelled simmering marinara and fresh basil, she felt awash in childhood memories.

Emma wrestled her gym bag from the backseat of her Escape and swiped her badge through Fitness Freak's card reader. In Blue Moon, one's options for late night entertainment were limited to drinks at Shorty's or sweating it out at the twenty-four/seven gym. Inside, the gym was empty. No one else had decided that Saturday night was the perfect time to work up a sweat within the lime green walls lined with weights and machines.

She changed, cued up her workout playlist, and packed up

her work clothes. She moved quickly, not that she was in a hurry to get on the rower, but it was just how she lived. Emma did everything at high speed. On busy nights at the brewery, it was a full shift of adrenaline. Even a finely tuned food service machine such as herself could be pushed to the limits on busy nights. No two shifts were ever the same, and that was what she loved about it.

While she ordered the rest of her life around measurable, timely goals, her desire for excitement and chaos, her own dirty little secret, was met in the restaurants she ran.

Emma pushed through the locker room door pulling her hair into a tail when she became aware of another presence.

Nikolai Vulkov's leanly muscled frame was ruthlessly banging out pull-ups on the rig across the room. His gaze met hers in the mirror, and he muscled out five more reps before hopping off the bar and turning to grin at her.

"You just made my night," he said in that throaty voice that served to both irk and arouse her.

Emma didn't like the flitter of excitement that raced through her at being all alone with the wolf. She debated ignoring him but decided that would only make him try harder. And it was already impossible to ignore him. Dressed in dark mesh shorts and a gray sleeveless tee, he offered a view even Emma couldn't help but enjoy.

"What brings you to Fitness Freak at this time of night?" She kept her tone polite, but the curiosity was real. If anyone should have Saturday night plans, it was the man before her. She was staring too long, pretending not to admire the sweat-slicked biceps and the hard-muscled thighs.

"My kind and generous hosts have been in bed since nine-thirty. I'm not used to such quiet, early evenings. Especially on a Saturday," he confessed, swiping his arm over his forehead.

"Ah, the charming culture shock of small town life," Emma

nodded in understanding. "I bet they cooked dinner tonight instead of going out."

He grimaced. "I've never seen anyone in New York use their kitchen for anything other than wine storage and catering space."

"It's a whole other world here," Emma agreed with a half-smile.

Niko took a swig of water and grinned. "There. That wasn't so hard, was it?"

Her eyes narrowed. "What wasn't?"

"Having a friendly conversation."

"I can be friendly," she argued. "But I can also recognize your type from a mile away."

"And what type is that?" he asked, stepping dangerously close to her.

Emma watched as beads of sweat trickled hypnotically over the sinewy curves of his shoulders and down his veined arms.

"The type that sees something shiny, plays with it until he gets bored, and then drops it when the next shiny object comes along."

"So a cat?" he drawled out, amused.

"Look, let's just get this out of the way, shall we? I'm not looking for anything—" she waved her hand at his spectacular torso, "that you have to offer."

"Not even scintillating conversation and foot rubs?" He was teasing her and enjoying himself.

"Nikolai, I'm sure you're a very good time. I'm just not in the market for a temporary good time. So the sooner you stop wasting your time with the flirting, the sooner we can settle into casual acquaintances."

His eyes narrowed as he watched her. "I find you fascinating."

Emma rolled her eyes. "It's because I said I'm not interested. Believe me, the novelty of my disinterest will wear off soon enough," she predicted.

"What can I say to make you like me?"

To prove that she could shove him as off-balance as he made her feel, Emma took a step closer. "Tell me you don't do casual." She felt a sense of satisfaction when he took a step back. "Tell me you're looking for something long-term. Tell me you don't date model after model after model because you're looking for something real." She advanced on him until she backed him into the eye-searing lime green wall behind him. "Tell me you've decided to pack it all in and move to Blue Moon to find a partner in life that will support you, challenge you, and be there for you day after day."

She poked him in the chest. "Tell me all that without lying, and I'll not only like you, I'll ask you out."

He opened his mouth, closed it.

"That's what I thought," she said, smugly. She felt like she'd won a small victory. At least until his hands lashed out, grabbing her by the shoulders. Nikolai spun her around, and now she was the one with her back to the wall.

"I don't need to apologize for my life choices," he told her. Their closeness, his dominance, had Emma's system zinging. He was tall enough that she had to look way up to deliver her glare.

"I'm not asking you to apologize. I'm trying to illustrate our basic incompatibility," she said snippily.

"Touché." He grinned down at her, placing a hand on the wall behind her. "Since we're putting it all out there, I find your distrust of me oddly fascinating."

Emma let out a groan. "Let's connect the dots. You don't do relationships, right?"

Niko pursed his lips in thought. "I do mutually beneficial casual."

"Good. Fine. Great," she shrugged, waving a hand. "I *only* do relationships."

"So I'm just supposed to give up?" he frowned.

"Yes!" Emma hadn't meant to shout the word, but at least the volume seemed to have gotten her point across. "Sorry. But we've just expressed our differing points of view and now we —and by we, I mean *you*—can start respecting each other's boundaries."

The sexy grin that curved his lips sent a warm feeling sliding through her stomach. "Because if I continued to pursue you after you've made it very clear that you're not interested, I'd be a douche."

"The douche-iest," she affirmed.

His smile was heart stopping.

"So then we'll just be friends," he decided.

"Friends?"

"You know, we'll talk, we'll laugh. You won't throw things at me, and we won't have sex. It'll be fun."

Emma remained skeptical. "In my experience, men and women who are physically attracted to each other never make it as friends." She realized her misstep immediately and blamed it on his proximity. It was hard to think clearly when over six feet of pure, gorgeous male was looking at her with an underwear-dissolving grin.

"As a gesture of my goodwill toward our fledgling friend-ship, I'm going to ignore the fact that you just admitted to being physically attracted to me." He gave her a wolfish look. "I want points for that, by the way."

"Fine. Five points, *pal.* Now if you'll excuse me, I'm going to work out." She ducked under his arm and made a show of shoving her ear buds in place as she strode over to the rowers.

Niko could say the "f" word as often as he wanted, but that didn't make her body stop reacting so strongly to his presence. She needed some space.

She climbed on the rower, set the damper, and tightened the straps around her feet. And frowned.

Even with '90s pop blaring in her ears, Emma knew exactly where Niko was in the gym. She'd never met anyone so magnetic, not even Troy, the player who'd played with her heart, and the fact that she was so aware of Nikolai annoyed her. She had made a deal with herself years ago that she'd never again be that girl, falling for a handsome face and plea-sure-promising lips that said all the right words.

She reached for the grip and noted the goose bumps that dotted her arms. "Seriously?" She yanked an ear bud out of her ear.

Niko was straddling the rower next to her. "What? We're friends, and now we're in the same boat."

"Cute," she said dryly, fiddling with the digital screen readout.

"Your sarcasm is one of the many reasons I treasure our friendship," Niko said conversationally.

She laughed. She couldn't help it.

"Friends work out together, you know," Niko explained.

"Whatever," Emma sighed and shoved her ear bud back in. The first few pulls served to wake up her arms and legs. Over her music, she could hear the steady whoosh of air being forced through the rower's fan.

She hit her stride with deep, steady strokes and felt her muscles warm. She tried to focus on the digital readout, not the virile sex god pumping his steel hard legs on the rower next to her.

His pace was faster than hers, which Emma took as a direct challenge.

Together, they stroked side by side, their skin sweat-drenched and flushed with exertion. Next to her ivory paleness, his skin was a dusky gold courtesy of ancestry and recent tropical sun, she guessed.

She couldn't hear his breathing over her music—now a Joan Jett anthem. But she could watch him out of the corner of her eye. He wasn't slowing his pace, so she refused to also.

Her breath was coming in ragged but measured gasps as the meters ticked up. Pulling, pushing, reaching. She dug deep until finally, finally she coasted over the two thousand-meter mark. *Damn.* She'd bested her PR by a full eleven seconds. *Maybe Nikolai Vulkov was worth knowing platonically after all?*

She glanced over at Niko who looked as if he'd just finished a leisurely walk around the town square. *Bastard.* He swiped a eucalyptus scented gym towel over his face. "What's next?" he asked.

"Look, I know we're BFFs now, but I really do prefer to work out alone," Emma said.

He paid no attention to her complaint and followed her to the weight rack where she chose a set of dumbbells. It was high-intensity interval night, and she really wasn't thrilled about having an audience.

Niko grabbed a pair of dumbbells double the weight of hers. "So what are we doing, buddy?"

She crossed her eyes at him in the mirror. "Squat press burpees, pal."

Emma had to hand it to him. Niko hung with her through burpees, squats, and press jacks. He used the plank intervals to fire questions at her.

"Did you get Reva to take the food last night?" he asked.

Emma tried to keep her voice steady even though her body was trembling in the plank. "She was reluctant until I told her it was a to-go order that no one showed up for. I asked

Beckett about her since he knows everyone. He said in his diplomatic, mayoral voice that the mother is 'troubled'—alcohol and generally poor life choices—and there's a younger brother," she told him, her abs vibrating as the seconds ticked down on her phone's screen.

"I'm glad Joey gave her a job at the stables," Niko admitted. He didn't even sound out of breath, and that annoyed her.

"If she hadn't, I was going to offer up a hostess job that we didn't have," Emma admitted.

"Softy."

"Don't let it get back to my staff. They're all appropriately terrified of me."

"As well they should be," he laughed. "Did Sunny and Rupert make up?"

"Caught them making out in the walk-in cooler when they were supposed to be doing side work. So, yes for now."

He shifted gears from work to life. "Where did you grow up?"

"How did you get involved in restaurants?"

"College?"

He didn't press when he asked about her mother, and she told him she'd left. Instead, he smoothly redirected and asked her how she felt about her father's upcoming wedding.

The physical exertion and the sweaty god-like scenery kept her walls down just enough that his persistent questions didn't bother her much.

He asked her about life in Blue Moon versus L.A. About her youngest sister and about her own culinary skills. By the time the interval timer on her phone buzzed, announcing the end of their self-inflicted torture, Niko knew her GPA in college and how old she was when she found out that Santa wasn't real.

Emma guzzled water from her glass bottle and felt her

muscles vibrate. She'd pushed herself harder with Niko there, a lot harder. His mere presence seemed to challenge her.

"What's next?" he asked.

She eyed him. "Yeah, you see that sweat angel I left on the floor over there? That means I'm done."

"But the night is young," he protested. "Emma, I beg you. Be a friend. Don't send me back to the house yet."

She glanced at the clock. It was nearly midnight, the dead of night in Blue Moon.

"Let me buy you a drink," he said suddenly. "Please, just tell me there's a bar that's still open."

She chewed on her bottom lip, considering.

"Just as friends," he added. "I'll let you ask me questions."

"Just friends," Emma clarified warily.

He held up his palms. "Platonic pals. I'll even let you buy the first round."

She was probably making a mistake. A six-foot two-inch, gorgeous mistake. But the offer was more appealing than burning off her post-workout buzz alone at home poring over sales reports.

Shit. When had that become her Saturday night? she wondered, horrified.

"Let me get cleaned up, and we'll go. I get to ask the questions. We drive separately. And if we run into anyone named Ellery or Rainbow, you're my first cousin."

"Do I want to know what that last stipulation means?"

Emma shook her head. "You really don't."

"Deal."

She was already regretting it when she pulled a hoodie over her sweaty tank in the locker room. Her hair was an unsalvageable nightmare, so she piled it on top of her head in a knot. She frowned in the mirror, remembering the care she used to take with her appearance for drinks on a Saturday night or dinner on her nights off with Mason. Mason, the nice guy who she probably would have ended up marrying had it not been for Jax's job offer. She'd given him little thought since her move to Blue Moon. It felt like light years ago. A different life, a different person.

She wrinkled her nose in the mirror. She smelled like gym socks, and her abs were a quivering mess from the planks, and she was about to go out on the town with Nikolai Vulkov, famed photographer and model-dater.

He'd impressed her, hanging with her through every plank, every interval. She liked a man who wasn't afraid to work hard. Those lean, hard muscles were clearly earned and not just from a genetic lottery.

She heard a loud thump beyond the locker room door and shoved her things in her bag before rushing out.

"What was that?" Emma asked, glancing around. "It sounded like a body hitting the floor."

Niko, who was sitting on a weight bench near the door, shrugged. "I didn't hear anything."

"Weird," she murmured.

He'd pulled on a long-sleeve tee that accentuated the broad expanse of chest and the rippled stomach beneath. The curling tips of his dark hair were still damp with sweat. There was no way around it. Nikolai Vulkov was perfection.

And she was making a huge mistake.

"You can follow me over to Shorty's."

6

_____

The parking lot of Blue Moon's only bar still had a dozen vehicles—including a handful of hybrids, rugged pickups, and one tractor—in it when they arrived.

Neon signs proudly promising ice-cold beer brands glowed in the windows. On the inside, it could have passed for any normal bar in any normal part of the country, except for the Jimi Hendrix and Woodstock art adorning the walls. Touches of tie-dye and wheat grass vodka shots listed on the menu reminded Niko that Blue Moon was closer to Oz than New York.

He followed Emma on shaky legs as she maneuvered her way through the tight tables to the L-shaped bar. Even after her shift of chaos management at the brewery and a workout for super heroes, she still moved with purpose. He, on the other hand, could barely stand.

The sound she'd heard at the gym was indeed a body hitting the floor. His after his knees gave out. Niko had always thought of himself as fit. He was a New Yorker, and as such, walked everywhere. He frequented a gym and often worked up a sweat. A brisk jog on the treadmill followed by crunches and weights was an enjoyable way to maintain his physique and keep up with any woman's demands in bed.

But what Emma had unintentionally goaded him into had been a holy terror of a workout. He'd just decided on claiming a fake hamstring pull or an emergency phone call when she'd finally declared the torture over.

Niko wondered if Emmaline Merill would be the first woman he'd fail to keep up with in bed. Not that they were lovers, of course. But if their friendship happened to evolve...

With great relief, he slid his aching body onto the barstool next to Emma's, stifling a whimper.

"Well, well, well. If it isn't the competition," said the point guard-sized bartender, winking at Emma as he doled out drink napkins.

"Gotta update my corporate espionage files." Emma wriggled her eyebrows, playing along. "Ed, this is Niko. Niko, Ed— or Shorty as he's affectionately known in his family."

"Runt of the litter," Ed explained and offered a dinner plate-sized hand over the bar. "Welcome to Shorty's."

"Thanks," Niko said, shaking his hand.

"What brings you two out so late?" Ed asked, handing over menus.

"We ran into each other at the gym," Emma said, perusing the menu. "Niko is staying with Summer and Carter who've been in bed for hours."

"Ah," Ed nodded in understanding. "New Yorker?"

"Born and raised."

"You must be enjoying the nightlife that Blue Moon has to offer," Ed joked.

"Ed here is a real comedian," Emma said dryly.

"So what post-workout beverages can I interest you two in?"

"Dirty martini, please," Emma decided.

"I feel like it would be culturally inappropriate of me to drink in Blue Moon without trying a wheat grass shot," Niko mused.

"You could be run out of town," Ed agreed. "Chaser?"

"Beer."

Ed headed off to make their drinks, and Emma raised a speculative eyebrow at Niko.

"What?" he shrugged. "I'm embracing the local culture."

"You know, there's something to be said for tried and true." She pointed at Ed pouring organic vodka into a cocktail shaker.

"But if you stick with tried and true, how will you know what you're missing out on?" Niko countered.

"I thought I was the one asking the questions?" Emma reminded him.

Ed set their drinks on the bar in front of them.

"Can I get another one of these for my open-minded friend here?" Niko asked, pointing at the vibrant green shot.

Emma wrinkled her nose when Ed set the shot in front of her.

"I'd think you'd be used to stuff like this, coming from L.A.," Niko said.

"Maybe I came here to escape cold-pressed juice and protein pancakes."

"Either way, I'm glad you're here to keep me company during my lonely nights."

"That's sounding a little too friendly," Emma warned him, shifting on her stool to face him.

He grinned. He liked seeing this softer, slightly less guarded side of her. In her cozy sweatshirt, with her messy hair, she was infinitely more approachable. Niko liked that she had no qualms about being seen in public without a blow out and a full face of makeup. He didn't know many women in the city who would be as confident without their armor.

He held his glass to hers. "To friends."

Her lips quirked. "To night owl acquaintances," she countered.

They knocked back the grass green liquid, and Emma immediately reached for her martini. "That tastes like a mouthful of mowed lawn," she gasped.

Niko studied his empty glass. "That wasn't bad."

"Wasn't bad? Now, there's a ringing endorsement," Emma grumbled.

"But you tried something new. Isn't the adventure alone worth something?"

"Uh-uh." She jabbed a warning finger at him. "I'm asking the questions now, Mr. Tall, Dark, and Friendly."

Niko picked up his beer and leaned an elbow on the bar. "Ask away."

"Why are you in Blue Moon indefinitely?"

He blanched. "How about we work our way up to that one? Let's start with some nice easy questions. Consider it foreplay."

Emma took a tidy sip of her martini. "Fine. We'll warm up with some softballs. How old are you?"

"Thirty."

"Books or movies?"

He smirked. "I live in Manhattan. We're all about live performances."

"I bet you don't spend much quiet time at home to read," she guessed.

"Mmm, not so much," he agreed. He didn't spend much quiet time anywhere, except when he was editing photos.

"So what are you doing when you aren't at home and you aren't working?"

Given the extra innocent look on her face, Niko knew she was setting him up. "Why don't you just ask me how many women I've dated?"

"Oh, is *that* what they're calling it these days?" she asked slyly. "Nikolai, we're friends." She put a hand on his arm. "There's no judgment here."

Oh, there was plenty of judgment in those meadow green eyes. "I like women," he acknowledged.

"But not one enough to stop seeing all the rest of them?"

"First of all, I don't 'date' more than one woman at a time. Secondly, I'm not against relationships. I just don't have time for them."

"Do your 'dates' know that?" Emma prompted. She was leaning in, and he liked it. Her cheeks had that rosy glow again, and her eyes sparkled. He liked seeing Emma enjoy herself, even if it was at his expense.

"Let's stop with the air quotes before one of us sprains a finger," he suggested, grabbing her hands out of the air. Her fingers stilled in his.

"I've never lied to get a woman into bed. Everyone I've taken there understands that I'm not looking for anything serious."

"And why aren't you looking for something serious?" Emma slid her fingers out of his grip and popped an olive between her plush lips. *What was it about her that drew him in?* he wondered.

"I told you. I don't have time for a relationship—"

"Cop out!" Emma fake coughed into her hand.

He glared at her, but she didn't back down. "Fine. I don't make time," he admitted.

"Better. Still-not-the-whole-truth." Emma's coughing fit was beginning to draw eyes.

"Tenacious," he accused.

"Friends don't lie to friends."

He looped a finger around the neck of his beer bottle, staring at the condensation rings it left on the bar top. "I don't know why," he said with a shrug. "I guess I haven't found what I think my parents had. I don't think you can work towards or 'date' your way to that kind of love. And until I meet the woman who makes me look at her the way my dad looked at my mom, I might as well enjoy casual and fun."

He glanced her way. Emma's eyes narrowed as she weighed his words.

"Your bronchitis clearing up?" he teased.

"I never would have pegged you, 'the wolf,' as a romantic," she confessed.

"I thought I was a player?"

"A romantic player," she amended with a smile that warmed him from the inside out. "You remind me of my sister Eva, ever hopeful that a sweep-you-off-your-feet love is right around the corner."

"Does that change your mind about going out with me?"

She shot him a bland look. "That makes dating you even less appealing."

"How is that even possible, Emma? How could wanting to settle down with the right girl be *worse* than serial one-night stands?"

"Not only are you sowing your wild oats now, but you're expecting this perfect woman to come along and make you want to give all that up so you can live happily ever after." She poked him in the chest. "That's unrealistic and setting yourself up for failure."

Fascinated, Niko shifted on the stool. His knee pressed against hers. "And what's your plan for success?"

"I'm going to choose a man with life goals that parallel

mine." She said it as if it were the most obvious solution in the world.

"That's so..." He couldn't quite come up with a word describing how depressing that was.

"Pragmatic? Realistic? Intelligent?" she offered, her expression cocky.

"Boring."

"I can understand how Nikolai 'A Different Model Every Night' Vulkov would think so," she sniffed.

"Is that judgment I detect?" he teased, taking a long pull from his beer.

"Not between friends," Emma said, fluttering her thick lashes at him.

"Smart ass. So, while you're waiting for Mr. Life Goals, why don't you want to have some fun?"

She shook her head, sipped. "Uh-uh. I don't need any distractions. I've got enough on my plate."

Niko leaned into her space, testing. She didn't pull back, and the air between them crackled with awareness. "I don't know whether to admire your delusions or feel sorry for you," he whispered as if imparting a secret.

Emma gave a husky laugh, and Niko felt the sound go straight to his gut. She was a dare, and it was the first time in weeks that he felt like rising to one.

"While you decide between those two sterling options, let's get back to the questions. You mentioned your parents. What are they like?"

"My mother was a wonderful, talented, amazing woman. She was a ballerina, actually. But when I came along she decided she'd rather be a mom. She still performed occasionally, taught more, but she was just this beautiful, warm, funny woman."

"Was?"

"She died when I was fifteen. Cancer."

Emma's hand covered his where it rested on his leg. He hoped that she couldn't feel the tremor of his muscles. "I'm sorry to hear that."

He gave a one-shoulder shrug. "It was a long time ago."

"But you never stop missing her," she guessed.

"And I never will," he predicted. "She and my dad married at eighteen and left Russia to start a new life here. My dad was a civil engineer. An engineer and a ballerina," he smiled wryly. "But they made it work. Our house was always full of music and friends. There were always extra plates set for dinner. I couldn't tell you how many times I walked into the kitchen to find my parents dancing."

"It sounds wonderful," Emma said.

"It was a great way to grow up. I hope someday I can give kids that kind of childhood." Niko frowned down at the empty shot glass. *And just where the fuck had that sentiment come from?*

"Are you and your father still close?"

He thought about it. "Not as close as either of us would like," he said finally. "Mom was the glue, and without her, our lives carried on in different directions. He remarried a few years ago. A nice woman." That he'd never really bothered to get to know, he realized. Niko picked up his shot glass. "What do they put in these shots? Truth serum?"

"Well, as long as you're feeling truthy. Let's talk about why you're here."

"What makes you think this isn't just a vacation?" he asked, evading the question. He nodded at Ed for another beer, and Emma asked for a water.

She watched him expectantly, her chin on her hand. He let her wait, and she rolled her eyes.

"I Googled you," she admitted and pointed a finger at him before he could gleefully accuse her of being interested. "Uh-

55

uh, Romeo. You travel to Paris and Rome and Berlin. Every once in a while, you and the lucky lady of the week head to the Caribbean or Mediterranean. You do not vacation on a farm in Blue Fucking Moon."

He liked a woman with a mouth on her, one who knew when to swear for emphasis rather than lack of vocabulary. "I want more points for not pointing out that cyber-stalking proves some level of interest."

She looked unimpressed and settled back on her stool to wait. "What better way to prove how seriously you're taking our fledgling friendship than by being honest with me?"

He studied the fresh beer Ed dropped in front of him. "Fine. But I'm already reconsidering our friendship. You're very annoying."

She gave him a swift, un-Emma-like kick to his bare shin.

"Ouch! Okay," he grumbled, rubbing his abused leg that immediately went into spasm. "It started a few months ago. I have the perfect life. Everything I've been working toward I already have. My job is interesting. I live in an overpriced loft in one of the most expensive cities in the world. I date beautiful women. I can buy just about anything I want."

Emma polished off the last of her martini but said nothing.

"And then one day, I woke up, and none of it felt like what I wanted anymore."

"Ouch," she winced.

"Exactly. Work went from this creative, high-energy experiment to me shooting on autopilot. The women I'd enjoyed seemed to lose all their color and appeal. I felt like I was shooting—and dating—clothes hangers."

She grimaced.

"Yeah? Imagine how I feel. My whole life revolves around photography and—" he shot her a glance. "Women.

But it feels as though the interest just dried up and disappeared."

"And you thought coming here would..." she prodded.

"If you repeat this to Summer, I will murder you and feed your dismembered body to a variety of farm animals," he warned.

Emma scooted closer. "Tell me," she demanded.

He took a deep breath and closed his eyes. "I thought if I came here, spent some time on the farm with Summer and the kids, that I'd remember how lucky I am and get excited about my own life again."

Emma's eyes were dancing with amusement. "You're slumming it in your best friend's life to feel better about your own choices?"

He clamped a hand over her mouth. "Why don't you yell that a little bit louder?" he hissed, looking over his shoulder. "I just thought getting out of my own life for a bit would remind me how much I actually enjoy it."

She pried his hand off of her face. "And you're hoping that comparing diaper duty and working in the fields and going to bed when you'd normally be heading out for dinner and drinks is going to reawaken your creative energy and your appreciation for beautiful women?"

He scrubbed his hands over his face. "When you put it that way, it sounds stupid and elitist."

"It's not," Emma laughed. "It's really not. I actually get it. I'm just trying to imagine Summer's reaction if she ever found out that you're using her life as a scared-straight 'thank God my life doesn't suck like yours does' comparison."

"You're not going to tell her are you?" Niko begged.

"Of course not," Emma replied, indignant. "I will, however, hold the information over your head and torture you with it whenever possible. It's the right thing to do."

"And I'm back to regretting this friendship."

Her playful expression had something stirring inside him, something that felt a lot like interest and want.

"Well, don't you two look cozy?"

Niko noticed that Emma recoiled from him at the chipper greeting from the woman who approached. Dressed in pinstripe slacks and a boxy blouse, the only hint that the brunette was a Blue Moon native was the peace sign belt she wore.

"Rainbow," Emma's smile didn't quite reach her eyes. "What are you doing out with the rest of the night owls?" She gave Niko's shin a nudge with her sneaker.

Rainbow? She'd warned him about someone named Rainbow. In any other town, he'd assume that this woman was the only one. But he just couldn't make those assumptions in Blue Moon.

Rainbow held up an empty wine glass. "Board of directors meeting ran late, so I thought I'd sneak in a chardonnay before bed. What are you sneaking in?" she asked, turning her appraisal to Niko. "Rainbow Berkowicz, bank president," she said, extending her free hand to give Niko a firm shake. "And you are?"

"Nikolai Vulkov, visiting photographer."

"He's my—"

"Friend," Niko interjected before the word "cousin" could come out of Emma's mouth.

"He's just visiting Summer and Carter for a few days before he heads back to the city," Emma explained hastily.

"We're having a post-workout drink if you'd care to join us," he offered and enjoyed the scarlet flush of rage as it rose high on Emma's cheeks.

"Oh, I wouldn't want to intrude on your date," Rainbow announced with the slightest upturn at the corner of her unpainted mouth. "I've got an early morning." She put her glass on the bar and walked out, whistling.

"Craaaaap." Emma slapped a hand to her forehead. "Crap. Crap. Crap."

"What just happened? Why are you afraid of someone named Rainbow?"

Emma dropped her hand and snatched his beer from him. She drank deeply and shot Ed a dirty look when he smirked at her.

"What the hell is going on?" Niko demanded.

Emma handed him his beer. "We just became targets." She slid off her stool and reached for her wallet.

"Targets of what?"

Ed leaned gleefully over the bar. "The Beautification Committee."

7

*N*iko felt the weight of Summer's judgment when he hobbled into the farmhouse's kitchen the next morning.

"Someone got home awfully late last night," she said conversationally to Carter, who was enjoying a cup of coffee at the island while the twins mashed bananas and strawberries between their fingers on their highchair trays.

Meadow spotted Niko and squealed a greeting to him. He booped her nose, stole a piece of banana from her brother, and limped over to the coffeepot.

"Someone's also walking funny," Carter observed. "We're going to have to ask. It's the neighborly thing to do."

Summer nodded. "So, Niko. How was your night? Anything you want to tell us about?" She blinked her wide blue eyes in feigned innocence.

"I went to the gym." He poured the coffee and fought the tremors in his biceps. His body felt like a tractor trailer truck carrying every flu virus known to man had hit it. He'd never had a workout decimate him like this before.

"Not the answer I was expecting," Carter admitted.

"What did you do at the gym?" Summer prodded.

"What the hell do you think I did at the gym? Learned to macramé? I worked out and overdid it. Happy?"

Summer was unfazed. "You went to the gym by yourself in the middle of the night and pushed yourself so hard you can barely walk." She eyed Carter. "I think we're missing part of the story"

Playing along, Carter pointed an accusatory finger at Niko. "Were you alone at the gym?"

"I went there alone," he hedged.

"Aha! You ran into a hot girl there and tried to impress her with your gym prowess!" Summer was triumphant in her hypothesis.

"And I'm paying the price now. Happy?"

"Did you at least get a date out of it?" Carter asked.

Niko shook his head, sipped the heavenly caffeine. "Struck out."

"Who could turn you down?" Summer demanded. She opened a cabinet by the refrigerator and fished out a bottle of aspirin.

"Apparently the female population of Blue Moon is immune to my charm," Niko said.

"No, seriously. Who would you have worked so hard to impress, and who would say no to all that perfection?" she frowned.

"Your husband is sitting right there." Niko pointed to Carter.

Carter stroked his beard. "Hey. He's right. I am right here."

"Oh. My. God. It was Emma, wasn't it?" Summer yelped. Meadow copied her mother's tone and shrieked.

"Don't worry, honey," Carter said to Meadow. "Mommy's just being nosy and excitable."

"Oh, I am so winning this bet," Summer rubbed her hands together.

"What bet?" Carter asked, plucking Jonathan from the highchair.

"I've got action on Niko getting a date out of Emma."

"How many units?" Carter asked.

"Two."

He let out a low whistle. "Let's hope you can pull this off, Romeo. We could use a win."

"What the hell is a unit around here? A skein of wool?"

EMMA LOCKED the front doors of the brewery behind Rupert and Lila as they headed out to their cars. For a Monday night, the crowd had kept them busy enough that Emma's dinner was still sitting under the heat lamp on the expo line.

Julio had left her an overly generous serving of shepherd's pie that she was looking forward to finishing over paperwork with a beer now that everyone else had gone home.

Not that the paperwork needed to be done tonight. She could just as easily come in half an hour early tomorrow if she wanted to do something... else. She'd thought of her Saturday night with Niko more often than she cared to acknowledge. And not just because of the lingering soreness from overdoing it at the gym that still had her clomping around with the grace of a drunken Clydesdale.

It also wasn't just his sweaty form that replayed over and over again in her head, though that certainly wasn't absent. She'd given his confession a great deal of thought, too. He was a man in the middle of an artistic crisis, or a life crisis, depending on how one looked at it.

And she had an idea on how he could begin to shake it.

Of course, that would involve seeing him again. And given her physical attraction to him, it probably wouldn't be wise to tempt herself with more alone time with Niko.

She stared at her phone debating for a solid minute before she decided. Emma called up Niko's contact information and typed up a text.

Emma: Hey, night owl pal. Interested in some shepherd's pie and some unsolicited advice?

His response was immediate.

Niko: Yes definitely and possibly. When/where?

Emma: Brewery. Back patio in ten.

She wasn't setting the scene of a seduction. Emma scoffed at the thought as she lit the fire in the brewery's patio fireplace and set up a tray stand behind the Adirondack chairs that faced the fire.

It was the warmest night of the year that Blue Moon had enjoyed since last summer, and she wanted to take advantage of the clear night sky.

Back in the eerily silent kitchen, she divided her dinner onto two plates, which she left under the heat lamp, before heading out to the bar to choose two drafts.

She trayed everything up and was carrying it out onto the concrete patio when the dark shadow of Niko appeared around the side of the building.

"A midnight picnic?" he asked, climbing the stone steps to take the tray from her and settle it on its stand.

"A *friendly* midnight picnic," she corrected him in case he'd gotten any objectionable ideas since Saturday.

"Is there any other kind?"

"You have your choice of an IPA or a lager," she said, gesturing at the pint glasses and ignoring his question.

He chose the IPA, and they took their plates to the chairs by the fire. They ate in silence for a few minutes, staring into the flames and enjoying the background chorus of crickets and frogs that sang from the fields and creek.

The inky night sky sparkled with a thousand stars. A sky full of stars was something Emma hoped she never grew accustomed to, never took for granted.

She finished her meal and leaned back to stare up. "You know how some people say that looking at the stars makes them feel small?"

Niko set his plate aside, nodded. "Insignificant specks. How do they make you feel?"

"Like I'm part of it all."

"A significant speck then."

She laughed lightly at the way they slid back into the rhythm of intimate conversation despite the fact that they were little more than strangers. "That's exactly it. I am a significant speck and part of the cosmos."

"When's the last time you left Blue Moon? I'm worried about what they put in the water here," Niko teased.

Emma bit her lip. She hadn't bothered taking any of the vacation time the Pierces had generously given her. When she'd started, there'd been too much work to do, and once she'd settled in, she'd talked them into expanding into catered events, which created even more work.

"Haven't you heard? Once you come to Blue Moon, you can never leave," she joked.

"They do seem to want to suck me in," Niko agreed. "Summer sent me into town for diapers yesterday, and I ended up shaking hands with half of Beckett's constituents who all pitched in to help me pick a brand."

"Okay, that's weird even for Blue Moon," Emma admitted. Usually they're nice to newcomers but not completely smothering. That happens after you buy property here."

"I feel like the whole town is really invested in making me like it here."

"Sometimes in Blue Moon, it's best not to know why Mooners do the things they do," Emma said sagely.

"Let's talk about this unsolicited advice you've got for me," he said, changing the subject.

Emma scooted her chair around to face his. "Before I get to the doling out part, do you remember why you got into photography?"

He nodded once, gazing into the flames. "I remember exactly why and when."

Emma pulled her knees up to her chest and waited.

"When my mom died, the funeral home suggested we pull together our favorite pictures of her so they could be displayed at the viewing." He leaned forward, elbows on knees. "I dug through every album we had. Mom was the amateur photographer of the family. There were hundreds of shots of me, dozens and dozens of my father and me. Christmases, birthdays, first days of school. But nothing of her.

"My father and I never thought of picking up the camera and turning it around on her. Sure, there were a handful of shots here and there but nothing that would be considered a documentation of her life. We'd lost her, and without pictures, we lost all those memories with her."

Emma reached out and laid a hand on his arm, her heart hurting for the young man and his father.

"We'd been lucky enough to have this wonderful, amazing woman in our lives, and neither of us ever thought to document her. To capture and keep her moments. And we lost the chance to when we lost her."

"So you became a photographer."

Niko nodded. "I was obsessed with it. Capturing the moments where you really see someone."

"And that's why you're so brilliant at it."

He shrugged, a desolate lift and drop of his shoulders. "It's what made me good at it. But if I've lost it... Why are we talking about this?"

"Because I have an idea. And you haven't lost anything," Emma told him.

"You sound confident in that assessment."

"You're just having some kind of creative crisis, and it's something that most artists struggle with from time to time." At least, she assumed it was. She didn't exactly have any strong data to back up her theory. "These stagnations usually occur right before the artist breaks into a higher level of their art."

"I get the distinct impression that you're bullshitting me."

Emma waved away his concern. "Bear with me here. You haven't suffered a physical trauma that would impact your skillset, correct?"

"I have not yet been kicked in the head by a cow, but Summer did let a goat chase me yesterday." He shuddered at the memory.

"Traumatic, but your issues began before Clementine. Are you suffering from a drug problem? Mental illness?"

"No, and I don't think so."

"Then I think we can assume that your creativity hasn't just collapsed in on itself leaving you with nothing but a black hole of nothingness," Emma continued.

"You're sure we can assume that?" Niko eyed her.

"Of course we can. You've still got your eyes and your shutter-pushing finger. What we need to figure out is how to get you back to the point where pictures were about capturing moments."

"And how do we do that?"

"My dad and Phoebe's wedding is coming up."

"Oh, no." He was already shaking his head.

"They don't have a photographer."

"Uh-uh. I don't do weddings."

"You did Summer's," Emma countered.

"That was different. She scares me, and she made me do it."

"You not doing weddings is the whole point," Emma said in exasperation. "We can't just shove you back into some fashion photo shoot. We have to take you out of what's familiar to break whatever psychological crap you've got going on. Which means you need a new challenge."

"I'll admit that has the potential to make sense, but I don't think adding the pressure of documenting the happiest day of someone's life is going to help me break out of my shitty mental funk."

"This isn't some bridezilla who needs fifteen bridal albums of Photoshopped bliss. It's Phoebe and my dad. They're just thrilled to finally tie the knot. We can use that to help you."

"We?"

It was Emma's turn to shrug. "Friends helping friends."

Niko rubbed his hand over the stubble on his jaw.

"Look," Emma tried again. "My dad and Phoebe have been looking forward to this day for a long time coming. It's the blending of two families. It's the beginning of new history. You're going to have moments out the ass to capture," Emma told him.

"Exactly! This *is* a big deal. What if I say yes, I shoot it, and I have nothing but lifeless crap to give them because I now suck at photography?"

"Drink your beer, Nikolai," Emma ordered gently.

He picked up his glass and sipped morosely.

"Look," she began. "They didn't want all of the traditional fuss. They just want to celebrate their special day with friends and family. You're not going to be doing group portraits and wrangling ring bearers. You're going to tote a camera around and capture the moment my dad sees his new bride for the first time. You're going to shoot me and my sisters crying like babies when we stand up there next to our dad and all of the Pierce kids running amuck. You'll have fun doing it. And that's the point. Take the work out of it and just let it happen naturally. Just see what you find behind the camera."

"What if I don't find anything?"

"Then we'll start looking for jobs for you around Blue Moon. How do you feel about auto detailing? Or do you by chance have any experience in the law? I'm sure Beckett could use a partner."

"Maybe I could wrangle goats?"

Emma grinned. "That's the spirit."

He looked at her and sighed. "I'll think about it."

She nodded briskly. "That's all I ask. Wedding's on Sunday."

Niko leaned in over the arm of his chair, his expression intent, and suddenly the evening chill was replaced with a wave of heat. His fingers brushed hers where they lay against the wood of the chair, and he picked up her hand, holding it in his.

"Why do you care, Emma?"

She looked away from the questions she saw in those dark eyes and instead focused on their joined hands. His grip was warm, solid. She felt her blood heat as if he had the power to warm her from the inside out with just a casual touch.

She should pull free, reestablish the rules. But Emma answered him first.

"I'm a fixer. You confided a problem in me, and now it gives me great joy to force solutions on you until the problem is solved."

She couldn't read the thoughts happening behind those serious eyes. But her pulse picked up, an instinctive warning. *Dangerous territory.*

She reclaimed her hand and put some space between them, ordering her heart rate to steady. *Just friends,* she reminded herself.

Niko shed his intensity like a jacket. "Now that we've worked through my creativity crisis, what's next on the evening's agenda?"

Emma produced a deck of cards. "Know how to play Dutch Blitz?"

8

---

*E*mma woke in the middle of the night. But this time, it wasn't dreams of a certain smoldery photographer who had walked her to her car at two o'clock in the morning and brushed her hair back from her face before kissing her lightly on the cheek that left her skin coated in sweat. It was much, much worse.

She barely made it into her broom closet-sized bathroom before losing the contents of her stomach in a spectacular, gut-wrenching fashion.

Long minutes later, when she could stand, Emma dragged her sweaty, shaky self back to her disheveled bed. Her head pounded as if a jackhammer had taken up residence in her skull, and the rest of her body ached down to the bones.

She was dying. It was the only answer that made any sense. She had moments left on this earth because her own immune system was trying to murder her. She couldn't remember if any of the kids had been pukey this week. Who could keep up with so many of them? Emma lulled her head to the side and peered blearily at the clock on her nightstand.

Maybe this would be just a quick bug, and she'd bounce

back in the morning. She could shake this and be back on her feet for work. The power of positive thinking.

Her stomach lurched. "Oh, God," Emma whimpered.

She inhaled with the desperation of a deep-sea diver, willing away the nausea. "I've got this," she whispered. "Piece of—"

Niko kicked back at the conference table in Thrive's open office and waited while Summer finished up a video chat with a freelancer. Sunlight slashed through the windows at the far end of the open space. She'd added a few tasteful, colorful accents since the last time he'd visited. The white walls and light pine flooring were warmed with touches of green from two plush arm chairs and stylish artwork that adorned the ship lap wall. Candles and knickknacks and framed photos breathed more life into the office.

Barely a year old, his friend's online magazine was, well, *thriving*. After years slaving for a high fashion rag, Summer had shifted her focus to tell the stories of real men and women in a lifestyle site geared toward health-conscious readers. It was a disruption to the system and still a bitter pill to swallow for her former boss, Katherine, who hated to see her ex-prodigy succeed on her own. Niko made sure to mention how well Summer was doing every time he did a shoot for *Indulgence,* knowing full well word would get back to the impeccably dressed Katherine behind her glass desk.

While Summer discussed the series on heart rate monitors with the writer, Niko examined the photos on the walls. He'd shot some of them. The one of Gia upside down in wheel pose had been part of the yoga series. He got up to study it closer. And found what he was looking for. The spark.

Every model had that spark of life in them, and he made it his mission to tease it out of them. *It was like catching a glimpse of someone's soul*, he thought. And it was what had been missing lately. Without that spark, that soul, a picture was just a picture. It didn't tell a story or provide a window into a life.

He wondered if he'd be able to find the spark in the bride and groom and do Phoebe and Franklin—and their family, one member in particular—justice if he said yes. He'd felt a low-level anxiety ever since Emma had broached the idea. He didn't *want* to do it, didn't want to fail. But it was practically impossible to say no when she looked at him with those sea goddess eyes alight with excitement.

God, he had it bad for her. It made him restless, constantly thinking of her. At night, he'd lay on his bed, hands stacked under his head and staring up at the ceiling as he thought about her smile, her eyes, that incredible body.

Niko turned his back on the photo and his problems. The basket of yarn balls on the table caught his eye, and he plucked up one the color of ripe grapes on the vine. He tossed it in Gia's direction when she charged up the stairs and made a beeline for her workstation.

She stuck her tongue out at him and chucked the yarn back at him. He lobbed another one in her direction.

Summer disconnected and clapped. "Locked down September's week one feature!"

She and Gia raised their hands for an air high five.

"Nerds," Niko smirked. "What's with the yarn? You take up knitting in your spare time?"

"It's a teaser for the Blue Moon blog. The Annual Knit Off is coming up," Summer said.

"When did you start a Blue Moon blog?" he asked.

"Readers are fascinated by Woodstock Jr.," Gia explained.

"Thrive is boosting tourism here. Eden at the B&B says she's booked solid through summer," she said proudly.

"Plus, it gives us more content for the site, and we can use local advertisers on the blog posts," Summer said, all business.

"Moving on to the Knit Off?"

"Apparently every spring, knitters from miles around congregate in One Love Park on the day of the Farmers Market Festival to race knit. The first knitter to hit ten feet of scarf or whatever the predetermined size is wins something weird," Summer filled him in.

"I think it's a year's supply of wine from Blue Moon Vineyards," Gia piped up.

"That's better than last year's prize," Summer smirked. "I believe Donna June Macomber walked away with a lifetime supply of organic fish bait."

Niko laced his fingers behind his head. "Okay, I know you two live here, and so you've probably been indoctrinated, but I've still gotta ask. Do you think this place is weird?"

"Oh, totally," Summer snorted.

"The weirdest," Gia agreed. "But we love it."

Summer nodded in agreement. "Best place in the world."

"Just checking," Niko told them.

Gia's phone dinged from the depths of her humongous bag. "Shit. Now what am I late for?" she muttered, pawing through baby accessories and adult woman trappings. "Oh, no! Emma's sick."

Niko leaned forward as if he could glean more information just by getting closer to Gia.

"Is it the stomach bug?" Summer asked sympathetically.

"She said she's praying for a swift death."

"Yeah. That's the stomach bug. Jonathan had it over the weekend."

Niko hadn't really noticed since it seemed like both kids threw up a lot, sick or not.

"Does she need anything?" he asked, coming to his feet. "I could take her some soup or some ginger ale..." He trailed off when he saw the looks of interest that passed between Summer and Gia.

"You'd better cool that puppy love before the Beautification Committee sniffs you out," Summer snickered.

"Oh, I've already met Rainbow."

"What! When?" Summer wheeled her chair to the side of her desk so she could see around her monitors.

"When Emma and I were at Shorty's—"

"Hold it!" Gia wheeled her chair around, too. "You and my sister were out together?"

"Yeah, we've been hanging out."

That shut them both up. They were gaping at him like hungry fish in a koi pond.

"Yes!" Summer pumped her fist into the air. "I'm so winning this bet."

"It's nothing serious," Niko reiterated. "She's not interested in dating me."

"You asked her out?" If Gia's voice got any higher, windows would start cracking.

"On multiple occasions." He shrugged. "She's a little stubborn."

"'A little' is an understatement. I can't believe we missed all this." Gia griped. "Babies really do ruin everything."

Summer wheeled back to her monitors and began to type furiously. "Son of a bitch. You're already in Blue Moon's Facebook group. How did we miss this? We're terrible friends. Technically Gia, you're a terrible sister, and I'm a double terrible friend," she said ruefully.

"Either one of you want to explain what's wrong with you? Limiting ourselves to this particular moment, of course."

Gia winged the ball of yarn back in Niko's direction. "You've been seen around town with Emma by the Beautification Committee. You're practically engaged," she explained.

"Look at his face!" Summer gasped. "He's not freaking out at that statement. Why aren't you freaking out?"

"I am too freaking out," Niko argued.

"Uh-uh," Gia shook her head. "You got this contemplative look on your face."

"You guys are freaking me out. I'm not dating Emma. I'm not looking to get engaged and move to Tie-Dye La-La Land. There isn't a place on earth that's a worse fit for me. I'll leave you to your crazy." He backed out of the office.

He was not *contemplating any of that*, Niko told himself. Well, maybe the dating part and definitely the sex part. He liked spending time with Emma, liked the sparks, liked the challenge. She was gorgeous, stunning even, but not in the way he'd grown accustomed to. Those willowy models with perfect pouts and sexy slinks didn't capture his interest the way Emmaline Merill had. He knew with an uncanny certainty that if they ended up in bed together, it would be better and bigger than anything he was used to.

Niko jogged down the stairs and out the side door of the barn. Interest didn't mean future. Interest meant present moment. Maybe he'd pick up a few things and drop them off at her place. That didn't mean he was looking to settle down. He was just being a good friend. Niko nodded to himself. He'd hit the grocery store, pick up a few essentials for the diseased, and drop everything off. *That's what friends did, right?*

9

*N*iko started at Farm and Field Fresh, the local grocer and discovered the produce and organics section to be sixty percent of the store. *Only in Blue Moon,* he thought, eyeing up the yards-long sprouts section.

He decided to entertain himself and hopefully Emma by texting her a running commentary on his shopping trip.

Niko: Deathbed deliveries arriving shortly. Any special requests? Ginger ale? Vomit bucket? Coffin lining samples?

He stocked up on tissues and tea and was studying the medicine selection when he felt a firm tap on his shoulder.

The woman had waist-length hair the color of the palest gold. She wore cowboy boots, jeans, and a plaid button down. She smiled at him, and her lavender eyes crinkled when she smiled. "You must be Summer and Carter's house guest," she said, shoving her hand at him.

He took it, intending to shake it, but she flipped his palm up and skimmed her fingers over the skin. "You have a very long, very fractured love line," she said matter-of-factly as if she were discussing the weather.

"Hi, I'm Nikolai," he said pointedly.

"Mmm, yes I know," she said, frowning intently at his hand. "My, eleven children is a lot. Oh! Silly me, that's your money line. My mistake!"

"I'm sorry. I didn't catch your name," Niko said with growing concern. The crazy meter in Blue Moon went higher than anywhere else he'd visited.

"Willa," she said in a breathy voice.

"Can I have my hand back, Willa?"

"Hmm? Oh, sure," she said. She made no effort to conceal her study of the items in his basket. She frowned, placing a hand on his forehead. "You're not ill," she announced. Strangers just didn't walk up to people and try to diagnose them in grocery stores in the city. Blue Moon was fucking weird.

"It's for a friend," Niko said, even as he warned himself that he didn't actually owe Willa an explanation.

"Of course!" Her eyes widened. "Your 'friend' Emma," she said, with an exaggerated wink.

"Yes, my *friend* Emma."

"Well, you're going to need some flu medicine because she refuses to go strictly holistic," Willa said, switching into I-play-a-doctor-on-TV mode. "And let's get you some bone broth and coconut water. Maybe some fresh yogurt full of probiotics. She'll need protein and electrolytes."

She floated off, and Niko wasn't sure if he was supposed to follow her or if he should just try to escape.

"Hurry up, Nikolai."

Niko: Think I'm being kidnapped by someone named Willa. She's trying to lure me into a van by promising me extra probiotics in my yogurt.

There was still no response from Emma by the time he left Farm and Field with four canvas bags of ingredients that Willa and the rest of the entourage they'd picked up around the store recommended to treat Emma's flu. Each item that went into his basket—and then cart when the basket overflowed—was Blue Moon-made. Niko felt like he'd gone shopping in the visitor's center gift shop.

Then, as if to prove how friendly the town was, Willa, the store clerk, an elderly farmer named Carson, his friend Ernest in grease-stained coveralls, and the girl in the meat department, all chipped in for a get-well card for Emma and signed it.

Niko tucked the bags into the backseat of his rental. He picked up the packet of loose tealeaves and shook his head. He had no idea what the hell to do with thistle weed tea. Hopefully Emma knew what to do with it. But first, he was under strict orders to hit OJs by Julia before stepping foot in Emma's house.

He found the shop, painted a bright green, situated on the corner of Main and Patchouli next to Abramovich's Jewelry. A bell jingled above his head when he ducked into the storefront. Benches and chairs with thick plum-colored cushions butted up against lime green wainscoting. The coolers, filled with mason jars holding a color wheel of juices, were highlighted under stainless steel spotlights. The chalkboard menu was artistically drawn, but still legible, and listed juices with catchy names like Beet Root Reboot and Berry Balance Blend.

He pulled out his phone and rattled off a text.

Niko: At the juice joint. How many prunes do you want in your smoothie?

"Nikolai, I presume?" A woman with a pink punk rock haircut and an eye-searing neon apron propped her elbows on top of one of the coolers.

"Word travels fast," he said, rubbing his temples.

"Especially when it involves 'six-feet-two-inches of walking sex.'" She laughed when Niko cocked an eyebrow at her. "I'm quoting Mrs. Nordemann, who caught a glimpse of you in the grocery store while buying out their selection of trashy romance novels. I'm Julia, by the way."

"I've met more neighbors today than I have in the three years I've lived in my building," Niko quipped.

"You'll get used to it if you stick around. People have even less privacy around here than they do living on top of each other in the city," she grinned.

"I'm getting the feeling that you're not kidding."

"Nope. So Emma's sick?" Julia asked as she danced out from behind the counter. She wore black skinny jeans and a paisley patterned tunic.

"So I hear."

"Willa called over and said you were on your way, so I pulled a couple of juices that should help," Julia said, pulling a paper bag out of the tall cooler in the corner. "This one is infused with ginger to help with the nausea," she said pulling out a jar filled with what looked like apple juice. Next came a pink one and then a green one. "This one's an immunity booster, packed full of citrus fruits for vitamin C. And this one is her favorite. So once she's back on her feet, she can enjoy it."

"Thanks, Julia," Niko said, pulling out his wallet.

"You're getting the flu season discount, even though it's not technically flu season," she said, slim fingers flying across the screen of her register.

"Thank you. That's very nice of you," Niko said, handing over cash.

"We're a nice town. A nice place to live," she said with a crooked smile. He got the feeling she was trying to pass him an encrypted message and was amused about doing so.

The back door of the shop opened, and two kids raced in ahead of a man in a hockey jersey carting a third.

"Gird your loins," the man called out in warning. "Here come the troops!"

"Mooooom!"

Julia's face lit up as the two ambulatory kids hurled themselves into her arms. "Hi, my lovelies!"

"Hi!" the little boy in an Avengers t-shirt and pajama pants chirped.

"Why aren't you wearing real pants?"

The little boy eyed Niko and gave him a nod. "Hi," he said suspiciously before turning back to his mother. "Because I didn't wanna. Dad's not wearing real pants."

Niko's gaze tracked to the man's well-worn gym shorts.

"Well, I guess I can't argue with that," Julia said, puckering up to accept a kiss from the man who was clearly her husband.

"Who's he?" Kid Avenger demanded, eyeing Niko suspiciously.

"This is Nikolai," Julia said by way of an introduction. "This is my husband Rob and our unruly mob."

"Ah, the famous Nikolai," Rob said, offering his child-free hand. "It's nice to meet you in person instead of just reading about you on Facebook."

"Robert!" Julia shot her husband a warning look.

"Uh, what?" Niko interjected.

"Trust me. You don't want to know," Rob assured him. "All you need to know is that Blue Moon is a wonderful place to live. Right, honey?" Rob's exaggerated wink at his wife told Niko there was a bit more to the story.

"The best," Julia said brightly.

~

AFTER THE JUICE CAFÉ, he'd been directed to make a quick stop at the home of one Elvira Eustace, president of the chamber of commerce and maker of organic, homemade household cleaner "guaranteed to cleanse the hell out of everything." Elvira, with her head full of silvery curls and her alpaca wool caftan, then made him promise to stop by the used bookstore in town for some kind of cleansing incense that the owner, a squirrely hippie named Fitz, sold.

Niko: Your flu-busting incense smells like pot.

By the time he pulled up in front of Beckett and Gia's stately Victorian, he was starting to wonder if the entire town of Blue Moon was fucking with him.

Everyone knew him on sight, plied him with discounts and chatter about how wonderful Blue Moon was, and cheerily sent him on to the next "helpful" destination. His flu-fighting arsenal had grown to six full shopping bags.

Niko: Your town is so weird. Haven't heard from you, so I'm violating your privacy and getting the key from Beckett if you don't answer your door. See you in five... or tomorrow if I meet any other townsfolk.

He could see evidence of the steadfast Beckett's taste in the manicured lawn and neatly trimmed shrubbery. Gia's presence was also notable in the tangle of wind chimes on the wide wraparound porch and the riot of wildflowers spilling out of jewel-toned planters.

He followed Fitz's instructions and instead of heading to the front door, followed the porch around to the side door and entrance to Beckett's law practice. He let himself into the sun-filled parlor and found himself face to face with a gothic princess.

She wore a short-sleeved black turtleneck with a crystal skull sewed into the chest, black jeans, and a pair of spiky black stilettos that looked sharp enough to turn murder weapon in a pinch. Her ebony hair was parted on the side and secured in a ponytail.

Her dark purple lips curved in welcome. "Nikolai! I didn't think I'd get to meet you for a few days."

"How does everyone know me before I walk in the door in this town?" he asked in exasperation.

"It's all part of the Blue Moon experience," she said, eyeing up his shopping bags. "I'm Ellery, by the way. What can I do for you?"

Niko mellowed slightly. "I just wanted to talk to Beckett for a second." If there was a God in this tiny town, he would make it across the twenty-five feet of grass that separated Beckett's house from Emma's before nightfall.

"That's easy enough. He's just in with some clients. Can I get you a cup of coffee while you wait?"

He wilted, losing the will to fight the Blue Moon mojo. "Coffee would be great, thanks."

"You can put your bags over there and have a seat," Ellery told him, pointing to a table and an overstuffed armchair next to a fireplace on the back wall. Niko dropped his bags on the table and sank into the leather.

He could see Emma's cottage through the tall leaded glass window. *So close, yet so far.* He snapped a picture and texted her.

Niko: Assuming you are incapacitated. Will be breaking down your door shortly.

"Cream or sugar?" Ellery asked from the coffeemaker.

"I'm surprised you don't already know," Niko said dryly. "Black, please."

A wisp of a smile teased her purple lips. "We're not that bad."

"I feel that I would not be exaggerating if I said that the entire town knows what color underwear I'm wearing."

Ellery handed him a sturdy mug.

"Now you're just being silly. You're new and shiny. Blue Moon loves new and shiny. Especially when it's a little mysterious."

"There's nothing mysterious about me," Niko argued.

"Oh, really? Famed fashion photographer Nikolai Vulkov shows up unannounced in little ol' Blue Moon with one suitcase and no return date, and we're not supposed to be curious?"

Niko sipped the coffee. "There's curious, and then there's shoving the 'best little town in the world' propaganda down my throat. I'm starting to think your town wants me to stick around."

Ellery didn't say anything so much as "hmmed" and left him to his brooding. He watched with interest as she bypassed the coffeemaker and instead opened a cabinet and produced a bottle of scotch. She poured a glass, set it on the shelf, and returned the bottle to its home. A minute later Beckett's office door opened and a middle-aged couple walked out all smiles. The woman was dressed in a flowing, fringed kimono in severe black. The man towered over her, looking like a banker on his day off in khakis and a striped polo.

They enthusiastically shook hands with a haggard-looking

Beckett before letting Ellery usher them out the door.

Beckett held up a finger at Niko before he could say anything and reached for the scotch. He downed it in a gulp.

"The Buchanans looked happy," Ellery commented when she returned.

"I suggested a trial separation period, and they countered with a trial togetherness period," Beckett said, eyeing the empty glass. "Why in the hell don't we have a therapist in Blue Moon?"

"A therapist couldn't handle all this crazy," Niko sighed.

"It's not craziness. It's cultural quirkiness, which is at the heart of this great community," Ellery said placing her hands over her heart.

Beckett pointed both index fingers at her. "No! I know what you're doing, and as your boss and mayor of Blue Moon, I'm ordering you to stop."

Ellery pouted.

"We have more than enough work to do that should take precedence over meddling in people's lives," he reminded her.

"Should I ask what's going on?" Niko wondered.

Beckett shook his head and started to unroll the sleeves of his shirt. "Trust me. It's better if you don't know. Now, what can I do for you?"

"Emma's sick, and I'm bringing over some supplies. Gia can't remember where the spare key is."

"Keys," Beckett corrected. "My wife wouldn't remember where they were if they were glued to her forehead."

"Poor Gia," Ellery sighed dramatically. "How would she feel if she heard her husband talking about her that way?"

Beckett glared at her, but Ellery merely batted her lashes at him.

"This is one of those people-drive-me-insane days," Beckett grumbled.

10

---

*P*recisely four hours after Niko had left Thrive's offices on his mission, he finally arrived at Emma's front door. He found the spare key exactly where Beckett told him it would be, under the squatting plaster frog by the pink azalea. He knocked once on the cottage's front door and peered through the glass windows of the glossy black door.

The kitchen and living room appeared to be lifeless.

He fired off another quick text.

Niko: Rapunzel, Rapunzel, let down your hair. Never mind, I'll just use this spare key.

There was no response, and he figured the thirty seconds he waited was long enough. Niko let himself in and closed the door behind him. Neat as a pin was his first impression. He could see evidence of Emma's urban roots tangling with Blue Moon's eclectic style.

The drapes were a rich navy and tied back with charming rainbow hued rope cord tassels. The tufted leather sofa that faced the fireplace was adorned with colorful throw pillows. He deposited his bags on the island countertop. Very nice crystal wine glasses hung from the underside of one white kitchen cabinet above a stoppered bottle of Blue Moon's own Merlot.

"Emma?" he called out. His only response was a faint groan coming from the narrow staircase off the kitchen. "I'm coming up," he warned.

At the top of the stairs, he saw the second floor was home to two bedrooms and one small bathroom. It was there that he found Emma, curled into the fetal position on the black and white octagonal tiled floor. Her head, arms covering her face, rested on the thick bath mat.

"Why are you here?" she groaned.

"Oh, baby." Niko stroked a hand through her sweat soaked tangle of hair.

"Just go," she croaked.

"How long have you been here?"

"One thousand years."

At least her sarcasm was still functioning, Niko thought.

Emma started to sit up and pointed him toward the door.

"I'm not leaving," he told her. "I'm here to nurse you back to—"

She interrupted him by throwing her limp body over the toilet and throwing up.

He grabbed her hair and held it loosely behind her neck until the heaving stopped.

She collapsed over the toilet seat and, with a shaking hand, reached up to flush.

"Just let me die in humiliated peace," she begged.

"Not gonna happen," he told her. Niko released her hair and took the washcloth from its hook. He ran it under cold water and wrung it out before placing it on the back of her neck. "We need to get you back in bed."

"Don't wanna throw up in bed." Her voice was muffled, raspy.

"I'll get you something to throw up in. You can't lay here on the floor." And with that, he gently scooped her up in his arms.

"Am I fighting you off? In my head, I'm fighting you, and you're putting me down."

"How high do you think that fever is?" he asked.

"I've never been more humiliated in my entire life, and I once fell down a flight of stairs carrying a tray of entrees. I smelled like veal marsala for the rest of the night."

Her skin was clammy. The oversized t-shirt she wore was soaked with sweat, and post vomit-shivers were wracking her body.

"I think you'll recover from your humiliation." He placed her carefully on the bed, and as she collapsed back against the impractical mound of pillows, he opened drawers of her dresser until he found a sweatshirt and leggings. "Here. Can you put these on?"

"Stop trying to see me naked," she groaned, teeth chattering.

"Baby, strip now, or I'll strip you," he said, turning his back to her.

Emma muttered and shivered her way through the clothing change while he examined her bedroom. Like downstairs, everything was organized and in its place. The room itself was plain with white washed plank walls and the light pine flooring. Long sheer curtains—white again—flanked the window and would billow nicely in the breeze if the glass was open. The bed, curvy yet quaint with its wrought iron frame, was topped with a thick, flowered comforter in reds, yellows, blues, and greens.

Red throw pillows and a red and yellow rug gave the room a cheery, feminine feel.

"Okay, sadist," Emma croaked from the bed.

He turned to find her huddled under the comforter, her t-shirt discarded on the floor. "Good girl." He lay a hand on her forehead and felt the heat pumping off of her. "I'm going to run downstairs and bring you some tea. Do you want anything else? Any toast? Soup?"

Her pallor went from white to green. "No, thank you. You can go," she told him, trying to dismiss him again. "I prefer to suffer in solitude."

"I'll just unload downstairs," he lied.

In the kitchen, he found a cleaning bucket under the sink and lined it with doubled up plastic bags. Niko jogged back upstairs and stopped in the bathroom to wet a fresh wash-cloth. Back in Emma's bedroom he put the washcloth on her head and slipped the thermometer he'd found in the medicine cabinet between her lips.

"I thought I told you to go away," she mumbled.

"Quiet," he told her. "If you have to puke, puke in that," he said, pointing at the bucket on the floor. While he waited for the thermometer to beep, he crossed the room and opened the window. Instantly the room felt less stuffy.

"What are you doing?"

"Julia and Rob said their kids had this last week. They said to get fresh air into the house so you don't marinate in the germs."

The thermometer beeped and Niko looked at the read out.

"Am I dying?" Emma murmured, eyes closed.

One hundred and three degrees. "Well, let's just say you're not going to work today."

Her response was a pained "ugh."

"Just get some rest for now and let the fever cook those germs."

She was too exhausted to respond.

Niko went back downstairs and, after texting Gia to let her know her sister was mostly alive, unloaded the shopping bags. Stashing supplies wherever he could find space in the refrigerator and cabinets, he opened the windows on the first floor and hoped that the sunshine and fresh air would murder the germs. He was organizing a tray when he heard the toilet flush upstairs.

"Emma?" He knocked on the bathroom door.

"Go away."

"Did you throw up again?"

Silence.

"Emmaline, don't make me come in there again," he said sternly.

He gave her until the count of three and, just as he was about to bust in, the knob turned.

She was at least standing. Sort of.

"Happy?" she grumbled.

There was a fresh sheen of sweat on her pretty, pale face, and it looked like it hurt her to stand.

"Baby," he crooned. "Come on. Back to bed." Niko tucked an arm around her waist and guided her back to her room.

"D-d-did Julia say how long this th-th-thing lasts?" she asked through chattering teeth.

"It's a short one. About twelve hours," he lied easily. "In fact, you should be feeling better soon." Hope was never wrong to give. He'd just hide her nightstand clock.

Niko helped her back into bed and tucked the covers around her tight. He used the washcloth to wipe the sweat from her face.

"Niko?" she shivered out his name.

"Yeah?"

"Are you going to shoot the wedding?"

"Go to sleep, Emmaline."

She kept her eyes closed, but the muscles of her face slowly started to relax, and when he was sure she was asleep, he slipped back downstairs.

He pulled out the spray bottle of suspect brown liquid and unfolded the handwritten instructions Elvira had given him on how to use her special cleaner. "What the hell does 'agitate until cloudy' mean?"

EMMA WOKE to an earthy spiced scent. She opened an eye and spotted a stick of incense sending lazy curls of smoke toward the ceiling that glowed yellow with the late afternoon sun. Carefully so as not to dislodge her head from her neck, she rolled to check the time, but her clock was missing. In its place was a glass with a sticky note that said, "Coconut water. Sip slowly."

Two capsules sat on their own sticky note. "Take me."

Nikolai. The memory of him holding her hair during Vomit Fest had her scraping her hands over her face. She hated being vulnerable in front of people, and at the given moment, there was no situation that she could imagine that was worse. She'd hurled in front of Niko, a man who looked like he was created just to torment women. And now every time he looked at her, he would be reminded of her barfing her guts out.

She would never live this down. Not that it mattered what he thought of her. They were just friends. Even if she thought he was too beautiful to look at. Just friends. Ugh. Her brain was too feverish to think straight.

Testing her body, Emma worked her way into a seated position and was pleased to find she no longer felt like vomiting into unconsciousness. She took a testing sip of the coconut water, and when her stomach didn't immediately rebel, she took a chance on the ibuprofen.

Easing her bare feet to the floor, Emma took stock of her body. She was still alive. The nausea was mostly gone, along with the chills, but the aches were still fighting for keeps. Her head pounded, and her bones hurt. With the careful moves of a ninety-nine-year-old, she hobbled into the little hallway.

She paused in the bathroom doorway, sniffed. It smelled like eucalyptus and something herby. The countertop and tile floor gleamed.

Had someone broken into her house and cleaned it? she wondered.

Carefully, Emma eased her way down the stairs.

"What the hell, Niko?"

Barefoot and at home in her kitchen, he stirred something on the stove. Her teapot whistled from the back burner.

"What the hell are you doing up?" he demanded, flipping the knob to turn off the flame under the pot.

"Walking into an alternate universe, apparently." The windows down here were open, and the cooling breeze swept through, bringing with it the fresh scent of Blue Moon spring and sweeping out the remnants of stale sickness.

Niko poured the steaming water over a tea bag in one of her favorite mugs. He wiped his hands on his jeans and steered her by the shoulders to the couch.

"Sit down before you fall down."

She sat and only put up the weakest of fusses when he bundled her up in a blanket. "This has got to be the most humiliating experience of my entire life," she decided.

"Then you haven't had nearly enough fun." He brought her the tea and sat next to her.

"Aren't you afraid of catching whatever death sentence this is?" she asked.

"Not with Julia's Miracle Immunity Booster juice that tastes like feet and radishes," he told her.

"You went to Julia's?"

"Did you miss all of my texts?" he asked, disappointed. "They were some of my finest work."

"I don't think I've looked at my phone since... my internal organs started trying to escape my body in the middle of the night. She made a move to get up, but Niko held her in place with one hand. "Not so fast, champ."

"I'm just getting my phone," she said, already short of breath from the effort to stand.

"I'll get it."

"It's on my nightstand." She watched him as he loped up the stairs. "Thank you," she called after him weakly.

He returned with the phone and her sheets. "Willa said you can't sleep on these or you'll risk reinfection. I think she's slightly crazy, but I'm going to play it safe."

Emma rested her head on the back of the couch and closed her eyes. "You held my hair while I threw up, scraped me off the bathroom floor, and now you're doing my laundry."

"It's all part of the friendly service."

"You'd do this for your other friends?" she asked, having only enough energy to open one eye.

"Hell no."

It brought a faint smile to her lips.

"In this moment, you're an excellent friend, Niko. And as an excellent friend, I'd like to propose that we never, ever speak of this day again."

"Whatever you want, Barf Queen."

He plied her with liquids, put fresh sheets on her bed while she took a shower, and watched four hours of early *How I Met Your Mother* episodes with her. She fell asleep on his shoulder, snuggled into his warmth.

He insisted on tucking her into bed before he left, and she was too tired to argue. But as soon as she heard her front door close behind him, she opened her text messages and reread every one he'd sent her documenting his efforts to get to her. Blue Moon was going to have a field day with Dr. Niko. And she wasn't as upset about it as she should have been.

It was beyond sweet how he'd ridden to her rescue. He cleaned her house, he did her laundry, and he dumped bone broth down her throat. No one-night-stand man in the history of one-night-stand men would have worked this hard for a potential lay.

Emma chalked her thoughts up to vomit-induced exhaustion, pressed her cheek into the cool, clean pillowcase, and fell asleep thinking about how much she really liked Nikolai Vulkov.

11

Niko planned to ignore the idea of shooting the wedding for another day or two and buried himself in life in Blue Moon. He weeded and planted in the fields with Carter, played creative director with Summer, and even lent a hand in the kitchen occasionally.

The twins seemed to get bigger and more advanced by the day. Niko was convinced that Meadow would be standing on Jonathan's shoulders to reach the knife block on the kitchen counter in a matter of days.

The physical labor and the simple routine of daily life in Blue Moon soothed his anxious brain of its "what ifs." And for once, he just let himself be.

He took walks around the farm every afternoon, never carrying a camera, but there were moments that he couldn't help but pull out his phone and snap away. He captured Joey working with Reva in the afternoons after school, the earnest girl absorbing Joey's orders and tackling every responsibility as if her life depended on it. He captured the farm's gardens and fields that took shape as the sun rose higher and stayed longer in the May sky. And he bared witness to the communal energy that was Blue Moon and Pierce Acres. There were no strangers here, only neighbors, each as much a part of the others' lives.

In the evenings, he enjoyed his role as Uncle Niko with the twins. He began poking his head into the stables to help Joey keep an eye on the hugely pregnant mare, Calypso. He hadn't seen Emma since her unfortunate bout with the stomach bug. She'd texted to thank him and reiterate that they should never speak of the horror again. But she'd blown off his attempts to see her since. She was avoiding him, and he was almost done letting her.

The only thing he was avoiding were the questions Summer and Gia peppered him with about Emma. He sidestepped those inquisitions in favor of toiling laboriously with Carter on the farm and was surprised to find that he enjoyed it. Niko could see the appeal of working so closely with nature rather than hustling down concrete and asphalt, rushing from building to building.

The rhythm of life here was different. Gone was the frenetic pace he'd grown so accustomed to in the city, and in its place was a patient, trusting flow. Rather than fighting or forcing successes, the victories here were found in cooperation.

There were little lessons everywhere, and Niko wondered if he would take them home with him when he returned to his real life. He could see how Summer was happy here. There was a tangible realness in Blue Moon that was too easily escaped in the city. There were no layers of artifice, no hidden agendas, no power plays—unless he counted the town's commitment to convincing him that this was the best place in the universe to live, work, and visit.

Blue Moon wasn't the departure he'd expected. Rather than convincing himself that his life in the city was exactly what he wanted, Blue Moon was raising questions Niko wasn't sure he was prepared to answer.

Two days before the wedding, Niko found himself wandering the parcel of land that Phoebe and Franklin called home. They'd built a tasteful Craftsman home on a corner of the farm nestled between trees and creek, tucked away from the beehive of activity. It was here that they would marry on the grassy lawn surrounded by loved ones and friends. *Another new start to build from*, he thought.

Niko admired the wide covered porch that wrapped around both sides of the house, taking full advantage of the views of rolling pastures and greening tree lines.

On impulse, he took out his phone and snapped a few shots, capturing the afternoon light. It was roughly the same time that the ceremony was scheduled to start, giving him an idea of lighting. It would be an intimate event. The guest list only included family and closest friends and him.

He could do it. Probably.

It wouldn't be work, at least not really.

"Getting the lay of the land?" Phoebe called out from the porch, a glass of iced tea in her hand, reading glasses perched on her head. She always reminded him of a literature professor with her silver streaked bob and tortoise shell glasses. The overweight pug at her feet sneezed violently.

Embarrassed at being caught trespassing, Niko scuffed his boot in the grass. "I take it Emma mentioned she asked me to step in as official photographer Sunday?"

Phoebe smiled warmly and gestured him up onto the porch. "She's awfully hard to say no to, isn't she?"

"I don't want to disappoint you," Niko confessed, leaning down to scratch Mr. Snuffles behind the ears. *Or Emma.*

"Niko," Phoebe sighed. "I don't want to force you into something you don't want to do. You're an incredibly talented photographer. I don't want you to feel strong-armed into shooting some little country wedding."

The little dog gave a snort.

"It's not that," Niko shook his head, rising back up to lean against the cedar railing. "I just haven't been shooting well lately, and I'd hate to give you subpar work. Not for you and your wedding day."

Phoebe patted his arm in a gesture only mothers have mastered. "My poor boy. Let me get you an iced tea and tell you how ridiculous that statement is."

Feeling like a teenager caught out after curfew, Niko slunk into the house behind her. Inside, with Mr. Snuffles on his heels, he found an expansive living space. The living room spilled into the dining area and kitchen, all sharing floor space under white washed beams.

Bookshelves were stuffed full with novels and family pictures. Couches in dog- and child-proof leather formed a U around the flat screen mounted above the whitewashed brick fireplace.

Phoebe pointed him to a stool at the kitchen island and opened the refrigerator to dig out a pitcher of tea. She set a glass of ice and tea in front of him and topped off her own.

"Let me tell you exactly what I'm looking for and then you can tell me if you think you can deliver. If not, no hard feelings."

He couldn't argue with that. "Fair enough."

"I want a picture of Franklin and I smiling without any food stuck in our teeth, one of me and my boys without bunny ears or middle fingers, one of Franklin and his girls, and a group shot of our combined families with everyone looking relatively sane."

"Four pictures?" Niko clarified.

"Four pictures," Phoebe nodded. "Franklin and I have both

been married before. We're old. We're laid back. We're not looking for some high-end portfolio of hundreds of shots of people posing for a toothpaste or sunless tanner commercial."

"You're not old," Niko argued.

"Aren't you sweet when you tell lies to old ladies?" Phoebe winked at him. "Now, I'd love for you to be there to snap a few quick pictures. But I'll be just as happy to have you there strictly as a food- and alcohol-consumer."

He squirmed on the barstool. How hard would it be to come up with a handful of shots to help the Pierces and Merills remember the day? He didn't have to get artistic and high-concept with the "assignment." It was a straightforward capture-the-smiles kind of plan.

Niko sipped the tea and caught the flavors of lemon and basil. "Fine, but if you're disappointed with what I shoot, you and Emma only have yourselves to blame," he warned.

"Let's talk about this 'subpar' work you plan to deliver," Phoebe suggested firmly.

An hour later, Niko felt surprisingly unburdened. He'd spilled his guts to Phoebe, and she'd listened without judgment until he'd finished. They'd switched to wine halfway through their chat and took it out onto the porch to enjoy the last of the afternoon light.

"So, if you're sure you'll be okay with whatever shots I can give you, I'd be happy to do it," he finished lamely.

"You know what I think?" Phoebe asked, patting his hand.

"That I'm blowing all of this out of proportion and I should just suck it up and pick up a camera?"

She shot him the look of a mother unimpressed. "No. I think that stalls in creativity are real, and they rarely result in a complete loss of skill."

"That's basically Emma's assessment," Niko told her.

"Hmm," Phoebe hummed, her eyebrows winging up.

"Oh, right. I'm not supposed to tell anyone we're hanging out. Something about the Beautification Committee."

"Really?" Phoebe's question was laced with maternal glee.

"You seem to say a lot with very few words."

"You're spending time with Emma and confiding in her. I didn't realize that you two knew each other so well."

"We're getting to know each other. Well, I'm trying to get to know her," he amended. "She's trying to make sure I stay in the friend box."

"Interesting."

"Now you're looking at me like the checkout lady at the grocery store and the bank president."

Phoebe topped off his wine glass. "I need to get on Facebook and catch up with everything I've been missing. It's going to be fun to see how this plays out."

"Uh. Okay."

"So she wants to be friends?"

"Just friends. I'm not her type," Niko explained and wondered why he was pouring his heart out to a woman he'd only met on a handful of occasions.

"What is her type?" Phoebe wondered.

"Stable, secure, in it for the long haul. Monogamous."

"And you're...?"

"I'm 'dangerous' and just out for a 'good time.' So Emma's put me in this position where, if I want to be around her, it's strictly as friends, and since she's been very clear about her intentions, if I pressure her to go beyond friends I'm..."

"An asshole?" Phoebe supplied.

He grinned, seeing where her sons got a very large chunk of their personalities. "Exactly. I like her. A lot. I like spending time with her, and I'm interested in being a hell of a lot more than friends, but I can't give her permanent."

"Oh, I can't wait to see how they orchestrate this," Phoebe murmured, half to herself.

"Sometimes I feel like this entire town is speaking a different language," Niko muttered.

"Oh, honey. You have no idea."

"So any advice you'd care to share in either of my situations?"

Phoebe pursed her lips. "My soon-to-be stepdaughter is a wonderful, headstrong woman, even if she's headed in the wrong direction. But my money is on you, Niko. Be smart, and you'll find a way to climb out of that friend box. Now, regarding your work issues, you should talk to Jax. He's dealt with writer's block. Maybe this is the same thing."

12

_____

"**Yep. Sounds exactly like writer's block," Jax agreed as he tossed the bale of hay onto the stack he was making in the barn.

Niko hefted the bale he carried up onto the stack next to Jax's. A dappled gray horse swung its giant head out of its stall and nickered until Jax pulled out a baggie of baby carrots.

"So how do you beat it?" Niko asked, pulling off his gloves and tucking them into the back pocket of his jeans.

Jax fed the horse a carrot and then popped one into his own mouth. "It's a bitch," he chewed. "You gotta get extra creative to break through shit like that."

"For example?"

Jax glanced over his shoulder, making sure it was still just them and the horses. "Okay, so the last screenplay I was working on, I got stuck right in the middle of it. None of my usual fixes—taking a day off, writing drunk, binge reading, chasing my wife around the bedroom—*nothing* worked."

He held out the bag of carrots to Niko, and he helped himself to one.

"So what did you do?"

Jax took another glance around the stables before continuing. "The days were ticking down to my deadline, and I was still stalled. Totally stuck. I was desperate. So in a last ditch effort, I put down the screenplay and started writing something completely different."

"How different?"

Jax cleared his throat and swiped his hand over his mouth and murmured something.

"It sounds like you said—"

"Romance novel. I started writing a romance novel."

"Okaaaaay." Niko wasn't sure where to go with that. "Did it help?"

Jax snagged another carrot, broke it in half, and held it out to the horse. "Worked like a charm. The book and then the screenplay just started pouring out of me. Now anytime I get stuck, I open up that document titled 'Crop Rotation Schedule,' and in a day or two, I can get back to my project with a fresh brain."

"So the novelty—forgive the pun—of something completely different helps to grease the wheels?" Niko rubbed a hand over his jaw and briefly wondered when he'd last shaved. Life on the farm was messing with his grooming habits.

"That's my theory," Jax said with a shrug. "Now, if you ever mention this to anyone, I'll tell everyone you're a dirty liar."

"Fair enough. So I should try something new," Niko decided.

"Go in a different direction, and see what happens," Jax advised.

"I'll start penning my Fabio-cover story tonight," Niko promised. Jax gave him a helpful shove and then tossed him a carrot. Niko chomped on it thoughtfully. *Fighting through it hadn't helped. Maybe finding something that flowed would. If the hippie woo-woo mojo of Blue Moon was pushing him in a new direction, who was he to ignore it?*

"Oh, look, Reva. We must have interrupted snack time." Joey's voice carried a teasing sarcasm. Jax jumped a mile and shot Niko a "keep your trap shut" look. Joey and Reva sauntered down the corridor with a wire-haired dog of dubious breeding trotting after them. Waffles gazed lovingly at his females. Reva's earnest eyes didn't show the flickers of amusement that Joey's did.

"Hey, gorgeous wife of mine," Jax said, offering her the bag of carrots with a mock bow. "I grew these especially for you."

Obviously amused, Joey reached for a carrot only to find herself being reeled into Jax's arms.

"Reva, why don't you go check the outdoor ring before everyone gets here for lessons," Joey suggested. "I'll catch up with you in a minute."

The girl nodded and hustled for the door, and Niko sank down to scruff up the dog's fur. "Hey there, Waffles." The dog dissolved in joy.

"She has yet to crack a smile," Joey said when the door closed behind Reva.

"How's she doing otherwise?" Jax asked.

"Smart. Eager. She'd put a new roof on the barn if I told her I wanted it done," Joey predicted. "But there's just something about her..."

"Sad and cagey," Jax assessed. "There's something going on with her."

"And you know how I just *love* getting involved in my employees' personal lives," Joey grumbled wryly.

"How does she get here?" Niko wondered. "Does she have a car?"

"Says she gets dropped off," Joey said. "But I've seen her

walking up the lane, so unless someone drops her off at the road, I think she walks."

"At least she doesn't look as hungry," Jax commented.

Joey looked embarrassed as she scuffed the toe of her boot into the sawdust. "I've been bringing in food and leaving it in the office."

"I fucking knew it!" Jax said, poking her in the chest with his finger. "I knew you didn't finish off all the pot roast leftovers, you little liar!"

Waffles yipped in protest at his mother being called a liar.

"Ugh!" Joey shrugged out of his grasp. "I knew I'd regret marrying an emotional eater!"

Jax grinned. "Please, the only thing you regret about marrying me is not doing it sooner."

Joey softened against him. "Prove it." Jax leaned in to kiss her, and Niko cleared his throat.

"I'm just going to go over here," he said, pointing toward Joey's office and the smell of fresh coffee.

"Relax, Niko. We save the really hot stuff for the tack room," Joey snickered.

"Remind me to stay out of the tack room."

A beautiful horse with a glossy chestnut coat and perfect white star on her nose shoved her head out of her stall, nodding her big head at Joey.

"Hey there, beautiful," Joey said, stroking a hand down the horse's neck. "When's that baby coming, Calypso?"

Calypso shook her great head, tossing her mane. She was hugely pregnant with the first foal of the Pierce Acres breeding program. A monumental start thanks to Jax's efforts to win Joey over with the gift of two spectacular specimens of horseflesh. Calypso and her stallion, Apollo, would cement the Pierces' place in the world of horse breeding.

"She looks like she could go at any time," Jax said, offering a carrot to Calypso, who took it gently with her velvet muzzle.

"Sammy the vet was here this week," Joey said. "She's predicting probably another week."

"We'll keep an eye on her," Jax promised.

"So this is where the party is." Emma, in stylish gray suede booties, picked her way over the straw-strewn brick to join them in front of Calypso.

Niko reacted to her the same way a dog offered a treat, eagerly with every fiber of his being focused on that delicious morsel. *Shit, he was in serious trouble.*

Emma was dressed for work in sexy black motorcycle pants and a slim fitting black sleeveless shell. Her hair, yet to be pinned back, floated in auburn curls around her face and down past her shoulders. And Niko couldn't stop staring at her.

The air in the barn changed as if a weather system had moved in.

"Don't step in any shit," Joey warned Emma with the stern point of her finger.

Emma glanced down at her shoes and grimaced. "God forbid. I wanted to check in with you about ladies' night tomorrow."

"Is that still on?" Joey frowned.

Emma sighed and tapped her foot impatiently.

"Get your head out of your horse's ass," Emma smirked. "We're throwing Phoebe a bachelorette party, and you're not getting out of it."

"I hate being social," Joey whined.

"Suck it up and be a big girl. There'll be a ton of booze."

Joey brightened. "Well, I do love my mother-in-law. What are you guys doing while we're partying it up?" she asked Jax.

"Babysitting all of the little people and playing poker. You in?" he asked Niko. "You'd better be because it's at Carter's."

Niko laughed. "Count me in. Wait, can we drink while we're in charge of children?"

"It's required," Emma, Joey, and Jax said in unison.

"So, then it's okay if I put you in charge of a couple of desserts since you're so bad ass with sugar and baked goods?" Emma clarified with Joey.

"Ugh. Fine. Sure. Just let me know how much I owe you for the..." Joey trailed off and looked at Jax.

"Entertainment?" Emma filled in.

"Yeah. That."

"Cool. Awesome. Great. Uh, if you two will excuse me, I need to take my husband into the tack room and do some... inventory," Joey said, curling her fingers into the neck of Jax's shirt and dragging him down the corridor.

"Inventory, huh?" Niko said, watching them go.

"If I start hearing screams of ecstasy, I'm leaving." Emma wrinkled her nose.

"You must be feeling better," Niko said. "I mean, you look better. Not that you ever don't look good..." *Shut up, asshole. Just shut the fuck up.* God, he'd turned himself into a gawky teenage loser who was too stupid to live.

"I assume you couldn't possibly be referring to the Situation That Shall Not Be Referred To Ever Again, and therefore, I will state for the record that I feel just fine. And I look amazing," Emma said, tentatively stroking Calypso's velvety nose.

"Glad you're done curling around the toilet in the fetal position," Niko said, stepping in on her. If he was going to act like a child, he might as well call on playground etiquette and pull some pigtails.

"If we were talking about it—which we aren't—I'd say thank you for being so... helpful." Emma swallowed hard.

"I feel like you just took my gold star and turned it into a shitty 'good job, champ.'"

"I'll get you a gold star if you promise to never bring this up again," Emma bargained.

"Deal."

Calypso nudged Emma's shoulder with her nose. "I'd better get out of here before I'm covered in horse slobber," she said, taking a step back.

Niko followed her and reached for her hand. "Hang on a second. I talked to Phoebe today."

She turned back to him, dust motes floating on the afternoon sunshine between them. "And?"

"And I'm shooting the wedding."

He didn't know how badly he'd wanted to say yes to her until Emma was squealing and throwing her arms around his neck. "I knew it! You're going to be amazing. and they'll love what you do."

She didn't pull back, and he didn't move his hands from where they'd settled on her hips.

"I'm glad you're happy," he said huskily.

"You didn't say yes just to make me happy, did you?" she accused.

"Not only for that. Though, at the moment, I'd have to say it was worth it."

"Niko." She unwound her arms from his neck and rested her palms flat on his chest. Yet, she didn't push him back.

He tucked a curl behind her ear and let his fingers thread through her fiery hair.

"What are you doing?" she sighed at his touch.

"Being friendly."

He'd love to capture her like this, in the softly filtered light with the wariness in her sea goddess eyes. His fingers itched for a camera. Emma was urban chic out of place in the quiet, dusty stables. But the desire was more than that. More than wanting to capture a moment, a perfect face. He wanted to experience her with no lens between them, nothing but skin to skin, need to need.

He could see her pulse flutter wildly at the base of her slim throat and knew that she was affected, too. "What are we doing, Emma?"

Her lips—so full, so soft—parted, but no answers poured forth. Her eyes were heavy lidded as they looked up at him. Long lashes curling delicately, framing eyes the green of spring meadows. She smelled like sin, all spice and temptation. His blood thrummed through his veins. He was hard, and all he wanted to do was to get closer.

Testing, Niko pulled her into him using his palms to guide the luscious curve of her hips. He lowered down to her, his lips skimming the sharp line of her jaw. He paused just behind her ear to taste that sensitive skin. She shivered against him, fingers digging into his t-shirt and holding him close. Emma let her head drop back, and Niko took it as an invitation to further explore.

He knew she could feel how hard she'd made him, yet she didn't pull away. He felt her heart beat against him as it matched the thud of his own when he dragged his teeth over the flesh of her neck.

"This is stupid," she sighed. "We're making a mistake."

But still she stayed, melted against him. Niko shoved his hands into her hair, gripping it.

"If it is, we'll have fun making it," he whispered, his lips lowering with impossible patience toward their goal.

Something solid shoved him from behind knocking him the last inch into Emma, his teeth gouging her sweet lip.

"Ow!" she yelped.

Niko swung around to meet their foe only to be faced with a very pleased with herself Calypso.

"Did that horse just make you bite me?" Emma gasped, holding her lower lip.

"Are you okay? Jesus, did I... puncture anything?"

Emma put her hands up when he made a move toward her. "I think we just proved that was a bad idea."

"I think we were doing just fine until someone butted in with her big, fat head," Niko said, glaring at the horse.

Emma shook her head. "I've got to get to work. I think it's for the best if we pretend this... situation never happened."

"You can't pretend to forget about every situation that doesn't fit into your plan, Emma," he called after her.

But she didn't stop, her heels clicking sharply on the brick floor as she exited the stables.

Calypso snorted and Niko narrowed his eyes.

"Cock blocked by a horse. I'm watching you, Calypso." He pointed two fingers at his own eyes and then back at her.

The mare gave a sassy toss of her mane and shoved her big, fat head in her feed bin.

13

"*D*amn, we're good," Emma sighed, taking in the transformed first level of the barn. Usually used for organizing Pierce Acres CSA shares, she, Summer, Gia, and Eva had turned the space into a decadent, feminine hideaway.

Sheer fabrics draped from the rafters and pooled on the floor behind cushions and borrowed furniture. Salt lamps and strings of lights bathed the room in a soft glow. The music was soft and spa-like. Separated from the main space by thick gold curtains, a massage table and candles waited with the shirtless masseuse, Corban, Summer had tempted in from the city. On the opposite end of the room was a mani-pedi station manned by Corban's cousin Helga, who was not shirtless. White linen tables held bottles of champagne and wine and a heavenly array of snacks and desserts. Monogrammed robes in silky shades of pink hung from a clothesline strung from the rafters.

"If goddesses hung out, they'd hang out here," Gia said with a satisfied nod of her head.

Summer clasped her hands under her chin. "I hope Phoebe loves it!"

"Do we have to wait for Phoebe before we try the Shirtless Hunk over there?" Eva asked. Her gaze locked on Corban's perfect pecs.

"Phoebe gets dibs," Emma said, giving her sister the eye.

"Secondsies," Eva raised her hand.

Gia slipped her arms around their shoulders. "Both sisters in the same place! I'm so glad you could come up for this, Eva."

Eva squeezed back. "I miss you ladies. I'm glad Dad's giving us an excuse to get together off-holiday."

A car pulled up outside, and Emma peeped through the window.

"Poker person, or Joey with the guest of honor?" Summer hissed.

"It's Joey!"

They scattered to take their places, and when Phoebe was escorted in—with Elvira Eustace at her side—Emma was ready for her with a glass of chilled champagne. Summer draped a Bride sash over Phoebe's shoulder and Gia settled a sparkly circlet crown on her head.

"Welcome to your bachelorette party," Emma said, dropping a kiss on Phoebe's cheek.

"Oh, girls! This is just spectacular!"

Joey bee-lined for the food table and started loading up a plate, which Summer slapped out of her hand. "Guest of honor first!"

Joey pouted until she spotted Corban and then admired him like she would a piece of horseflesh. "Not bad, ladies. Not bad."

THE PARTY WAS A HIT, Emma thought with satisfaction.

Phoebe, in her ivory robe and glittering crown, peeped out from under the cucumber slices on her eyes to reach for her glass of champagne while Helga applied a candy pink polish to her toes.

Seated on a bejeweled meditation cushion, Joey shoved pie in her face. She'd refused a manicure but had relented on the toes, letting Helga slather a sexy deep purple on the nails. Summer and Gia were enjoying their childless night out with glasses of wine and plates of Joey's sinful cheesecake brownies. Gia and Elvira—who was piling her salt and pepper curls on her head in preparation for her turn on Corban's table—chatted about town business both chamber- and gossip-related.

"I heard a rumor about our Emma here." Elvira's gossipy smile drew a collective "oooooh" from the group.

Emma downed her glass of champagne in one gulp and reached for another. "Niko and I are just friends," she said firmly.

"And I was just interviewing Carter," Summer supplied.

"And I was just Beckett's tenant," Gia said with a shrug.

"And I could never get past my hate of Jax," Joey snickered smugly.

Emma was not impressed.

"Oh, no dear! You misunderstand." Elvira shook her head making her ringlets dance. "Of course you're not dating Nikolai. I was referring to the rumor that you've decided to make your move to Blue Moon permanent."

Emma felt a swift rush of conflicting feelings. *What exactly did Elvira mean by "of course" she wasn't dating Nikolai?*

"Are you really staying?" Gia demanded. "Please say yes!"

"I gave myself a year to decide whether or not Blue Moon was a good fit for me, but honestly I can't imagine leaving."

Gia's fist rose victoriously. "Yes!"

"Oh, that's wonderful, dear," Elvira clasped her hands together. "Now you can start looking for a place of your own."

Gia tapped a finger to her chin. "Hmm, if you move out, that means Beckett and I could have a sex cottage instead of getting it on in all the hiding places in the house."

"You know what I find interesting is that your mind went straight to Nikolai," Phoebe told Emma, admiring her newly painted nails.

"He is gorgeous," Summer agreed. "I've never met a model who wasn't awestruck just by looking at him."

Emma pointed triumphantly. "And that is exactly the reason we're just friends. He's a womanizer. A charming one, but I'm in the market for forever, not an incredibly gratifying one-night stand."

"People change," Gia said innocently.

"No they don't," Emma argued. "I'm not going to change my mind, and Niko isn't going to suddenly become the settling down type. And I don't care what the Beautification Committee is cooking up. It's not going to happen."

Elvira gave a dainty shrug. "I haven't heard a peep out of them on the matter. I don't think you're even on their radar."

Emma frowned into her champagne. Not on their radar? Was it because they recognized a terrible match when they saw one?

"Don't worry, Emma. I'm sure once you're a permanent resident the BC will find some poor schmuck to hook you up with," Joey said, helping herself to a fresh glass of wine.

Elvira frowned at Joey and Joey shrugged. "What?" she asked, all innocence.

Emma pointed with her wine glass. "What's going on with you two?" she demanded.

Elvira reached for her bag and pulled out her phone and

reading glasses. "Nothing at all, dear. I'm just going to send a quick text."

"Sucker," Joey mouthed at Emma.

Emma was beyond thankful when everyone moved on from her as a topic. She tried to settle back into the festivity of the night but couldn't shake the feeling that everyone else knew something that she didn't. She wondered what the Beautification Committee's reaction would have been if they had spotted Niko and Emma and their almost-kiss in the barn.

Annoyed with everyone, including herself, Emma shook it off and decided to forget about it all for the night. She plopped down on a cushion next to Phoebe and Eva followed suit.

"Phoebe, since you're about to become our wicked stepmother, I feel like we should know how you and our dad fell in love," Eva said.

"Yes, do tell," Emma agreed, tucking her feet under her.

Phoebe's face lit up. She snuggled into her robe, settling in for the story. "Girls, before I begin, I hope you're not as prudish as my boys are when it comes to my love story."

"They don't approve?" Eva was appropriately horrified.

"They had a hard time accepting it in the beginning," Summer said diplomatically. "But to be fair, they didn't know anything about Franklin until they caught him shimmying off of Phoebe's porch roof at six o'clock in the morning in his bathrobe."

"No!" Emma gasped in disbelief.

"My boys can be a little..."

"Overprotective?"

"Opinionated?"

"Ridiculous?"

Phoebe's daughters-in-law all chimed in with suggestions.

"I was going to go with insane," Phoebe laughed.

"*Our* father was caught sneaking out of *your* bedroom?" Eva asked, her glee barely contained.

"His legs were dangling off the roof, and they pulled him down," Summer recalled.

Emma tried to imagine her father, the man who'd grounded her when she'd slunk in four minutes after curfew, sneaking half naked out of his lover's bedroom. Summer and Phoebe gave the blow-by-blow of the event and put them all in tears.

"I'm never going to let him live that down," Emma announced, wiping a tear from her eye. "And just look at you two now."

Phoebe pinked up. "I never thought I'd have a second time around, let alone one so wonderful."

Emma felt her throat tighten with emotion. Seeing her father devastated by her mother's abandonment had added another layer to the grief and anger she'd felt toward her mother. But watching Phoebe glow as she talked about him as one of the two great loves of her life pulled the pieces of her heart back together just a little tighter. "I've never seen my dad so happy," she offered.

Phoebe took her hand and squeezed.

"Your father is a wonderful man."

"He's one of a kind," Emma agreed.

"So when did you know that he was *the one*," Eva demanded, her eyes bright.

"Oh," Phoebe sighed. "It wasn't a grand gesture or some kind of a climactic finale. He was standing in my kitchen washing my dishes after dinner one night, lecturing me on proper knife care."

Emma laughed, knowing well her father's speech on blade maintenance.

"That's it? He was washing dishes, and you were like 'I can't live without this man?'" Eva sounded disappointed.

Phoebe laughed. "It was more like a resounding 'yes!' I saw him standing there in my little kitchen, whistling Tosca, and I felt like a truck had hit me. I knew that, no matter what else happened in life, I wanted Franklin by my side for it. We were friends first, not looking for love, and that ended up being the best foundation we could have had."

"I changed my mind," Eva sighed. "That's incredibly romantic."

Emma's eyes prickled with fresh tears. "I couldn't imagine a better partner for Dad," she whispered, wrapping Phoebe in a one-armed hug.

"Oh, sweetie," Phoebe sniffled. "You're going to make me blubber."

"You're going to make us all blubber," Gia's voice cracked.

"Hell. I should have gone to poker," Joey muttered, noisily blowing her nose into a pink napkin.

The roar of an engine from outside drowned out any further comment. It revved once, then twice.

"That's not the entertainment, is it?" Emma demanded.

"It appears to be a sexy man on a sexy motorcycle," Gia said, peering out the door.

It was a stampede. By the time Emma made it through the door, the men and kids had poured out of the house to admire Nikolai in jeans and that damn leather jacket astride a gleaming machine.

It wasn't the warm Sunday dinner kind of love brought on by a man washing dishes, it was a hot fist of lust that socked her right in the stomach. He caught her eye, and that crooked, cocky grin of his went straight to her core. Friends or not, she wanted him fiercely.

And he knew it.

"Sweet wheels," Jax whistled admiring the chrome and curves of the hulking bike.

"Thanks," Niko said. "Got it from Ernest Washington outside of town. Had to turn the rental in and needed a set of wheels. And she spoke to me."

The men nodded and grunted in approval as they circled up to admire the machine while the women appreciatively eyed the man.

"Just how are you supposed to resist that?" Phoebe asked Emma quietly.

"I have no idea," Emma murmured.

The women flocked down into the driveway, mingling with the Pierces.

Nikolai dismounted and stepped back, letting Jax and Carter get a closer look. He ambled over to where Emma stood on the edge of the circle with her arms crossed.

"Want to go for a ride?" he whispered in her ear. Her blood turned to molten lava as a dozen visions crashed through her imagination. Not a single one of them involved her on the back of a motorcycle. But there were plenty of her on him, under him.

"Where are the seatbelts?" she asked lightly.

"I got a helmet for you just in case you want to throw caution to the wind and embrace a little adventure," Niko told her.

"I like seatbelts and airbags and air conditioning," she said primly.

"I think you'd like feeling the wind race over you when we lean into a corner." His lips brushed her ear. "All that power between your legs? It's an experience you shouldn't miss."

Damn if he didn't turn her fair skin six shades of fuchsia.

She took a self-preserving step back and glared at him when he laughed.

"Friends, remember?"

"Emma, I'm feeling awfully friendly toward you right now." Niko's meaning was clear. He was the wolf, and she was Little Red Riding Hood. Only there was no woodsman to save her from herself.

The women, blowing kisses to their men and children, began to meander back to the barn. But Emma couldn't quite drag herself away from Niko's gaze. The evening air crackled with energy between them. It wasn't fair. She wasn't into bad boys. Why couldn't her body back her up on this?

"Miss Emma? Are you ready for me?" The shirtless Corban waved a champagne flute at her from the barn door.

Niko's face went slack, and it was Emma's turn to laugh. "Gosh. I'd better go. Duty calls," she said with a wink and sauntered back to the barn.

14

*P*oker with the Pierces and a passel of kids was memorably chaotic. The handful of games he'd attended in the city had been catered affairs in private rooms with high stakes. It was an entirely different experience in Blue Moon. The twins were already in bed, and the baby monitor sat on the kitchen counter.

Franklin, who had decided to forego an official bachelor party in favor of babysitting and poker, pulled two golden bubbly lasagnas from the oven. "Vegetarian one is on the left," he told Carter, pointing with a spatula. Jax and Beckett made appropriate disparaging remarks about vegetarians.

They tried settling Aurora in the dining room with a giant bean bag, a bag of chips, and a tablet streaming a bug-eyed kid cartoon, but the little girl was much more interested in being involved in the action. She pulled her beanbag up to the table and stood on it next to her brother Evan who eyed the cards Niko dealt him like a professional poker player.

"Is Fitz coming tonight?" Franklin asked Beckett, glancing over his reading glasses.

Beckett shook his head and tossed a chip in the pot. "No. He said something about a last-minute work obligation."

"Damn," Franklin sighed. "I was hoping to win back some of what he took last poker night."

"He's a burned-out hippie who runs a used bookstore. What kind of obligations does he have?" Jax wondered.

Beckett shrugged. "I don't ask Fitz questions, mostly because I'm terrified of the answers."

"Cardona will be here soon," Jax said, dropping his phone back on the table. "Some kind of riot over at the park over warring popcorn vendors."

"I'm gonna need some background on that statement," Niko said, picking up his cards.

"Cardona's town sheriff. We went to high school with him. Mediocre poker player but all right guy all around. It's movies in the park on Fridays, and there's this popcorn vendor whose been selling for years. Apparently tonight, some enterprising kid set up a competing popcorn stand with lower prices and a white cheddar flavor," Jax said, tossing his chips in. "All hell broke loose when the first vendor accused the second of trespassing and the second vendor accused the first of..." he picked up his phone again and read. "'Being a bourgeois fat cat capitalizing on the hungry.'"

"Cardona texted all this to you?" Carter asked, picking up his beer and clinking it against Aurora's cup of chocolate milk.

"Huh-uh. That last part came from the Blue Moon gossip group," Jax said.

Beckett rubbed his forehead. "I hope to God this doesn't come up during the next town meeting."

Jax looked at something on his phone and smirked. He handed the phone to Carter who glanced up at Niko and back at the screen.

"Have you been to a town meeting, Niko?" Carter asked.

"I have not had the pleasure. How many cards?" Niko asked Jax.

"Two. You really should go. They're a highlight of life in Blue Moon."

Aurora peered over Beckett's arm at his cards. "You have a lot of faces on your cards," she said.

A collective "crap" went up around the table, and everyone threw their cards down.

Beckett, who wore a sleeping Lydia strapped to his chest, grinned and handed Aurora a dollar. "Nice job, kiddo."

"Played by a first grader," Franklin shook his head in disbelief. "You promised you'd only cheat for Grampa!"

Aurora giggled. "Next hand," she said in a loud whisper. "Bucket?"

"Yeah, Shortcake?" Beckett ruffled her hair.

"Can we play makeover?"

The collective fear around the table was palpable, and Niko got the feeling this wasn't the first time a game of makeover had been suggested.

"We'll play next weekend," Beckett promised.

Franklin saved them all. "Why don't you come help me play poker?" he suggested. They all sighed with relief when Aurora climbed into his lap and started counting his chips.

The action around the table continued. Jax kept up a running commentary on all the joys of life in Blue Moon, which seemed to amuse everyone else at the table for reasons Niko couldn't quite understand.

Beckett dropped a steady stream of chips and snacks on Lydia's head until Carter covered her cute, bald head with a napkin.

"Nice beard, by the way," Carter snarked at his brother.

Beckett rubbed a hand over the early stages of a full beard. "Thanks. I think I'm going to keep it, let it get a little fuller."

Niko picked up on the twitch of Jax's shoulders as he picked up his cards. "You definitely have the face for a beard," the youngest Pierce said amicably.

"It looks good on you," Evan chimed in with an evil smile. "Don't you think so, Niko?"

Niko felt the need to play along just to see how it all shook out. "It's a great beard."

"Thanks," Beckett beamed.

Carter glared at him and stroked a hand through his own beard. "I thought you hated facial hair."

"Where did you ever get that idea?" Beckett asked innocently.

Carter threw his cards down on the table. "Oh, I don't know. Maybe because of every snide comment you've ever made about my beard in the past five years?"

"What are you talking about?" Beckett feigned confusion. "I've said nothing but nice things about your beard."

"Bullshit!" Carter shouted, pointing at his brother. "Bull. Shit. 'Don't get beard hair in my food, Carter.' 'You look like a wookie, Carter,'" he mimicked in a falsetto voice. "Bull fucking shit."

Aurora giggled into her fingers, and Franklin put his hands over her ears.

"What's gotten into you, man?" Beckett asked, not even bothering to hide his shit-eating grin. "You're gonna wake up Lydia. I've never said anything derogatory about your face."

"Can we get back to telling Niko how great Blue Moon is?" Evan asked.

"Why is everyone educating me on Blue Moon?" Niko demanded.

"Grampa! All your cards are red," Aurora announced.

Cards were slammed down all around the table, and Lydia woke up with a wail. While Carter and Beckett continued to bicker, Niko got up to help himself to the stuffed mushrooms Franklin had brought with him. Jax grabbed a fresh round of beers from the fridge.

"What's with the beard wars?" Niko asked.

"Last week, Beckett bet me I couldn't eat two dozen deviled eggs without puking. He completely underestimated my gastronomic prowess."

"So you made him grow a beard?"

Jax grinned. "I've been trying to make this gag happen for years. Beckett hates not shaving. He's been busting on Carter for his since he grew it when he got out of the Army."

Beckett joined them in the kitchen and pulled a baby bottle from the fridge. "It was my idea to fuck with Carter over it," he said proudly.

"So this is what having brothers is like?" Niko asked.

"Pretty much," Jax grinned, handing him a cold beer.

It actually made Niko a little sad to be an only child.

They got back to the game with Carter still glowering at Beckett. Aurora had lost interest in cards and was under the table painting Valentina and Meatball's toenails with sparkle polish.

Niko spotted headlights from the driveway.

"Is that Cardona?" Beckett asked, making a show of stroking his beard when Carter looked up.

Franklin poked his head out of the window and frowned. "No. It's... Fitz? But he's going into the barn, and he's dressed like a cop?"

The table emptied as the men crowded around the window.

"What the hell is Fitz doing dressed up like a cop—" Beckett began.

"Emma did mention they hired 'entertainment' for Phoebe," Niko said.

"There is no fucking way on the face of this earth that they purposely hired Fitz to strip for them," Jax said, staring in fascination as Fitz pulled a patrolman's hat down lower on his head.

"Wait. Someone paid Fitz money to take his clothes off?" Evan asked, looking more than a little confused.

"There's no way," Carter shook his head.

"Do those pants have snaps down the leg?" Franklin asked, squinting.

They all watched as Fitz knocked on the side door of the barn and walked in.

"Oh, this is going to be amazing," Beckett predicted.

"I'll get the baby monitor," Carter said.

"I'll get the beer," Niko volunteered.

They piled out of the house and grabbed chairs off of both porches and set up in the driveway. It took about four seconds for the screams and shrieks to start.

"My eyes!"

"Put it back on!"

"Why would you do that?"

The men were in tears as the police cruiser eased down the driveway. A tired-looking Donovan Cardona got out of the car. "What the hell's going on in there?"

"Get out!" Someone shrieked from inside the barn.

"Hey, Cardona, isn't it illegal to impersonate a cop?" Jax asked.

Another set of screams erupted from inside.

The sheriff sighed and settled his hat on his head and stomped toward the door. He knocked, but no one inside could hear him over the chaos. He shoved the door open and went inside.

"For the love of God! Put your pants back on," Cardona shouted from inside the barn.

Franklin cracked open a new beer as the brothers gasped for breath.

"Is someone recording this?" Carter asked.

"Live streaming it," Jax said, holding his phone up.

The women flooded out of the barn looking like the survivors of an atrocity.

"He's just so pasty," Joey whispered over and over again and walked into Jax's open arms.

"I've seen him in his yoga briefs a hundred times, but this was so much worse," Gia shuddered.

Emma came out next, her arm around Phoebe's waist, both looking like a deer in headlights. Phoebe walked straight up to Franklin and snatched the beer out of his hand. "I'm going to need a case of these to forget what I just saw in there."

"Why in the hell did you hire Fitz to strip?" Carter demanded.

"We didn't!" Summer insisted. "He just showed up and said he heard there were some naughty ladies who needed to... to... take the law into their own hands. Oh, I think I'm going to be sick."

Cardona came out with a handcuffed, pantless man. Beckett covered Lydia's eyes. Bill Fitzsimmons couldn't weigh more than 140 pounds soaking wet and wearing cement shoes. His skinny rattail of hair hung out from under the hat that was askew on his head.

Carter and Beckett hung on each other laughing while their wives clung to each other for comfort. Franklin's glasses steamed from the tears that streamed down his face and Jax's shoulders shook with silent laughter.

Emma met Niko's gaze and shook her head. "He just started flailing around like a scarecrow. It was awful, but I couldn't look away."

Elvira Eustace sashayed out of the barn and jogged up to

Donovan's patrol car. "Excuse me, sheriff?" Donovan stopped trying to shove Fitz into the backseat.

Elvira leaned around him and stuffed a wad of bills into Fitz's shirt pocket. "Nice job in there, cutie. Call me when you get out of jail."

Eva shrugged. "I don't know what all the fuss is about. He wasn't *that* bad."

Gia looked at her sister like the woman had grown a second head.

"What?" Eva asked.

The baby monitor lit up, and an unhappy wail sounded through the speaker. "I think this party is over," Summer said. "I'll take the first crier."

Carter followed her back toward the house. "Hey, you know that Beckett hates beards, right?"

Emma turned to Phoebe, whose tiara sat crookedly on her head. "I'm sorry to end your night this way. I don't know what happened to the scheduled entertainment, but I will find out and demand a refund."

"Oh, please don't. This was an... unforgettable night," Phoebe said with a laugh. "I wouldn't change a thing. Well, except Bill's pants. Those should have stayed on."

Donovan yelled through the back window at Fitz to keep his sweaty balls off the upholstery. The rest of the crowd began to disperse around them.

"Are you okay to drive?" Niko asked Emma.

"I only managed to down two glasses of wine and half a dozen brownies before that hot mess arrived. If I would have had more, the scene in there would have scared me sober," she said. "I'm going to get this straightened out with the sheriff and then take my sister home."

"Then I'll see you at the wedding?" Niko asked.

"See you at the wedding." She nodded toward the barn.

"Will you tell Carter we'll take care of clean up tomorrow? I don't think anyone wants to go back in there right now. It's too fresh."

He watched them go, Donovan beside him. "So, we're seriously not going to play poker?" Donovan wondered.

Niko tilted his beer to his mouth. "I'm game. But don't you have a prisoner?"

Donovan gave a one-shouldered shrug. "We can cuff him to a chair and play a few hands."

15

*T*he day of the wedding dawned warm and bright with a gentle breeze that fluttered the walls of the white tent in Phoebe and Franklin's front yard. Niko arrived early, camera gear at the ready and his wardrobe adhering to the casual dress code.

The yard was already overrun with caterers and early arrivals. Niko spotted Franklin directing the catering company into the house. Emma was deep in discussion with the event coordinator, ticking items off the list on her tablet.

She looked like a woodland fairy in her blush pink dress, her red hair down in a riot of curls. Her eyes sparkled with the excitement of the day, and when she spotted him, the smile she sent him from those perfect lips went straight to his gut. When had it happened? When had he fallen for the untouchable girl? Looking at Emma now, Niko couldn't remember a time that he hadn't felt this longing, this need.

They had just met. They hadn't even slept together. *How could he have such strong feelings for a woman he barely knew?*

She laughed at something the guy in the coveralls said,

and Niko's world tilted. It wasn't possible, but that didn't change the fact that it *was*.

She came to him, skimming over the grass as her dress floated around her legs like that of a goddess.

"Hi." Her voice was soft, her eyes bright.

"You look incredible. Stunning," he breathed.

She twirled for him, kicking up the layers of skirt as the spring air caught beneath them, and before he was even conscious of it, he was raising the camera and snapping the shot.

Emma stopped spinning. "Oh! Save your shots for the bride and groom!"

"This one's for luck," Niko said. "Thanks for making me do this."

She wrinkled her nose at the dig. "You'll be thanking me sincerely later," she predicted.

"Let's hope so or else Phoebe and your father will only have a handful of shitty shots to remember their special day."

She gave him a playful shove. "You're going to be just fine, Nikolai. Trust yourself." She rolled her eyes when he raised a skeptical eyebrow. "Fine, then trust me."

She tucked her arm through his. "Come on. I'll take you to the bride."

Looking stunning in a simple floor-length gold lace gown, Phoebe Pierce wed Franklin Merill in a pool of afternoon sunshine as their children, grandchildren, and closest friends looked on. Phoebe's sons, in white button downs and khakis, lined up behind her for the ceremony while Franklin's daughters in their blush dresses did the same for him. Groomsmaids and bridesmen, they'd called themselves.

Niko snapped a handful of test shots as the ceremony began but didn't get the tingle of the magic until the moment that Emma discreetly passed Gia a tissue. The happiness of the ceremony, the simplicity of the vows spoken, the bonding of two families was its own magic. There were tears and watery smiles on both sides as two became one.

And when the minister mentioned the joy that those who were gone from this world must certainly feel for the happy couple, the brothers marked the moment spontaneously by laying a hand on the other's shoulder. Jax to Beckett, Beckett to Carter. Magic. Family. Love.

Niko caught it all, finding the flow in the swooping flight of the butterflies released from their white cardboard prison. The reception bar had opened before the ceremony, and the guests happily lifted their glasses in a spontaneous toast when Phoebe and Franklin were introduced as husband and wife.

Niko felt his own throat tighten just a bit when he watched a tearful Emma blow her father a kiss as he and Phoebe dashed down the aisle to wild cheers.

He caught it again when the bride and groom held their three youngest grandbabies in celebration and then again when Carter reached out to cup Summer's face in a sweet, private moment.

He was there for the laughter of Jax and Eva's toasts. He caught Aurora swiping an extra piece of cake and sneaking under the gift table to eat it. Calvin Finestra, Blue Moon's go-to contractor, and his wife led the guests in a complicated line dance that had the band cranking up the speakers a little louder.

Niko watched Emma twirl around the dance floor laughing in her father's arms. Here in the Blue Moon sunshine, he found real. He found love.

"I LOVE SEEING you so happy, Dad," Emma laughed breathlessly as Franklin twirled her in a tight circle. The Wild Nigels, Blue Moon's favorite garage band, blared out a swing song. Fran, Fitness Freak's mohawked front desk worker, rocked out on her bass, her wheelchair festively decked in pink and gold ribbons.

Franklin dipped Emma, making her squeal. "I feel like I have everything I ever wanted," he said, the smile nearly splitting his face.

"I just wish you could have found this the first time around," Emma told him. She hated that he'd been hurt so badly by her careless mother, hated that he'd had to suffer quietly while putting on a brave front for three scared little girls.

"Emmaline, my girl, let me tell you a secret," Franklin said, pulling her back into his arms. "I wouldn't trade a second of that heartache because everything since then has been leading me here to this perfect moment."

She hugged him tighter, and a tear slipped out between her lashes. "I just wish you could have gotten here without the pain."

"Don't be afraid of pain, or less-than-perfect, daughter of mine. That's where the real joy comes from. Life gets its color from challenges and adversity. You can't plan your way to happiness, you know."

Emma frowned. *Is that what her father thought she was doing? Is that what she was doing? Trying to orchestrate chaos into the most agreeable outcome?*

"Now, no worrying today. Today's only for celebrating. I think there's someone who could use a little distraction."

Franklin nudged his chin across the dance floor where Niko was capturing the Pierce boys and their beers at the bar.

Niko was mouth-watering as always in charcoal pants that made his ass look even more spectacular than usual and a pale blue shirt, the sleeves rolled stylishly to his elbows. She could see just a hint of the ink from his tattoo peeking out under the sleeve. He'd shaved for the occasion, but Emma realized it didn't do anything to lessen the bad boy vibe. God, he was gorgeous.

Evan galloped up to Emma and Franklin, a laughing Phoebe in tow. "Our grandson can certainly dance," she said.

Evan gave a little bow. "Ladies like a guy with moves," he said wisely and turned the bride back over to the groom.

"Why don't you two enjoy a dance," Emma suggested. "I have a photographer to distract."

She made her way through the crowded dance floor and swung by the bar. She ordered a martini and a beer from Cheryl whose tip jar was overflowing with wedding goodwill. Off duty and out of uniform, Donovan Cardona leaned against the bar nursing a beer and staring into the crowd.

"Did you get everything straightened out with Fitz?" Emma asked, nudging him.

Donovan shook himself back to the present. "Apparently our pal Fitz took an online Stripping 101 course a while back. He's the understudy to whoever you actually hired. That guy couldn't make it last night because he's the understudy for the lead in an off-off-Broadway of *The Full Monty,* and the lead fell down a flight of stairs and broke his leg after someone slapped him on the shoulder and told him to break a leg."

Emma shook her head. "Was this Fitz's first gig?"

Donovan laughed. "Here's the unbelievable part. Apparently, the little weasel's been picking up jobs here and there and clearing an extra grand a month shaking it for book clubs and knitting circles."

Emma shuddered. "I'm never joining a book club or a knitting circle."

"Here you go, boss," Cheryl pushed the drinks at Emma with a wink. "You going to go hydrate that gorgeous photographer?"

"I'm thinking about it," Emma said slyly.

"Hot damn." Cheryl moved down the bar to take another order, and Emma looked around the crowd again. She saw Aurora sharing a piece of cake with a little boy in jeans and a too-small polo shirt.

"Do you know who that boy is?" Emma asked Donovan, tilting her head in Aurora's direction.

"That's Reva's little brother, Caleb." For a second, Emma saw Donovan go from wedding guest to cop as he studied the boy. "There've been some rumors around town about their mother. I've been trying to call her, but the house phone's been disconnected."

"What's going on?"

"Rumor has it the mom skipped town with her latest boyfriend. She stopped showing up for work last month, and no one's seen her since."

"Then who's taking care of Reva and Caleb?"

"That's what I'm worried about," Donovan said.

Emma watched Caleb's big eyes get bigger as Aurora spooned a huge portion of cake onto his plate.

"Well, hell," she said. She could only imagine what would happen if it turned out their mother had abandoned them. Foster care, separation, instability. "I hope for their sake the rumors aren't true."

"I hope so, too," Donovan admitted. "But I don't have a good feeling about it."

"Let me know if there's anything I can do," Emma offered.

When Donovan didn't respond, Emma followed his gaze to Eva as she spun around the dance floor with Evan, laughing and gasping for breath.

Emma bit her lip. The town sheriff with a crush on Eva? Now that was interesting.

"Maybe you should go ask her to dance," she suggested to him.

Donovan turned six shades of red and fumbled his beer.

"And don't even pretend you don't know what I'm talking about," she warned him when he opened his mouth.

"Is she seeing anyone?"

"No one serious. But she appreciates a man who can keep up with her around the dance floor." Emma left him pondering her suggestion and tracked down Niko who was capturing Mrs. Nordemann kicking up her bare feet on a table with a piece of cake in her lap.

"You're officially off duty," Emma said, handing him the beer.

She saw the glaze of his eyes and knew he'd found his way back into it all. The grin she flashed him was pure cockiness. "Looks like someone's remembered how to be a photographer."

The teasing brought him all the way back to her. "No one likes a smart ass," he countered.

"Not true. You like me, and you're well aware that I'm a smart ass."

"You're my friend. I'm required to like you, warts and all."

She took a fortifying sip of martini and set her glass on the table well away from Mrs. Nordemann's bunions. "Dance with me, Nikolai."

It took no convincing for him to put down his camera, take her hand, and lead her out onto the dance floor. The sun was setting, and the band shifted into a slow, smooth song about love and heartbreak. Someone plugged in the strings of lights looped around the tent casting a soft glow over everyone beneath it.

Niko fit her body against his, and the rightness of it zipped through her like electricity. They danced closer than friends, closer than they should, but Emma didn't want to pull back to put that space between them. She wanted him close enough to touch, to taste.

"What's gotten into you, Emmaline?" Niko asked, his lips moving against her ear.

"Just listening to my elders."

"Whatever they said to put you here, I agree with one-hundred percent," he said, his voice husky. He ran his hands up and down her sides, fingers splaying over her hips and waist. "You look like a goddess."

"You look like a very enjoyable bad idea."

He pulled her hand to his mouth and laid his lips across her knuckles. "Emma, you're sending me mixed signals," he warned.

"I know," she said, biting her lip. "I'm thinking."

"Thinking about revising our friendship?" he asked.

She nodded.

He bent her backwards in a dramatic dip. She laughed and wrapped her arms around his neck. "Think fast," he suggested darkly.

"Nothing would change," she stipulated. "You aren't planning to give up your life and move to Blue Moon, and I'm not leaving here."

"That doesn't mean we can't enjoy ourselves with the time we do have together."

"How much longer are you going to stay?" She wasn't asking for planning purposes, Emma realized. She was asking for her. "You've obviously had some kind of breakthrough today, thanks to your incredibly intelligent friend."

"Incredibly intelligent, sexy, stunningly beautiful friend," he corrected her.

"I like all those things about me."

"I do, too. And I'm planning to stick around a while longer. We can't know for sure that I'm completely cured."

"That's true," Emma mused. "We should take our time and make sure your recovery is a permanent one. We don't want to rush anything…"

On impulse, she pressed her lips to his neck and felt him go hard everywhere against her. His fingers dug into her hips. "I have never wanted anyone or anything the way that I want you."

"When you say it, it doesn't sound like a line," Emma whispered back.

"Emmaline, everything with you is real."

"You guys are kinda ruining the formation," Evan hissed at them, appearing from nowhere. Emma realized they were surrounded by dancers including Aurora, Caleb, and Evan's junior high girlfriend, Oceana, all of whom were doing the same steps. The song had changed at some point to one with a peppy beat, and neither of them had noticed.

Rainbow and Gordon Berkowicz had their heads together with Bruce Oakleigh and Bobby from Peace of Pizza. They all looked rather pleased with themselves.

"Well, that should give everyone something to talk about," Emma said, feeling the flush creep over her cheeks. "I'm going to go track down my martini."

"Want to dance with us, Niko?" Aurora asked sweetly.

"Uh, sure?"

16

The party lasted until almost midnight with the guests reluctant to leave the fun.

"Come on, guys. Let's let the newlyweds go do what newlyweds do," Joey yawned. She didn't see the color drain out of Beckett and Jax's faces, but Niko did, and it made him laugh. "I want to get out of this dress," she complained to Jax.

"I'm happy to help you, Mrs. Pierce," Jax teased.

Emma organized the cleanup and helped Cheryl pack up the portable bar.

Niko took a moment to flip through some of the pictures on his camera display. His pulse quickened. They were good. Really good. And there were more of them than he'd expected. Phoebe might just be getting herself a wedding portfolio after all.

It was all there. The laughter, the tears, the love, and the land. He breathed a sigh of relief and turned the camera off, repacking the flash and extra batteries in his bag.

"How do they look?" Emma asked.

"Uh-uh. Bride gets dibs on these," he told her.

Emma pouted. "Are you sure the friend who strong-armed you into this doesn't trump the bride?"

He ran his thumb over her lower lip and wished they were alone. "Pretty sure. But maybe you could try convincing me." He watched her eyes go dark and wanted more than anything to move in and sample her.

"You guys ready to head out? Reva's bringing the wagon back around to pick us up," Joey said, jerking her chin toward the sound of hooves and the creak of the hay wagon.

"Yeah, let me just grab something quick," Emma said, backing away from Niko.

She dashed over to the caterer and returned with two big bags.

Reva pulled the team up in front of them and climbed down. Wordlessly, she nodded at everyone and bundled her brother into his jacket. "Get up on the wagon, Cale," she ordered.

"I'm tired, Ree," the little boy yawned.

"I know, buddy. We're going home now."

"Reva, we're divvying up leftovers. These are for you guys. Does your mom like chicken?" Emma asked, handing Reva the bags.

"Mom's on vacation," Caleb said sadly. "I miss her, but Reva doesn't."

"Okay, time to go," Reva said quickly, shoving Caleb toward the wagon. Niko saw Emma and Donovan share a glance.

"Horses do okay for you?" Joey asked Reva, changing the subject.

"No problems," the girl answered solemnly as she carefully packed the bags up on the seat next to her.

Niko took pleasure in lifting Emma onto the wagon. He

climbed on behind her and pulled her into his side when they sat.

"Everybody on?" Reva called from the front.

"All clear," Jax reported.

The wagon lurched forward, and Niko wondered if life could possibly get any better than this moment. A beautiful woman curled into his side, the night sky filled with stars, and a day of fun behind them.

He saw it, the quick flash of a shooting star across the midnight blue of the sky. He glanced around, but no one else had noticed it. There was only one thing to do with a shooting star. So he wished. He didn't know the how or the why, but those didn't seem to matter. All that did was the who.

Emma.

They returned to the brewery parking lot and unloaded. Jax and Carter unhooked the wagon and led the team back to the barn to untack.

Summer left to help Gia load up her car and search Aurora for contraband cake. "How many pieces of cake did you have?" Gia asked her daughter as they walked toward the parking lot.

"Thanks for the leftovers and for letting my brother come. Our neighbor couldn't watch him tonight," Reva said quietly to Joey. "We're gonna go home."

"Who's here to pick you up?" Joey asked, fussing with the strap of her dress.

"Uh, our mom. She's probably down by the road," Reva said, putting her arm around Caleb.

"I don't wanna walk, Ree," the little boy yawned.

"Hush. It's not that far," she told him.

"It is, too. It's a million miles."

"How about I drive you down and meet your mom," Donovan said. It wasn't an offer. It was closer to an order.

"No, that's okay," Reva said quickly.

"Is Mom really here?" Caleb asked hopefully.

Niko could see the tension radiating off of Reva.

"Reva," Beckett said quietly. "What's going on?"

"Nothing," she shook her head. "Nothing, we just gotta get home. It's late."

"I'll drive you," Donovan said again.

"You can't," Reva said flatly.

"Why can't he drive you?" Joey asked frowning.

"Because it'll ruin everything, okay?" Reva threw her arms up in the air.

"Don't be mad, Ree. It's okay." Caleb patted his sister's arm.

"It's not okay. And you guys are going to ruin everything!"

"Where's your mom, Reva?" Emma asked.

"She left. Okay? She left us three weeks ago."

Joey let out a string of curse words that had Caleb's mouth falling open. "Those are *all* bad words!"

"My wife has a spectacular vocabulary, buddy," Jax said, reappearing with Waffles at his heels. He ruffled Caleb's hair. "What's going on?"

"Reva's mad 'cause mom left us to go on vacation, and she won't let Mr. Sheriff drive us home even though I don't wanna walk 'cause it's so far an' I'm tired," Caleb explained.

"Well, shit."

"You can't split us up," Reva said to Donovan. "I won't let you."

"Reva, I don't want to separate you from your brother."

"But if you put us in foster care, that's what's going to happen. I'll be eighteen in ten months. I can be Caleb's guardian then."

"But you can't freaking raise yourselves until then," Joey argued. "What the hell, Reva?"

"Okay, hang on. We need an adult pow-wow," Emma said.

"Stay right there, and don't even think about running away or I'll have Waffles hunt you down," Joey threatened Reva.

"Okay, here's what happened," Donovan began when they huddled up. "Reva's mom asked you two to watch her kids while she went on vacation," he said pointing at Joey and Jax.

"Us? We don't know what to do with kids!" Joey complained.

"Please," Jax snorted. "Reva is more mature than the two of us combined."

"True. Continue."

"We're going to take them to their house, make sure the mom isn't there, pack up some of their shit, and they're going to stay with you two until I can figure out a way to make sure they don't get split up," Donovan decided.

"You heard the sheriff, Jojo," Jax said. "We got ourselves a couple of house guests."

"Good thing we put that addition on the house," Joey muttered.

NIKO AND EMMA went with Donovan, Reva, and Caleb to the house to pack while Jax and Joey readied the guest rooms.

Reva stared sullenly out the window of Donovan's SUV while Caleb fell asleep against Emma's arm. Emma felt an ages-old rage roil inside her. How were mothers still abandoning their children? And in this case, there wasn't a second parent ready and willing to step into the void. She and her sisters had been lucky. Franklin had been father and mother and therapist and friend to them all. But who did Reva have? And who did Caleb have besides Reva?

Emma understood Reva better than the girl could know. She knew the bitter taste of betrayal just as she knew the determination to keep the rest of her family intact. She just hoped the system wouldn't damage them even more.

Without directions, Donovan pulled into the dirt driveway of a ramshackle ranch. Once a shade of white, the siding shown dingy gray in the headlights. Paint peeled from the shutters and front door. But the grass was neatly trimmed and the porch light glowed a sad welcome.

"Come on, Cale," Reva whispered to her brother. "We're home."

Inside, Reva flipped on lights revealing a worn but spotless interior. The threadbare carpet was vacuumed. The shelves holding a handful of framed pictures of Reva and Caleb were dusted. The kitchen was immaculate and empty save for a box of peanut butter crackers and a bag of apples on the counter. There was no food in the cabinets or the refrigerator.

"I was going to go grocery shopping tomorrow. I got paid this weekend," Reva said defensively as Donovan systematically opened and closed cabinets.

"Reva, there's not a one of us that's gonna say you did something wrong. So get that through your stubborn head," Donovan said. "We're here to help, and we're going to do whatever it takes to keep you and your brother together. So if you're gonna be pissed, be pissed at someone who deserves it."

"You mean like my mother."

Niko knelt down to Caleb's level. "Hey, man. Want to show me your room? We can pack up some stuff for your sleepover at Jax and Joey's."

Caleb trotted down the ribbon of hallway tugging Niko behind him.

"Look, we're not here to judge," Donovan began.

"But you are," Reva countered. "I come from a woman who loved pills and booze more than her own kids. That's in me. She made me."

Emma laid her hands on Reva's shoulders. "You aren't your parents any more than any of us are. My mom left, too. And I take great pleasure in not being her. It doesn't matter who made you. It matters what you choose to be."

"Do you know where she is, Reva?" Donovan asked quietly.

She shook her head. "Said she was going away for the weekend with her boyfriend. That was three weeks ago. She emptied the checking account."

"Go pack whatever you need," Donovan ordered quietly.

Emma gave her a minute and then wandered down the skinny hallway with its flattened, stained shag carpeting. She paused outside Caleb's room and listened to Niko explain how to pack his Buzz Lightyear suitcase so he could fit his teddy bear in it.

"Wow!" Caleb said in wonder as Niko zipped the bag shut. "You pack good."

"Lots of practice, kid."

"Niko?"

"Yeah, bud?"

"Do you think Jax and Joey will have Marshmallow Munchies at their house?"

"What are Marshmallow Munchies?"

The little boy moved in and leaned his tired head against Niko's arm. "It's my favorite cereal. I had it one time at a sleepover."

Niko cleared his throat, and his voice was gravelly when he spoke again. "Yeah, buddy. I think they'll have Marshmallow Munchies."

Her throat thick with emotion, Emma moved on to the room Reva had entered and knocked lightly. "Need a hand?"

Reva was sitting on the bed, silent tears tracking down her

face. "I'm not sad," she said quickly, wiping a hand under each eye.

"You're pissed, and you have every right to be," Emma said, sitting down next to her. "Be mad at her. It'll fuel you better than sad ever will. But don't forget that you still have a life to live, and it's going to be good. Really good."

"You think so?" Reva sniffed.

"This is Blue Freaking Moon, Reva. We take care of our own whether you want us to or not. Now, shove your crap in a bag and let's get your brother home to bed."

It was another hour before they had Reva and Caleb settled in at Jax and Joey's. Waffles was beside himself with excitement over the house guests and couldn't decide who he wanted to sleep with.

"I can't believe they've been on their own for almost a month," Niko shook his head as they walked back to Emma's car in the brewery parking lot.

"That is one determined girl," Emma agreed, wrapping her arms around herself to keep warm. Noticing, Niko pulled her up against his side, and the heat pumping off of him warmed her immediately.

"Is there an all-night grocery store around here?" he asked.

"In Cleary, about thirty minutes west," Emma told him. "Why? Are you hungry?"

"I'm gonna go pick up a couple of boxes of Marshmallow Munchies."

And just like that, she broke. Hard and fast and without any hope of ever recovering her sanity.

"Damn it, Niko!"

She grabbed him by the shirtfront and dragged him down

to meet her mouth. Her body, it seemed, had been waiting for this exact moment forever. The heat and pressure of his lips against hers sent magic zinging up her spine as every cell in her body flamed to life.

He caught up quickly, spinning her and pressing her against the door of her SUV. Cold metal at her back and the hot, hard lines of Niko's body at her front. She felt him harden against her and welcomed it when he leaned into her, grinding hips against hips.

She whimpered against his lips, and he used it to gain access to her mouth. His tongue swept into her like an army invading, and Emma could see the stars brighten behind her closed lids. Closer. She needed to be closer to him. His belt bit into her belly, but it only excited her more.

He skimmed his hands over her shoulders, down her arms to her waist and hips, the silk of her dress begging to be ripped away.

She shoved her fingers into his hair, keeping him on her, and gave up all need for oxygen as she poured herself into the kiss. *Swept away.* As if her common sense and her carefully laid plans were caught in the unceasing current of a river.

It's what he was doing to her, what she was allowing to happen.

Her lips bruised themselves against his, finding the pain worth it now that the wait was finally over. She belonged right here, right now, devouring and being devoured under the night spring sky. Nothing but now mattered.

"Baby," Niko whispered, his breath ragged. "We've got to stop, or I'm going to take you right here on the hood of your car."

"There are worse places," Emma said, nibbling on his lower lip.

He growled darkly. "You deserve better, Emmaline. And I'm going to give it to you."

She lost her breath again at that promise. "My house. Tomorrow night. Tonight," she corrected looking up at the night sky. "Dinner. I'll cook for you and then after—"

"I'll make you very, very happy," he promised. He pulled back slightly and stared up at the sky, swore. "Are you sure, Emma? I know you want to be friends, and I've got to admit, I've become pretty dependent on having you as a friend."

"Niko, you're driving an hour round-trip to buy a little boy you just met cereal that he had one time and loved. This after spending hours documenting the happiest day of my father's life, all because I asked you to do it. You're not just gorgeous on the outside. You're beautiful on the inside, too, and I'd be an idiot to not take advantage of whatever time we have together."

"Jesus, Emma. You gut me," he said, resting his forehead on hers.

"Nikolai, you're going to feel a lot more than gutted when I'm done with you."

His erection flexed hard as steel against her belly at her words. "I'm worried I won't survive you," he admitted.

"There's only one way to find out. Seven. Don't be late. And you might want to catch a nap this afternoon so you're rested up."

17

*E*mma congratulated herself on having had the foresight to take Monday off at the brewery. Originally, it had been in anticipation of a spectacular champagne and happiness hangover. But after a few hours of sleep, she'd woken hangover-free and excited. She was going to have sex with Nikolai Vulkov, and after that kiss last night—the one that had left her hot, breathless, and weak in the knees—she would need the day to prepare.

But first, she popped by McCafferty's Farm Supply on the square. She had planned to pick up what was supposed to be just a few items of clothing for Reva and Caleb and somehow ended up with an entire wardrobe for them both.

She'd dropped them off at Jax and Joey's and found Caleb snuggled on the couch with Waffles and a blanket.

"Hi!"

"Hey, Caleb. How's it going?"

"Jax and Joey said I didn't hafta go to school today since I was up so late last night. I had Marshmallow Munchies for breakfast, and they were the best ever!"

"That sounds like a really good day," Emma agreed. "Is Jax or Joey here?" God, she hoped one of them was.

"Jax is in his office writin' stuff. He made me grilled cheese for lunch!"

"Cool. Well, I'm going to go say hi to him. But first, I saw this and I thought you might like it."

She pulled the stuffed pony out of one of the shopping bags and handed it over to him.

"For me?" he asked, incredulous. And her heart broke just a little bit for him.

"I thought you'd like it since you're staying here with all the horses."

"Wow! Thanks! What's his name?" Caleb asked.

"You get to name him. He's yours."

"Hmm. Joe? No. Horsey? No." His little face was serious as he examined the pony from ears to tail, trying on names for size. She left him to it and wandered around the staircase to Jax's office.

He and Joey had added an addition to the cozy cabin that nearly doubled the square footage. The second floor now boasted four spacious bedrooms, while downstairs, Jax got a study for himself and Joey got a sunroom.

Emma knocked on the doorframe and watched Jax drag himself out of the story he was telling.

"Oh, hey," he yawned, stretching his arms overhead. "Trouble at the brewery?"

"When have I ever brought you a problem I couldn't handle?" Emma demanded, dumping the bags by the door.

"Good point. Are you clothing an army?" he asked, nodding at the bags.

"I noticed Reva and Caleb didn't have a ton of clothes when they were packing last night, so I thought I'd pick up a few essentials."

"And a few essentials turned into the entire second floor of McCafferty's?" Jax laughed.

"Pretty much."

"Between you and Niko, these kids are going to be swimming in iPads and diamonds," Jax predicted.

The delight she got out of just hearing Niko's name was ridiculous.

"So Niko made his cereal delivery?" she asked innocently.

"He texts me at three this morning and asks if it's okay to leave a few 'groceries' in the kitchen for the kids. So I let him in, and he's got four bags of frozen pizza and cereal and chips and mac and cheese. Comfort food, he called it."

Emma felt her heart warm.

"What's with the face?" Jax demanded.

"What? What face?"

"I tell you Niko dumps eighty-two thousand calories in our kitchen, and you get all soft and dewy."

"Shut up. I did not."

Jax leaned across the desk. "Those crazy Beautification Committee bastards got to you two, didn't they? When's the wedding?"

"The Beautification Committee has nothing to do with me being *friends* with Niko. In fact, I have it on good authority that they have no interest in pairing me off with him."

"Yeah, you keep telling yourself that. Also, they don't call going all doe-eyed at the mention of some guy's name 'friends.'"

"You're ridiculous!"

"He's a good guy," Jax said, shifting gears into serious. "You could do a lot worse."

"He's not staying in Blue Moon, and I am," Emma reminded him.

"Emma, Emma, Emma," he sighed. "Never underestimate the power and pull of this insane town."

Caleb ran into the room, hugging the stuffed horse around the neck. "Emma! I picked a name!"

"You did! That's great! What is it?"

He held out the horse for his introduction. "This is Cloppy." His face fell momentarily, and the little boy looked worried. "Are you really sure I can keep him?"

Emma's eyes met Jax's, saw her own sadness mirrored in his, before answering. "Of course. I got him just for you."

Satisfied, Caleb smiled and then threw his arms around her legs. "Thanks! Hi, Jax!" he waved before scampering out the door. "Come on, Cloppy!"

"Everything that kid says is like a hammer fist to my heart," Jax said, rubbing a hand absently over his chest. "How could anyone just walk away from him?"

"You never know why people make the decisions they do."

"Does this stir up a lot of stuff for you about your own mom?" Jax asked.

Emma raised an eyebrow at him, and Jax looked chagrined. "Sorry. Nosy writer habit."

"Things are simmering. But that was a long time ago for all of us, and we had my dad. And it looks like Reva and Caleb have you and Joey."

"For better or worse, it looks like," Jax joked.

The timer on his phone went off.

"What's that for?"

"It's my 'check on Caleb' to make sure he's alive and not ingesting forty pounds of chocolate alarm."

～

AFTER JAX'S, Emma convinced Eva to put down her work, and the two headed off to the Snip Shack for some pampering. She was due for a trim and let Claudette, the stylist, work her magic on her curly tresses. Next came facials and the pedis they'd both missed out on due to Fitz's untimely arrival.

As their feet soaked in the tubs of warm, scented water and the mud on their faces hardened, Emma broached the subject. "So listen, Eva. You know how I said you could stay with me as long as you wanted?"

Eva glanced up over her reading glasses and took a sip of her diet soda. "I'm getting the feeling you're about to give me bad news."

"I need you to stay somewhere else tonight."

"Why? Are you getting the place fumigated?"

"Niko's coming over for dinner and... dessert."

Eva straightened, nearly launching the magazine she was reading into the foot water. "Are you serious? Oh, my God! This is the most incredible news! What are you going to wear? What are you going to cook? How are you going to do your hair?"

"So you're not mad that I'm kicking you out?"

"Ems, I'd go sleep in the forest in the middle of winter if I thought it meant you were happily getting laid by that gorgeous, smoldering piece of hotness."

"He's not just eye candy," Emma said, disapprovingly. "He's pretty great on the inside, too."

"That's quite the change from 'I know his type. He's just another womanizing bad boy.'" Eva said, mimicking Emma's previous stance on Nikolai Vulkov. "Not that I'm complaining that you changed your mind," she corrected quickly.

"Could have fooled me."

"I just mean that after you meet him, anyone can see that Niko's not your standard wham-bam-thank-you-ma'am guy.

Sure, he's super intense, but there's this genuine interest in there like even if he doesn't want to sleep with you, he'd still like to know you as a person. Even though he totally wants to sleep with you."

Emma stared blandly at her sister. "What goes on in your head?"

Eva grinned. "Trust me, Ems, you don't want to know. Let's get back to what you're going to wear."

BY SIX FORTY-FIVE, Emma was dressed in a simple yet sexy dress in a fresh, springy green. Its sweetheart neckline was cut low enough to be very interesting while the slim-fitting skirt stopped an appropriate three inches above her knees. Her hair, expertly styled by Claudette, hung in glossy ringlets that begged for a man's hands. She'd gone for a little bit of drama with smoky eyes and a sexy gloss on her lips.

The meal she'd kept relatively simple with stuffed mushrooms for the appetizer followed by Florentine style cuts of porterhouse and a light prosciutto and pine nut salad. Dessert, if they got that far into the courses, was a decadent tiramisu that she'd picked up from her father's restaurant.

A bottle of cabernet was breathing on the table, and there was a box of condoms tucked into her nightstand.

They would enjoy wine and appetizers in the kitchen before moving to the table for the meal. Conversation between them had never been a problem before, so Emma wasn't anticipating any awkward moments there.

She was ready. At least, she should be, given all her preparations. Her legs were shaved, and her sheets were fresh. The brewery staff was under strict instructions to only bother Jax or Carter with any emergencies tonight. Eva was ensconced in their father's house with Mr. Snuffles while Franklin and Phoebe jetted off on their surprise Bahamas honeymoon, a gift from their kids.

Everything was perfect.

She pressed a hand to her belly where a squadron of butterflies dive-bombed into each other. Was she crazy? Was she literally insane for thinking that she could enjoy a couple of nights of "no strings attached" sex with Niko before they both went on with their separate lives?

Emma plopped down on the couch and closed her eyes, determined to calm her racing heart with one of Gia's breathing exercises. *It was just sex*, she reminded herself. Divine, possibly mind-altering sex, if that kiss last night was any indication. But still. Sex was sex. There was nothing to be nervous about. A careful seduction that would lead to a mutually satisfying evening with a man she enjoyed spending time with. She should be glad Niko mattered to her. It should make intimacy with him easier. In the past, she'd often found it difficult to completely open up to men, always holding a few pieces of herself back. It was safer that way.

But Nikolai wasn't one to settle for part of anything. Though they had no future together, she imagined his demands on her in the present would be total.

Stop thinking, she ordered herself. Focusing on alternate nostril breathing, Emma forced herself to think only of her breath.

The knock at her door jolted her from her tenuous Zen.

She leapt up, rapping her shin on the coffee table, and limped to the door. One last breath, and she opened the door.

Nikolai looked beyond gorgeous in charcoal trousers and a slate blue oxford shirt that he wore open at the neck. His glossy cognac loafers matched his belt. He held a rapturous bouquet of spring flowers in shades of red and pink. He wasn't smiling. He was watching her with an intensity that had her stomach doing cartwheels. It was the single most tempting picture Emma had ever seen in her life.

"Hi," she said breathlessly.

"Hi back." There it was, that slow, sexy smile that melted both inhibitions and underwear. "Can I come in?" he asked.

Emma jumped back from the doorway. "Of course, come in." *Get it together, girl,* she growled to herself. "Would you like some wine?" Her voice was coming out a full octave higher than usual as she hurried into the kitchen at a half-jog.

"You're not scared, are you, Emma?" Niko asked with a wolfish smile.

She fumbled the wine glass and laughed nervously. "Of course not. What's there to be nervous about?" *Losing a piece of your soul to sex so good everything else for the rest of your life will pale in comparison. Falling for an unkeepable guy and suffering the devastation of loss.* Her brain helpfully filled in the answers.

His hand closed over hers on the stem of the glass.

"Let's just get this out of the way so we can both stop thinking about it."

18

He meant to just kiss her. He'd thought of nothing else since last night when Emma launched herself at him. He was hard before she even answered the door. That's what she did to him. Her mouth on his had almost leveled him, nearly stripping him of his control, and he wanted the experience again.

He'd kissed and been kissed but not like that. Never like that.

Emma had taken something from him last night, and Niko wanted it back.

There was nothing gentle about the way he crushed his lips to hers. He was the aggressor this time. He was in charge. Fisting his hand into her hair, he dragged Emma's head back, changing the angle of attack. When her lips parted for her to draw in a breath, he sealed his mouth over hers and swept inside using frantic strokes of his tongue designed to over-whelm her.

She responded to him as if he were the sun and she a flower blossom. Opening and blooming under him, she came to life and stole his breath with the beauty of her need for him. Emma's fingers knotted in his shirt holding him to her. His hands busied themselves worshipping the perfection of her curves.

There was light here, color and heat, too. Her flavor sang through his veins and ignited a desire more akin to addiction than anticipation. The sexy little moans coming from the back of her throat had his body begging to be let off the leash.

It was supposed to be just a kiss. And it was anything but that.

He spun them, accidentally rapping her head off of the cabinet door. She swallowed his muffled apology with those precious, perfect lips, urging him on. He dragged his hands up over her hips, coasting around her waist to rest under the full curve of her breast.

Emma reached fast fingers under his belt and worked the buckle free. Niko palmed her breasts through the soft fabric of her dress and was rewarded with a sigh of pleasure from her.

"If you like this dress, you need to get out of it in the next two seconds, or it's going to be destroyed," he warned her.

Emma pushed him back a half step and slid the thick straps off her shoulders. She was wriggling it down her hips when he lost patience, shoving the garment to the floor. Her breasts overflowed from the lavender lace that lifted them like an offering to him. Dainty briefs in the same delicate lace had his fingers itching to shred them from her body. But the artist in him wanted to savor the moment... the flawless ivory of her skin, the glorious fullness of her curves, the single-minded quest for fulfillment that sparked behind those meadow green eyes.

He wanted to capture her like this, wearing power and need like an aura, a halo. She was a goddess made with the sole purpose of rendering him speechless.

"You're perfection," he murmured, holding her hand as she stepped out of the dress.

"Don't stop now," she said on a breathless whisper.

"I've got to catch up." And calm down. If he let himself loose now, he'd take her here on the floor.

She worked the buttons on his shirt open, slipping her palms under his shirt to slide them over his chest. Her touch ignited an awareness so intense, Niko wasn't sure if anything beyond this room existed anymore.

When she reached for his zipper, Niko stilled her hands with his. "Bedroom, Emma. I want you in a bed this first time."

Her heavy-lidded eyes opened wider, and she rose on tiptoe to reclaim his mouth. "Hurry," she murmured against him.

It was all the encouragement he needed, boosting her up and wrapping her legs around his hips. He growled when she cuddled against his raging hard cock. He gripped her ass and made the mad dash up the stairs. They smacked into the wall at the top and a framed picture tumbled to the floor.

"Keep going," she demanded, feeding on his lips.

Niko kicked the bedroom door open, and then they were tumbling to the mattress. He should be going slow. He wanted to savor her body. But then she was wrestling his pants free, nudging them down with her heels hooked around his hips, and there was nothing he wanted more than speed and need.

"Hurry!" Emma ordered.

He kicked off one pant leg and then the other before pressing his face to her breasts, loving the thump of her erratic heartbeat against his cheek

"So beautiful," he murmured, plying those voluptuous curves with kisses.

She arched up, sliding the straps off her shoulders. Niko reached under her and released the clasp with one hand.

"Show off," she teased.

"Baby, just you wait."

The lace slipped, and he took a moment to slide it off her breasts like the unveiling of a masterpiece.

"Worth the wait," he breathed. Her nipples, perfect pink nubs, hardened in anticipation before his eyes. God, she was perfection. She had the magic. Women like her had been the temptation of men for centuries. And tonight, she belonged to him. He nuzzled softly, reverently, before bringing the soft pink bud into his mouth.

"Nikolai!" On a shout and a sigh, Emma fisted her hands in the comforter. His name from her mouth was a spell. He licked and tasted before sealing his mouth over her nipple and sucking. She arched harder against him, and he took more, feeding their desire.

She writhed against him when he switched breasts, teasing the ignored bud until it strained for more.

"My Emmaline," he whispered reverently, slipping down her body, blazing a trail with his lips over her flat stomach to the curve of her hip. He hooked his fingers in the front of her gossamer thin underwear, dragging it down. His mouth followed, and he felt her quake against him when his tongue dipped between her legs to sample her.

She was wet and ready for him, and he'd barely touched her. Niko drew the tip of his tongue through that wet slit and reveled in her gasp. She was so much more than he'd anticipated. So much more than he deserved. The hurry, the desire to claim, returned in force, and Niko slid one finger into her.

"Niko. I'm going to—"

He dipped his tongue to the sensitive, swollen nub, stroking gently. She fell apart on his finger and mouth, muscles closing around him as she came and came and came.

He was so hard, so ready, he thought he might go with her just from the sound of her voice breaking on a sob.

He should have felt a dose of pride for bringing her here, for making her sob his name. But all he felt was need. He needed to be inside her, to claim her, to feel her come around him.

But before he could move, she was wriggling free of his grip and pushing him onto his back.

"You tasted me. It's only fair." Those sea goddess eyes teased him, promising him pleasure, as she coasted down his body, dipping her tongue over his chest and abs to the sensitive skin just inside his hip bone.

There was nothing playful about the way she took his cock in her mouth. When she slicked down over his shaft, his hips levered up off the mattress, his entire body tensed at the sensation. Her mouth was hot as it licked up to his tip that leaked copiously from the seam.

She tasted him there, and her tongue traced a path over every vein, every inch, until he was panting with desire. One hand in the comforter, he shoved the other into her hair and gripped. Hard. She bobbed up and down, fisting him from root to tip. Sliding over him like a fucking popsicle. Over and over again, harder and faster.

She was going to kill him. He was going to die right here with his cock in her mouth without ever having fully had her.

The thought was enough to have him dragging her up his body by the hair and rolling. He settled between her legs just outside her weeping entrance.

"God, condom!" she gasped.

He was glad one of them still had the power of thought. Niko reared up, looking for his pants.

"Nightstand," Emma pointed with a shaking hand.

He dove for the drawer and, finding the box, shredded the cardboard open.

The purr from her throat when he tore the wrapper with his teeth had his hands shaking as he rolled the rubber on. He fisted his shaft, and Emma, eyes at half mast, licked her lips.

He wanted to remember this moment forever, commit it to memory, capture it on screen so he could relive it again and again. The moment Emmaline became his. They were both breathless and wide-eyed as he guided the broad head of his erection to her entrance. He didn't have to tell her to look at him. She was staring into him as he eased into her inch by inch until he was buried inside her.

Emma's eyelashes fluttered, and her jaw clenched as she fought the fullness.

"Just relax, baby," he breathed. "Relax for me."

Her breaths were short, sexy little gasps, but little by little, he felt her muscles give until his last inch slid into her. Those green eyes, the knowing and the wonder in them, convinced Niko that he'd never forget this exact moment for as long as he walked the earth.

With a patience he didn't know he had inside him, Niko slowly pulled out, gritting his teeth at the sensation. He took his time, sliding back into her until they were one. It was her throaty little moan that pushed him over the edge. That and the fingers she stabbed into his shoulders. Emma's legs opened wider, welcoming him, and he snapped.

He took and took until sweat slicked their skin, driving into her as if powered by a primitive force deep in his DNA. His feet dug into the mattress as he drove himself home. Emma's hips pumped in sync as they climbed together.

She fit him, clamped around him, and every stroke, every thrust, was an unimaginable pleasure.

He worried he was being too rough, but when he

murmured that concern into the curve of her neck, she only begged for more. Emma hitched her legs around him, pulling him as deep as he could go.

There was nothing beyond this bed, this room, that mattered anymore. Niko knew his reason for being writhed under him in a quest for release, and he would take her there.

Their mouths met and tangled again as his body fed on hers. She gave him everything he asked for, met every thrust with an eager arch. He was hanging on by a fine silver thread when he felt her begin to quicken around him.

"Yes, baby. My Emma," he breathed into her. He shifted just slightly, changing the angle of his thrusts and let them both go. He came with her, that first shuddering contraction around his dick forced him over the edge. He held on long enough to match her wave for wave, losing himself into her until he was empty and she was quivering and blind beneath him.

19

He'd branded her soul, Emma thought as she fought her way through the bleary aftershocks of pleasure. Nikolai Vulkov had just destroyed her for any other man, past or future. She was ruined. And she couldn't care less.

He'd collapsed on her, spent and satisfied, before rolling to the side and gathering her into him. And here she rested, lips smugly curved and the scent of their lovemaking hanging in the air.

She'd never be able to look at this bed without seeing him ranging over her, his dark eyes possessive and lustful.

God, she was going to have to get a new bed when Niko left Blue Moon. Hell, she was going to need a house that didn't carry the ghosts of sexual perfection.

"You're smiling." Niko's lips moved against her hair.

"I don't think my face is capable of anything but this right now," she sighed, refusing to open her eyes.

"Do me a favor and stay there," he said, slipping out of bed.

Emma obliged, finding no desire to get back to life. She

wanted to bask here, her body loose and wonderfully used, perfectly sated.

She snuggled into the pillow and thought of nothing but how good she felt.

The quiet click of a shutter had her lazily opening one eye. *Click*.

Naked and unapologetic, Niko stood over her, camera held to his eye. "Just like that. Satisfied, smug, fucking beautiful."

She arched an eyebrow at him, and he clicked away. "Is this a photographer's version of a sex tape?" Emma asked, working her fingers through her tangle of curls.

"Very funny. This is a photographer's version of perfection. So shut up and smile at me like you own me."

She did just that and laughed as his shutter clicked in rapid succession.

"What are you doing?" she asked finally.

"Trust me, Emma. You're going to love these," he told her, putting the camera on the nightstand and sliding in next to her.

"Don't even think about showing those to anyone ever," she warned him.

"When you see these, you'll want the world to see them."

"I doubt that very much."

He merely hummed an answer against her skin.

"Sounds like someone got over his slump," Emma said, tracing her finger over his chest.

He was perfection beneath her hands, she thought. The muscled fullness of his chest and shoulders gave way to lean, shredded abs tapering to a still-hard cock of spectacular proportions. His thighs were strong and muscled. And that face, that fallen angel face with dark eyes and a cocky smile, looked at her with as much heat and need as when he'd knocked on her door.

"It's hard not to with this inspiration," he fired back.

Emma rose up on her elbow and teased her fingers down his chest, over every ripple of abs.

"Are we still friends?" she teased.

Niko grinned. "Baby, we're *best* friends now."

"Am I going to get to see those pictures you just took?"

"They're as much yours as mine."

"Good. How do you feel about cold stuffed mushrooms and a glass of cabernet?"

He nuzzled at her neck, teeth grazing her skin and nipping at her shoulder. "I'm feeling amenable to room temperature anything," he teased.

"Thank God, I'm starving." Emma hopped out of bed, feeling Niko's eyes follow her. "Clothes or no clothes?" she asked over her shoulder.

"Definitely no clothes," he decided.

"You have excellent taste, Mr. Vulkov." Emma tossed him a saucy wink and yanked the bed sheet off of him, knotting it between her breasts.

"Baby, don't I know it."

Wrapped in bed sheets, they sat cross-legged on the couch drinking wine and picking at the mushrooms with their fingers. They laughed and flirted, teasing each other with soft kisses and long, silky touches, enjoying the peace and quiet of the long night before them.

They both jumped when Emma's front door burst open.

"Aunt Emma! Do you wanna bake cookies with me?" Aurora skipped inside. Emma yanked the sheet up to her chin and shoved Niko down on the couch cushions.

Aurora stopped and frowned at them. "Are you making a couch tent? Where are your clothes?"

Beckett burst through the door at a run, shielding his eyes. Diesel the dog bounded in on his heels with a happy bark.

"Sorry, sorry, sorry. She got past me. Don't tell Gia!" Beckett picked Aurora up, tossed her over his shoulder, and sprinted through the door with the little girl giggling. It slammed shut leaving them in stunned silence.

Diesel sauntered over and put his big, gray head on Emma's lap looking mournfully at the mushrooms.

The door burst open again. "Shit. Sorry," Beckett stumbled around the table into the living room and grabbed Diesel much the same way he'd carted Aurora out and hauled ass for the door.

Niko picked up his glass of wine. "Well, that's never happened to me before."

"Did that really just happen?" Emma covered her face and groaned. "My step-brother-in-law boss just witnessed our post-coital bliss."

"That should make the next family get-together fun," Niko quipped.

"I need to get my own place," Emma decided. "I've been putting it off because I wanted to be sure I was staying, but I cannot live in my sister's backyard forever."

"We'll go house shopping," Niko said, leaning in to taste her neck. "After."

"After what? Dinner?"

"I was thinking maybe we should skip straight to dessert and circle back around to dinner."

HOURS LATER, wrung out and sated, Emma laid her head on Niko's chest in the dark. She listened to the thud of his heart as it slowly returned to a measured pace. "Would it be wrong to say I'm so glad you had a life crisis? Because I'm feeling rather grateful at the moment."

He laughed softly, lips moving against her hair. "I'm not feeling particularly regretful myself."

She sighed and used the pads of her fingers to trace meaningless patterns on Niko's chest. He let her play in silence for a few minutes before drawing her fingers to his mouth to kiss each tip. "How are you not taken, Emmaline Merill?"

"The pickings around Blue Moon can be... an acquired taste," she said diplomatically.

"What about before? In L.A. There's no way you were single out there."

"I became very particular when I lived there," she admitted. "It's a long story."

"I've got time unless Aurora is going to jump on the bed and ask to sleep over."

Emma debated with herself. Opening up about past mistakes made her feel uncomfortably vulnerable. But Niko had been nothing but honest with her. She cleared her throat and took the plunge. "When I first moved to L.A., I was very young, very naïve," Emma sighed, fighting the internal flinch at the memory of her own stupidity. "There was this guy who was several years older than me, more experienced, incredibly good looking."

"He sounds like a dick," Niko said, squeezing her hand.

She gave a wry smile and returned the squeeze of his hand. "He would surprise me with flowers, gifts. There were fancy dinners out, a weekend in Napa. It was enough to keep me from questioning why he never answered his phone when I called or why we never spent the night at his place."

She could tell he knew where she was going with this story.

"I was just a shift manager at the time, so I'd work catering jobs on the side to make ends meet. I was mixing a Manhattan at a fundraiser when I saw him. He was supposed to be 'out of town on business.' But he was there with an aspiring model/actress. Beautiful, young, naïve." She gave a sad laugh.

Niko threaded his fingers into her hair and stroked but said nothing.

"I controlled my considerable temper and bided my time. He wandered off to make a phone call—me on my cell, oddly enough—and I approached her with a tray of canapés and a line about how handsome her date was. They'd been 'dating' for two months. *I* was the other woman."

"So what did you do?"

"Because you know I did something." This time her smile was real. "I dragged Thandie—that's her name—into the ladies' room. I broke the news, maybe a bit harshly." She regretted that, but it couldn't be helped now. "When she recovered, we took a selfie together and texted it to him."

"Cold. I like it," Niko grinned.

"He called me first, which hurt Thandie even more and pissed me off even more. After I gave him a piece of my mind and hung up on him, he called her and gave her the same apologies, the same promises."

"Did it work?"

"Not then but eventually. They got married a year later and divorced a year after that."

"What about you?"

"I became much more selective about who I dated. I'd been seeing someone leaning toward serious when Jax showed up in L.A. with a job offer."

"What happened to 'leaning toward serious'? He didn't want to switch coasts?"

Emma sighed. "He wouldn't have wanted to. His life and job were there. It wouldn't be fair to ask him to uproot everything for me." She hadn't actually asked Mason, hadn't given him the chance to say no. But it was for the best. They'd both been disappointed that things hadn't worked out, disappointed but not devastated. *It was*, Emma thought, *how adults parted ways, civilly and without drama.*

"What made you choose here over him?"

"Family," Emma said without hesitating. "I missed my dad, and with Gia and the kids here, the decision was a no-brainer. I missed birthdays and Sunday lunches and pop-ins. I'm happy here. I feel like I belong and what I do matters to people here."

"That's a good feeling."

"Nikolai?"

"Hmm?"

"When are you going to let me see the wedding pictures?" she whispered.

He pinched the flesh of her arm and made her squeal. "One-track mind."

She trailed her fingers lower over his abs and then lower still to wrap around his shaft. "Maybe a two-track mind."

BLUE MOON NIGHTS were quieter than the city, and Nikolai couldn't remember ever enjoying a night more than this one. Emma slept soundly in his arms, her leg thrown over his, one hand resting over his heart.

In his considerable experience, there'd never been a woman who had captivated him, body and soul, like Emmaline. What happened here tonight had changed everything for him, and he needed time to process, adapt, refocus. He'd lost himself in her and in that loss had found something bigger and more essential than what he'd known before.

It was love between them, of that he was certain. He didn't

understand what it meant, yet. But he did know he wasn't letting this woman out of his arms.

Emma cuddled closer to him in her sleep, and his lips curved. She wasn't so concerned with vulnerability in her sleep. His serious, reserved girl needed him to tease out the adventuress in her. And he would show her what lay outside the lines, just beyond the rules.

20

_E_mma was in her kitchen, dreamily putting away dishes and recalling every detail of the night before when an insistent knock on her front door broke through her reverie.

She found her sisters on her doorstep, Gia looking annoyed and Eva looking guilty. Mr. Snuffles, her father and Phoebe's pug, cocked his head to the side at Eva's feet.

"I have to find out from my *husband* who spotted Niko's motorcycle out front this morning that my incredibly picky sister is dating?" Gia snapped. She was dressed for yoga and had her hands on her hips.

Behind Gia, Eva was gesturing wildly and shaking her head at Emma.

"And I have to find out from my other sister that my oldest sister is dating without having any prior knowledge myself? That's just unacceptable, Emma," Eva said when Gia turned to look at her.

Emma had to hide her smile. Eva was playing the victim so Gia wouldn't be mad at her, too. *She'd let Eva play it out and hang it over her head later*, Emma decided. Same with Beckett who hadn't come by the knowledge due to a bike on the street but an eyeful of naked people on the couch.

"Jesus, guys. It's not like that exactly, and it literally just happened in the last twelve hours!"

"That is practically a century in Blue Moon gossip time. Now you owe me details, and I'm not leaving until you give me some. And a snack. I'm hungry and grumpy." Gia shoved past her into the kitchen and flopped down on a barstool.

"Come on in. Make yourself at home," Emma said sarcastically, stepping aside and let Eva in too. "Whoa, do *not* let that snot machine anywhere near my nice furniture," she warned Eva.

Eva scooped up Mr. Snuffles and cuddled him to her chest. "Don't you listen to your sister, Mr. Snuffles. She loves you. She just shows it by being bossy."

Emma knew better than to argue with Gia and pulled the orzo salad out of the refrigerator. She produced three forks and leaned on the opposite side of the island.

"So what do you want to know?"

"How did this happen? Are you out of your mind? Niko is the opposite of your type. How serious is it? Have you had sex? And was it amazing?"

"Yeah, all those things she said," Eva agreed innocently.

"Okay, first of all, let's clarify something. We're *not* dating. We were friends, and then we had sex," Emma explained.

"That is so not you. Did you sustain a head injury? Have you been getting weird headaches?"

"Just the two sitting in my kitchen," Emma said blandly.

"Sex makes you grumpy," Eva teased.

"I do not have a head injury, and I'm not grumpy. In fact, I'm deeply and incredibly satisfied if you must know."

"Hang on. So if it's just sex, I don't know if I lost. I have to check with Summer," Gia muttered, digging into the salad with gusto.

"Why do you have to check with Summer about my love life?"

"We had a bet. I said there was no way you and Niko would get together because you're immune to the whole sexy, danger-ous, bad boy type. Summer thought Niko would wear you down. I just don't know if we clarified between sex or relation-ship." Gia frowned. "You know what? I'm not even going to tell her. We'll just wait and see what happens."

"You have lived in this town too long!" Emma accused. "You can't bet on my sex life."

"Can and did," Gia shrugged. "You can bet on mine if you want."

"How can you possibly have a sex life?" Emma demanded. "You have three children."

"Beckett is very creative about timing, and we're very moti-vated," Gia said smugly.

"Wow," Eva sighed.

"I'm impressed," Emma agreed.

"So what else have I missed out on?" Gia demanded. "Did you two run off and elope? Eva, are you secretly starting a second career as a stripper?"

Eva dropped her fork and studiously avoided eye contact. "You know me. You can't keep me away from those technical manuals."

Hmm, Emma thought. *There was something there. She'd need to browbeat it out of her sister later when she wasn't expecting it.*

"Did you know that Jax and Joey have two kids living with them?" Emma ventured.

"Now you're just messing with me," Gia laughed, scooping up a forkful of orzo.

"Nope. Dead serious. Reva and Caleb moved in Sunday

night after the wedding. Their mother abandoned them three weeks ago, and Reva's been trying to hide it so she and her brother can stay together."

"Oh!" Gia's face went through the stages of shock and sadness. "Oh, those poor kids. What do they need? Does Caleb need toys? Roar's due for a purge. How about some dinners? We can alternate."

"What about school supplies? I'd be happy to take the kids shopping?" Eva offered.

Emma smiled. Her sisters were damn good people. "I think what would help them out the most is an attorney. The goal is to keep Reva and Caleb together, and if they go into foster care, that's going to be tough."

"I think I know where we can find the best, sexiest, smartest attorney in the state," Gia said, pulling out her phone.

"What about their father?" Eva asked while Gia texted Beckett.

"Not in the picture," Emma shook her head.

"We were lucky, weren't we?" Eva sighed.

"Very."

Gia's phone rang, and they listened as she filled Beckett in.

"You're the best, smartest, sexiest, most amazing man in the universe," she chirped. Emma and Eva mimed throwing up when Gia hung up. "Okay, Beckett is going to talk to Jax and Joey and Donovan."

"Speaking of our fair sheriff," Emma said, eyeing Eva. "Did you two enjoy your dance?"

"Oh, my God. Eva!" Gia pounced. "You need to move here and marry Donovan, and then we'll all be together!"

Emma and Eva rolled their eyes. "What is wrong with you?" Emma demanded.

"I think it's post-pregnancy hormones. I've been thinking about joining the Beautification Committee," Gia confessed.

"If you do that, I'm disowning you," Emma gasped.

"That's what I love about you, Em. You're so non-judgmental," Gia teased.

"What exactly is the Beautification Committee?" Eva asked.

"It's a secret committee that spends their free time trying to pair off unwilling townsfolk to create the illusion of happiness and stability."

"Really?" Eva's interest was piqued.

"It's a non-consensual matchmaking service," Gia corrected.

"I love you, but you're insane," Emma told her.

"Agree to disagree. Now, let's get back to sex with your gorgeous Russian friend," Gia said, pushing them back on track. "What does this mean? Are you seeing each other? Is it going to happen again?"

Niko lined up the memory cards on the island and wiped his palms on his jeans. He'd put off reviewing the wedding pictures for a day. Emma had consumed his every waking thought since that first life-altering kiss under the stars. Their stolen night together, so fresh in his mind, was a turning point for him.

And now it was time for another.

It was nerves, a fear that the flow and energy of the day's shoot had resulted in shit.

But there was only one way he'd find out. Niko shoved the first card into the slot on his laptop and drummed an impatient beat on the granite while the images loaded.

Was it just him, or was the house too quiet? he wondered. The twins were at daycare, Carter was outside running a new fence line, and Summer was hibernating in her office master-minding magazine matters.

He opened a playlist, and eighties metal drowned out the silence.

The pop-up on his screen told him the images had successfully uploaded to his cloud. "Let's see what we've got," he murmured to himself.

Diving in, he clicked at random, opening a ceremony shot.

It wasn't bad.

Phoebe was laughing at something the minister was saying while her sons were peering over her shoulder. Franklin, smiling his biggest smile held her hand, while his daughters laughed. There was some life there. If he were editing, he'd sharpen the focus on Phoebe and Franklin and soften the rest. Maybe go grayscale and up the contrast.

"Okay, one acceptable shot," he muttered. "What else is in here?"

The next was better and the next even better than both of the previous. "Now we're talking."

He grabbed that one, a shot of Phoebe and Franklin looking deliriously happy on the dance floor, and played with the highlights until he was satisfied. One down and three to go before Phoebe's request was fulfilled.

He lost track of time and count of the images he'd pulled for editing. There was one of the brothers ranged around the bar in easy camaraderie, a round of beers in their hands. There was another of Phoebe dancing with Beckett, his fore-head resting on hers as they grinned at each other. Another of Franklin surrounded by his daughters as they all hoisted flutes of champagne skyward.

There was another that tugged at him. Franklin and

Emma taking a turn around the dance floor. He'd caught them over the shoulders of other dancers and sharpened the focus, blurring everyone else to isolate them. Franklin smiled tenderly at Emma. But it was Emma's face that went straight to his heart. Tears in her eyes and a tremulous smile on her sweet lips. It was a beautiful moment between father and daughter, one that could be treasured forever now.

He hit pay dirt with another ceremony shot. Their heads bowed in a spontaneous moment of remembrance, Jax's hand resting on Beckett's shoulder, Beckett's on Carter's. A bond of brotherhood and grief and hope for the future. Emma, her own eyes glistening, handed tissues to her sisters behind her. Phoebe and Franklin squeezed hands and bowed their heads.

No one could look at that picture and not *feel*.

He sat back, rolling his knotted shoulders. He'd already edited twenty shots that were damn good. But there was one more he wanted to see. The very first shot of the day.

He scrolled to it and opened the file.

Emma.

He'd captured her mid-twirl, looking over her slim shoulder at him, the blush of her dress highlighting the happy flush of her cheeks. The green of her eyes didn't need enhancing as they sparkled with joy. Her lips, glossed and pink curved in feminine knowing. Her hair, a fiery red under the spring sun, flowed out with the momentum of her turn. She looked like a fairy princess who would lead him down a forest path and never let him escape. She was luring him in, and he was too enamored to be afraid.

He stared as if hypnotized by emerald eyes and the smile that promised a life of laughter. He was still staring when his phone rang next to him.

"Yeah?"

"Hello to you, too." Amara was too used to dealing with

temperamental talent to take offense to a brusque greeting. She'd been his agent for three years now and had landed him every dream gig he could have envisioned. And never once complained about a thing.

"Sorry, Am. I was working. What's up?"

"Working? Well, that's a good sign. I was beginning to think you were going to give it all up to play scarecrow up there."

He hadn't exactly explained to Amara why he was taking a sabbatical, but she was smart enough to put two and two together.

"I have no plans of giving up Manhattan for Blue Moon," he promised. But his gaze tracked back to the screen where Emma beguiled him.

"I know you're not taking assignments right now, but I thought I'd pass this idea on. You know how if you're off the scene longer than it takes to recover from rhinoplasty, everyone in the industry forgets about you?"

Niko picked up an apple out of the bowl on the counter and bit into it. "Uh-huh, sure."

"Well, I've got an idea that could tide everyone over until you're back from playing farmer. I've got a friend of a friend who owns a gallery in SoHo. He's looking for a new exhibit, and I thought you could pull together some shots. Maybe do a retrospective with some of your favorites?"

He stared at his screen again. "Actually, I have a better idea."

By the time he hung up, his agent was ecstatic and he was feeling a little psyched himself.

21

*N*iko found Emma in her office at the brewery swearing at her computer screen. "Unfreeze, damn you!" She slapped a palm down on top of the desk. The office had been built into the barn's original silo and was tucked away from the chaos of the brewery and its kitchen, which was probably one of the reasons Emma spent very little time in here. He'd noticed she preferred to work from a laptop in the restaurant where she could keep an eye on things.

"You're beautiful when you're annoyed."

Emma startled and then smiled a sleek, female grin when she spotted him in the doorway. "Well, isn't this a nice surprise? Miss me already?" she teased.

"Maybe," he admitted, crossing to her. He eased a hip on the corner of her desk and stretched out his legs. "How are you today?"

Emma pushed back from the desk and swiveled her chair to face him. She looked up at him through her thick curtain of lashes and wet her lips. He went instantly hard.

"A little sore and a lot satisfied. How about you?" There was a smile in her voice that he liked hearing.

Niko tugged on the end of a red curl. "Not nearly finished with you. That's how I'm feeling."

He couldn't quite gauge her reaction. Emma was a little too good at masking her thoughts. "Is that so?" she asked innocently.

"Before we explore this in-depth," Niko winked, "I need to know if we're still friends."

Emma cocked her head to the side. "I feel very friendly toward you," she promised.

Everything this woman did or said seemed designed to make him want to tear her clothes off and pleasure them both.

"It looks like you're feeling pretty friendly, too," she said, eyeing his erection through his jeans.

"Stop looking at me like that. You're making it worse," he groaned.

"I could probably help you out with that," she said, trailing a hand up his thigh.

"Jesus, woman." He stilled her hand with his own. "Let me get to the point before I lose any more blood flow to the brain."

She leaned back in her chair looking pleased with herself and opened her palms. "By all means."

"I need you to look at something and tell me what your honest opinion is."

"Your cock is spectacular, and you know it."

"Emmaline." His voice was stern. "This is serious."

"I was being completely serious."

He tossed the envelope on her desk.

"What's this?"

"Open it and find out, smart ass."

She slid the stack of pictures free, and Niko found himself holding his breath.

"Oh! The wedding!" She looked up at him, eyes dancing,

lips parted. He shifted away, straightening from the desk to pace. He didn't trust himself to not bend her over the desk when she looked at him like that.

He shoved a hand through his hair. "I emailed them to Phoebe and she was... pleased." She'd been thrilled. The number of exclamation points in her email outnumbered the words she'd used. But Niko didn't trust that she wouldn't be just as enthusiastic if Aurora and the twins had recreated the wedding in crayon and macaroni.

Emma was watching him closely. He pointed at the pictures. "I want to know what *you* think."

She gave him one last searching look before dropping her focus to the stack of photos he'd printed.

"Oh, Niko," she breathed, holding up the first, a photo of Aurora hiding under the table with her contraband cake. "It's perfect. Absolutely perfect."

He said nothing and waited while she paged through the stack.

Her breath caught on one, and she stared at it for a long minute before carefully shuffling it to the back. "Are you trying to murder my heart?" she asked, holding up the last shot. It was the one of her and Franklin sharing a dance.

Niko shoved his hands into his pockets. "Well?" he asked her.

Emma paged through the photos once more before tucking them carefully back into the envelope and stood. "Nikolai Vulkov, how can you possibly doubt yourself after that?"

He blew out the breath he'd been holding. "You like them?"

"They're beautiful, and I'm keeping them. Phoebe can get her own when she comes back from the Bahamas."

"Is that so?" he asked, hooking his fingers into the front of her very sexy black Oxford and drawing her in.

"Not in the office," she warned, putting her fingers over his lips.

"Jax and Joey do it in the tack room," he argued.

"Stop distracting me. Tell me how you feel about the photos," she ordered.

"They're good. But I wanted to hear you say it so I'd know if I was delusional."

She laughed, hooking her hands behind his neck. "My delusional artist friend."

"While I have you softened up, I've got a proposal for you," he said, brushing a tendril back from her face.

"We're definitely not getting married," she smirked, batting her eyelashes at him.

"We'll put that in the To Be Discussed pile," he shot back. "I've been thinking a lot about..." his eyes raked her. "Us."

"There hasn't been an 'us' for a full twenty-four hours yet," she reminded him.

"Our friendship goes way back," he insisted, and Emma laughed.

"Please continue."

"I'm going to be here for a few more weeks," Niko began. "And there's no way what happened last night was a one-time thing."

"Hmm," she said blandly.

He tickled her under the ribs until she cracked. "Okay! Okay. I wouldn't say no to a repeat performance," she gasped.

"Now, you know that I don't do relationships, and I know you don't do anything casual."

She was looking suspicious now and tried to take a step back but he followed her. "What are you suggesting?"

He backed her up against the desk caging her between his

thighs. "I'm suggesting we both step outside our comfort zones and see where this goes."

She wet her lips, and it drove him crazy. "Huh?"

"I'm saying I'll be monogamous with you if you'll be willing to give up your ideal end game for me so we can continue enjoying each other."

Emma's green eyes narrowed. "I'm trying to think about the multitude of reasons why this is a terrible idea. But I can't because you're too close." She slapped a hand to his chest, but it didn't move him an inch. He merely leaned in over her to tease her jaw with his teeth.

"Say yes," he ordered.

He felt her shiver beneath him and skimmed his hand down the curve of her breast, over her waist and hip, until it found bare leg where her black skirt ended.

"What are you doing?" she whispered against his mouth.

He shifted his stance so his thighs parted hers, and he let his hand trace its way up the inside of her thigh. "I'm sweetening the deal."

He found the satin of the thong already damp and growled low in his throat. "The things you do to me, Emma." He brushed the wet satin with the pads of his fingers and watched her head fall back in surrender. "What's your answer?"

Those slick cherry lips parted, but no words came out. Niko slid his fingers under the edge of the material and used his knee to force her legs farther apart. He was gentle at first, circling slowly before dipping two fingers into her honeyed entrance. She moaned, bucking her hips against his hand as he thrust in and out.

"Tell me you want me, Emma. Just me," he said, using his thumb to brush that sweet nub.

Her knees buckled, and she gripped his shirt to keep from falling. "Say the words, baby, or I'll stop."

"Don't you dare stop," she gasped.

"Tell me."

She was riding his hand now urging him on.

"I want you, Niko. I want you."

"You'll be mine... for now?" he clarified.

"Y-yes."

"Good girl." She tightened around his fingers, muscles clenching down as he took her over the edge.

She opened her mouth, and Niko clamped his free hand over it, muffling her cry of surprise as she came. She went limp, sagging against him. He withdrew his fingers and enjoyed her look of shock when he slid them into his mouth.

Her flavor was on his tongue, and he wanted more.

"Damn it, Niko! Not at work," Emma hissed, recovering her sense of propriety.

He should've been sorry, but he wasn't. Not when he got to witness Emma's physical response to him first-hand.

"You don't even look sorry," she grumbled, straightening her skirt and shoving her hair over her shoulders.

"I'm never going to be sorry about making you come." It was her turn to clap a hand over his mouth.

"Let's get one thing straight. I got carried away, but this can't happen again at work. My job is important to me, and I don't want to jeopardize anything for a quick fuck on my desk," Emma told him coolly.

Niko took her by the hands, feeling a stirring of guilt. "I'm sorry. I got carried away, too. That's the last thing I'd ever want you to feel about what we do." She wouldn't look him in the eye, so he nudged her chin up. "I'm sorry, Emma."

She set her jaw. "As long as you understand, work is off-limits. So if you want any help taking care of that," she looked down pointedly and tapped the erection that was trying to claw its way out of denim with her knuckles, making him draw in a sharp breath. "Then you're going to have to wait until my break and meet me outside."

"Have dinner with me."

"What?"

"I'm not leaving you feeling like this," he told her, stroking a hand over her cheek. "Have dinner with me on your break. We'll eat in the bar."

"If we do that, then everyone's going to know!"

"Know what?" The question came from the doorway.

Emma jumped a mile and backed into her desk. "Holy shit, Joey," she said, clutching a hand to her heart. "You scared the hell out of me."

Joey, in boots and riding breeches, smirked and crossed her arms to lean against the doorjamb. "You look pretty occupied. Maybe I should come back later."

Emma tried to swat Niko out of the way, but he stayed put. "Wait right there," Niko pointed to Joey and dragged Emma to the far side of the office. "We have to tell her."

"Tell her that you just gave me an orgasm in my office?" Emma hissed in disbelief.

"That we're dating, baby. The orgasm thing is up to you," he whispered.

"But we just decided... I don't know if I'm ready." Emma looked up at him, her green eyes wide and searching.

"What's going to happen if we don't tell her?"

"Well, she's going to know anyway and probably blab to Jax who has a huge mouth."

"His mouth is pretty regular sized. Beckett has a bigger mouth," Joey corrected her from across the room, and Emma went scarlet.

"You heard that?"

"Good acoustics," Joey shrugged. "Congrats on the orgasm by the way."

"I'm going to die right here on this spot," Emma moaned.

Niko took matters into his own hands. "Joey, Emma and I are... dating." He didn't exactly choke on the word, but it didn't flow either.

"Okay. Anyway, Jax and I were going to bring the kids in tonight for dinner. Is that cool with you?" Joey asked Emma, unfazed.

"Uh, sure. We only have a handful of reservations. All small parties."

"Cool." Joey shoved away from the door. "See you at seven?"

"Seven's fine," Emma said, nodding harder than necessary.

Joey frowned thoughtfully. "You might want to work on your delivery, by the way. Maybe lead with the orgasm thing." And then she was gone.

"That was easy," Niko said when she was gone.

"I guess we're committed now," Emma groaned.

Niko brought her hand to his mouth and kissed her knuckles. "I guess we are."

22

*J*oey and Jax insisted that Niko and Emma—on her break—join their party for dinner. Forty-eight hours had changed a lot for their little table, Emma thought. Reva and Caleb were both wearing some of the new clothes she'd delivered this morning. Joey listened as Caleb delivered a dissertation on every kid in his kindergarten class. She looked over his head at Reva. "Is there an off button?"

Reva gave a small smile, the first Emma had seen from the girl.

Emma was relieved for the distraction of extra dinner guests. It was a slow night at the brewery, and she and Nikolai would have had entirely too much time together.

Her head was still spinning from last night, from this afternoon. Everything about Niko pushed her off balance. The way he'd made her feel in bed—and then again in her office—was so intense, she needed time to adjust, to get used to it. She'd played it cool when he showed up in her office, but on the inside, adrenaline was thrumming through her veins the second she'd looked at him and remembered how it felt to have him over her, under her, in her.

Then he'd thrown her again with his "see where we end up" suggestion. She must have been temporarily insane to have agreed to something that ridiculous. They couldn't possibly have a future together. Why waste the time?

She looked across the table at him and when his dark gaze met hers she remembered *exactly* why it was worth wasting the time. He was so effortlessly gorgeous, so incredibly talented, and still so interested in her. While their friendship had started as a joke, Niko never made her feel like he didn't value the time he spent with her.

A heated debate broke out over appetizers. Joey and Caleb wanted wings while Jax and Reva were staunchly in favor of the beer-battered onion rings. "Why can't we get both?" Joey grumbled.

"Because we're feeding kids, and we'll stunt their growth or give them high cholesterol if we feed them like this," Jax argued.

"Shit." Joey looked down at Caleb. "Sorry. Crap."

"It's okay. Our mom says 'shit' all the time." Caleb patted her hand.

"We're getting both appetizers," Joey decided. "But just this once," she added sternly.

Reva's lips quirked again, and Emma thought that maybe miracles did happen.

She looked over at Niko and smiled when he winked at her.

"So you two, huh?" Jax grinned from the head of the table.

Emma shot Joey an accusing look.

"What?" Joey shrugged. "You didn't swear me to secrecy. He's kinda my husband. We have to talk about stuff."

Emma took a deep breath. "Yes, we're... dating."

"How do you think the Beautification Committee's going to handle this?" Jax asked.

"We're not even a blip on their radar," Emma paraphrased Elvira. "I'm sure they've got bigger fish to fry."

Joey snorted. "Don't be too quick to believe everything you hear," she warned.

"The Beautification Committee has better things to do with their time than worry about us," Emma argued.

"You'd think, but no," Jax put in.

The appetizers arrived and were divvied up and the conversation turned to how life at the Pierces' was going with two new additions.

"My commute's a lot shorter," Reva joked.

Niko grinned approvingly at her humor, and the girl flushed to her roots. Emma bit her lip and hid her smile. Nikolai Vulkov's charm had quite the effect on women of all ages.

They ate and talked and laughed and the normalness of it all had Emma hiding her panic and excusing herself under the guise of brewery business. She ducked into the kitchen and checked up on Julio who was training a new cook. Her dishwasher, Shane, waved cheerily from his spotless work-station.

"I like the apron tonight, Shane," Emma winked at him and made him laugh. She'd hired Shane through a nonprofit program that paired workers with disabilities and traumatic brain injuries with local employers. He'd been her favorite hire to date, and everyone on the staff loved him. Shane's claim to fame was his rotating wardrobe of colorful aprons. Tonight's was a Blue Moon original in flaming tie-dye colors.

She took the kitchen's back stairs down a flight to the keg room. She took her time hefting each tapped keg to make sure it would last the night. Cheryl, the head bartender, ruled the keg organization with an iron fist, and Emma was pleased to see everything was in order after this week's kegging of the new lager.

She took a moment to sit and breathe. Sitting across the table from Nikolai felt too... right. If she was going to make this "see where things go" relationship work, she had to forget about the end game and focus on the now. This was painfully new to her. She was nothing without her goals and long-term projections. At one point, she'd thought that Mason was her future, yet when she'd broken things off, she hadn't felt overly disappointed. The fact of the matter was, she just hadn't felt much at all besides secure when it came to Mason and their future.

There was a hell of a lot more emotions that came to mind when she was with Nikolai. Lust, need, anxiety, terror.

If she was going to enjoy this, she needed to let go of the what-ifs temporarily. Eventually, Niko would move back to the city and pick up his life where he left off, if the photos today were any indication. And she not only needed to be okay with that. She needed to enjoy the time they had together.

Pep talk completed, Emma took a rallying breath and stood, straightening her skirt, and marched back upstairs. She handled a few voids on the POS, gave a birthday discount, and busted Sunny and Rupert's make-out session in the supply closet before returning to the table.

Niko eyed her speculatively as she approached, and she winked. She could do this. She could be fun. Temporarily.

She took her seat and a flush-faced Rupert scampered over. "I have your soup in the kitchen," he told Emma. "I didn't want it to get cold."

"Thanks, Rupert," Emma said.

"I'll go grab it for you, and sorry about... you know... in the closet." All eyes were on him, and Emma bit back a sigh.

"Soup, Rupert."

"Yep. Cool. Okay." He hustled off.

"You're such a mean boss," Joey snickered in appreciation.

"Me? I'm sure Reva here could tell us stories about your dictatorship in the stables," Emma shot back with a grin.

"I plead the fifth," Reva said, studying her sandwich as the table erupted into laughter.

THEY DINED and drank and laughed. The kids provided an unexpected level of entertainment to Niko. He didn't usually run in circles that involved kids of any age. The fact that many of the models he worked with were closer to Reva's age than his own was enough to make him feel a mild sense of shock. The comparison was interesting. In some ways, world-weary models of eighteen or twenty had miles more life experience than Reva. And in other ways, Reva's maturity outclassed many of the women in their mid- to late-twenties that he'd photographed.

Blue Moon was proving to be quite the learning experience.

"I've got to go take a lap," Emma announced.

"Make sure no one's burning down the kitchen," Jax agreed.

"More like make sure no one's making out in the supply closet," Emma said with a head jerk in Rupert's direction.

She rose, and Niko stood with her. He followed her a few steps away from the table. "Do you need any help in the closet?" Niko whispered.

"Not right now, but maybe after hours," she said with a slow grin that had his blood pooling south.

"Looking at you and not being able to touch you is driving me insane."

"I knew you were a masochist," she teased. She glanced around them and gave a little "what the hell" shrug. When she moved in and rose up on her tiptoes, he was too surprised by the kiss she placed on his cheek to respond. He watched her leave, the chiffon pleats of her black skirt swirling around her spectacular thighs.

"Hey, Romeo, you want the last wing?" Joey called from the table.

"All yours," he said, returning to his seat.

He liked Joey and her smart mouth, liked watching her with Jax when they put down the boxing gloves and played nice when they thought no one else was watching. More, he liked the rest of the family. It really was something that was lacking in his life. He had no solid circle of friends, no strong family ties that kept him rooted. Until now, he'd preferred casual acquaintances that could be called upon on the rare occasions that he was in the city and not working. Summer had been, and still was, his best friend. And he'd done nothing to replace her since she'd moved.

He thought of the wedding, the joining of families, the interconnectedness they shared as naturally as if they'd all grown up together. It made him think about his own father and how distant he'd allowed that relationship to become.

When his own father had found his second wife, he hadn't felt an ounce of the joy that the Pierces felt when Phoebe married Franklin. In fact, he hadn't even been officially invited to the wedding. It was a courthouse deal, and he'd been on a shoot in Paris. His father said he didn't want Niko to feel obligated. He remembered feeling relieved when he found that his presence hadn't been necessary.

In some ways, he'd expected his father to always remain

faithful to the memory of his mother. But he was beginning to understand that life inevitably carried on and though new beginnings explored undiscovered paths, the past didn't have to be forgotten.

He was wondering if perhaps he should reestablish a stronger relationship with his father and stepmother when a man with shaggy blond hair peeking out from under a ball cap ambled up to the table.

"Colby," Jax greeted him cheerfully. "I didn't know you were here. Pull up a chair."

"Love to, but I think you guys are gonna want to head to the barn," he said, taking his hat off and swiping a hand through his hair.

"Why..." Jax began the question, but Joey's comprehension was faster.

She stood up so fast she knocked her chair over backwards. The other diners quieted and turned to stare. "Calypso?" she whispered.

"We're havin' a baby," Colby nodded.

Joey whooped in victory. "Get your asses moving! We're not missing this!" She dragged Reva out of her chair while Jax grabbed Caleb and threw the boy over his shoulder.

"You coming?" Jax asked Niko.

"Let me get my camera. You're going to want some baby pictures," he predicted.

They hustled toward the brewery's front door where Niko promised to call Emma and let her know what was going on. When Jax and Joey's entourage headed toward the stables, Niko peeled off to the house.

He burst through the kitchen door to the surprise of Summer and Carter who were stirring something on the stove.

"Geez, where's the fire, Niko?" Summer said, patting a hand over her heart.

"Can't talk! We're having a baby!"

He ran for the stairs.

"Holy shit! Calypso?" Carter yelled after him.

"Grabbing my camera!"

Niko snatched his camera bag off the desk and thundered back downstairs. He heard a cry from the twins' room and grimaced. "Sorry sorry sorry," he said, running through the kitchen.

"I got this," Summer said, pushing Carter after him. "Go see your baby horse!"

They hustled off the porch when she opened the screen door behind them. "And don't think for a second I'm not going to ask you where you spent the night last night, Niko!"

Niko and Carter jogged along the dusty path connecting farm and stables. The night was alive with crickets and fireflies. "So you and Emma, huh?" Carter said conversationally.

"Yeah. It's pretty new," Niko said, realizing he'd never had this conversation before. How had he made it to thirty without ever telling a friend he was seeing a woman?

Carter pumped his fist in the air. "Yes!"

"I didn't realize you were so invested in my love life," Niko said wryly.

"I am when my wife bet Gia two nights of babysitting that you and Emma would hook up."

"*That's* what a unit is?"

"Two glorious twin-free evenings," Carter grinned. "Beckett's gonna freak. This almost makes up for the beard."

THREE HOURS LATER, Niko watched as Calypso's foal struggled to his feet and took his first toddling steps. He had the coloring of his father, Apollo, the dark, arrogant stallion, and a white star on his nose that exactly matched his mother's.

Joey knelt quietly in the doorway of the stall. Jax stood behind her, resting his hands on her shoulders. Niko snapped a shot of them, catching the reverence and excitement that passed between them. Reva rested her chin on her hands as she peered over the front wall of the box stall, a ghost of a smile on her lips.

After making sure all was well with baby and mother, Carter had headed home to catch some sleep so he could check on the horses early.

"Well, we've got our baby, Jojo. What do you think?" Jax asked, stroking a hand through his wife's hair.

"I think he's pretty fucking awesome," Joey said softly. Catching herself too late, she looked over her shoulder. "Shit. Sorry. Pretty freaking awesome."

Reva gave a soft laugh. "It's okay. Cale's asleep."

Niko snapped the six-year-old curled up on a bale of hay wrapped in an old quilt, sound asleep.

Calypso leaned down to gently nose her foal, and the baby's tail twitched as if in recognition.

Instant family was fascinating to Niko.

"Is the baby here?" Emma appeared in the corridor now wearing serviceable flats and a hopeful expression.

Niko beckoned her closer, and she joined him next to Reva.

"Oh! How precious! Boy or girl?" Emma asked.

"Boy," Joey said without taking her eyes off of the foal.

"He's perfect," Emma sighed. "What's his name?"

"Thunder?" Joey threw out.

"Right because we want to name the founding member of our breeding program after every kid's pony ever."

"Fine, smartass. You suggest something."

"Green Light?" Jax suggested.

Joey shook her head. "Too Hollywood."

They all took turns throwing out and rejecting suggestions. "The Dark Knight?"

"George."

"Octavius."

"Clippy?" A sleepy Caleb roused himself to offer the suggestion. "We can't call him Cloppy 'cause we already got one of those."

"Eclipse," Reva offered.

The stables were quiet as everyone mulled it over. Joey nodded. "Yeah. Yeah. Eclipse. I like it."

"Nice job, kid," Jax said, ruffling Reva's hair. "You just named a horse."

Caleb yawned and settled back down on the hay bale.

Joey rose and stepped into Jax's arms. "It looks like we've got ourselves a good start, Jackson Pierce." She kissed him hard on the mouth before releasing him. "I'm going to make some coffee, and we need to get Caleb to bed or he'll miss another day of school this week."

She was grinning when she floated past.

23

Normally, Emma enjoyed a busy week at the brewery. However, the busy-ness was cutting into her time with Niko. And for the first time in a long time, she was interested in enjoying her social life.

Unfortunately, right now, she was stuck on the bar since Cheryl had come down with a head cold that was "suffocating the life out of her."

For the first time since Rainbow had spotted her with Niko at Shorty's, Emma didn't even flinch when known Beautification Committee conspirators bellied up to the bar. Her fears over any meddling in her love life had been allayed, and she offered Rainbow's husband, Gordon Berkowicz, a smile and a pint. His hairline was receding on top, making it look like his hair had just shifted back into the long ponytail he wore down the back of a Janis Joplin cover band t-shirt. His jeans looked as though they'd lived through the sixties. He and his son, Anthony—a skinnier glasses-wearing version of his father— was enjoying a mango margarita.

Gordon peered over his reading glasses at the bar menu, debating between appetizers.

"Have you gentlemen decided?" Emma asked.

Gordon put down the menu and nodded at his son. "We're going to go with the rockfish bites." He elbowed Anthony in the side, and Anthony coughed.

"So, Emma. You've been in town a while now. What do you think of Blue Moon?"

Anthony was the editor of *The Monthly Moon*, Blue Moon's monthly community newspaper. Emma was aware that anything she said to Peter Parker could end up in an article.

"What's not to love about Blue Moon?" she asked, taking their menu and keying in the order on the POS.

"So then you're definitely planning to stay permanently?" Anthony prodded.

Emma rolled her eyes before turning around. She knew full well that Elvira Eustace would have already reported back to the entire town that she'd decided to stay.

"I'm considering," she hedged. Of course she was staying. Her father lived here, one of her sisters lived here, and she loved her job. But that didn't mean she had to put all her personal business out there.

Gordon cleared his throat. "I imagine you'll probably want your own place eventually. Something a little bigger than the guesthouse?"

Emma thought of Aurora bursting through her front door and finding Aunt Em and her friend Niko naked on the couch. "I wouldn't be opposed to it."

The Berkowicz men looked pleased.

"I'd be happy to give Bruce Oakleigh a call for you. He's a part-time real estate agent, you know," Gordon offered.

"That's very kind of you, but I'm not sure I'm ready to move forward—"

"Oh, it's no problem," Anthony said brightly. "We're happy to help."

Emma spotted Ellery a few stools down lifting her empty wine glass. "I don't want you to go to any trouble for me. When I'm ready, I can call Bruce myself," she smiled sweetly. "If you'll excuse me."

She grabbed Ellery's glass. "Ready for a refill?"

"You look ready for a break," Ellery smiled.

"Just escaping some well-meaning Blue Moon snooping," Emma winked, uncorking a fresh bottle of Blue Moon Vineyards Shiraz. She poured Ellery a glass.

"That just means you're family," Ellery chirped. "I bet you're enjoying having your whole family in one place at the same time."

Emma had the distinct feeling that she was walking into a setup.

"It is great," she admitted. "I can't remember the last time we were all together like this."

"Eva works from home, doesn't she?" Ellery crossed her arms and leaned forward on her elbows.

"She does," Emma confirmed.

"Wouldn't it be great if she decided to stay in Blue Moon?"

Emma raised a skeptical eyebrow. "It would be. What exactly are you getting at, Ellery?"

Her purple lips curled. "Well, I happened to notice that she and our very own Sheriff Cardona shared a very sweet dance at the wedding."

"Ellery! Are you suggesting we work some Beautification Committee magic and conspire against Eva and Donovan?"

"Conspire *for* them. There's a huge difference," Ellery clarified. "You had to have noticed how Donovan looks at her."

"Why are you bringing me into this? Isn't this B.C. business?" Emma tilted her head.

"Who's going to have more influence over Eva, a bunch of

weirdo strangers?" Ellery cocked her head in the direction of Gordon and Anthony. "Or her big sister?"

Emma shook her head and ducked back into the kitchen for a breather. What the hell? Why was the Beautification Committee suddenly so enamored with the idea of a romance for her sister? *What the hell was she?* Emma wondered. *Chopped tofu?*

She rested her forehead on the wall for a moment. She was losing her damn mind if she was jealous that the nosiest people in town wanted to meddle in her sister's life instead of her own. They were crazy people. And they were making her crazy.

Emma put Sunshine on the bar and squeezed in a fifteen-minute break for herself with a cup of soup at the end of the bar.

She stirred the minestrone pensively. She knew Ellery was on the Beautification Committee, Gordon and Anthony, too. Yet all the Berkowiczs wanted to do was drum up real estate business, and Ellery was more interested in convincing Eva to move to Blue Moon to fall head over heels for Donovan Cardona. None of them were fishing for information about Emma and Niko. His motorcycle had been parked on the street the handful of nights they'd managed to enjoy together before Franklin and Phoebe returned from their honeymoon, ousting Eva from her position as house- and dog-sitter.

Why weren't they trying to secure a future for her and Niko? Emma wondered. Worse yet. Why did that bother her? Did the B.C. think she and Niko had no chance in hell at making this work? Isn't that what she thought, too? The complete disinterest was mind-boggling to Emma. Blue Moon had been so fascinated by every single facet of her life up until Niko...

"Oh for fuck's sake," she muttered to herself. She wasn't used to such internal turmoil. This is why she was goal-oriented. There was always an end game in mind and every choice, every decision, could be weighed against the final result. Will this get me closer or further away from my goal?

Everything was too confusing when the goal was "see what happens." The things that she knew for sure were that she was staying in Blue Moon, and she was *really* enjoying her time with Niko. She had no idea that the human body was capable of living on food and sex alone. Emma had felt more energetic this week than she had on her usual seven and eight hours of sleep. That physical connection she'd found with Niko had to mean something. *Didn't it?*

She'd never felt so... unleashed with a partner before. He seemed to enjoy taking her to her limits and letting her decide to go just a little farther.

She spooned up her soup and stared at it. She should be enjoying their time together. Not worrying about where it could or wouldn't go. And certainly not being offended that the Beautification Committee couldn't be bothered to take an interest in her love life because they saw no future in her relationship with Nikolai.

She shoved her fingers into her hair before realizing she was wrecking her bun.

"Ugh!" This damn town and that damn man were ruining her peace of mind.

Her phone signaled a text, and Emma swiped the screen and read the message from Niko.

Niko: *What are you doing right now?*

She nibbled on her thumbnail and then typed her response.

Emma: *Thinking about you.*

Wait. Was that too much? she wondered, thumb hovering over the send button. Emma wasn't sure where the lines for "casual" were drawn. She started to delete the text and then stopped.

"Boss, you're frowning at that screen like it just told you it was calling off tonight." Julio, his dark hair pulled back in his stubby ponytail, grinned at her as he helped himself to the soda gun behind the bar. He had a gold canine tooth and a scar that sliced from forehead to just below his eye, yet he had the charisma of a Latin soap opera star. He'd been married three times, and his current girlfriend was fifteen years younger. He was an expert on love affairs.

"Julio, what does it mean when a guy says he wants to 'see where things go'?"

He sipped his ginger ale and eyed her thoughtfully. "It's a hell of a lot better than 'not looking for anything serious.'"

Emma perked up. "Really? So texting someone who wants to see where things are going that you're thinking about them wouldn't be too terrifying?"

"Boss, anyone ever tell you you think too much?"

"Only about three thousand times since elementary school," Emma admitted.

"Future or no future, there's no point in toning yourself down for any guy. Got it? Say what you want to say. Do what you want to do, regardless. Otherwise you're just building a house on a shaky foundation. You know?"

Emma frowned in thought. "That was shockingly good advice, Julio."

"I'm not just a pretty face," he winked.

"That's good to know because next time there's trouble in paradise, I'm sending Rupert and Sunny to you."

He raised his cup as he headed back to the kitchen. "That's what wisdom's for. Sharing it with the young and the dumb."

Emma looked back at her phone and, after a moment of lip chewing debate, hit send.

Niko's response arrived before her screen dimmed.

Niko: Available for a late night date?

Emma: My sister's still at my house.

Niko: Not a problem. We're going out on the town.

She felt a stirring of disappointment and immediately felt guilty. She wanted alone time with him, alone *naked* time. But beggars couldn't be choosers.

Emma: Shorty's?

His response had her wheels turning.

Niko: Even better. Meet me at the park when you get off work. Come hungry.

Niko had something up his sexy sleeve, and she couldn't wait to find out what it was.

24

*E*mma raced through closing and made it into town at a very respectable eleven-thirty. The streets were empty at this time of night, the lampposts shining their beams on empty sidewalks. The only businesses open now were Shorty's and Fitness Freak.

She parked in front of Gia's yoga studio and texted Niko.

Emma: I'm here. Where are you?

He responded with a picture of strings of lights woven around whitewashed wood beams.

Niko: Come find me.

One Love Park was decked out for the Sunday farmers market and Knit Off. Empty stands that would be full of produce and products and teeming with neighbors, sat in shadow. She spotted the gazebo on the far end of the park. It was lit up with dozens of strings of lights.

Niko stood at the top of the steps, holding a pizza box,

waiting for her. Emma's pulse raced. Just looking at him had her body reacting in the most basic, instinctive ways. Something like this wasn't sustainable. Not when just a smoldering look from his dark eyes sent her adrenaline spiking, her core tightening in anticipation. Drawn to him, she followed the sidewalk to the steps of the gazebo.

"Hi, beautiful." His voice was low, a little rough.

"I see you've upped the ante on the midnight picnic," Emma said, eyeing the ice bucket and thick quilt spread over the gazebo bench.

"I got the very last pie from Peace of Pizza and thought you'd like to share it with me," he said, reaching for her hand.

She took his and let him draw her up the wooden steps. "How did you arrange this?"

Niko shrugged. "I just happened to have a conversation with Wilson Abramovich at Overly Caffeinated today—the cold brew is fantastic, by the way—and he mentioned that the gazebo is available for rental for private parties."

"So you rented it?" Emma laughed, letting him pull her into him.

"I missed you." He said it simply as if it explained everything.

"You saw me two nights ago. *All* of me, if memory serves," she teased.

"And short of dragging you to a hotel in another city, I thought this would be an enjoyable way to spend some alone time together." He put the pizza box down on the bench and shoved both hands into her hair, drawing her in for a slow, sweet kiss.

When they broke apart, a little breathless and a lot aroused, Emma patted a hand over her racing heart. "The things you do for me," she said on a sigh.

"Almost as good as the things I plan to do *to* you." His devil's grin had her laughing.

She shook her head. "I can't believe I could have missed out on this."

"Good thing I'm irresistible," Niko agreed. "Now, catch me up on what I missed while we dine on cold pizza."

She filled him in on the Beautification Committee's sudden interest in Eva and Donovan.

"Would you like having Eva live here?" Niko asked, topping off her plastic cup with a very nice chardonnay.

"Well, of course I would, but it seems a little underhanded to guilt her into moving here only so some ridiculous committee can try to marry her off."

"How far do these people go to arrange marriages?"

"Well, let's see, they convinced Joey that they were going to push Jax into the arms of Moon Beam Parker. They made Beckett think that they loved Gia's ex-husband. With Phil and Fred, they set up a fake night of speed dating at Karma Kustard and only invited the two of them." She ticked the infractions off on her fingers.

Fascinated, Niko laughed. "Wait, how often does this work?"

"How often do the poor suckers fall in love and get married?"

Niko nodded.

"Perfect track record."

He shook his head in disbelief. "There's no way."

"*The Monthly Moon* posts write-ups on their triumphs. I believe they are 30 and 0, currently."

"What is in the water here?" Niko wondered.

Emma shrugged. "My guess is hallucinogens."

"So the entire town is in love?"

"They claim that happy, stable residents in happy, stable

relationships make for a stronger community."

"Can you imagine something like this flying in New York or L.A.?" Niko asked.

"No! People understand the importance of boundaries there. No one wants to dig into their neighbors' lives."

They sat in silence for a few moments, and Niko threaded his fingers through hers. "I guess there are worse things," he ventured.

"I suppose. But I think being manipulated into a relationship is no better than falling head over heels for some stranger you don't even know. Why can't people just meet, assess their compatibility, and move forward based on that?"

"You're such a romantic," Niko teased. "Come on. Let's take a walk." He tugged her to her feet.

"I don't have anything against romance, you know. I just don't think it plays a role in building a partnership. It's all artifice. Does it really matter if he sends you a dozen roses or takes you on long walks on the beach, or does it matter that you agree on retirement and school districts?"

Nikolai's laugh warmed her even though it was at her own expense.

"You are one-of-a-kind, Emmaline."

"Now you're making fun of me." She glared up at him in the darkness.

"Only a little. You fascinate me."

"Then I'll keep going," Emma announced haughtily.

"Tell me everything."

"Fine. You know what else I don't like about 'romance?'"

Niko slipped his arm around her shoulders and pulled her up against his side. "If you say puppies as part of marriage proposals you're inhuman."

Emma rolled her eyes. "Ugh, no. It's the whole grand gesture to prove your love to someone. It's so... over-the-top," she decided. "Like being willing to spend the rest of your life with someone should be big enough. You shouldn't have to dress it up by chasing someone down to throw yourself at their feet and beg for forgiveness or surprising them with a spontaneous week in Paris or a Mercedes with a big red bow on it."

"You'd say no to a Mercedes?" Nikolai asked with mock suspicion.

"Well, not if there was a puppy in the front seat. But do you get what I'm saying? The crap these insecure men surprise their indecisive women with should be decisions that are made jointly after carefully weighing the options."

"You're an incurable romantic," Nikolai said, plucking a black-eyed Susan bloom from the edge of a flowerbed and tucking it behind her ear.

"I'm a realist. If you want to fall in love, go for it. But if you want to choose someone to spend the rest of your life with, you should make sure you're choosing wisely."

Nikolai stopped in his tracks. "Wait a minute. Are you saying that instead of marrying for love, people should marry for—"

"Security," she filled in for him. "Love is too volatile. You can fall out of it too easily. My parents certainly did. But if you pick someone who wants the same things as you, you can be a team."

"So, no love?" he asked, his expression still shocked.

"I like to think of it more as mutual respect."

"What does your sister have with Beckett?" he asked, as they began to walk again.

Emma smiled softly. "I think they're the lucky few. I think they got both. I can't see Beckett getting sick of their life and packing up and running off. They make a great team, a united front, and I think they genuinely love each other."

"You have a very pragmatic view of the world, you know that?"

She grinned at him. "It works for me. It's better than floating around like my sister Eva expecting love's thunderbolt at any second."

"Is it?"

She gave him a shove. "What about you, Niko. What do you believe in?"

He stopped again and grabbed her wrist. He pulled her in half a step until their toes met and Emma felt her body reacting to his nearness.

"I believe in the kind of feeling that stops you dead in your tracks and changes everything you ever believed. I believe in a love so swift and sure that it knocks the wind right out of you and leaves you lying on your back staring up at the sky wondering what just hit you."

Her lips parted, but no words came out.

"I believe in an ever after that isn't even a choice because you can't imagine your life without the woman in front of you."

Emma's breath left her in a rush. His words brought to the surface a need she didn't know existed.

"I think you're pretty new at this dating thing. You could give girls ideas if you talk like that to them." Emma said nervously. "For future reference."

"Future reference?"

"When you go back to New York and you finally meet the woman you've been waiting for."

She slipped from his grasp and took a few steps off the path. He was bringing up too many feelings in her. For just a second, she could imagine him saying those words to her. Loving her. Wanting her. Emma pressed a hand to her belly to calm the nerves that took flight there. She wasn't one to fall for romantic, late night walks and soft words.

Feeling the weight of his gaze, Emma faced him. He was dark and dangerous, as always, but there was something else in his expression now. Something she didn't recognize. Maybe she'd taken Julio's advice too far. There was probably a difference between being herself and lecturing a sex partner on her world view.

Wanting to regain some of the playfulness they'd lost, she went to him. "Tell me. When you rented the gazebo, did you also get use of the park?" she asked, gripping his leather jacket with both hands.

"What did you have in mind?"

"I've been missing you, too," she confessed, leaning up and brushing her lips against his.

He held back, just a bit, at first. But she teased him until he went from neutral to willing to desperate. And she was right there with him. Nikolai could have her body revving in seconds as if under a spell. That's what it was, she thought distantly as his lips slanted over hers again and again in rising greed. Her body was enchanted by his existence. He merely had to look at her, and she wanted him, needed him, lusted for him.

Her white knuckled grip on his jacket wasn't necessary. He wasn't trying to get away. He was trying to get closer. He stroked under her cardigan, squeezing her waist and molding the curves of her hips with his palms.

She felt him, hard as granite against her belly, and purred into his mouth.

"You make me feel so crazed for you," he murmured, devouring her with teeth and tongue.

"You make me feel craved," she sighed back.

They were the last words exchanged. Their bodies

communicated on an entirely different level. Emma didn't have to tell him where to touch her because he was already plunging his hands into the top of her wrap dress, baring her to the night air.

On a growl, he dragged her further off the sidewalk into the shadows of a copse of trees. There was a bench, secluded away in greenery.

Emma shoved him down on the wood and straddled him. She loved the feel of him. The hard steel of his erection grinding against her, separated by too many layers of clothes. She could come just like this, but she wanted it all. She wanted to take him into her and claim him as hers.

He was yanking the V of material down her breasts and—after half a second of admiring the sexy balconette bra she wore beneath the dress—he was shoving the cups down. Niko breathed reverently over her exposed breasts. Admiring them, he cupped them in his palms and Emma delighted at the feel of his thumbs brushing over her nipples.

Dark, sinful eyes met hers as he leaned into one peak and licked gently. Emma's eyes fluttered closed. The warmth of his mouth against her sensitive nipple was almost too much to take. And when his lips closed around it to suck, a whimper escaped her throat. He took long, deep pulls that she felt echoed in the empty clenching of her core.

She grinded against him and felt the length of his cock drag across her aching nub. Without breaking contact with her breast, Niko clutched her to him, leaning to the side and yanking his wallet free.

Understanding, Emma fumbled it open and found the condom inside.

She wanted to pause, to consider the consequences of making love here in the middle of town. But for once, her pragmatism was absent, and in its place was a desperate need to take. She rose up on her knees, her breast releasing from Niko's mouth with a pop. The cool night air teased her wet, aching nipple.

Together, they freed his hard-on from the confines of his slacks. His head fell back against the bench when Emma rolled the condom down his thick shaft. She would have stroked him, toyed with him until he was desperate and wild. But there was no time for gentleness or play now, only reckless desire.

Niko gripped her hips hard enough to bruise as Emma positioned herself over his broad crown. She pulled her underwear to the side and took a shaky breath as she lined him up with the wet heat of her entrance. She was already slick and ready for him with a greediness that scared her. Easing down, she accepted the first inch and then another and another until she was impaled on his throbbing cock.

She watched in fascination as the cords on his neck stood out as if he was in great pain. She took a moment to give her muscles time to soften around him, and Niko used the seconds to fasten himself on her other breast.

Slowly, achingly, Emma began to ride. The pull at her breast echoed in her now full channel, promising pleasure too intense to prepare for. She took what she wanted, and still it wasn't enough. She needed more, and it was terrifying, but she wasn't stopping. Not now. Not tonight. She wanted this more than she wanted to be safe.

The heat built and built until Emma felt like the sun had come out to bake them both under its rays. He was carrying her to the sun, burning away everything but ecstasy.

Every stroke, every nuzzle, every pull of his mouth, sparked an awareness so intense, Emma thought she might not survive. Everything was so clear here, possessed by him, adored by him. *This* was exactly right.

She took them both higher and higher, riding harder, faster, until neither could catch their breath. Wild and free. She let her body do what it was made to do.

The light inside her was breaking apart, and she felt the build. It was happening, and there was nothing they could do to stop it. Emma felt herself close and tighten on him. The pained groan that rumbled in his chest told her he was with her. Harder and faster, they chased it together. Until under the moon and stars, they came apart around each other. Like lightning striking through her over and over, Emma shattered around Niko's swollen cock as he released into her, desperate sighs and moans mixing with the night noises.

She quaked around him with a never-ending orgasm that shattered her to pieces. Gasping for breath against his chest, Emma tried to come back to earth.

"Not done. Need more," Niko demanded. He lifted her off of him and groaned when his still hard cock slid free.

He put her hands on the bench's back and closed his fingers over hers. "Hang on," he ordered.

Emma bent forward and gasped when he drove into her from behind. How could she want him again so soon? She could still feel aftershocks, yet her greedy center was begging for more.

Niko gripped her hip and palmed one of her breasts as he worked himself in and out of her. "You feel so good, baby. I can't get enough of you."

He wasn't gentle, and she didn't want him to be. She liked this needy side of him, knowing that he wanted and craved her as much as she did him. Emma spread her feet wider, and he groaned his approval. Her senses were so full of him, his scent, the slick slide of his flesh against hers, the taste of him still on her lips. This was special, this was once-in-a-lifetime, and Emma was beyond grateful that he was hers for tonight.

Harder and harder he thrust into her to the hilt. Emma bit her lip hard to keep quiet though she wanted to let loose a stream of pleading cries. She wanted to come again, tightening on him as he flexed into her, losing himself in her depths. She wanted that joining, that closeness that nothing else would ever accomplish.

There was nothing in the world that she wanted as badly as that.

"You're going to come with me," Niko demanded, slipping the hand at her breast between her legs and stroking her wet slit. "There it is," he growled. The pads of his fingers found her, working her until she saw nothing but light in the darkness.

"Now, Emmaline. Now," he whispered harshly. The first pump of his orgasm ripped her over the edge with him. Her vision went black as she came violently on his cock and fingers. He rode out his own orgasm, using her body to milk himself dry.

He spun them around so he could cradle her in his lap. Emma was shivering, but it wasn't from cold. It was from being hurtled into the heavens and not knowing if she could find her way home. Seeming to understand, Niko wrapped his arms around her and held her against his chest, anchoring her to him.

Emma closed her eyes and let the rest of her senses slowly come back to life. She could smell him, that spicy woodsy scent that drove her insane. The beat of his heart was steadying itself back to a normal rhythm under her ear.

"Niko?"

"Yeah, baby?" He stroked a hand through her hair, gently, reverently.

"I'm never going to look at this bench the same way again."

25

*E*mma had decided that they could make their public debut at Blue Moon's Annual Farmers Market Showcase and Knit Off. The juxtaposition of a public debut in Blue Moon versus New York was, on the surface, remarkably similar. The couple would appear in public together, and then gossip would run rampant. However, instead of the city's rabid appetite for sordid affairs, Blue Moon rooted for happily ever afters one new couple at a time.

He'd been warned, by Emma, Summer, and most of the Pierce family about the interfering ways of the Beautification Committee. And when no marital manipulation attempts were made in his direction, Niko wondered if perhaps the town felt he was not marriage material. Instead, the whole town seemed to be working overtime to convince him that Blue Moon was the destination of his dreams.

If he dreamed in Technicolor tie-dye.

And wasn't it interesting that after just a few weeks in town, his natural avoidance of monogamy and planning for the future had given way to a curiosity about such things?

The late May sun warmed Niko's back as he guided his

bike down Blue Moon's eclectic streets to Emma's place. Since she'd decided they'd be making their debut, he'd decided they should do it in style. Carter had bet him twenty bucks he wouldn't get Emma on the back of the bike. Summer already knew better than to bet against Niko and put her money on him instead.

He parked against the curb and followed the curving brick walkway around the side of Beckett and Gia's stately Victorian to the backyard.

Emma answered his knock in slim cut cropped jeans and an off-the-shoulder cashmere sweater the color of morning fog.

He had intended to say "good morning," or "hi" at the very least. But her sunny smile hit him in the gut like a fist, and he was backing her into the dining table with a kiss that took both their breath away.

"Wow. Good morning to you, too," Emma breathed when he finally released her.

"You shouldn't answer your door looking so gorgeous," Niko told her, cupping her face in his hand.

Emma raised a suspicious eyebrow. "Are you trying to get out of the farmers market by seducing me?"

"For future reference, everything I do is to get you naked. So if it's not before the farmers market, it's after."

"Good to know, Don Juan." She shoved an armful of canvas shopping bags at him. "I figured we could shop for dinner tonight. Eva's in the city overnight doing vague Eva work-related things," she said, planting a kiss on his cheek.

"I'm not going to say no to a night with you. Though I can't believe I'm heading to the farmers market on a Sunday morning with my girlfriend." He saw her hands fumble her house keys.

"The 'g' word?" Those green eyes watched him keenly.

Niko slung an arm around her shoulder and drew her out the door. "I figured it was better than calling you my 'lady friend.'"

"Agreed. What would you be doing on a Sunday morning in New York?" she asked, locking the door behind them.

"I'm guessing same as you in L.A."

"Sleeping off Saturday night?" she winked.

"Pretty much. This isn't so bad though," he said bringing her knuckles to his lips to kiss.

"Aren't you charming this morning?"

"I'm buttering you up," he admitted, walking her around the side of the house.

"For future reference, with you, very little needs to be buttered to get me naked."

"I'll file that away, but for right now, your chariot awaits." He steered her toward the bike.

"Oh, no. Nope. Nope. Nope." She shook her head and sent her curls flying.

"When's the last time you were on a motorcycle?"

"That would be never because I don't have a death wish or a moronic need for speed."

"Where's your sense of adventure?" Niko prodded.

"That's what people say right before they go base jumping and their chute doesn't open or the alligator they're wrestling turns around and bites off a limb. Why do we need to ride anyway? It's just three blocks."

He turned her argument back on her. "Exactly. It's just three blocks, Emmaline." Niko traced a finger over her bare shoulder. "Don't you want to see what it's like to have that power between your legs?"

Emma looked down at his crotch. "I think I already have a pretty good idea."

He tried again. "It's important to me."

She rolled those emerald eyes heavenward. "Fine. But I want to be cremated, and I want 'Down in a Blaze of Glory' played at my funeral."

Niko grinned in victory and handed her a helmet. "Safety first."

"If that were an actual consideration, we'd be driving my car," she snipped, sliding the helmet over her head. She let him secure it under her chin, and he gave her head a friendly pat before pulling on his own helmet.

"By the way, in the interest of honesty, I bet Carter that I'd be able to get you on the bike. He didn't think it was your thing. So if you want him to be right, you can still back out."

Emma glared up at him. "I'm starting to get a little tired of people thinking they know what I will and won't and should and shouldn't do."

"That's the spirit." Niko slid a leg over the bike and patted the seat behind him. "Come on. It's only three blocks, and I'll split Carter's twenty with you."

He saw the rise and fall of her shoulders, her sigh of defeat.

Reluctantly she climbed on behind him. "What do I do with my hands?" she asked as he revved the engine to life.

"Hang on to me. Tight."

It took her only two blocks to warm up to the bike enough that she demanded that he loop back so they could ride longer. Happy to oblige, Niko drove them out of town and grinned until his jaw hurt at Emma's joy. He'd known she'd like it, known it would unlock that part of herself that she kept tamped down with rules and schedules and shoulds and shouldn'ts.

He had suspicions it had to do with her mother and needing a sense of control over her own life. Emma thought she could control her way through life and, in doing so, cut herself off from fun. He'd caught glimpses of her desires that ran that vein. There was nothing controlled or regulated about the girl who rode him to the stars on that park bench. He liked prying her open, liked delving beneath that prickly surface.

Emma tightened her arms around his waist, and he felt like all was right with the world.

She whooped in his ear as he accelerated down a straight-away, pasture on their left, woods on their right. He stuck to the speed limit, mostly, and let the roads lead them for another ten minutes before turning back toward town.

They made an entrance onto Main Street and drew even more eyes when, upon dismounting, Emma yanked off her helmet and gave him a smacking kiss on the mouth.

"Liked it, did you?"

"I want one," Emma said definitively. "I want you to teach me how to ride, and then I'm getting one."

"My pretty little bad ass." He tapped her nose with affection. "How about we market—or whatever the appropriate verb is—first, and then we'll go for a long ride this afternoon?"

"And maybe an even longer ride tonight?" Emma asked coyly.

"I see you two rode over," Carter interrupted, standing on the sidewalk behind the handle of the double stroller.

"When I saw Niko brought his bike I just begged for a ride," Emma said, batting her lashes at Carter. "I've always wanted to ride a motorcycle."

Carter dug out his wallet. "You are so full of shit, Emma."

She snatched up the twenty he pulled out and grinned. "Don't bet against me, Carter. You'd be surprised what I'd do just to prove people wrong."

Niko and Carter watched her sashay across the street to the market.

"Women," Carter grumbled.

"Yeah. Women," Niko grinned. "Where's yours?"

"She's helping man the stand while I walk the twins to sleep."

Niko glanced down at two wide-eyed toddlers. "It doesn't look like it's working."

Carter peered over the roof of the stroller. "Damn. I'd better walk faster."

Niko grabbed his camera out of the bike's saddlebag and jogged across the street. He found Emma pretending to admire the braided candles at a stand run by a woman who was a hundred and ten if she was a day.

"Ear wax melts the most evenly," she was explaining to Emma.

Emma very carefully set the candle back down and wiped her hands on her jeans. "There you are!" she said to Niko in bright desperation. "It was nice seeing you Mrs. Allmamen."

She latched onto Niko's arm and steered him into the crowd. "Hurry before she tries to sell us breast milk yogurt."

Niko stopped in his tracks. "Are you sure you don't want a couple of nice ear wax candles for your dining table?" He jerked his thumb over his shoulder. "Because I could go back and get them for you."

"That's disgusting. You're disgusting. And what's with the camera?"

Niko shrugged. "I thought I'd shoot a little if the mood strikes me."

"Well, well, well," Emma said smugly.

"Don't act like you're going to take credit for my newfound enthusiasm for work." Even though he was pretty sure that's exactly where credit was due.

"I'm not saying a word," she said innocently. "I'm just glad your talent didn't wither up and die inside your black hole of creativity."

He captured her hand and squeezed hard until she yelped.

"Oh, gee, I'm sorry." Sarcasm dripped from his words.

"You're mean." She wiggled her fingers in his grip. "Mean and strong."

"What's Carter buying us for dinner tonight?" Niko asked, letting her lead him through the throngs of people. It looked to Niko that the entire town had turned out for the market.

He'd been here before, shooting the Pierces for a magazine piece Summer had worked on before she made the move here permanent.

It had been colorful chaos then and hadn't changed an iota since. Stands under awnings in every color of the rainbow flanked the park's wide brick sidewalk. Generations of people representing varying degrees of hippie culture wandered around eating, laughing, talking. Even the transplants like Emma eventually showed signs of assimilation, he thought, eyeing the silver peace sign anklet she'd donned for the day.

The vibe here is a good one, Niko thought as he tucked his lens cap in the back pocket of his jeans and raised the camera to catch earwax candle lady lean out of her stand to follow the path of a butterfly.

Summer and Phoebe waved from the Pierce Acres stand, and Niko and Emma began to work their way over. It was slow going, though, with Emma pausing to talk to neighbors and complete strangers greeting Niko welcoming him to town.

"Nikolai!" Willa waved frantically. "Over here!"

Not seeing an easy or polite way to ignore her, Niko left Emma with a Mrs. Nordemann and her book recommendations and headed into Willa's tent.

"Hey, Willa. How's it going?"

"Oh, fine, fine. How about with you? It looks like you nursed Emma back to health."

"I couldn't have done it without your help," he told her.

And your ninety dollars of organic remedies, he added silently.

"I've been hoping you'd stop by the store." She let the words hang there in the air, candy coated with guilt. "But since you didn't, I thought I might see you here today. I have a pair of boots I think would be just perfect for you."

Niko eyed the contents of her stand. The fabric walls were lined with cowboy boots with purple stitching, t-strap sandals in colors never before seen in nature, and dozens of patterned socks.

"I don't know if this is really my style..." he began diplomatically.

Willa waved away his concern. "Don't be silly. I know a perfect match when I see one. And I saw the one for you. Let me just dig them out—"

She disappeared under a table and box lids and recycled tissue paper exploded into the air as she rifled through her inventory. "Aha!"

She reappeared with a price tag stuck in her hair and a box in her hand. "Voila!"

Willa pried the lid off the box.

Niko was relieved when he didn't have to fake his interest. They were motorcycle boots in sleek, black leather. He weighed one in his hand, solid construction, beefy soles, thick laces. "Wow, Willa. These are nice. Really nice."

"Vegan leather, waterproof, hand-stitched." She reeled off the qualities. "And a very special friend of Blue Moon discount for you."

"I don't know if they'll fit," he said, already looking for a place to sit.

Willa cleared a space on a short wooden bench. "They're your size," she promised. "I can always tell the size of a man even from a distance."

Niko bit back the half a dozen penis jokes that surfaced in

his brain at her comment and instead slipped on the boot and laced it up. Sure enough, the fit was perfect.

Niko looked up just as Emma walked past deep in conversation with Evan and Aurora who were entertaining her with a story. The sunlight hit her just perfectly that her hair was a sensual spark of flame. Her eyes danced as she listened to her niece and nephew. And when she laughed, that husky sound went straight to his gut.

"What did I tell you? A perfect match," Willa said slyly.

He paid a fraction of what he would have for the same shoes in the city and thanked Willa profusely.

"It's what we do for our neighbors," she said waving away his thanks. "Have a lovely Blue Moon day."

He caught up with Emma at the Pierces' stand.

"I bring you to a farmers market, and you buy shoes?" she snickered at his bag.

"Don't knock Willa's stuff," Summer warned Emma. "That's where I got those sandals that you slobber over every time you see them."

Suddenly interested, Emma gripped Summer's arm. "Does she have any more?"

"Only one way to find out!" Summer shoved Niko behind the stand. "Help Phoebe. Emma and I have important shoe business."

Niko didn't have a chance to get his bearings as Mrs. Nordemann was demanding parsley, lettuce, beet greens, and a pound of asparagus. He juggled, bagged, and chatted. And when there was a pause in the action, he shot the scenes he saw from behind the Pierce Acres stand.

As far as Niko was concerned, Phoebe had the "flow." She'd perfected the art of gossiping and upselling. She remembered the names of everyone's children and pets, knew who was recovering from surgery, who was visiting colleges.

"You love this don't you?" Niko asked, lifting a rubber-banded bunch of fresh dill to his nose.

Phoebe grinned. "This is the highlight of living in Blue Moon. Everyone coming out every Sunday to support their local farmers and artisans, kids running free while their parents catch up, and you know that something that you grew with your own two hands is going to end up on a neighbor's table for dinner tonight." She sighed. "I wouldn't want to live anywhere else."

"It's like a giant co-op," Niko winked.

"It takes a village," Phoebe laughed. "A crazy, nosy, complicated village."

Niko watched as her face lit up and had the presence of mind to snap the picture. "There's part of my village now!"

Jax and Joey wandered up with Reva and Caleb in tow, and Niko thought that the world would be a better place if all parents and grandparents greeted their offspring with that sense of excitement. His mother had done the same. Every time he walked in a room, she looked at him as if he were bringing the light with him.

"Who's ready for lunch?" Phoebe asked, doling out hugs.

"I am," Caleb piped up. "Joey says you're taking us for Italian?"

Phoebe ruffled his hair. "That's right. Franklin's joining the three of us for lunch at his restaurant while these two goofballs man the stand."

Joey sauntered behind the stand, tugging at the hem of her Pierce Acres shirt. "Let's get this over with," she grumbled.

Jax pressed a kiss to her head. "Excuse Jojo the Grump. She doesn't like leaving Eclipse yet."

"Not when the freaking three of us are here," she said gesturing between herself, Jax, and Reva, "and he's all by himself."

"Colby's there," Reva reminded her. "He said he'd keep an eye on him."

"Whose side are you on, anyway?" Joey grumbled.

"Quit your whining and go sell some eggs and asparagus," Jax suggested. "If you're a good girl, I'll buy you a funnel cake."

"With extra powdered sugar?" Joey asked hopefully.

"Anything you want." He kissed her, and Caleb made gagging sounds.

"Just you wait, Cale. Someday you're going to be real excited about kissing girls," Jax warned him.

"That's disgusting," Caleb announced.

"Well, let's leave them here to be disgusting, and we'll go have ourselves a feast," Phoebe suggested.

"Woo Hoo!" Caleb raced off.

Reva rolled her eyes. "He doesn't even know what car you drive," she sighed at Phoebe. "I'll go get him." She turned and loped after her brother.

"Thanks for taking them to lunch, Mom," Jax said, giving Phoebe a kiss on the cheek. And for one second, Niko missed his own mother fiercely.

Phoebe patted Jax's cheek. "It's my pleasure. It's not often that I magically receive spontaneous grandchildren."

She headed off in the direction Reva and Caleb had taken. And Niko thought of circles opening and closing.

"So how is it being a mom?" Niko asked Joey.

"Are you asking about the horse or the kids?" Jax joked.

Joey smacked him in the chest, and Jax rubbed absently at the spot. "You're hilarious, Captain Hilarious Pants."

Niko hid his smile.

"The kids are great. Funny, smart. I don't know why Summer and Gia are whining about how hard it is. Reev and Cale made us pancakes for breakfast today."

"Maybe having already potty-trained kids with some sense

of impulse control is a little easier than twin toddlers or Aurora and a baby?" Niko offered.

"I think we're just better at it than they are," Joey said with a shrug and a grin.

"Yeah, make sure I'm not around if you decide to offer my brothers that nugget of insight," Jax warned her.

Joey rubbed her hands together. "I'm still working on my delivery. I can't wait to see Summer and Gia's faces when I say it. They're going to freak."

"See why I love my diabolical wife?" Jax asked Niko.

"It would be hard not to," Niko agreed.

"Where's your woman?" Joey asked. "I wanted to ask her for her bruschetta recipe. My parents are coming tonight to meet the kids."

"That reminds me, I need to swing by the brewery and pick up a six-pack," Jax said, rubbing his palm over his chin.

Joey raised an eyebrow.

"I guess I'd better make that two six-packs," Jax amended.

"I never would have thought in a billion years that you and my dad would be all BFFy," she said shaking her head.

Jax gestured at himself. "What's not to like?"

"What did your parents say about you two becoming instaparents?" Niko asked.

Joey grinned. "Nothing yet."

"Jojo!" Jax whipped around to face her. "You didn't tell them?"

She shrugged. "You know how they are. If you give them too much of a head's up, they think too much."

"So you're just going to spring a seventeen-year-old and a six-year-old on them?"

"They think they're coming to meet Eclipse."

Jax groaned. "Diabolical."

26

$\mathcal{E}$mma returned—with two shoe bags—and they abandoned the stand to Jax and Joey. They spent the rest of the morning visiting and shopping, teasing each other with bites of fresh cheese and samples from OJs by Julia.

This was what a community felt like, Niko decided, raising his camera when Aurora threw her arms around Gia's neck in a sticky-fingered hug. Warm, welcoming. He wouldn't mind experiencing more of this.

Maybe it was time to start really thinking about the future? What was it that he really wanted? More of the same, or something different? Better.

Emma was irresistible, he thought, watching her haggle over salad greens and free-range chicken breasts with Farmer Carson who, though in his nineties, clearly had a crush on the redhead. Niko loved watching her swing into action, loved her unshakeable confidence, her attitude. He couldn't remember ever spending time with a woman like this. The ones he'd dated casually had been more interested in talking industry gossip and not eating because of whatever shoot they had the next day.

Had he been missing out his entire life?

Chicken and greens purchased, they picked up gyros from the Greek stand and carried them to the gazebo where more than twenty knitters were setting up.

"This is why I have to live here," Emma said, shaking her head in wonder as men and women readied what looked like large, colorful logs of thick merino wool yarn.

"I've never seen yarn like that," Niko said, raising his camera.

"They're race arm knitting blankets for the children's hospital over in Cleary," Emma explained.

Niko dropped his camera. "I don't understand that particular combination of words."

Emma laughed and took a bite of her gyro. "Just watch. The contest is first team to one standard sized blanket. They'll trade off every time they swap out yarn," she explained.

Niko gave her an incredulous look.

"What? It was in *The Monthly Moon*," Emma explained.

Ellery was onstage readying herself behind a stack of black-as-midnight yarn. She waved in their direction.

"Some poor kid in the children's hospital is going to end up with the blanket of death," Niko quipped.

Emma elbowed him in the ribs. "Very funny. Get your camera ready, they're about to start."

Niko forgot all about his gyro when the action started. Arms blurred with speed, and chunky sections of yarn turned into thick rows of knit blankets. The competition was fierce and filled with good-natured cheating. He captured Bruce Oakleigh sweating over a skein of pink wool while Mrs. Nordemann, Elvira Eustace's knitting partner, crawled over to tie his loose yarn in a knot around his chair leg.

An out of town knitting duo sang off-key folk songs so loudly that the team next to them kept missing stitches and shooting them dirty looks while Bobby, the dreadlocked proprietress of Peace of Pizza, "accidentally" kicked another team's yarn off the makeshift stage.

Ellery was clearly a pro. She settled noise-cancelling headphones over her ears and her yarn between her feet where no other contestants could get to it. Any time anyone invaded her personal space, she stomped her Frankenstein shoe on the stage. The intimidation appeared to be working as she was a full row ahead of the competition.

Niko shot the action and the crowd until Emma covered his lens with her hand. "Okay, Annie L Leibovitz. Let's enjoy the fun without a camera for a minute so I can make sure you know how to live on the other side of the lens."

"One more," Niko insisted. He called Evan over. "You mind taking a picture of us?" he asked.

Evan handed the dripping ice cream cone he'd been working on to a friend and wiped his hands on his jeans. "Sure!"

Niko looped the padded strap around the boy's neck and gave him the point and click instructions. He returned to Emma and wrapped his arms around her waist.

"Smile pretty for the camera."

"You go from not wanting to pick up a camera to wanting to capture every second of the day?" Emma teased. "Don't you know how to live in the middle?"

Niko gave her a pinch. "Where's the fun in that?"

∼

FORTY-FIVE MINUTES LATER, the knitting action came to a climactic finish when Bruce Oakleigh and his wife, Amethyst, edged out Ellery for the big win by two stitches. Emma hid her smile when Niko rushed forward with the crowd to capture the awarding of the prize. Davis Gates, the young and dashing owner of Blue Moon Winery, presented the year's supply of wines to the ecstatic Oakleighs. Bruce's victory speech lasted twelve minutes until Bobby, her silver dreads sparkling in the sunshine, elbowed him out of the way and thanked everyone for coming out to show their support of race arm knitting.

Niko returned to her, grinning at the screen of his camera as he flipped through his bounty.

Emma crossed her arms in amusement. "If I didn't know better, I'd say you were starting to like Blue Moon."

"What's not to like?" he asked, looking up from the screen, his grin irresistible. "I've got a beautiful girl who's going to grill dinner for me tonight."

"Emma! Yoo hoo!" They turned to catch Bruce Oakleigh bouncing on the balls of his feet to peer at them through the crowd. He waved frantically. "Emma!"

She waved back, a sunny smile plastered on her face. "Now what do you suppose Blue Moon's race arm knitting champion wants with me?" she asked without moving her lips.

"He probably wants you to weigh in on the powdered wig debate. I hear it's getting heated," Niko whispered behind his hand.

Bruce dodged and weaved his way to them arriving in a huff of breath. He combed one hand through his silvery beard and another through his fluff of hair before straightening his cranberry sweater vest.

"Congratulations on your big win," Emma said extending her hand. Bruce shook it enthusiastically.

"Thank you! Amethyst and I have been practicing all hours of the day and night for this, and the effort really paid off. It's nice to finally meet you, Nikolai," he said, offering his hand to Niko.

"Now, I'm sure you're wondering why I flagged you down

like a crossing guard." Before Emma could answer, Bruce launched into his explanation. "I'm glad I ran into you, Emma. Gordon mentioned you were interested in looking for a place to call your own, and the whole town is just thrilled to death that you're staying. Now is the time to buy. It's a buyer's market in Blue Moon, and there are so many wonderful properties available. I took the liberty of speaking to Rainbow at the bank, and she assures me a loan would be no issue. And to top it off, I have the perfect property for you. It just came on the market yesterday."

He paused long enough to breathe and wait for a response. Bulldozed and open-mouthed, Emma merely stared.

"So what do you say? I've got a few minutes before Anthony comes to take our victors' picture for the paper. It's only two blocks from here, and we could just pop in and take a look around. Nikolai, you should come too. See what square footage you can get here as opposed to the city."

Hearing no opposition or verbal noise of any kind, Bruce clapped his hands. "Excellent. Now you just follow me, and we'll be there before you know it."

"He's taking us house-hunting," Niko whispered to Emma as they followed Bruce's nimble strides down Patchouli Street. "Does that mean he's going to ambush us with a marriage license and a reverend?"

"He's taking *me* house-hunting," Emma hissed back. "He didn't even ask how many kids we were planning on having. I think this is about making a sale, not a match."

Bruce led them two blocks north of the park to a shady street and a lot with what looked like a round garden shed. "Well, what do you think?" he asked, his enthusiasm made Emma wonder if perhaps he could see something other than the garden shed.

"Is that a tool shed?" she asked with a frown.

"Oh my goodness, no! It's a yurt," Bruce announced with fanfare. "Come in. Come in. You're going to love it."

She hated it.

They walked into a space that looked like a pantry with a futon. Freestanding shelves were stacked with canned goods, books, toilet paper, and clothing.

"Now this would be your living/storage room/closet," Bruce announced. "Aren't the high ceilings spectacular?"

"Hmm," Emma hummed.

Niko elbowed her and winked behind Bruce's back. "It's something, isn't it Emma?"

"Now around this half wall you'll see the previous owner cleverly combined functions," Bruce said, walking the two steps into the next room. They crowded in after him.

"Why is there a drain in the kitchen floor?" Emma asked with great trepidation.

"This is the clever part." Bruce pointed to the suspended showerhead above them.

"There's a shower? In the kitchen?" She said the words slowly, not quite believing that they were coming out of her mouth.

Niko let a laugh slip and covered it with a cough.

"Oh, not just a shower! The under the sink cabinet pulls out and that's your toilet!" He pulled the slider out with the flourish of a magician revealing a rabbit.

"Is that even legal?"

Bruce frowned thoughtfully and wagged a finger. "You know, I'm going to have to check the municipal codes on that and get back to you."

"What would you call such a multi-purpose room?" Niko wondered.

"That's the best part." Bruce leaned in as if he was going to share a secret. "It's called the bitchen."

27

_J_une arrived with a mellowing of temperatures and an excess of sunshine. The farm was in full swing as produce poked its green fingers through freshly turned soil. The days were longer and busier. Niko lent a hand whenever he could on the farm. The brewery was booked with bridal showers and baby sprinkles and anniversary celebrations, and Emma was working overtime to keep up with it all.

He was shooting everything these days. The deadline for the upcoming show this month served as creative motivation, and Niko spent long hours capturing his subjects and even longer hours editing. And when he wasn't doing that, he was reassuring his agent Amara that he hadn't fallen off the face of the planet or forgotten how to work a camera.

Bruce Oakleigh hadn't given up on his quest to find Emma the perfect home. Despite her repeated objections that she wasn't really ready to look for a house, she'd seen a yurt, a tree house, and an eight-bedroom brick mansion that until two months ago had been a funeral home. While Niko enjoyed tagging along with her to view the properties, he'd begun to wonder if Blue Moon had any normal residences.

When they weren't working or shopping for real estate, he and Emma made up for lost time in the midnight hours. Eva had returned to her Virginia home and, while Emma was sorry to see her sister go, she and Niko took advantage of having the cottage to themselves. Keeping the front door securely locked, they explored each other with the desperation of teenagers.

It worked. They worked. But Niko knew they were both wondering what would happen next. He couldn't leave his life and work in New York forever. Eventually he would have to return. And what would that mean for his relationship with Emma?

Antsy and needing a change for the afternoon, Niko packed up his laptop and drove his bike into town. He had work to do on the photos he'd culled out for the show. Overly Caffeinated, a spacious café on the corner of Main and Lavender, promised free WiFi and necessary caffeine.

He ordered a coffee from a teenage girl with a spiky cap of orange hair and settled in at a table facing the wide expanse of glass that overlooked the park. He'd already culled out thirty shots for the show. They were different from any of his other work, and that was the beauty of them, he supposed, of going from high fashion, orchestrated photo shoots to capturing and freezing real life moments.

Each picture carried with it a story and a feeling. Hope, friendship, victory... and more. *Much more*, he thought, opening his favorites of Emma.

It was no surprise how often she'd shown up in the shots for the show. If he were to look at her pictures objectively, as if they were someone else's, he'd assume that the photographer had strong personal feelings for his subject. There was a kind of magic that translated through the lens when model and photographer were bonded. He could see it in these, he thought slowly clicking through the files.

Emma mid-twirl in her groomsmaid dress. Emma shaking a cocktail behind the bar at the brewery. Emma lecturing staff before the dinner rush. Emma kissing her father at his wedding.

Yes, there were strong feelings there, he thought. Strong, complicated feelings.

There was another one he'd taken recently that he thought might fit. Emma sleeping, the sheets draped and wrapped around her naked body, a hint of a satisfied smile on her lips. They'd made love, and she'd fallen asleep when he went downstairs for water. He hadn't been able to help himself snapping the picture. The intimacy of the moment, the power of her even asleep.

He inserted the camera card into the slot and waited while his files uploaded.

"Excuse me," the café's orange haired barista was back. "We just made these, and we need a taste tester. Fresh organic oat bars," she said, offering up a smile and a plate with what looked like a granola bar on it.

He wondered what it would be like to go back to New York where no one tried to bribe him with free stuff into liking the community.

"Thanks," he said, accepting the plate.

The girl wandered off again, and Niko took a bite while he flipped through the pictures. The Knit Off, in its blur of color and action, filled his screen, and he entertained himself flipping through the files. There were a few shots that he could use for the show, he decided, culling them into a separate folder to be edited.

He closed one image and clicked to open the next one, and

his organic oat bar lodged in his throat. It wasn't a shot he'd taken. It was the one he'd asked Evan to take.

Emma was looking up at him and laughing, her hands splayed across his chest as he pulled her into him. But it wasn't her face that demanded his attention. It was his own. He'd seen that look before, knew it so well that it pulled him back to another time. He hadn't noticed it. It had crept up on him. But in the picture it was clear that the resemblance to his father was striking as was the expression on his face. Niko was looking at Emma the way his father had looked at his mother in those quiet, private moments when they thought no one else was watching.

It was love.

The realization hit him harder than a ton of bricks dropped from above. He was leveled. He'd known he had feelings for her, strong ones. He just hadn't realized until this second what those feelings were.

He collapsed back in his chair and stared through the glass to the park where life continued on without any indication that the world had turned upside down.

STILL REELING FROM HIS DISCOVERY, Niko jumped at the invitation to Man Night Poker at Beckett's. Emma was working, and he wanted to distract himself with something until he could process his epiphany and decide what, if anything, to do about it.

He arrived early, carting a six-pack and the three footlongs he'd picked up from Righteous Subs. His knock was answered by the adorable, mischievous Aurora and her guard dog Diesel, an overgrown gray beast that had flunked doggy obedience school twice.

"Hi!" she greeted him with enthusiasm.

"Hey, kid. Are you seven yet?"

"Not yet," she shook her head. "But soon and then I'll get presents and cake and there'll be a party. You can come!" she offered.

"Wouldn't miss it," he said. "Is Beckett home?"

"He and mom are here somewhere. I'll go find them, and you can play with Diesel and my Barbie," Aurora said, shoving her doll into Niko's hand.

The little redhead charged up the stairs calling for "Bucket" and her mom. There was a moment of silence and then a loud thump and a muffled giggle that came from the coat closet.

Niko watched as the doorknob turned as if by invisible fingers. A disheveled Gia poked her head out of the closet into the hallway.

"Crap. Busted," she whispered over her shoulder.

Beckett, still buttoning his shirt stepped out behind her. "It's just Niko, not a kid," he sighed with relief.

"I'm early," he announced unnecessarily. He tried not to look at them directly in the eye.

Beckett's hair stood up in tufts. Gia's skirt was on sideways and her neck was red. She scratched at it absently as the sound of a baby crying wafted down from the second floor. "Damn it! Beard burn," she muttered. "Hi, Niko. If you tell any of our children where we were, I will make you babysit."

"I saw nothing," he promised. Diesel whimpered longingly at the bag of subs. Gia yanked Beckett's mouth down to hers for one hard kiss before dashing barefoot upstairs.

"Mama's coming!" she called out.

"So..." Beckett said, buckling his belt.

"So..." Niko looked at his feet.

"Beer?"

"Definitely."

~

"Thanks for coming with me," Emma said to Phoebe as she signaled a left turn.

"It's my pleasure. With all the houses your father and I looked at before we decided to build, I kind of miss exploring the weird and wonderful real estate that Blue Moon has to offer."

"I've seen more weird than wonderful," Emma sighed. "But Bruce was awfully firm about this house being 'the one.'"

"Did you at least make sure it has a separate bathroom and kitchen?" Phoebe asked.

"I did this time. He assures me it's a dream home, but I'm afraid that translates into nightmare." She spotted the house number and parked at the curb. "Oh, this can't be it," she breathed.

The red brick house rose three stories high and was tucked into a fenced in lot with an abundance of trees and ferns. The leaves of the dogwood tree in the front yard fluttered in the evening breeze.

"This is... lovely," Phoebe decided, opening her car door.

"I must have gotten the address wrong," Emma frowned, checking her phone for Bruce's text.

"I don't think so," Phoebe said, pointing at the for sale sign with Bruce Oakleigh's mug on it against the sidewalk.

"Maybe the inside is terrible?" Emma murmured, following the brick walkway to the front porch.

"Oh, it wraps around both sides," Phoebe sighed. "Just think of a porch swing right there and morning coffee and evening wine."

"Termites. There's probably an entire termite colony living

here," Emma predicted. "Or black wallpaper. Or maybe a murder-suicide happened here."

"Only one way to find out." Phoebe nodded at the front door.

Just as Emma raised her hand to knock, the door flew open and Bruce grinned at them. "Right on time, ladies! Right on time. Now, come in and take a look around. I think you're going to really like this place."

An hour later, Emma was in love and trying to talk herself out of it. She could see it, could see herself living here. She'd walked into the stunningly appointed kitchen, with its sexy as hell quartz counter tops and six-burner stove, and envisioned lazy brunches at a table tucked into the bay window. The kitchen opened into the family room at the back of the house. A wall of glass showed off the backyard that begged for a fire pit and a dog.

The formal dining room had soaring ceilings and room for at least a dozen. The master bedroom was four times the size of her postage-stamp sized room now. She smiled, realizing Niko wouldn't have to duck to get under the showerhead in this bathroom. The third floor library space would be a perfect studio and office for Niko.

And that's when things fell apart.

Emma wasn't just envisioning herself in the house. She was picturing Niko editing photos upstairs, sprawled out in front of the fireplace in the formal living room, joining her in the glass shower in the master bathroom.

"Did you see the molding around the doors?" Phoebe gushed as they returned to the first floor via the spectacular staircase at the center of the house that was designed for teenage girls to make their grand entrances on prom night.

"Mmm-hmm." It was all Emma could get out. Somehow her brain had taken a vacation, and her imagination had built a life around Nikolai Vulkov and this house. Maybe there really was something hallucinogenic in the water in Blue Moon? But she knew the danger in trying to turn "see where this goes" into a concrete future.

"Well, what do you think?" Bruce asked, clasping his hands in front of him.

"It's wonderful," Emma admitted. But she needed to decide if it was wonderful because she'd fantasized Niko all over the house or if it really fit what she wanted in a home. "Maybe a little big for just me?"

"It's a home to grow into," Bruce said, suddenly serious. "Just imagine all of those bedrooms full with children and guests. Think of how much happiness these walls could hold."

Emma cleared her throat, trying to dislodge the emotion that had settled there. She could see it. Thanksgivings and birthdays. The gallery dedicated to Niko's work in the stairway that rose three floors up. She could *feel* it.

"It's a possibility," she said finally.

POKER NIGHT WAS EXACTLY *what he'd needed*, Niko decided, taking another bite of superb Italian sub. They crowded around a table on Beckett's third floor in a spacious room with gabled ceiling and thick carpet. All three Pierce brothers, the off-duty Donovan Cardona, the fully clothed Fitz, and Evan, who at thirteen had a surprising aptitude for the game, settled in for the evening.

Franklin missed the fun to fill in as host in his restaurant, and Niko wasn't disappointed. He'd never spent time with the father of anyone he was seeing. Though he'd known the man for a year, things were different now. And with everyone around the table knowing that he and Emma were having sex and more, Franklin's absence was a relief.

"How's it going with the kids?" Niko asked Jax.

Jax scratched his jaw and discarded. "Good. Really good. It's definitely an adjustment, but I don't know who it's harder on, us or them."

"Still can't believe you and Joey for all intents and purposes are parents," Beckett said stroking his beard with a disbelieving shake of his head.

"Said the man wearing a baby," Jax shot back. Lydia was curled up in her wrap, sound asleep against Beckett's chest.

"Gia took Aurora to the studio. Lyd's easy when she sleeps." Beckett picked up his sub and took a healthy bite.

"Nothing about babies or kids looks easy," Donovan argued. "First you have babies who are completely dependent on you for everything. Then they turn into kids and teenagers who will do anything to be independent of you. It's insane."

"You ever planning on having a family?" Carter asked Donovan, washing down his veggie sub with a swallow of cold beer.

Donovan shrugged his shoulders. "Yeah. Probably. Eventually. If I find the right future Mrs. Cardona."

"Family's easier with the right partner," Beckett agreed, folding.

"Someone like Eva Merill?" Niko asked with a sly grin. He had no problem throwing others under the significant other bus.

Donovan shot him a look that made Niko glad the man wasn't carrying his service weapon.

"You and Aunt Eva?" Evan asked, studying Donovan with a frown.

"What? He's bang— uh, dating your aunt Emma." Donovan pointed an accusatory finger in Niko's direction.

Evan laid the evil eye on Niko and shook his head slowly. "I think they both could do better," he sighed, straight-faced.

The table busted up, and Niko put Evan in a headlock and ruffled his hair. "Smart ass."

Evan smirked. "Just be respectful of them and treat them well, and we won't have a problem."

Beckett threw his stepson a salute. "Listen to the kid. Because if either of you fuck with either of them, Evan and I are going to start taking names."

"And kicking ass," Evan added.

An "ooooh" echoed around the table.

"What? Beckett says I can swear up here as long as I don't tell Mom or do it at school."

"I like this kid," Niko said, jerking his thumb in Evan's direction.

"I'm telling you. Kids are fucking magic," Carter grinned, swiftly dealing the cards.

"And fucking monsters," Beckett said, winking at Evan.

"Magical monsters," Carter corrected. "It's not something anyone can prepare you for. If I were to tell you that starting a family is like the best worst thing I've ever done, you wouldn't get it until you were staring at your sleeping baby who spent the last four hours screaming and vomiting on everything you own."

"It's the challenge," Beckett agreed. "Like 'no, I'm not letting this tiny person break me.'"

Niko glanced down at his cards and tossed more chips into the pot. "I've never really thought much about having kids, starting a family," he admitted.

"Joey and I have been on the fence about it, too," Jax admitted.

"Really?" Donovan interjected. "I thought you two would

end up with a family big enough to require one of those cargo vans."

Jax shrugged and took a swig of his beer. "We're not baby people. Give us an Evan and an Aurora, and that'd be awesome."

"Thanks, Uncle Jax," Evan said, raising his bottle of root beer in a mock toast.

Jax winked at him. "I think that's why we're adjusting pretty well to Reev and Cale. But looking at Puke-a-saurus Rex over there?" he said, pointing to the drooling, unconscious baby strapped to Beckett's chest. "That terrifies me to my very soul. Besides, can you imagine Joey pregnant and not being allowed to ride?"

Carter shuddered. "You're right. Don't do it. We can't take over the stables and riding program for her."

Nikolai smirked at the Pierce banter. "So does no babies mean no family?"

Jax frowned. "Not necessarily. Before all this, we hadn't really talked about anything other than how gross babies are and how awesome it is to sleep in and not be covered in someone else's puke. You should know we've been gloating about how superior our lives are since the twins and Lydia came," he grinned.

"You paint such a romantic picture of parenthood," Beckett snorted. Lydia chose that moment to throw up on him in her sleep. "Shit. I hate when Uncle Jax is right." He reached for his napkin and started mopping up his daughter.

Evan snickered.

"Is there any news on their mom?" Carter asked.

Beckett and Jax shared a quiet look.

Donovan took a drink, set his bottle down. "We tracked her to a motel in Virginia Beach a week ago and then poof. Into the wind. She'll turn up eventually."

"What happens in the meantime?" Niko wondered.

Jax cleared his throat. "We're talking to Mr. Mayor here about drawing up guardianship papers."

"No shit? Are you serious?" Carter demanded.

"Early talks yet. And we haven't brought it up with them yet. They may want to wait it out for their mom, or they may not want to stay with us. But Caleb's learning to ride, and he's really into cars. Reva's Joey's freaking right hand in the stables, and she's doing better in school now that she's not trying to support her brother on her own."

"What made you guys decide to make it permanent?" Niko asked.

Jax ran a hand over the back of his head. "Honestly, we thought our lives were perfect before. Awesome sex life, my career's great, the breeding program is off to an epic start. But the longer they're there, the better it feels. They just kinda fit. And they fit in this space that we didn't even know was empty.

"Plus, and this is really important, neither of them has ever puked all over me," he grinned.

"Asshole," Beckett muttered.

"Well, congratulations," Donovan raised his bottle. "If this works out, you'll be cutting down on my sleepless nights worrying about dumping those two in foster care."

"I'd appreciate if you all could keep your traps shut about this until we find the mom and see where everything stands," Jax said, holding up two fingers for cards.

"She's got to sign over custody," Beckett explained. "And she may not be willing."

"Fuck that," Niko argued. "She abandoned them."

Beckett finished mopping up Lydia and himself. "The law's the law. And we need to be on the right side of it when we're talking about kids and families."

"What about you, Fitz? You ever regret not having kids?" Jax asked.

Fitz ran his hand down his braided rattail. "I thoroughly enjoy my bachelorhood."

"I guess a wife and kids would really interfere with your stripping career," Jax mused.

"You're going to have a kid in college," Carter grinned. "How's that gloating going?"

"Hey, what are you guys all going to do when your daughters start dating?" Evan piped up.

Niko grinned watching the color slowly drain from the Pierce faces.

"Yeah, Reva's probably already dating," Donovan said, feeding the beast. "Have you met any of the guys, or do you think she just sneaks out to meet them? You wouldn't believe the places I find teenagers making out."

Jax's knuckles whitened on the neck of his bottle, and Niko got the feeling he was reminiscing about his high school exploits with newfound regret.

"Can you guys imagine when Aurora starts dating?" Evan mused. "She's barely controlled chaos now."

"Hell no. I fold. None of them are ever dating," Beckett decided, shaking his head. "I can't handle that. I know what guys are like at that age."

"We *all* know what guys are like at that age. We *were* those guys," Carter groaned, tossing his cards on the table.

"They actually start younger now," Donovan said helpfully.

"Oh yeah, I had to chase off a couple of preteens who were necking behind my dumpster at the store," Fitz agreed. "Turned the garden hose on 'em."

"Maybe we can send them all to a private all-girls school?" Beckett wondered.

Jax pulled out his phone. "I'm out. I gotta see if there's an all girls college with an equestrian program. No way in hell Reva's going away to school with slobbering, pimply, walking freshman hard-ons."

Evan raked in the pot and grinned smugly.

"You've got baby barf in your beard," Carter smirked at Beckett.

"Let's get back to Fitz's stripping career," Niko demanded. "I have a lot of questions."

28

"I can't believe you talked me into this." Emma stared out the train window as upstate New York zipped past. "Three days in the city," she sighed.

Niko grinned at her. "Excited?"

She dropped her head to his shoulder. "Beyond. I thought it would be harder to get the time off, but Jax told me they were on the verge of forcing me to take a couple of vacation days."

"You're family to them," Niko said, lacing his fingers through hers.

"Funny how that happens. So tell me again everything that's on the agenda," she demanded.

"Tonight, we're having dinner with my father and his wife."

"Your stepmother," Emma corrected.

"My stepmother," Niko nodded. He didn't need to tell Emma that part of the reason for their visit with his family was so he could wipe the slate clean with his father's new wife. She'd already guessed and was fully in his corner. It wasn't that there'd been tension between Niko and his father. Almost worse, there had been an impenetrable layer of disinterest as his father built a new life. Things would change, starting with this visit.

"Tomorrow you'll be accompanying me to a photo shoot where you'll be so overcome by my genius that you'll barely be able to refrain from tearing off my clothes. But we'll enhance the torture by going out for a traditional New York date, dinner and drinks, and delay the gratification until we're in danger of being arrested for lewd conduct."

"You do make interesting plans," she teased. But the catch of her breath told him she was already anticipating a playful night of flirting, touching.

He leaned in closer, lips brushing her ear. "Then I'll take you home and make love to you in my bed until the sun comes up." Emma trembled against him, and he went achingly hard.

Her hand squeezed his. "Then what?"

"Then we sleep, eat, and make love until the show."

The smile spread her lips slow and sexy. "You sure know how to show a girl a good time."

He traced a finger over her cheek and down the knife-edge of her jaw.

"I can't wait to have you all to myself," he admitted. "No brewery, no Blue Moon, just you and me."

"So there won't be any children sprinting through your front door while we're naked?"

"None." His teeth grazed her earlobe, and Emma sucked in a breath.

"You'd better behave yourself while we're on public transportation," she hissed, gripping his hand.

He shifted gears again from intense to playful. "How was the house you saw this week? I noticed you didn't say anything about it. How terrible was it?"

Emma felt herself pulling away, tightening up. "Oh, it was

fine. Nice actually." *Really nice*, she reminded herself. "But I think it was too big for just me."

"I seem to recall you being worried about that before," Niko teased.

"You're an ass," Emma gasped.

"That wasn't the body part I was talking about."

NIKO'S APARTMENT was everything Emma had fantasized it would be from the concrete floors to the soaring ceilings. It was an industrial space, made more comfortable with leather couches, colorful area rugs, and spectacular art on the brick walls.

"Wow," she murmured, admiring the view from the windows. "Judging from this space and that view, you're a bigger deal than I gave you credit for."

He came up behind her and tugged her hips back against him. "Baby, I'm the biggest deal," he joked.

She felt the steel-hard length of his erection at the small of her back. "I already know exactly how big your deal is. What I need to know is do we have time to enjoy your deal before dinner tonight?"

They had time and made good use of it. Staring up at the ceiling from the acre of bed, Emma stretched her sated body. She'd declined to join him in the shower, knowing full well it would lead to another round and then they'd be late. He was nervous about reconnecting with his father, and she thought it was incredibly sweet. Did it mean something that he'd brought her to meet his father? He was bringing her with him for a very personal, very private reconciliation? It felt important.

She sat up and swung her legs over the side of the bed.

And now she was nervous. Emma skimmed a hand over her belly. This was a big deal and quite possibly a misstep. She'd met Mason's parents, but, at the time, that had made sense. The way their relationship had carefully progressed in the right direction, meeting them was proper timing.

She'd packed carefully for this trip, planning for each outing and adjusting according to the weather report. Yet, she'd failed to actually consider the significance of the trip. Niko was introducing her to family and work associates and friends. Didn't he understand how serious that was? How could she not take it seriously?

They were just seeing where things went. There were no future plans, no team goals. This wasn't the step they should be taking at this stage.

The water in the shower shut off and a naked, wet Niko appeared in the doorway. "Stop panicking."

"What makes you think—"

"I could hear your brain working all the way in here," he said, giving her that crooked half grin. "You're worrying about what this means and what happens next."

"There's nothing wrong with that," she argued, trying not to be dazzled. But it was impossible. Naked Niko was just that. Dazzling.

He crossed to her, and sank down in front of her. "I want you here because you've been, among many other things, a good friend. Reconnecting with my dad, jumping into a shoot? It's a lot. And I need you there to remind me that I can do it."

Great, now she felt like an ass for making it about her.

She pasted on a bright smile. "I'm happy to be here for you, Nikolai."

He cupped her chin and made her look him in the eye. "I want you here."

"I want to be here."

"Good. Now go get dressed and be ready to help me repair fifteen years of shitty relationship."

No pressure.

~

THE DRIVER EASED up to the curb of a quiet street in front of Vadim Vulkov's Brooklyn townhouse. They'd moved out of Niko's childhood home shortly after marrying, and Niko realized he'd never been to his father's new home.

He had no emotional connections to the three stories of yellow brick, and he wondered if he'd find an emotional connection with the man that lived within those walls. There had been no argument, no irreparable rending, just a son's disappointment and a father's disinterest.

"Ready?" Emma asked, squeezing his hand.

"Maybe we should just go out tonight?"

She squeezed harder. "Nice try. Now slide your perfect ass out of the car," she ordered.

Niko did as instructed and helped Emma out after him before leading her up the concrete steps to the front door. It had been a year since he'd last seen his father in person. A hurried lunch in Manhattan with lingering silences that had highlighted the gaps in their relationship. A whole year, yet the Vadim Vulkov who answered the door looked somehow younger.

"Nikolai!" His greeting was large and warm, just like the man. Broad shouldered and barrel chested, Vadim looked more like a barroom brawler than a civil engineer. He'd grown a mustache, thick and dark and yet to show the silver that the rest of his hair was sporting.

"Dad." Niko extended a hand and, when his father took it, pulled him in to slap him on the back. "It's good to see you."

"It's been too long," Vadim agreed. "Now, who is this beauty you're hiding from me?"

Thirty-three years in the country had mellowed the Russian from his accent, but it was still detectable.

Niko reached for Emma, pulling her into the fold. "Dad, this is Emma."

His father's hand engulfed Emma's. "Emma, it's a pleasure to meet you. Did you know you're the only girl Nikolai has ever brought home?"

"I have a feeling he may have snuck a few past you into his room earlier in life, Mr. Vulkov," Emma quipped.

His father chuckled and clapped a hand on their joined ones. "Please, call me Vadim. And you clearly know my son well."

He ushered them inside, and Niko got his first good look around his father's home. The living room was organized around a small marble fireplace. The furnishings were worn, comfortable. There was a basket of kids' toys next to an over-stuffed chair and its mismatched ottoman.

His father noticed the direction of his gaze. "Toys for the grandchildren when they visit Papa and Oma."

"You have grandkids?"

"Greta's oldest has two. Her youngest is unmarried like you." He turned and bellowed in the direction of the back of the house. "Greta! Our guests have arrived."

Niko, struggling to absorb the fact that his father was a grandpa, started to turn in the direction of his father's call when his gaze pinned to the mantel of the fireplace. He blinked, not understanding. It was a picture of his mother, one of the few. She stood *en pointe* in a spotlight graceful as the long neck of a swan, her arms stretched overhead. A single white rose in a delicate bud vase sat next to the heavy gold frame.

He was still staring at the picture when Greta bustled into the room. She was a sturdy sort of woman. Taller and softer than his mother, but her smile was just as warm. Her hair was a soft, fluffy blonde that was beginning to streak silver. She had a dishtowel thrown over her shoulder that she tossed in Vadim's direction.

"No drinks for our guests, Vadim?" she teased. "They'll never want to come back!"

Her voice was louder, more boisterous, than the soft whisper of his mother's and held notes of Germany, her country of birth.

"Where are my manners? I must have been so distracted by the beauty of the girl Nikolai brought with him or the smell of your cooking," Vadim said, raising a flirtatious eyebrow.

"Oh, I can see why you are the way you are." Emma raised her eyebrows at Niko, and Greta laughed.

She offered Emma her hand. "I am Greta, married to this incorrigible flirt."

"It's lovely to meet you, Greta. I'm Emma, and I'm dating incorrigible flirt junior."

Niko surprised Greta by swooping in and offering her a peck on the cheek. "It's nice to see you again, Greta."

"You, too, Nikolai. I will get you a vodka," she winked. "Emma, would you like a glass of wine?"

"I'd love one. We brought a bottle with us if you'd like to open it." She offered the raffia bag to Greta.

"Wonderful. We shall drink, and we shall dine."

The doorbell buzzed, and Greta clapped her hands. "They're here!" She rushed to the door.

"I hope you don't mind, but we invited Greta's daughters," Vadim said, looking at his feet.

Niko felt Emma slide her arm through his. "The more the merrier," she insisted. "Right, Niko?" Her smile, slow and sweet, soothed the rough edges, and he wrapped his arm around her shoulders.

"The more the merrier," he agreed.

AND MERRIER IT WAS. Greta's oldest daughter, Adele, brought her husband, Tony, and their two kids, London, age six, and his sister Maria, age four. The presence of the kids made it impossible for awkward pauses. Katrina, Greta's younger daughter, was the only ice cube of the evening in Niko's mind. Katrina had her mother's blonde hair cut in a short nearly platinum cap.

She had no qualms about being up front. When Greta called them all to the table for dinner, Katrina stepped in front of Niko.

"I don't like anyone who doesn't like my mother."

Emma's eyes widened, and she brought her wine glass to her mouth.

Niko looked her way for help, but Emma shook her head. He was on his own.

"I don't *not* like your mother," he argued.

"They've been married almost two years, and this is the first time you come to their house. That doesn't exactly scream supportive son."

She hit her target with that one. Just because his father hadn't been extending invitations didn't mean Niko shouldn't have been putting forth the effort.

"I'm here now," he said evenly.

"Good. Now try not to fuck it up," she warned before filing into the dining room behind her brother-in-law.

Emma let out a breath. "She's scary. I like her."

Niko guided her in front of him like a human shield. "You would," he murmured.

"Don't worry, Nikolai. I won't let her hurt you."

They dined on chicken Parmesan in honor of Emma and blini and spätzle to round out the international representation. The bottle of wine Emma chose had been opened and emptied as had two more that Greta produced from the kitchen. Watching his father's interaction with Greta's family made Niko feel as if he'd been absent for years. It was an easy dynamic, one that he and Emma were welcomed into—with the exception of Katrina.

The conversation never lagged, not with so many mouths around the table. Greta was a research scientist in plant sciences. She and his father enjoyed animated if technical discussions with Adele, who was a biochemist. Tony was in finance. Katrina ran a salon and was a bit prickly about it, but Niko got it. She was from a family of science and logic. Growing up, he'd had his mother to support and understand his creative hobbies.

Emma entertained them all with stories of dinner shifts gone horrifically wrong, and the kids gave a running commentary on their day in school and daycare.

When London and Marie, now dressed in pajamas, demanded Papa read them a bedtime story, everyone crowded into the living room to listen to Vadim voice the characters. It hit him then. Niko realized he could have been part of this family—one that shared striking similarities to the Pierces—had he bothered to put forth an effort.

Yet his father hadn't welcomed him into his new life. Was Niko just a painful reminder to him of the woman they no longer shared? Was his mother the glue? Could there be a father-son relationship without her?

Niko wasn't sure, but he wanted to try. His time in Blue

Moon had shown him what family could be, and it was something he knew he wanted in his life now. He rose with his father when Adele and Tony said their goodbyes.

Katrina was the next to bow out with the excuse of an early morning appointment. She kissed his father and then her mother on both cheeks, offered Emma a sincere "nice to meet you," and then coolly shook his hand.

"No longer a full house," Greta sighed, shutting the front door behind Katrina. "Always bittersweet."

"Bitter because we miss them when they're not here," Vadim said.

"And sweet because now we can put our feet up and enjoy the quiet," Greta supplied, winking a blue eye at her husband.

"Greta, let me help clean up," Emma offered.

"We can enjoy another glass of wine and talk about how handsome and stubborn these two are," Greta said, slipping her arm through Emma's guiding her out of the room.

The silence they left in their wake was immediately awkward. Vadim slipped his hands in his pockets and jingled the change he found.

"Do you still like brandy?" Niko asked, eyes again returning to his mother's photo.

"I do. Though I don't have any in the house. It seems to evaporate right out of the bottle," he said with a twinkle in his eye.

"I thought that might be the case," Niko said, digging into the bag they'd brought and producing a bottle. "I brought a spare, just in case."

Vadim looked at the label, and his caterpillar eyebrows lifted. "Very nice. Very nice, indeed." He opened a cabinet built into the corner of the living room and produced two snifters.

They sat, his father in an ancient recliner and Niko on the couch, and he poured the amber liquid into the glasses.

They sipped in silence, listening to the sounds of running water and laughing women floating from the kitchen. It was a homey scene, yet Niko felt wildly uncomfortable. Words needed to be said, questions asked, but that didn't mean he couldn't ease them both into it.

"You and Greta seem happy," he said. It was the truth. He'd been used to thinking of his father as two men, one headily in love with his mother, the other darkly mourning her loss. But this Vadim was different. He and Greta shared common ground, mutual interests. They weren't held together by passion. They were fortified by commonality.

"Yes. Very happy," Vadim said gruffly. "I enjoy her company very much."

"A good match," Niko said, thinking of Willa and her boots.

"Do you think so?" Vadim asked, and Niko thought he heard a hopeful note in the question.

"I do. I'm glad you're not alone, that you're not still mourning."

"I still mourn," Vadim said, staring into the brandy. "I will always mourn. Your mother was one of a kind."

"And Greta?"

The corners of his father's mouth lifted under his mustache. "Greta is one of a kind, too. I am a lucky man."

"Why aren't we better, Dad?"

Vadim didn't pretend not to understand the question. His pause was thoughtful. "It started with a mistake I made. I thought if I gave you space, you'd come around willingly rather than me forcing you to accept things you were not yet ready to accept."

"Giving me that space made me feel like you'd not only

moved on from Mom, you'd moved on from me. New wife, new home, new family." Niko looked around the living room, shelves stuffed with relics of two lives combined into one. His senior picture, his college graduation, his moments were tucked in with the rest of their highlights. Greta and Vadim's wedding, Adele and Tony's wedding, London's first day of school, Maria's first birthday, Katrina at her salon looking fierce.

His father looked down at his hands, and for the first time, Niko recognized their resemblance to his own.

"I am sorry for that. We Vulkov men are not good with feelings. Perhaps that's why we lean so heavily on our partners. Greta's been demanding that I drag you back here since before the wedding, but I was stubborn."

"I don't know if I'm mad at you or disappointed in myself. I didn't know you had grandchildren. I've never been to your house. I didn't know Greta was a research scientist." Niko shook his head, bitter at the time lost the two would never get back.

"Perhaps you can be mad *and* disappointed. Neither of us is innocent."

"You have Mom's picture on the mantel." Niko finally got the words out. "Why?"

"Just because she is gone doesn't mean she never was. Greta believes in honoring the past. And she does not mind when I remember fondly your mother."

"Greta sounds like a good woman." Niko raised his glass to drink.

"So was your mother," Vadim told him. "And so is Emma."

"We have excellent taste."

29

The driver closed the town car's door after them and Emma snuggled into Niko's side. "I'm the teensiest bit drunk," she whispered her confession. "Your stepmother has an incredible tolerance for alcohol."

Niko smiled at the slur of her words and brushed his lips over her hair.

"Thank you for being there with me," he told her, watching the lights of Brooklyn neighborhoods pass by his window.

"Thank you for asking me," she yawned. "Did you and your father talk?"

"We did. It's a start. He and Greta are coming to the show at the gallery."

Emma lifted her head, smiled. "Really?"

Niko nodded. "I can't believe I waited this long."

Emma snuggled in against his neck. "Don't be too hard on yourself. You both are stubborn, distracted men."

"Drunk Emma is a little too honest," Niko teased.

"Sober Emma is honester," she insisted.

EMMA CONSIDERED the dull headache she carried with her the next morning worth it. They'd tumbled into bed the night before exhausted from good alcohol and the rebuilding of family. It had been the first time Emma had spent the night with Niko without sex, and she had to admit, falling asleep curled around him somehow took their intimacy to a new level.

She felt a little off-balance as if things had somehow shifted between them last night. But the breakfast Niko had delivered, the easy conversation over coffee and crepes, put her back on mostly even ground. Niko seemed pleased with the way dinner with his family had gone the night before, but he was distracted. And Emma could see he was shifting gears into professional photographer mode. She was just as excited about today as she had been about last night. It was another glimpse into Nikolai Vulkov's life. And she was honest enough to admit that she wanted more than just glimpses.

Someone had secured the pre-construction fourth floor of a warehouse turning multi-million dollar loft project for the shoot. Three thousand square feet of brick pillars, scarred wood floors, and dingy walls of windows that overlooked the murky Hudson waters and the Manhattan skyline.

It was strange to see such life breathed into the space. There were make-up artists, hair stylists, assistants, magazine reps, the model and her entourage of bored-looking friends whose phones were glued to their hands.

Niko had his head together with the ad agency's creative director for the campaign and the brand representative from the watch company. Others scurried about adjusting huge filtered lights and draped backdrops. Wardrobe shoved racks of clothing at the model who, pre-makeup, looked to be about fifteen. There was a table laden with dozens of watches in their open cases, their jeweled faces winking under the lights. A man in a security uniform stood guard and frowned fiercely as he paced tight laps around the watches.

Another table along the wall opposite the windows held a catered lunch spread fit for a vegan model and her entourage. Thankfully a tiny sliver of the table held normal foods for normal people.

It was a hive of energy that reminded Emma of Friday nights at the brewery. Everyone had a purpose, a task. Each part of the whole was as essential to accomplishing the common goal as the other.

She liked watching Niko at work like this. He was calm and focused. Listening as the creative director, between texts and emails, pounded home the exact look they were going for. Niko waved Emma over to him and slid his arm around her waist when she joined them.

"Nat, have I ever let you down?" Niko asked, covering the screen of the director's phone with his other palm.

She slapped his hand away. "No, but you do make me work hard to keep you in line and within budget," she answered with a dry look over the rims of her glasses.

"Relax. Introduce yourself to my girlfriend and pretend you're a human for a few minutes while I go talk to Branka." Niko dropped a kiss on Emma's cheek and, with a wink, disappeared.

"Girlfriend?" Nat's eyes goggled, her phone forgotten.

"Emma," Emma said, offering her hand.

"Nat." She shook with efficiency if not effusive warmth. "I've known Nikolai a long time, and I've never heard the word 'girlfriend' cross his inhumanly sexy lips before."

Emma laughed. "It's new. Very new."

"Well, this certainly explains his mysterious sabbatical,"

Nat surmised. "I had to grovel for him to come back for this shoot."

"He's an amazing talent," Emma said, watching him make small talk with Branka the model through her Slovenian translator.

"A bigger talent with much smaller asshole tendencies than my other options," Nat said, consulting her phone. "How did you two meet?"

"He came into my restaurant while I was yelling at a supplier," Emma reminisced.

Nat grinned. "So you're not even a model?"

Emma shook her head. "Nope. Regular person, regular job."

"I hope you're wearing something fabulous tomorrow. You're certainly braver than I am. Coming face-to-face with a long line of model ex-lovers?" Nat shuddered in mock horror. "I'd need a year of therapy to recover."

"I'm sure it will be fine," Emma said with flagging confidence. She hadn't considered the possibility of facing down a bunch of gorgeous, perfect women who had all enjoyed naked Niko the way she was now. God, what if he took one look at her next to them and came to his senses?

Nat excused herself to make a call. And Emma was left alone with her panic over Niko. As if she'd called him by name, their gazes met across the space, and he cocked his head to the side, questioning. She gave him a weak smile.

Emma pulled out her phone. She needed her sisters.

Emma: Why did I not consider the consequences of meeting Niko's model exes tonight???

Eva was the first to respond.

Eva: What are you going to wear? Make sure it shows off your boobs. Models don't have boobs. Not enough body fat.

Gia, the yoga instructor and mother of two young daughters, had a different take.

Gia: Do not imagine yourself in some idiotic lady competition with them! Be confident in yourself and Niko's feelings for you.

Eva chimed in again.

Eva: G's right on the girl power. I'm right about the boobs.

Emma's lips quirked. She could always count on her sisters.

Emma: Thanks for talking me down. I hate acting like an insecure teenager.

Gia responded sagely.

Gia: Just remember we're all insecure teenagers on the inside

Beneath the pulsing beat of a hair band ballad, Niko got the shoot underway. Branka had been transformed into a high fashion model in a sleeveless silk jumpsuit in bone white and a delicate gold watch with an onyx face that cost more than a year's rent for Emma's L.A. townhouse. She pouted prettily on a floral divan against a white backdrop.

The shift from fresh-faced youth to made-up fashion model was startling to Emma. The girl didn't look like the same person who had walked in in jeans and flip-flops. The woman before her was fierce and mysterious.

Niko, casual in jeans and a tee, orbited around her, giving instructions through her translator.

"Cheat your chin this way."

"Tilt back. Back. Back. Perfect."

"Elbows forward. More. Right there!"

He put her through her paces, and Nat looked pleased with the results she saw appearing on the portable monitor behind Niko.

After several minutes, Niko handed the camera over to an assistant, and wardrobe descended upon Branka, stripping her with the efficiency of a NASCAR pit crew and redressing her in a body clinging sheath dress in magenta. A stylist fashioned Branka's dark hair in a bulbous bun at the base of her neck while the makeup artist touched up her lips.

In no time, Niko was shooting again, this time in front of the raw brick of an interior wall. He continued an endless stream of encouragements and instructions. Tiny, imperceptible movements made each image better than the next. Emma looked on in fascination.

While the images on screen looked perfectly fine to Emma, she sensed that Niko wasn't pleased. He was taking longer and longer to review the shots before trying some new pose or outfit or backdrop.

Finally, he announced they were taking five and handed the camera over to his assistant. He gestured Nat over, and they put their heads together.

Emma caught enough of the conversation to get that Nat thought they already had something they could use, and Niko was insisting they hadn't gotten there yet.

"Time is money, Niko," Nat reminded him.

"Do you want acceptable or incredible?" he shot back.

"What's the difference?" she muttered. "Keep in mind the

VPs that will be looking at these pics aren't going to know the difference."

"You'll know it when you see it." Niko scrubbed a hand over his mouth. "Let's do this. You still want behind-the-scenes shit, right?"

"Yes. We need it for the blog and social media," Nat confirmed.

"Let's put her in a robe and do the interview while hair and makeup get her ready for the next look."

"You're the creative weirdo," Nat said with a shrug.

"Your faith in me is uplifting," he told her, winking at Emma.

"Yeah, yeah." Nat stalked off to set up the interview, and Niko crossed to Emma.

"Not happy? The shots look great from here," Emma told him.

Niko crossed his arms and paced restlessly in front of her. "She's too wooden. I can't get her to loosen up. I'm missing the 'it.'"

"The 'it'?"

"That spark that makes a picture a story."

"Ah. I get it. Okay, so how do you make that spark appear?"

"Well, you can't force it."

"You're not wallowing on the inside and thinking it's your fault there's no spark, are you?" Emma asked him, poking him in his very firm stomach.

He stroked his hands down her waist. "No wallowing. I promise."

"Good. I like watching you work," she confessed.

"I like having you here. It keeps me from yelling at people and throwing tantrums."

Emma slapped him lightly on the arm. "Very funny. I think you're more a stony silence kind of guy than a drama queen."

Niko pulled her in, hands settling on her hips. "You know me pretty well, don't you?"

Emma shrugged. "I'm enjoying getting to know you. And I think your idea to get to know Branka in the interview will help."

Niko rubbed a thumb over Emma's lower lip. "Grab yourself a sandwich and watch the master at work."

Emma laughed and let him push her toward the food table. As much time as she'd spent hating cockiness, Niko's confidence in his abilities was somehow reassuring rather than obnoxious.

She picked up half of a chicken salad sandwich and watched assistants hurry to set up two chairs against one of the exposed brick walls. Niko took one chair, and Branka was guided to the other. With hair and make-up working on her, Niko charmed the model out of her shell with amusing questions and a healthy dose of that panty-melting grin.

Branka, it turned out, was twenty and a little homesick. She was the oldest of six and the first of her family to move away from home and was excited and terrified to make a name for herself, to make them proud. Niko walked her through a mix of personal and professional questions, and Emma watched Branka begin to relax and enjoy herself.

She missed her mother's *potica* bread and walking her younger brothers and sisters to school. But she loved not having to share a bathroom with anyone now. Niko talked about his background in photography, and they both worked in a plug for the watch brand.

By the time hair and makeup were done and the interview wrapped, Branka looked yet again like a completely different person.

"Let's try something new," Niko said, addressing Branka. "I want you to pick the watch you want to wear."

He escorted her over to the table and waited while she browsed. Her fingers paused over one before moving to the next. She looked up at him questioning.

"Whatever one calls to you," he told her.

Victoriously, she plucked an oversized men's watch from its box and held it up to him.

"Perfect. We can work with this. Now, let's talk wardrobe."

Fifteen minutes later Branka, dressed in only a crisp white men's oxford and murderously sharp stilettos, leaned against the dingy window surveying the city sky line. Her watch hand was planted firmly on the glass, her other at her hip. Nat was pouting in the corner after having lost a round of "this isn't the look we were going for" with Niko.

Impervious to the drama, Niko consulted his light meter, made a few adjustments and started with the test shots.

He checked the screen and grunted in approval. "Okay, let's do this before we lose the light." He moved in, alternating his distance to Branka, capturing full body shots and close-ups. Emma could tell he was still warming her up, feeding her translator instructions. Her anticipation built.

"Okay, now I want you to look at that city like you own it. Manhattan is yours."

The translator fed Branka the line and even from her vantage point, Emma could see the slight curve in the models lips, the change in her eyes.

"Yes! That's what I want!" Niko announced from behind the camera. There was no language barrier to his enthusiasm, and Branka went with it. A queen surveying her kingdom, the men's watch catching the light on her wrist.

Click. Click. Click.

"Oh, hell yeah," Niko said, handing the camera over to an assistant. He offered a palm to Branka, and she slapped him an enthusiastic five.

They crowded around the monitor setup clicking through the shots, and Branka clapped her hands when they saw it. The spark. The woman who owned the world.

"Damn you, Nikolai," Nat sighed. "That's not what we were looking for."

"Tell me it's not perfect," he dared her, a cocky grin pulling on his lips. "Tell me."

"Let me send the test shot up the ladder and see what the powers that be think."

She instructed one of the set assistants to upload the file, and Niko strutted back to Emma. He pulled up a stool in front of her. "So what did you think?"

He was incredible. Magical. Watching him work left her a little shaky and breathless just knowing what genius lay beneath that beautiful exterior.

"You are really, really good at your job," Emma admitted. "And I definitely want to tear off your clothes."

30

_____

They celebrated in true Manhattan style with dinner reservations at a trendy bistro, and Emma dressed the part. Her simple ivory sheath dress had elbow length sleeves and stopped several inches above sedate. Niko, still buzzed from his shoot, couldn't take his eyes off of her.

"I've missed this," Emma sighed, letting her gaze travel the restaurant. Nine o'clock on a Thursday and the place was packed. Blue Moon didn't have the energy of the city. And she was pleased to find New York's vibe was edgier, busier, than L.A.'s.

"You know," Nikolai said, leaning in conspiratorially across the table. "We could just ask them to pack up the entrees to go." He was dashing in a dark suit. He'd skipped the tie and left the top two buttons of his tailored shirt open. And Emma wasn't the only female in the place who couldn't take her eyes off of him.

She laughed. "You're insatiable." He'd proven that fact yet again when they returned to his apartment after the shoot. They'd very nearly missed their dinner reservation.

"You look beautiful," he said, lifting her hand to his lips. "It's not my fault that I can't get enough of you."

"You Vulkovs certainly know how to pour on the charm," she said, fanning herself with her napkin.

"Emma, you know you're special to me, don't you?" Niko asked, his dark eyes intent on hers.

She glanced down at the table, fighting the blush that threatened her face. "I am aware that you have certain *friendly* feelings toward me."

"It's more than that, and you know it," he argued. "And you're going to see it tomorrow at the show. I don't want you to feel ambushed."

"You used pictures of me?" Emma's heartbeat picked up.

"I asked your permission," he reminded her. "I would have shown them to you in advance, but I really wanted you to experience them as part of the whole."

She did vaguely recall Niko demanding in the throes of passion that she allow him to use her images and was also fairly certain she'd shouted or sighed out "Yes, God" about a hundred times after that.

"Oh, Jesus, I'm not naked in any of them, am I?"

"Let me put it this way, you can't see anything."

"Oh, my God, Nikolai!" she hissed.

He grabbed both her hands, squeezed. "Emma, I would never do anything that I thought would hurt you. Maybe push you a little outside your comfort zone but never anything that I thought would really hurt you. Okay?"

"I'm not feeling inclined to trust your judgment right now." She felt panic, slick and hot in her belly.

"How many pictures of me are there?"

"Five."

"*Five?*"

"Too many or too few?" Niko asked.

"One feels like too many!"

Niko signaled the waiter and ordered another round of drinks. "Emma, please don't make me tell you what an inspiration you are to me. It's corny and embarrassing to have the 'you're my muse' conversation."

She glared at him. "And I wouldn't buy it anyway."

He sighed. "Please trust me. You know I wouldn't do anything to hurt you."

She wasn't happy about it. But maybe having pictures he'd taken of her would lessen the sting of meeting a bunch of beautiful women he'd slept with. "For future reference, don't ask me to make important decisions during sex. I'll just say yes with no concept of what I'm agreeing to."

A wicked grin lit his face.

"You sneaky bastard. You did that on purpose!"

"Are you mad?"

"I'm certainly not thrilled right now."

He released one of her hands and cupped his palm to her face. "I'm sorry, Emma."

She slapped his hand away. "Don't try to charm your way out of this. I'm going to withhold judgment on how much trouble you're in until after the show."

"That's fair."

"How many of your ex-dates will be there, by the way?"

He grimaced as if considering it for the first time. "A few probably. Will that be a problem?"

Emma leaned in and traced a finger over the back of his hand. "Let's just turn the table for a moment. How would you feel if I was taking you to an event where you would be meeting 'a few' of my ex-lovers?"

She had the great pleasure of watching the color slowly drain from his face and the tic in his jaw appear.

He swore quietly, and she smiled.

"Good. I'm glad we understand each other."

He released her hands and pressed his fingers to his eyes. "I think I'm having a stroke."

Emma smiled smugly. "Oh, good. Here comes our food."

DINNER WAS FOLLOWED by drinks and music at a boutique club with chic white walls, purple neon, and thumping music. Niko, still ashen faced from dinner, ordered a bottle of wine before collapsing back against the plush cushion of the booth he'd scored for them.

It had taken them a while to get to the booth since they'd been stopped every few feet by people Niko knew. But he'd been distracted, cutting conversations and introductions short and dragging her toward their private oasis.

Finally alone, he leaned forward again, elbows on his knees. "Emma, I never thought how meeting women I'd..." he swallowed hard before continuing, "*known* would make you feel."

"Yes, I can see that," she said, offering a small, amused smile.

"No," he shook his head. "No. I mean it really didn't occur to me at all."

The server returned with their bottle in a chiller and two glasses.

Niko drank deeply before continuing. "What I mean to say is that they don't mean anything to me. Which now sounds incredibly callous, but there was never a woman who after-wards I wanted to..." He groaned and shoved his hands through his hair. "I don't know how to be honest without sounding like an asshole."

"Just spit it out," Emma sighed. "Get it out, and we'll work through it, or if it's really that bad, I'll dump this ice bucket on you and cause a huge scene."

"None of them meant anything to me. Not compared to you. With them, each one was just a temporary distraction. You? You're different."

Emma ran her tongue over her teeth and waited.

"I meant what I said at dinner. You're special to me. Very special to me, and I think you're going to see that tomorrow night. But I never thought how difficult it might be for you to meet other women that I've—"

"Fucked," Emma supplied.

Niko winced. "Shit. I'm fucking everything up, aren't I?"

Emma took pity on him. "Niko, relax. Seeing you feel bad makes me feel better."

He shot her a look, and she smiled brightly. "Gee, thanks," he muttered.

"I just wanted you to understand how uncomfortable it might be for me tomorrow."

"I feel like an asshole. I never even considered... no one has ever meant anything to me before you—and I get that that makes me a callous asshole—but you're going to see that tomorrow night at the show. You're going to really get it. And that's all that I was thinking of. Not about anyone else. I think since they didn't mean anything to me, it didn't occur to me that they'd mean anything to you. But if you dragged me into an event with men you'd slept with?" His knuckles whitened as his fists balled. "It wouldn't mean nothing to me."

"As ungraceful as that was," Emma said, sliding onto Niko's lap and slipping her arms around his neck, "it does make me feel better."

Niko held on tight and dropped his forehead to hers. "Emma, please know that you mean the world to me. Your friendship and stubbornness got me back to where I need to be professionally. And the way you look at me when you're under me? The way you make me laugh when we're having breakfast, the way you make me sweat at the gym when I'm trying to show off? I've never felt like this about anyone."

Emma could hear her heartbeat pounding in her head. She knew, *knew* what he wanted to tell her. But she couldn't hear it, couldn't let him say the words. She wasn't ready. She wasn't sure it was right.

So she kissed him. She cupped his face in her hands and kissed him until she couldn't breathe, kissed him until he was hard and throbbing beneath her. Here they were even. Here she could give as well as she got. Here they could forget everything else if even just for the moment.

He broke the kiss with a shaky breath. "Are you sure you're okay?" The tenderness in his eyes slashed her across the heart.

"Take me home, Niko, and make me forget to breathe."

HE CALLED FOR THEIR DRIVER, and the second the door closed behind them, Niko's hand trekked up her thigh as he kissed her, drawing the skirt of her dress indecently higher. The driver climbed behind the wheel and pulled into traffic. Emma clamped her hand on Niko's. "Don't you dare," she whispered to him in the dark.

Of course he took it as a challenge. Her resolve weakened and then failed completely when he nibbled at the sensitive flesh of her neck. Dark deeds in the backseat of a Lexus. With the brush of his lips, Nikolai Vulkov managed to convince her to do things she'd never do if left to her own devices.

When his hand coasted higher again, making her throb with anticipation, she didn't stop him. His fingers found the apex of her thighs and prodded gently, warm flesh over white silk.

"Open." He whispered the command against her ear, and Emma shivered with need. She spread her knees an inch wider, teasing him as much as herself.

"Emmaline, I have twelve blocks to make you come."

Her knees fell open of their own volition, welcoming his clever fingers. He probed and stroked, touching her only there with the exception of the gentle brush of his mouth over hers. And it was enough to have her soaked with desire. Her nipples tightened, and her breasts felt heavy and full with the aching need for his touch.

She wanted to whimper, to beg, but the driver's presence kept her silent. Instead she trembled when Niko slipped his fingers under the edge of her silky thong. He used the pads of his fingers to circle her greedy nub.

Streetlights flashed past the tinted glass of her window, but Emma was oblivious to anything beyond the leather backseat. Her legs spread wider still, begging without words for more, and Nikolai obliged, sliding back and forth through her drenched sex. Teasing her with gentle circles before dipping just the tips of two fingers into her.

He brought his mouth back to her ear to whisper dark promises. "Imagine my mouth between your thighs, Emma. Do you feel me tasting you?"

When she shivered, his teeth sank into her ear, and she had to cover her gasp.

"Five blocks, Emmaline."

Ruthlessly, he worked her up. She was so close to coming that she was terrified she wouldn't be able to stay quiet. Emma began to fight against his hand.

"Let it happen, baby. Let me take care of you."

She could feel his erection against her hip and bit her lip.

He could make her come like this, but it wasn't going to be enough until he was inside her.

She clamped a hand over his shaft through his pants, and he groaned in her ear. "Imagine me pumping into you, Emma. Nothing between us. Bare, raw, slamming into you until you shatter around me." His words carried her up the steep cliff-side, those perfect little circles nudging her along. She bucked her hips against his hand. "Imagine me coming inside you, Emma, filling you up with every drop I have while you squeeze me with your sexy little pulls."

With one masterful flick, he shoved her off of the cliff into her release. She felt it spread like a spotlight from her toes up her legs until the orgasm unfurled in her core.

"Fuck," he growled in her ear. "I could come right now just watching you, baby."

She barely heard his words through the mist in her mind. Her body felt hot and heavy, her limbs useless as the aftershocks made them tremble.

Lightheaded and still needy, she didn't even realize they'd arrived until Niko pulled her skirt back in place. "Just hang on to me, baby." He half dragged her out of the car and, with an arm around her waist, pulled her toward the building.

She couldn't make eye contact with the driver or the doorman, but Niko smoothly thanked both of them and shoved her inside. In the elevator, any evidence of the controlled Niko was gone. He yanked her underwear down her thighs and, when gravity didn't work fast enough, ripped them from her.

He shoved two fingers into her and groaned as if he'd been desperate to be inside her. Emma fisted her hands in the lapels of his suit holding him against her. "I want your cock inside me now."

"Greedy girl," he murmured, nuzzling her neck and flexing his fingers inside her.

She felt her muscles clench around him, and he growled his approval.

He withdrew his fingers from her and brought them to his mouth. She watched in fascination as he slid them between his lips to taste. God, was there nothing that wasn't erotic about him?

The elevator dinged, announcing their floor, and by the time they made it to his door, her dress was off her shoulders and being worked down by a determined Niko. He shoved open his door with a violence that had her shaking with anticipation.

Dragging her across the foyer, he kicked the door closed and pushed her back up against it. With one swift yank, her dress gave way and crumpled to the floor.

She gasped. "That was a very expensive—"

"I'll buy you ten more," he promised, his eyes glazed as he looked his fill. Her breasts were rounding over the top of the sexy lace cups of her bra. Barely contained when she'd put it on, her breasts were spilling out now, swollen with the need to be touched.

"You are my fucking ideal," he said softly. He didn't move fast enough for Emma's liking. So she moved for him. In her bra and heels, she dropped to her knees and worked his belt free.

"Baby, don't do that. I'm too close—" His argument ended with a pained groan as she slid her mouth over the wide crest of his engorged cock. He put his palms flat on the door behind her and let her take.

Emma brought him to the back of her throat, taking as much of his shaft as she could. He whispered praise to her as she sucked and licked the length of him. And when she settled into a wicked, mesmerizing rhythm, he met her eager mouth with shallow thrusts. She knew he was close, could taste him as he leaked into her mouth, and it excited her knowing she could take him to the edge so quickly.

And then he was yanking her to her feet. "Bed. Now."

This time, it was Emma who didn't move fast enough, and Niko swept her up, throwing her over his shoulder. He tossed her none too gently on the bed and shrugged out of his jacket. She kneeled in the middle of the bed and watched as he shed his shirt next followed by his pants and underwear. When he was naked, magnificently naked, she reached for the closure of her bra, but he shook his head.

"Let me," he said.

He crawled onto the bed and, reclining against the pillows, pulled her over him. She straddled his hips and gasped when she landed with his erection nestled between her thighs.

With a deft flick of his wrist, he opened her bra and spilled her breasts free against his face.

Yes. Her body sang as he finally cupped her heavy breasts. He slid down lower on the mattress and ordered her to lean forward, bringing her nipples in perfect line with his mouth.

He took one hungrily between his lips, and Emma felt lightning explode in her veins. She felt it all, every stroke of his tongue, every change in the pressure of his mouth. She was electrified. Restlessly, she grinded against him, and when his cock slipped between her wet folds, she moaned.

It felt so good, so perfect, to have nothing between them. He released her first breast and moved to the next, nuzzling her flesh gently before latching on to suck and stroke.

She rolled her hips, reveling in the friction of him against her. "Nikolai," she breathed. "I need you. I need you inside me."

Her nipple popped free of his mouth. "Hang on, baby. I need a condom."

"No," she whispered the word, and he froze. She bit her lip. "I want you like you said in the car."

His fingers flexed on her hips. "Are you sure?" He wanted it so badly that she could feel his entire body coil as if to pounce, yet he still held back to make certain. And that convinced her.

"Positive."

"Are you—"

"Birth control," she answered.

And then they were rolling, Emma on her back with Niko over her. He was already testing the resistance at her entrance, already probing with the thick tip of his erection.

She brought her knees up, begging him with her body to take her.

He looked into her eyes, into her soul, and she saw a tenderness she didn't know was possible in those dark eyes. Carefully, patiently, he pressed her arms over her head and braceleted them with one of his hands.

His weight was on her, pressing her into the mattress, and instead of feeling trapped, Emma felt powerful, desired.

His eyes seemed to darken, and with excruciating patience, he worked his way into her. Emma had luxuriated in having Niko inside her before, but this? This raw fullness was unlike anything she'd ever experienced before. Stretched, stripped, bared. They were one. He pierced her with his gaze, dark and possessive and wondrous. And then he began to move.

She thought he'd lose himself to the speed and the craving for fulfillment. Thought they would race to the finish, but instead Niko took his time worshipping her body with his. He brushed his lips over her forehead and cheeks and jaw, skimming a hand over the curve of her breast and hip while stroking in and out of her with something that glowed like... love.

He moved in her with reverence. There were tears that clouded her eyes. It was too much. He made her feel too much. But her body wasn't afraid. Her body wanted more of this beautiful, gentle pleasure.

With steady, venerating strokes, Niko primed her body. She was so slick around him that he moved easily in her, yet she felt every thick inch of him, every vein and ridge. He was grunting softly with each thrust, and the sound of his pleasure drove her mad.

She wanted him wild and fast but couldn't fight the sweet, torturous pleasure complete surrender had given her. Every breath, every stroke, every whisper was golden and perfect. Their bodies warmed and slicked with sweat. The exquisite fullness she felt when he was sheathed in her was an impossible joy. The ache when he withdrew was an unimaginable torture.

They shared no words, only shallow breaths and whispered moans as each thrust brought them closer. He pulled back just enough so that she could see his face.

He knew her body so intimately, knew that she was seconds away from losing herself to the bliss that his body provided. Emma wanted him to go with her. She felt the first warning flutter deep inside her.

"Now, Nikolai," she whispered.

And that was all it took. She was coming, and everything behind her eyes went black before glowing gold. The first wave closed her around his shaft, and she felt him come, not just in the stuttering jerk of his hips but how it let loose deep inside her. It took her pleasure to new levels, feeling him fill her, and she went blind again as she came and came and came, shattering around his release until they were coming as one.

He buried his face in her neck, grunting softly, hips thrusting, until he was empty, and she was so full. The beauty of it, the incredible cohesion brought the tears back to her eyes.

~

HE WAS PLAYING with her hair, toying with fiery strands. "I've never had sex without a condom before."

Her fingers paused in their tracings over his chest and stomach.

"Neither have I," she confessed.

"Why with me, Emma?"

Leisurely she returned to stroking his skin, making it sing under her touch. "Because you're special to me."

She used his own words, and he smiled softly. He knew what he was saying with those words, but she didn't. Not yet. She'd know tomorrow night. For better or worse, he was painfully, irrevocably in love with her. And once she saw the pictures, she'd know.

There were so many things they needed to discuss. Where would they live? How would it affect their work? What compromises needed to be made? But they could figure it out. Together.

He'd never anticipated this. Not when he'd shown up on Summer's doorstep, expecting to remind himself how perfect his life was. He'd ended up finding what he was desperately missing. Family, love, *Emma*.

She'd hit him harder and brighter than a bolt of lightning, and what he'd thought had been a case of lust at first sight had quickly transformed into a love he'd never imagined. She was his other half, his inspiration and conscience. And she needed him, needed him to push her to feel, to do, to let go of her strict rules every once in a while. Together, they had something special, essential. And he didn't want a life without it, without her.

He only hoped Emma was prepared to accept his love. Because, if not, it would be one hell of a fight to make her see the light.

31

$\mathcal{T}$he gallery was a contemporary space in SoHo squeezed in between a sushi joint—that left Emma with a deep and abiding regret that Blue Moon had no such fare—and a jazz club that billowed clouds of blue smoke every time the front door opened.

The gallery was packed by the time they arrived fashionably late. The grip on her hand was the only indication of Niko's nerves. With one settling deep breath, he opened the glass door and guided her inside. Within a matter of seconds, they were surrounded. Niko switched her to his left arm so he could keep her close while shaking congratulatory hands and accepting the accolades.

She met Niko's agent, Amara. Emma guessed at the Korean heritage in her gorgeous, exotic face. She wore her dark hair in a razor sharp bob. Her purple framed glasses gave her a trendy, artsy vibe, and after thirty seconds with her, Emma could see why Niko liked her. Amara didn't deal in bullshit. She made connections, pushed when necessary, and seemed to have great patience for the artist's temperament.

"I'll admit I was a little skeptical when you told me what you wanted to do, Niko. But as usual, you were right."

"Proving once again why I'm the client and you're the agent," he teased.

Amara rolled her dark eyes. "Yeah, well, smartass, you've already sold seven pictures and had four offers on the one that's not for sale. Which reminds me, Emma, you've got a lot of people asking after you."

"Me? Why?"

"Take a tour around and you'll see," Amara said circling her finger in the air. "Gotta go circulate and earn my keep."

As soon as Amara drifted off into the crowd, Vadim and Greta appeared, all smiles. The resounding slap Vadim laid on Niko's back had Emma's eyes going misty. *The man's turning me into an emotional basket case*, she thought.

"Nikolai, it's wonderful. You have such a talent," Greta gushed, and Niko grinned.

He dropped a kiss on each cheek. "Thank you. I'm excited you both could be here."

"We would not be missing this," Vadim said. "Not the exhibit of my son." He made the last statement proudly at announcement volume so that several heads turned.

Emma laughed, well familiar with embarrassing parental pride.

"Not too shabby, Nikolai," a cool voice announced behind them. The unsmiling Katrina was dressed in Manhattan's favorite uniform, head-to-toe black. Her sexy sweep of platinum hair was set off by dangling earrings with stones that glittered. She crossed her arms and studied him.

"I'm glad it meets your approval." Niko's sarcasm was playful.

"I've seen worse," she mused.

"That's a ringing endorsement from Katrina," Greta told them with a wink.

Amara reappeared with a photographer. "Hey, let's get you and your family and your muse together for a shot."

It was more of a command than a suggestion. And Emma was starting to get anxious about what she would find on the walls if she was labeled Niko's muse. They clustered together, all smiles, and when Katrina tried to step back out of the shot, Niko pulled her back in. "Come on, *sis*, it's family. Smile nice." Emma grinned as Katrina shot him a look that could have frozen a pond solid in August.

In the blur of introductions and greetings and photo ops, Emma had yet to make it more than ten feet inside the door to glimpse any of the actual art. A leggy brunette strutted up in suede thigh-high boots, a micro-mini dress, and a pout. Emma recognized the look in the woman's eye. An ex-lover, she was sure of it. It was confirmed by the way Niko's gaze slid from Slenderella's face to Emma's.

Okay. She could do this, Emma decided, blowing out a quiet breath. Internal pep talk time. No, she wasn't six-foot-one and eighty-seven pounds. But she was the one who'd spent last night naked and satisfied in Niko's bed. She was the one whose hair he'd held while she vomited profusely. She was the one he'd put on the walls of his exhibit... though she'd yet to see those pictures. God, what if he'd taken pictures of her barfing?

No. Get a hold of yourself, Emmaline Freaking Merill. She'd held up during understaffed Friday dinner service with a twenty-five top with no reservations. She could do this.

Slenderella didn't wait for Niko to finish his conversation. She was a woman who waited for no one.

"Neekolai! You disappeared on meee," she purred in an Eastern European accent.

Emma almost laughed when she realized Niko was running through his memory banks for a name.

"Vladia. So nice to see you. I'd like you to meet my girlfriend, Emmaline," he said, reeling Emma into him like a trout on the line. "Emma, Vladia is a model."

"I can see that," Emma said, offering her hand. "It's lovely to meet you, Vladia."

Vladia stared blankly at her hand and blinked at Niko. "Girlfriend? Her?"

Niko's friendly smile chilled a few degrees, and he made a show of sliding his arm around Emma's waist. "I couldn't believe I got this lucky either."

"You are not joking?"

Emma rolled her eyes. "Afraid not." She hid her snort when Vladia slowly accepted Emma's hand and shook it.

"Well, it is nice show. Where is the bar?"

Amara stepped in and ushered her off with a smirk.

Niko leaned down. "Okay. That was awkward," he whispered.

Emma raised an eyebrow.

"Don't even ask because I have no idea what I was thinking," he admitted.

Emma glanced back in the direction Vladia had loped off in. "Oh, I think I have an idea of what you were thinking."

"Smart ass. Are you okay?"

Emma nodded. "It helps that you didn't immediately shove me to the floor and start kissing her feet."

"I don't know if you noticed, but she has huge feet. Size thirteen if memory serves. She pissed off a creative director once by acting like an entitled asshole, and the guy told her to get her canoes off his set."

Emma snorted and clamped a hand over her mouth. "You're horrible."

"Technically, she's horrible. I was just stupid."

There were two other awkward introductions. One to a stunning Swedish swimsuit model whose bubbly laugh added to the blonde bombshell image and a sweet, six-foot-tall Southern belle with glossy chestnut hair and a Miss America smile. Thankfully, neither woman was rude enough to give Emma the once over. In fact, Gone with the Wind was sweet enough to introduce them to her fiancé, a short, thin man with glasses and a shy smile. Emma felt an immediate kinship with him when he sized up Niko and lost a bit of color in his face. It was hard being normal and facing the spectacular past of one's lover.

Deeming the worst over, and with Vladia nowhere to be seen, Emma convinced Niko to let her wander around to see what all the fuss was about.

The gallery was, by design, a blank canvas. Stamped concrete floors butted up against plain white walls or rough brick. Lighting on wire tracks shed light on key points for the optimal art experience. In this case, it was familiar faces everywhere she looked.

The first picture she spotted was Aurora sitting on her knees under a table at the wedding, the skirts of her dress poofing out in a mound of tulle. She was staring at the hefty wedge of cake she'd stolen as if it was the love of her life. *The perfect sliver of the time of her life*, Emma thought with a soft smile.

She walked a path and took it in, picture by picture. Ellery's supreme concentration at the Knit Off, a goth girl knitting a goth blanket. There was Julia doling out a rainbow of juice samples at the farmers market. Willa, her hair long and free and a dreamy smile on her face as she stared off into space. Phoebe, the beautiful bride, laughing with her sons at the brewery. There was the one of Emma and her sisters with Franklin on the dance floor at the wedding.

Joey on Apollo, mid-gallop, a wicked grin on her face and the trees behind her a blur of speed and movement. Reva, straight-faced and so quietly pretty, leading a speckled pony into a sunbeam in the indoor riding ring.

There was Summer sharing a belly laugh on a quilt with sweet Meadow and Gia cuddling Lydia and Aurora on her yoga mat. Eva, a whirl of color and energy on the dance floor with Evan, while Donovan looked on longingly.

She didn't know why, but her heart felt so full looking at these moments, these slices of life. There were more, so many more. Phoebe listening with the rapt attention of a grandmother to Caleb as he chattered on about something clutching the stuffed pony Emma had given him. Mrs. Nordemann, eyes wide, behind the cover of what was sure to be a very graphic erotic novel. Rainbow Berkowicz and Bobby from Peace of Pizza laughing over glasses of wine at Shorty's.

There were more of her. The mid-twirl before her father's wedding. An artsy black and white shot of her clad in black leaning against the brewery's bar as if surveying her domain, a look of smug satisfaction on her face.

But the piece that came next was more, so much more. It seemed to hold the rest of the exhibit together, serving as a keystone of sorts.

The canvas was huge, wider than she was tall. It was a shock to see herself beyond life-size. He'd taken this shot of her in bed at her cottage. Soft focus, filtered light from the nightstand lamp. The sheet draped over her like a gown. One hand in her hair, a riot of curls spilling over skin and pillow and sheet. Her face was the focus. Eyes closed, the slightest curve of her rosy, swollen lips. She looked like a goddess, a well satisfied one.

She swallowed hard past the lump in her throat. Was this how Nikolai saw her? This languid, powerful beauty?

"What do you think?" Behind her, his voice purred low and raw.

She didn't turn away from the photo but brought her fingers to her lips. "I don't know what to say, Niko. These all are so wonderful, so beautiful. It's like... it's like you love us."

He turned her then, gently forcing her to face him, nudging her chin up until she met his gaze.

"I do."

She sucked in a breath as if she'd taken a hit. The words echoed inside her like a wave that kept crashing against the shore.

"What do you mean?" she demanded.

"I mean I'm in love with you Emma. And this is how I thought I could best show you. Do you see it?"

Emma inhaled on a gasp. There wasn't enough oxygen here. Too many people, too much noise. She turned away from him and back to the picture of herself. But that was too much, too. She couldn't live up to those expectations, those ideals. She couldn't give herself up to a love like this. She'd lose herself. Who knew where she'd end up if she gave the reins to Niko. Did he expect her to give up everything she'd worked toward to follow him around the world?

It wasn't fair. It couldn't work. She couldn't give herself over to someone like Nikolai Vulkov. She'd end up broken and damaged, just like her father had.

"Emma?" Niko's touch was gentle on her arms. "Just tell me what you're thinking. I know it's a lot to take in. I know we weren't planning this. But you are it for me, and I've known that for a long time."

She shook her head trying to block out the words. "I can't do this, Niko. I can't be this woman." She gestured at the picture. "That's not me. That's some filtered, edited version of me."

"Emma." Niko's voice carried a warning now. "I understand this is a lot to take in, and I'm not asking you for a permanent commitment right now. I just need you to know that I love you. That?" He pointed at the picture. "That's not some edited ideal. That's *you*. That's how I see you. I know you, Emma."

"Niko, I can't do this."

"What can't you do?" He skimmed his hands gently over her shoulders and down her arms. "Tell me what you need."

She pulled away and it cost her. "I need space. I need to think."

"Baby—"

But she was already backing away. "I'm sorry, Niko. I don't mean to ruin your night. Your work is... amazing. But I can't be here."

He grabbed for her arm. "Emma, you can't just leave. I'm not letting you wander the streets of New York alone."

"I'm going home."

"What? How?"

"I'll take a cab to the train station," she decided. "I just have to go. I'm sorry."

She bolted out the exit she spotted and found herself in an alley. Blinded by tears, she ran toward the streetlights. Behind her, the door bounced off the brick, and she heard footsteps running after her.

He caught her easily, yanking her back against him and then forcing her against a wall. His breath was ragged in her ear, yet he said nothing. When she trembled against him, choking out a sob, he ever so gently turned her to face him. With supreme care as if he was holding fragile glass, he tucked her under his chin and wrapped his arms around her.

"I know you're scared, Emma. I know you are. It's a scary thing—frankly, I'm fucking terrified, too—but I'm here, and I'm not going anywhere. I promise." His lips moved against her hair, his broad hands stroked her back gently as she sobbed into his chest.

She wanted him. She wanted to love him, wanted to just throw caution to the wind and jump. She wanted to follow him, to build a life with him. Desperately. But she couldn't do that. That's how people ended up damaged. Nikolai could break her. Long ago, when she'd had her heart broken, she'd vowed to never let anyone put her in that position of vulnerability.

But here in Niko's arms, all of that resolve blurred. Everything she knew to be true wavered.

"I love you, Emma," he whispered the words as he held her. "I'm not going to let you go."

That's what she was afraid of.

"I can't stay here like this, Niko."

His hands stilled for a moment before beginning their soothing path up and down her back. "How about I take you back to my place?"

She shook her head. "I don't want you to leave. This is a big night for you. I'd feel like the worst human being in the world if I dragged you away."

"You're what's important to me," he argued.

"I'll take a cab," she offered.

"I'll call you a car if you promise you'll be there when I get home tonight."

She nodded, still not sure that she was telling the truth. All Emma knew was she needed to be alone, needed to think. Niko didn't follow her rules.

He reached into his pocket and dialed the car service.

"I'm going to wait with you out front until the car comes for you." He left no room for argument.

"I'm sorry, Niko," Emma whispered. She wished she could be what he wanted, wished that she could love him and worry about the rest later.

"It's okay, baby," he said, stroking a hand through her hair. "I've got you."

The car arrived mercifully fast, and Emma slid into the backseat, once again promising she'd be there when he got home, once again not knowing if she was lying or not.

SHE SLEPT, fitfully, in Niko's bed, barely registering when he crawled in next to her. In her sleep, she had no issues with snuggling up to him, resting her head on his chest and throwing her leg over his. In her sleep, she knew she was safe with him.

Nikolai woke in stages, the low-grade headache that usually followed an event was present and nagging. Last night came back to him in a flood of color and feelings. The show, his father and Greta, Emma. *Emma.* He hadn't expected it to go perfectly. He'd known a declaration of love would throw her. But he hadn't quite anticipated the abject panic he found in her eyes. That had stung.

He wasn't about to let that stop him from chipping away at her resolve. Obviously she had trust issues, had earned the right to be cautious. But he had found the woman he loved, and he wasn't going to let her get in their way.

He rolled to take her in his arms, to reassure them both, and found the bed empty. Her bag was missing. His feet hit the floor, and he prowled naked into the living room, scouring his place for evidence of Emma. She was gone. And in her place she'd left a politely apologetic note for him on his table.

She needed time and space to think, the note said, and she hoped he would understand. He crumpled the paper in one hand and flung it in the direction of his trashcan.

He grabbed his phone, checked his messages. Amara had left him about a dozen texts and voicemails demanding he call her back, but there was nothing from Emma. He resisted the urge to throw his phone across the room.

Emmaline Merill was about to learn an important lesson about pissing off a temperamental artist.

32

Emma tried to bury herself in work at the brewery. Saturdays were busy days, and there was plenty to do, but she kept catching herself freezing and staring off into space. There was a constant feeling of dread that had settled into the pit of her stomach. Her staff had read her mood and was avoiding her like the plague. She'd actually seen Shane, her always positive dishwasher, duck into the supply closet when he saw her coming and felt relieved that at least that was one conversation she wouldn't need to have.

This was supposed to be home. Yet she felt like an alien exploring a new planet. Everything was wrong, and she wasn't sure she could blame Niko for it.

The Pierce brothers had shown up to do some brewing and had taken one look at her before retreating to the first level. She knew they'd texted their wives when Summer, Gia, and Joey showed up at the bar with sympathetic eyes. Well Summer and Gia looked sympathetic. Joey just looked bored.

Emma stepped behind the bar, needing to put the physical barrier between them.

"I'd ask what brings you three out on a Saturday afternoon, but I have a feeling it's your big-mouthed husbands."

"Why are you back early?" Gia demanded. "You're still supposed to be in the city."

Summer crossed her arms. "Where's Niko?"

"Can I have a menu?" Joey asked, squinting at the beer taps.

Emma, in an immature display of temper, slammed a menu down on the bar in front of Joey. "I came back early because I was ambushed. Niko is where he belongs—in New York. And we have a wing special for the afternoon happy hour. Happy?" she snapped.

"I think we need alcohol for this," Summer predicted. They ordered beverages from Cheryl, and Joey got an order of wings.

"Let's go back to this ambush," Gia suggested, sipping her beer.

With nothing better to do while waiting for her food, Joey kicked back on her barstool and crossed her arms.

"First, let's talk teams," Emma insisted. She pointed at Gia.

"Team Emma of course," her sister rolled her eyes.

"Team Niko," Summer announced, "unless he did something incredibly stupid, which I'm not putting past him since he has a penis and all."

"Team Hot Wings for now," Joey said when Emma pointed at her. "I'm withholding judgment on the conflict until I hear the whole story."

"Fine. Here's what happened. We're having a great time in the city. I meet his family, he and his dad are patching things up, and I think I'm really getting the hang of this 'see where we go' thing. And then bam!" She slammed her palm down scaring Ellery who was splitting a pizza with Anthony

Berkowicz a few stools down the bar. "He takes me to the show where apparently I'm his muse, and now he's in love with me."

Summer choked on her chardonnay. "I'm sorry, what? Nikolai Vulkov professed his love for you?"

Emma handed her a napkin.

Gia covered her eyes. "Hang on, girls, my sister's about to tell us how stupid she was."

Emma sniffed indignantly. "I told him I needed some time and space to think about it."

"And?" Gia prodded.

"And then I snuck out of his apartment at five o'clock this morning and caught the train back."

Summer put her head down on the bar. "Emma, Niko has never told a woman he loves her. Never. And you just run out on him? You probably just scarred him for life!"

Joey was finally interested in the conversation. "Hang on. Catch me up here. You are like Madam Monogamy, aren't you?"

Emma shrugged.

"Yeah, you are. You're all 'step one, step two, step three' and then 'oh hey look, perfect life,'" Joey pressed. "So why would having someone who looks at you the way Bad Boy Biker looks at you be a bad thing?"

"Because he's not the settle down and build a life kind of guy," Emma said in exasperation. "He's the 'let's jet off to Paris in the middle of the week so I can do a photo shoot' guy. Niko is not the let's refinance our mortgage and talk about retirement guy."

Gia chugged her beer and set the empty glass down on the bar. She burped and signaled for another drink.

"So you're saying you'd rather have mortgages and retirement than Paris?" Joey frowned.

"Exactly!" Emma pointed a finger in Joey's face. "See? She gets it. I'm not crazy."

"No, you're batshit crazy. Don't try to pull me into your delusion. You can have a mortgage and a retirement with literally anyone with a pulse. Now, Paris? You only get that once in a lifetime, and you just ran away from that. Team Niko," Joey decided.

"You could have had mortgages and retirement with what's his face." Gia waded back in.

"Mason?"

Gia snapped her fingers. "That's the one. What was he? An accountant? Why didn't you just go off and start a 401k with him?"

"Mason wouldn't have been interested in leaving his life and moving across the country to Blue Moon," Emma argued.

"But Niko would," Summer put in.

"Niko's life is in New York and whatever other fabulous destinations he travels to. He doesn't fit into my life. That's why the Beautification Committee never came sniffing around us. They knew we wouldn't make a good couple."

"Then why did you date him?" Summer demanded.

"Could you say no to that?" Emma's voice was shrill. "How could anyone pass up Nikolai Vulkov? He's sexy, smart, funny, sweet, rides a motorcycle, looks even better naked than he does wearing clothes, and he looks damn good wearing clothes." She ticked the points off on her fingers. "I just wanted to see what it was like to be with him and not worry about the future for once."

Ellery and Anthony had given up all pretenses of minding their own business and were watching in rapt fascination.

Then they all heard it. The whole bar tuned in to the revving of a motorcycle engine.

Emma felt the color drain from her cheeks. "Shit."

"Heeeeeee's baaaaaaaack," Joey sang.

The engine cut out.

Emma was debating whether she should just crouch down behind the bar or try to make a run for the back door when Niko strode inside. He proved her point to a tee, wearing jeans, boots, and a leather jacket over a fitted gray t-shirt. His hair was tousled, and the thin line of his mouth and the sharp, dark eyes told Emma he was beyond pissed.

"You want to explain why I wake up to an empty bed and then have to rent a fucking car at the train station to get back home, Emmaline?"

She blanched. She hadn't actually expected him to return to Blue Moon and hadn't felt guilty about taking her car from the station.

Joey leaned in. "I'm just going to point out that he just called Blue Moon 'home,'" she said in a stage whisper.

"Shut up, Joey," Emma said without looking at her friend. "Don't you guys have some place else to be?"

"Oh, hell no."

"Nope."

"I'm very comfortable right here."

Niko stalked right behind the bar and grabbed her arm. "Let's talk."

"I don't want to." She sounded like a three-year-old.

"I don't give a shit."

An "oooooh" from their audience echoed off the rafters.

"This is my job. You can't come in here and pick a fight with me!"

"I'd rather fight with you at my place, but you snuck out in the middle of the night!"

Emma shot a scathing look down the bar silencing the next "oooooh."

"Fine," she shrugged. "You want to have it out in front of

everyone? I rejected you, and you're pissed off. Let's deal with it. I live and work here in Blue Moon. You live and work in the city. Why don't we just get back to our separate lives and forget any of this happened?"

Niko slammed his hand down on the bar, and Emma flinched. The girls pulled their drinks out of the danger zone.

"I have *never* met a woman that made me want to strangle her like you do," he growled.

And why exactly did that admission get her just the tiniest bit hot? Emma wanted to know. Her body was a god damn traitor. Just Niko's presence had her blood pumping and a painful throb intensifying in her core.

"Threats of violence? That's a great way to win over a woman," Emma sneered.

"That's it." The words cracked like a whip. "We're finishing this, and you're going to listen." He pulled out his wallet and threw some bills on the bar and eyed Cheryl. "Next round's on me. Sorry for the disturbance."

Before Emma could argue, Niko's fingers closed around her wrist, and he was dragging her in the direction of her office.

～

"You're taking this scorned lover thing to extremes," Emma complained, yanking away from him and stepping inside. Her relief at finishing this in private wavered when he slammed the door shut hard enough to rattle it on its hinges.

"Emma, I'm warning you. If you keep pushing me, I'm going to end up saying something we'll both regret."

She rolled her eyes. Fighting the panic in her belly, she led with anger. "What did you expect introducing me to your ex-lovers? What woman in her right mind would be okay with that?"

"Bull. Shit. You were handling it. And handling it like a fucking champ. You didn't flip the panic switch until I told you I loved you."

Emma was shaking her head, ready to deny. "You walked me into an event full of women you'd slept with."

"And you're comparing me to that asshole in L.A. that hurt you when you were younger and I'd like to say dumber, but clearly that's not the case."

Emma jutted her chin out. "There are more than a few parallels."

"That's not fair, Emma. I never lied to anyone I was with. I never made false promises." His voice was low and very, very dangerous.

"But some of those women still got hurt!" Emma argued. "Why else would they be hunting you down at your show?"

"And I'm sorry for that. But I can't control everyone else. And unlike you, I have no desire to do so."

Emma's eyes narrowed. "So I call you on your bullshit, and now I'm a control freak?"

"Look at you!" Niko stalked away and back again. "You get defensive and start to attack."

"I'm not attacking you," Emma seethed.

"You need everything and everyone in your life to be just right or you get scared. I scare you. I terrify the fucking hell out of you. You know why?"

Emma clenched her jaw and refused to answer.

"I'll tell you why, because it's beyond time that someone did." Niko gripped her chin and made her look him in the eyes. "You are trying to protect yourself from the feelings you had when your mother left. So everything has to be neatly ordered and everyone has to fall into place or cracks start to appear and that anxiety, that pain starts to show through."

Emma shoved his hand away and stared at him coldly. "I don't know when you decided to psychoanalyze me, but you're wrong. I got over that a long time ago."

"Burying and getting over are two very different things," he argued. "You love me, Emma, and it terrifies you."

She shook her head as if she could unhear the words by denying them.

"Look at me," he ordered. "You love me, and I am head over heels in love with you. Have been since about the first second I saw you yelling on the phone. My life needs to change to make this happen, and I'm willing, I'm fucking thrilled, to do it because I need you."

"Stop it," she whispered, her voice ragged, pained.

"I love you, Emma. We have something here, and I'm not going to let you walk away from it because it doesn't fit in your nice, neat box."

"You're not right for me! You aren't what I want!"

She could see the words hit him like arrows, wounding him with their barbed tips. "Now you're lying to yourself. I know you love me, and I know you're scared, and I hate that anyone ever hurt you before. But I am your friend, Emma. Jesus, you're the fucking best friend that I've ever had, and I'm going to return the favor because you need to hear it."

"Hear what? You don't know me! You don't know what I want! You think you're Nikolai Vulkov, God's gift to women. You can't comprehend that there's a woman out there who wouldn't want you."

He paused, choosing his next words carefully. "You've sabotaged every safe relationship you've ever had because it's not really what you want."

"You don't know anything about what I want," she snapped.

"Yes, I do. You don't want some safe, stable guy who's never going to challenge you, never going to push you to be more, feel more. You don't want easy."

"You're just pissed because I don't want you," she said, jutting out her chin.

"You're scared," he accused. "And I am, too. I've never wanted anyone the way that I want you. It's like you're inside me, you're in my veins. When I see you, everything in me lights up. That means something, Emma. You are the one I've been waiting for. You're the one who makes me look at you the way my father looked at my mother. And I'm sorry you're not happy about it. I'm sorry that it's inconvenient for you."

"How dare you—"

"Oh, no, baby. How dare *you*. If you turn your back on this because you think that finding a nice, safe, stable guy will protect you from pain, you're throwing away something real."

"This is just another fling for you. You're not capable of love!"

"Bullshit, Emma! Why won't you hear me? I fucking love you, and you're cutting my heart out with this fear."

She didn't respond, couldn't, because her throat closed on itself, but a tear carved a path down her cheek.

He tried again. "Baby, you deserve a life of love and passion and adventure. Not some coma of boredom. I can give you what you need, what you've been telling yourself is wrong and scary. And I can still protect you. Let me give you what you need. Let me love you, Emma."

She shook her head back and forth, tears seeping from the corners of her eyes. "I can't love you, Niko. You aren't what I want."

"God damn it!" Anger flashed white and bright from him. "What do you want then?"

"I want someone I can count on—"

"You had that. You had it with the guy before me, and it still wasn't enough to make you stay," Niko argued. "You know what you really want? You want someone who makes every damn day of your life an adventure. Someone who's going to fight for you if you ever try to give up and walk away. You want someone who will make you *feel*."

His lips crushed down on hers in a volatile kiss that stole the breath from her lungs like an inferno. She clung to him even as she tried to push him away. She would not give in to this, would not feed the need that threatened to consume her. This wasn't the life she had planned for.

She couldn't control Nikolai... or survive him.

Yet she couldn't stop herself from opening for him, welcoming him into her mouth with a hunger that would never be sated. She let the heat scorch her, let it begin to thaw the ice that was forming in her chest.

Why did she crave this from him? Why did he make her feel alive? He wasn't safe. Nikolai Vulkov was a threat to her. He could hurt her. Deeply. He could leave her wrecked and heartbroken, too devastated to pick up the pieces.

She shoved away from him even as her fingers curled into his shoulders to keep him close. "You're wrong. I don't want this."

He cupped her face in his hands, his eyes hard, his breathing ragged. "You have to stop denying yourself, Emma. You can't protect yourself from everything and still call it a life."

"You don't know," she said, her voice breaking to betray her fear.

"I know I fucking love you, Emmaline. I know that I'm fighting for you right now."

"What kind of a life would we have together, Niko? Your life is in New York. Mine's here."

"The how isn't important right now." His hands skimmed to her shoulders where they settled heavily. "It's the why, and I'm giving it to you. I love you. I want to be with you. I want a life with you. If you want it, we'll find a way to make it work."

"The how matters to me!" She hated that her voice broke. Hated the desperation she heard in it. "I need to know that it will work. I want a guarantee that I'm not jumping into a huge mistake."

"Life doesn't come with guarantees. You don't get a warranty or money-back guarantee with love." The frustration she heard in his tone grated at her. He didn't understand. He was fearless. Like her mother.

"You remind me of her," she said softly. "My mother thought that life was a big adventure. She dreamed big, and I loved her so much."

He squeezed her shoulders reflexively as if he could ward off the pain with his touch. But there wasn't anything anyone could do to protect her from what she'd already let inside. "She left us when we weren't big enough or exciting enough for her anymore. I'm not going to give you the chance to leave me. I barely survived it when she did, and I know I wouldn't if you would." Her teeth were chattering as she spoke the words that clawed their way out of her throat.

Nikolai took a step back as if she'd slapped him. His face was ashen, his broad shoulders tense.

"Do you think I'm not deserving or worthy of your love?" he asked quietly.

"What? No!" She didn't believe that. He was deserving of

anyone's love. "This isn't about you deserving love. This is about you being able to hurt me."

"Anyone you love has the capability to hurt you, Emma! It goes with the territory of opening yourself up. I'm here. I'm open, and you're the one hurting me."

She shrugged out of his grasp, unable to think clearly when he had his hands on her. "I need some time to think, some space."

"You need to run away. Again. You need to walk out when the going gets tough. Now who reminds you of her?" Nikolai said the words quietly, but that didn't dispel their force. Nor did it dull the pain they inflicted.

Emma gaped at him. He said he wanted to fight for her, yet here he was proving her exactly right. He could and would hurt her because she cared too much. But it wasn't too late to protect herself.

"Goodbye, Nikolai," she said with a cool layer of calm that she mustered from her shaking soul.

He didn't stop her when she turned her back on him. But he also didn't leave quietly.

"I lost my mother, too. But that pain didn't turn me into a coward."

He stalked out, and she listened as his footsteps disappeared behind her. When she was sure he was gone, Emma slammed the door hard and sat down to cry.

She allowed the tears for five full minutes before dragging herself back together. The broken pieces rattled like shards of glass in her belly. She had to get out of here. Needed space to think. What was so wrong with that?

She'd worked her way back up to a full on mad by the time she returned to the bar. The Pierce women had been joined by their husbands, and all conversation stopped.

Jax, the bravest or the dumbest of them, straightened away from the bar.

"What do you need?"

And her heart broke just a little more. Family. The Pierces came through for her even when there was a possibility that she didn't deserve it.

"I need the day off."

"Done," Beckett said, and Carter nodded.

"Em—" Gia began. But Emma was shaking her head at her sister. She didn't need a pep talk or another verbal beat down. She needed peace. She was still shaking her head when she ran out the front door.

33

 $\mathcal{N}$ iko pulled into Summer and Carter's driveway and gunned the bike's engine before cutting it off. He had taken off from the brewery and the bad feelings there and gone for a ride but found no peace in the spring sunshine.

Nothing had dulled the razor's edge of anger that cut at him since Emma had dismissed him. He guessed that it would be a long time before that anger mellowed. He hadn't been prepared to say goodbye to this town and its oddball occupants, but some time and space would do both him and Emma some good.

She'd compared him to the mother who had abandoned her. And that had pissed him off. In a fit of temper, Niko hurled his helmet at the fence. It hit the white wood with a satisfying crack. Satisfaction was quickly replaced with guilt when the pasture gate swung open, its lock broken and wood splintering.

"Shit." Niko muttered. He was more than old enough to know better than to give in to fits of temper.

He heard a squeal and then another one, and two massive pigs trotted into the pasture from the barn.

"No, no, no!" Niko ran for the gate, but the pigs were faster, muscling their way through the opening and jogging into the driveway. "No! Get back in your pasture," he ordered.

His demands were ignored, and the slightly smaller pig started up the driveway at a gleeful trot. *At least it wasn't running for the road*, he thought ruefully. The second pig followed suit, and Niko found himself jogging after them. His pig wrestling skills were untried, and he felt woefully inept to tackle either hulking beast. Besides, carrying them back was not a remote possibility.

He settled for yelling for help, then jogging a few steps, and yelling again. Repeat. Again and again until the farmhouse and its pastures receded behind the crest of a hill. The pigs paid him no attention, and it seemed to Niko that, for the third time that day, he was truly screwed.

Where in the hell was the entire meddling town when you needed them? Niko cursed his fate and faithfully followed the pigs wondering if they'd all eventually be stopped at the Canadian border before he spotted salvation. Another person, an honest to God human being, crested the hill of a field to the west and waved.

"Looks like we've got trouble!"

It was Emma's father, Franklin. Niko could tell by the Hawaiian shirt and cloud of silver hair. He'd never been so glad to see another man in his entire life.

"Help!" Niko yelled back. "I have no idea how to catch a pig or what to do with one once it's caught."

Franklin hustled down the hill, his red and blue Hawaiian shirt billowing in the breeze. "Maybe we can herd them into a pasture," he suggested when he reached Niko's side.

It was the best idea Niko had heard all day. "Yes! Let's do that!"

"You run ahead of them and try to scare them back this

way, and we'll see if we can't coax them into the north pasture over here. I'll man the gate," Franklin offered.

Niko's reply died on his lips when a yellow-eyed, brown-furred blur galloped between them on the path.

"Oh, shit."

"Clementine." Hands on hips, Franklin watched the goat charge down the farm lane. "Going after Jax," he predicted.

"Is that bad?"

"You might want to text him and tell him to get to higher ground," Franklin suggested.

Texting. Why hadn't he thought of that? Niko wrestled his phone out of his pocket and fired off a text to Jax warning him about the furry brown missile and then another one to Carter and Beckett begging for assistance.

Carter responded immediately.

"How in the fuck did that happen?" which was quickly followed by *"On my way."*

There was no time to explain, not with four hundred pounds of pork hightailing it toward freedom. And Niko sighed with relief. "Okay, Carter's on his way."

His phone chimed again. "And so is Beckett."

"Well, let's see if we can at least get Dixie and Hamlet turned in the right direction before they get here," Franklin suggested.

"Good call. I'll run. You man the gate." Niko loped off. The sweat was starting to work its way down his spine. He shed his leather jacket and dropped it in the grass and cut around the pigs that were happily stomping through a swath of wildflowers. They paid him no attention as he circled back to them from the other direction.

Great. He was in position. Now what?

Franklin, hanging on the open pasture gate, waved his arms in a shooing motion.

"Right, okay." Niko raised his arms. "Shoo, pigs. Shoo!"

The bigger pig, Hamlet, Niko presumed, shot him a nonplussed look. Niko tried it again, waving his arms harder. "Shoo!"

Hamlet went back to nosing around in the flowers.

"Come on, guys. I've had a shitty day." *And now he was pleading with pigs. Fucking perfect.*

"Fine. We'll do this the hard way then," he said, hoping his warning tone would convince the pigs to take him seriously.

Dixie rolled on her back in the dirt.

Desperate, Niko stomped his foot on the ground and clapped his hands. "Let's go!" he yelled.

Dixie stopped rolling, one ear flicking.

"Move!" But there was nothing that hinted that the pigs were even aware of his existence.

"Fine. You asked for this. Just remember that. You could have been good pigs, but no. I have to do it this way." Niko lunged for them, startling the pigs. They took off in opposite directions, and Niko went after the smaller one. "Get your ass back here, Dixie!" She started uphill, of course, and he hit a dead run behind her. He'd lost a lot today. He was not going to lose a battle to a pig. That was his last thought until his boot caught on a root. He caught air and time slowed long enough for him to brace for the impact. He sprawled face down into the dirt, a cloud of dust rising all around him.

He was debating on whether he was ever going to get up again or just let the turkey buzzards find him when the sound of raucous laughter reached his ears over the buzz of bees and the joyful squeals of pigs being assholes.

He half-rolled, half-flopped onto his side and spotted the source of the noise. Carter and Beckett hung out of the top of

Carter's Jeep laughing themselves stupid. Beckett was in tears as Carter clung to the roll bar gasping for breath

Niko held up his middle finger. It only made them laugh harder.

"Yeah, keep laughing, assholes. It's your pigs running wild."

"It was worth it just to see you Superman into a dust cloud," Carter howled.

Franklin ambled up, the urgency of the task passed, and had the good grace to only chuckle quietly.

Carter finally took pity on him and, still snickering, hung out over the windshield. He raised a bag of potato chips in the air and shook it. "Here, pig, pig, pig!" he called.

Niko watched in fascinated misery as the two walking slabs of bacon trotted back to the Jeep, tails wagging and ears twitching.

"I hate you," Niko called out.

WITH THE PIGS cheerfully following Beckett's trail of potato chips out of the back of Carter's Jeep, Niko was tasked with the unsavory job of rounding up Clementine and leading her back home. She'd been heading toward the stables, and he was hoping she had a similar vice for people food that he could use to his advantage.

He jogged into the stable, noting that nearly every exterior door was open in appreciation of the warm spring day. Voices carried from the indoor riding ring at the far end of the building. Niko headed in that direction, looking left and right for any sign of Clementine.

"It doesn't make sense that way," Jax yelled, dropping the

rake he'd been using to coax the sawdust into a neat layer inside the ring.

"Of course, it makes sense," Reva said, teenage annoyance in her tone.

Niko peered over the shoulder-high wall and took in the argument in progress

Jax shook his head. "No way. I'm not comfortable with that. You can't just catch a ride with a guy."

Reva looked baffled. "Why not? He lives just down the road. I'm on his way."

"You might not be aware of this, but I was a teenage guy with a car once, and I know what teenage guys with cars are thinking when they offer a girl a ride to science camp!"

"He's offering me a ride, not a teenage pregnancy!"

Jax's growl of frustration echoed off the rafters as he paced away from the wheelbarrow and then back again. "You're damn right you're not getting pregnant! You are forbidden to date! Ever."

Niko stifled his laugh. At least someone else was having a shitty day, too. Joey, amusement written all over her pretty face and Waffles at her heels, bellied up to the wall on the other side of the gate. She stood on tip toe and finding the view lacking, climbed on top of an upside-down bucket. The dog wasn't about to be left out and scurried over to the gate and sat as if he too were eavesdropping.

Oblivious to the audience, the argument continued. "Jax. I'm seventeen." Reva sounded like she was talking to a toddler. "And it's not a date. It's a ride into town for a week for advanced placement prep."

"You're not seeing the danger here!"

Jax wasn't either, Niko realized when he caught a movement across the ring. A black and brown head poked around the door to the outdoor ring. *Clementine.*

"You're overreacting," Reva argued. You make it sound like I'm asking permission to attend the senior class orgy!"

Niko wondered if Joey could see the goat, if she'd call out a warning. He shot her a look and judged by the amusement on her face, Joey was perfectly content to watch it all unfold.

"Christ!" Jax shoved his hands through his hair. "It's like arguing with your mother!"

Jax and Reva froze as the weight of the words settled over them. Joey pressed a hand to her mouth.

"You're not talking about Sheila," Reva said, finally. She scuffed the toe of her boot into the sawdust.

Jax ran a nervous hand through his hair. "No. I'm not. Shit. I'm sorry. I just got caught up—"

But then Reva was hugging him hard. And the way her shoulders shook, Niko bet it was about a decade of stored up emotion that she was releasing. Carefully, as if he was afraid he might scare her or break her, Jax wrapped his arms around the girl.

It was the intimacy of the moment that had Niko opening his camera app and taking one quick shot. The first moment that she realized she had a family. The first moment that she really let herself believe. It went straight to his gut.

Joey felt the moment, too, Niko could see. The normally stoic smartass pressed her fingers to her lips, eyes glistening with unshed tears. Waffles' tail swished side to side silently over the floor. Niko shifted just a little to add Joey to the frame and clicked again. They were connected, the two adults who chose each other and a girl who'd found her way to them. And if that motley crew belonged together, then he and Emma had a chance. A real one. They both deserved it, if she would just get out of her own way.

And just like that, the anger in him dissipated. Family wasn't just blood and biology it was a commitment. A hard-headed refusal to accept anything but the best for the ones you chose and the ones you were gifted. He had that here with Emma, whether she liked it or not.

"I'm not trying to be a hard ass here, Reev." Jax insisted, drawing Niko's attention back to the action in the ring. "It's my job to protect you from guys like I used to be. If you stop crying, you can ride with that jackass."

Reva's shoulders still shook, but Niko couldn't tell if it was tears or laughter.

"Sorry, I mean *that guy*," Jax amended. "After Joey and I meet him and Cardona runs a background check on three generations of his family."

Before Reva could reply, she was interrupted by a psychotic farm animal.

Clementine, bored with the scene, bleated out an enraged battle cry and charged into the ring. Niko swore the goat's eyes rolled back in her head. Jax shrieked like a five-year-old girl coming face to face with her favorite Disney princess and shoved Reva in front of him like a human shield.

Joey, peals of laughter wracking her body, fell off the bucket she'd been standing on. Waffles dodged her falling body and scuttled into the ring, determined to protect her human father from the demon interloper.

"Don't let that yellow-eyed asshole kill Waffles!" Jax shouted, shoving Reva forward toward Clementine and reaching protectively for the dog.

"You can't be serious. You're not afraid of this sweet little goat, are you?" Reva wandered right up to the goat and stroked a hand down the fickle Clementine's neck. This time when the goat's yellow eyes rolled back in her head, it was in pleasure. "See? She's just a sweetheart."

"Do not let go of her," Jax warned, backing away. "Joey, if

you can stop pissing your pants laughing, I'd appreciate it if you could get a damn lead rope or something!"

"I think she's going to need a few minutes to get back on her feet," Niko announced, leaving the relative protection of the wall and stepping into the ring. He grabbed a rope off the hook inside the gate and stepped up next to Jax. "I'm here to collect this creepy-eyed lady and take her back to Carter's."

"Yeah. Great. Whatever." Jax grabbed Niko by the shoulders and pushed him in the direction of the goat. "Stay where you are," he hissed at the goat.

Niko, remembering his own experience being chased by Clementine, advanced slowly. "Now, let's just stay calm. We're just going to put this rope on your disturbing little neck, and you're going to walk out of here real nice."

Reva, amused at their caution, helped Niko hook the lead rope around itself on Clementine's neck. "There that wasn't so hard, was it, you big babies?"

Something like victory lit Clementine's ghoulish eyes, and Niko looked over his shoulder at Jax. "Uh, she looks like she's going to –"

His tentative warning was too little, too late. The goat lunged past Reva and under Niko's arm. He threw himself over her bristly back and hung on for dear life, but no one was fast enough to stop a determined goat.

Reva's "oh shit" sounded to Niko's ears like it came in slow motion as Clementine met her target with a creepy ear-piercing bleat.

"Ah! She's got me! She's got me!" Jax screeched as the goat latched onto his jeans. "I don't have any cookies, you psycho bitch!"

Niko and Reva wrestled whatever goat parts they could find while Joey sobbed with laughter behind the wall.

"I'm so pissed at you right now," Jax yelled at his wife.

"Looks like they've got the situation under control," Beckett called from the entrance to the ring where he stood with Carter.

"Get your asses in here!" Jax screamed while Niko tried to get Clementine's neck in a headlock to pry her face off of Jax.

Carter took a handful of chips before passing the bag to Beckett. "Just another day on the farm," he crunched.

34

*E*mma had taken her keys and bag with her when she'd left the brewery, but the idea of confining her pain to her car was too constricting. She needed to move, to walk, to breathe. Blindly she followed the dirt path that connected farm and brewery.

Spring was edging toward summer already with an explosive blooming of wildflowers in the field. The trees were full and green, the grasses in the meadows and pastures a riot of life. *How could she feel so much pain while surrounded by so much beauty,* Emma wondered?

But the icy feeling in her gut wouldn't go away. She *hated* hurting people, and hurting Niko had been the worst thing she'd ever done. She wondered, for just a second, if her mother had ever been cognizant of the pain she'd caused others.

Emma trudged up a small hill, not bothering to look at anything but her own feet, and stopped when she realized she'd found the Pierces' picnic pavilion, the very spot she'd surprised her sister and father almost exactly a year ago with the announcement she was moving to Blue Moon.

She'd been so excited about the possibilities, the future. How had it all gotten so screwed up? Emma buried her face in her hands.

"What is wrong with everyone?" she demanded to no one.

"Well, I like to think there's a little something wrong with all of us."

Emma clamped a hand over her racing heart. "Jesus, Phoebe. You just scared eight years off of my life."

Phoebe slid off the picnic table she'd been perched upon. "Imagine my terror when a raving lunatic approaches shouting into the void."

"Touché," Emma offered a watery smile.

Phoebe patted the bench next to her. "Come sit. We don't have to talk."

Too emotionally exhausted to make an excuse, Emma sat. They stared quietly out over the hills and creek, the green and the blues and browns.

"So are you having a freak out, too?" Emma asked, breaking the silence.

Phoebe laughed. "If you call talking to the dead a freak out, then yes."

"John?" Emma asked. John Pierce was Phoebe's first husband, the father of her sons. He'd died years before, and the hole in the family was still felt. They'd built this pavilion on the spot where they'd scattered his ashes.

Phoebe smiled sadly. "Yes. I come up here regularly to fill John in on what he's missing out on. Not that he's not hovering over us all and pulling strings, of course."

"Of course." Emma's lips quirked.

"I was just filling him in on Reva and Caleb."

"They're really good kids," Emma sighed.

"So are you and your sisters," Phoebe said pointedly.

"Is that your way of leaving an opening for me to pour my heart out?"

Phoebe grinned, leaning back and resting her elbows on the table. "I've got nowhere to be."

So Emma told her. The whole ugly story.

"The things he said to me," she shook her head. "I just can't believe someone who loves me would say those things."

"Honey, I'm not going to give you advice because the person who knows what's best for you is you. But I will tell you something that I think you need to hear."

Phoebe grasped Emma's hand and squeezed.

"Love is an incredibly beautiful thing. Love is the reason your father keeps a handwritten list of things for me to come here to tell John about. Because Franklin loves me so much that he doesn't see me still loving John as a betrayal."

Emma took a shuddery breath and laughed when a tear fell. "That's my dad."

"And that's love. It can and should be the source of your greatest strength, not your biggest fear. Don't forget that, Emma."

Emma sniffled and took a breath. "You know, Phoebe, if I got to pick my mom, she would have been you."

Phoebe pulled her into a hug. "Oh, sweetie. Now you're going to make me mushy. I love you very much, and I want you to be happy and safe."

"I love you, too," Emma hiccupped.

"Do you want to come back to the house and drink a whole pitcher of margaritas?"

Emma laughed. "Thank you, but I think I need to walk and think some more."

"Well, the offer stands. Anytime you need it," Phoebe said.

~

THE WALKING HELPED her work back up to mad. It was a safer emotion than sad or hurt. And she was fairly certain Niko had earned her wrath. She replayed his words over and over again in her head.

How dare he? Emma fumed as she stalked through the field away from the brewery. How dare he presume to understand her. Just because she'd rejected him, he'd lashed out at her with ugly accusations. She'd been right all along to be reluctant getting involved with him.

She ignored the lovely warmth of the sunshine even as it coaxed her face upward and trudged on down the skinny dirt path that paralleled the pasture fences.

She should have listened to her instincts, Emma railed against herself. They'd always protected her before, but Nikolai had tunneled under her defenses only to plant a Trojan horse in her heart.

She wasn't her mother, and she sure as hell wasn't a coward. She was steady, stable. She didn't run away.

Except she had. The thought stopped her in her tracks.

Hadn't she? After all, she'd been the one to walk away.

Emma sank down on the bench, oblivious to the riot of flowers, the buzz of long dormant bees. She'd carefully constructed a life that wouldn't ever open her up to the kind of pain she'd known when her mother left. She'd chosen men for their steadiness, their lack of threat to her independence and her heart. She'd quashed desires and behaviors in herself that she deemed too much like her mother.

Yet Nikolai had revived them. The thrill of being on the back of his motorcycle had reawakened her sense of adventure. Exploring his naked body had sparked a physical craving for pleasure, one she'd never known before. Those intimate late night conversations that had laid her bare...

He'd used it all against her. He'd fulfilled her two biggest fears, confirming that he had the ability to hurt her like no other and drawing parallels between her and the woman who had broken her family. Nikolai Vulkov was the bad guy.

Unbidden, a hundred memories of his heart, his kindness, his creative genius swamped her. But she fought them off. It had to be him. She needed him to be wrong. It couldn't be her.

Her sisters would tell her. They would back her up. He was all wrong for her, always pushing her to be someone she wasn't. Always taking her past her comfort zone.

She turned back to the brewery. She was right. She needed to be right or else she'd just made the most unforgiveable mistake of all.

EMMA SHOVED through Gia's front door, nearly tripping over the dancing Diesel. Beckett was jogging down the stairs with his brother's twins, one under each arm. Jonathan giggled with delight. Aurora was hot on Beckett's heels, peppering him with questions.

"Two nights of babysitting," he muttered under his breath. He glared at her. "This is all your fault, Emma. I blame you."

"Ah, the bet. Well, it didn't last so maybe you can weasel out of the second night?" Emma said morosely.

He headed down the hall toward the kitchen, and Emma followed him.

"Evan!" Beckett shouted for his stepson and pushed open the kitchen door with his foot.

From the hallway, Emma could see Evan sitting at the island, enjoying a popsicle and some peace and quiet.

"I will give you $20 to take these two outside and play with them in the backyard for half an hour."

"Deal."

"You have to keep them alive, and don't let them eat too much dirt or too many bugs."

"On it," Evan agreed.

Emma heard Gia giggle, and Beckett set both twins on the floor and pointed in his wife's direction. "No laughing. I blame you for making the bet in the first place. I need half an hour to finish this deposition. They're all yours until then." He stormed back down the hallway muttering under his breath.

Emma poked her head into the kitchen and stumbled when she spotted Eva sitting at the breakfast nook table across from Gia.

"You're back?" Emma asked.

"Damn it! You ruined the surprise," Gia groaned.

"Surprise. I'm moving here," Eva said with a wry smile. "Now what the hell's going on with you and Niko? I hear from a reliable source that you had a fight."

Emma ignored her sister's question in favor of her own. "You're moving to Blue Moon? Permanently?"

"I didn't want to be the only Merill living hundreds of miles away. I can do my job from anywhere. So I thought why not here?"

Sensing Emma's mood, Gia nudged Aurora out the back door to play with Evan and the twins in the yard.

"You look like you just accidentally murdered your best friend. I take it you and Niko didn't make up," Gia said.

Emma shocked herself and her sisters by bursting into tears.

"Oh shit. Oh my, God. What happened? I thought it was just a fight?" Gia rushed to her side.

"Niko." It was the only word Emma could get out.

"What did he do? Did he get you pregnant? Cheat on you? Call you a crazy bitch?" Eva bombarded her with possibilities.

"Worse," Emma sniffled, regaining some semblance of

control. "So much worse. He said he loved me and got mad and said all these horrible things when I told him I didn't love him, didn't want to be with him."

She wasn't too hysterical to miss the long look that passed between her sisters.

"What?" she demanded.

"Why don't we sit down, and you can start from the beginning," Gia suggested. "I'll make us some tea."

So Emma sat and sipped her tea and told them everything. And when she finished, she still didn't feel unburdened. If anything, it all sat heavier.

"He just didn't want to understand that he's not the kind of man I want to spend my life with," she said, wrapping her hands around the sturdy mug, hoping the warmth would seep into her body.

Eva and Gia shared another look.

"If you two don't stop with the mental telepathy thing and spill, I'm going to add you to the list of people who have really pissed me off today."

Gia interlaced her fingers on the table. "Do you want some well-meaning honesty or only sisterly support right now?"

"Why can't I have both?" Emma demanded.

"Because you're wrong." Eva picked up her mug and took a nonchalant sip.

"You can't be serious." Emma shook her head. "You know me. You know what I want in life, what I've always wanted. A stable partnership. Not some womanizing bad boy that thinks every day is a ridiculous excuse for ignoring responsibilities."

"I've known you my entire life," Gia began. "And I've never seen you happier than these past few weeks. What makes you think you don't love Niko?"

Emma's jaw strained under the pressure to keep it tight. "Ugh!" she groaned. "Fine. Okay. I do love him." She loved him so much it hurt her to breathe. "He snuck up on me with the whole 'we're friends' thing. But that doesn't mean that love is enough of a foundation for a life together."

"Love is the foundation of everything, dumbass," Gia snorted in very un-yoga-teacher-like fashion.

"What is it about him that scares the crap out of you so badly?" Eva asked.

"What *doesn't* scare the crap out of me? He's this restless artistic type who has had so many women that I don't think he even knows what number I am. He's never committed before. Why would he commit now? Why would he want to? I'm not some millionaire super model. I run a brewery."

"That's bullshit," Gia said cheerfully. "And I'm not even going to dignify that with a rebuttal because you know it's bullshit. Niko loves you. A blind idiot with no sense of romance could see that. So stop with the 'woe is me, I'm not a six-foot-tall model crap.'"

"Be careful," Eva warned Emma. "You're going to piss her off, and she's going to take us out to the shed to punch us instead of the heavy bag."

"I *am* getting pissed because you are purposely turning your back on a wonderful man who loves you just because he doesn't fit your unrealistic control freak goals."

"Oh, so you think I have control issues, too?" Emma demanded.

"Yes!" her sisters shouted back.

"What's with all the yelling? Did Aurora try to make an indoor Slip 'n Slide again?" Beckett, looking slightly more relaxed, pushed through the swinging door, took one look at their faces, and turned back around. "Call me if you need help with a body."

"See!" Emma gestured toward where Beckett had been. "That's what I want."

"You can't have my husband, you weirdo," Gia announced firmly.

"Not your husband specifically. But someone steady and stable like Beckett. You know he's always going to want to be here."

Gia blinked. "I'm sorry, did I not tell you about the time he broke up with me because he thought that I should remarry Paul?" Her voice was entering dog whistle range.

"That was a misunderstanding," Emma argued. "He thought he was doing the right thing for your family."

"He thought me being with the man who was incapable of providing any emotional, physical, or financial support for my family was the right thing. And now I'm getting mad about it all over again, and he's going to have to apologize again," she yelled toward the closed kitchen door.

"I'm going to the flower shop and taking the kids," Beckett yelled back.

"Bring back pizza," Gia shouted after him. They heard the front door slam behind him, and she smiled smugly. "My point is, my darling husband was an idiot, but I was magnanimous enough to forgive him. But you, sister dear," she said pointing at Emma. "You're the idiot in this situation."

"There is nothing wrong with prioritizing stability—"

"Okay, let's just cut to the chase here," Eva suggested. "We think you make all your life's decisions around keeping yourself safe so you don't feel the pain and abandonment you felt when Mom left."

Niko had held the same theory, and she'd eviscerated him over it.

"Do you honestly believe that?" Emma asked.

"Yes!" Eva and Gia answered together.

Emma crossed her arms, shook her head. "I still don't see what's wrong with that. Mom leaving was devastating to our family, and I think it's smart to make sure I'm never in the position to give someone that power again. Nikolai is too much like Mom. He's never given the future more than a passing thought. He's always looking for the next exciting thing, the next beautiful woman, the next assignment. There's no long-term plan there. He wouldn't want to live here. We're all finally in the same place at the same time, and you want me to just pack it all in and follow this guy to New York?"

"Relationships are about compromise—" Eva began, but Emma cut her off.

"No, they're about figuring out exactly what you want in life and then finding someone who fits those goals."

Gia's laughter bordered on hysterical. "Oh, my God. Can't breathe."

Eventually she regained control. "I get why you feel that way. I totally do," Gia told her. "But the problem is, even though you say you want stable and safe, you still walked away from Mason. You didn't want him so you didn't even give him the option to follow you here. You made the decision for both of you, and you walked away."

"Just like Mom," Eva added.

There was no blame in her tone, no anger. Just the cold, hard truth.

"And now you're walking away from Niko because your feelings for him scare you. No, he's not what you thought you wanted. But he is what you want, and you walked away." Gia glanced at Eva who nodded at her. "Just like Mom."

Shit. Shit. Shit. Shit.

"Why aren't you two carting around baggage over Mom?" Emma asked quietly.

"Our baggage is just smaller," Eva insisted.

"Because we had you," Gia said, reaching across the table to squeeze her hand.

"Mom may have walked out on us, but you stepped up for us," Eva nodded, reaching for Emma's other hand. "You did my hair for prom."

"You bought me condoms when I told you I was thinking about having sex with Billy McBride," Gia added. "You didn't say 'I told you so' when Paul and I got divorced. You just showed up on my doorstep and helped me pack."

"You used your own money to buy us presents that first Christmas Mom was gone," Eva remembered. "You took a thousand pictures of my college graduation."

Emma felt tears prick her eyes again, though these were of a different kind. "Oh, my God. This place is turning me into a sobbing lunatic," she lamented. "I never used to cry before I moved here."

"You stepped up as the mom we deserved," Gia said softly. "And it kills us to see you push something real and beautiful away just because it makes you feel."

"Fuck."

Gia and Eva nodded in agreement.

She did the walking away so she wouldn't get hurt. It wasn't any better than what her mother had done, walking away because she got bored.

35

*E*mma sat at her kitchen island morosely stirring the oatmeal she'd made for herself after realizing she'd missed lunch... and dinner. After a very long day of mental torture, she was no closer to making peace with her decision. Niko's words, Phoebe's, her sisters', all crowded into her head bringing with them a very large dose of doubt.

Had she made the mistake that everyone else thought she had? Emma worried.

She almost ignored the knock at her door. She didn't want to see anyone, didn't want to put on a brave face or listen to yet another person tell her that her coping mechanisms made her a coward.

However, her front door had enough glass in it that whoever was knocking had probably already seen her pouting into her bowl. She heaved a defeated sigh and shuffled to the door.

At least she could be certain it wasn't Nikolai on her doorstep.

She was, however, completely unprepared for the man she did find there. Tall and slim, his blond hair was neatly combed in the style he'd worn since junior high. He stood in his green golf shirt with his hands in the pockets of his khaki shorts.

"Mason?"

He rounded his shoulders. "Hey, Emma. I was just in the neighborhood."

She hadn't seen him in a year and wondered how it was possible to feel like she was meeting both a stranger and a ghost from her past. "What are you doing here?" She was gaping at him and didn't know how to stop.

He shifted his weight from foot to foot. "Do you mind if I come in?"

Still dumbfounded, Emma opened the door wider. "Of course, I'm sorry. I'm just... surprised."

Mason walked past her. Hands still in his pockets he surveyed her living space. "Quite the change from your place in L.A.," he ventured.

Emma mustered a soft laugh. "That's an understatement."

"It seems like a nice town, though," Mason continued.

"Can I get you something to drink? Coffee? Water? Wine?" *Perhaps an entire bottle of liquor?*

"Water would be great."

Right, no caffeine after six, Emma remembered. It had been his steadiness, his sense of responsibility that had attracted her to him. He made plans. He followed through. Dating him had been a relief. If he said he made reservations, he had. If he promised to call, he would.

Emma filled a glass with ice and, remembering his preference, added a sliver of lemon.

"Thanks," he said, accepting the glass and drinking deeply.

He looked nervous.

"I'm sure you're wondering why I'm here," he began.

"Very curious."

Mason cleared his throat, his brown eyes darting around the room. "I've been thinking that we may have made a mistake when we ended things last year."

Emma, fearing that her knees might give out, sank down on the couch. "What kind of a mistake?"

Mason sat on the opposite end of the couch. "We had a good, solid relationship, and I wonder if letting a move end things for us wasn't the right choice."

"I'm not considering a move back to the West Coast," Emma said gently.

"No, of course not. Your family is here," Mason shook his head. "I was thinking I could move here, live here, and we could—" he cleared his throat again. "I thought we could get married."

Emma wasn't completely clear on what happened, but Mason was suddenly leaning in and staring hard into her eyes.

"Are you okay?" he asked.

"Uh, yeah. Fine. Sure."

"Because you haven't spoken or blinked for a full minute." He glanced at his watch to verify. "Closer to two minutes."

"Uh. Fine. Yeah."

"I'm sorry for springing this on you. You have no idea how sorry," he said under his breath. "But it was something that needed to be said. Something that needed to be put on the table."

"You think we should get married?"

"Emma, you're an amazing woman, and any man would be lucky to have you."

"What about your job? You're a partner with the firm."

"I could start my own practice. People in Blue Moon pay taxes, right?"

"Probably some of them, but I wouldn't put all my eggs in that basket."

"Well, that's something I could figure out. I'd move here, and you could stay with your family and keep your job. We could live here if you want." He glanced around the cottage's living space and drained the rest of the glass.

"What brought this on?" Emma asked, still feeling as if she'd been blindsided by a steamroller.

"Like I said, it was something that needed to be put on the table." He put his empty glass on the coffee table and rose. "Okay, so I'm going to go."

Emma stared up at him. "You just proposed, and you're going to leave now?"

"You like to think things over. I wouldn't expect you to just jump into something. It's a lot to consider."

Mouth still agape, Emma nodded. She walked him to the door and considered the possibility that she was asleep and dreaming all this. It seemed more likely than her ex-boyfriend flying across the country to propose a year after their break up.

He turned in the doorway. "You have my number if you want to talk."

She nodded, mutely.

He scratched at the back of his neck. "Okay, well. It was good to see you, Emma. You look great."

"Thanks, Mason. You too…"

And then he was disappearing across the lawn.

EMMA WOKE Sunday morning on her couch after a fitful night of mental debates. She'd nearly worn a trench in her bedroom rug from pacing and trying to understand all that had transpired in the past twenty-four hours.

Nikolai had told her he loved her. She panicked and ended

their relationship because she didn't see how they could make it work. Mason showed up out of the blue and proposed. Oh, and everyone she cared about told her she was a scaredy cat who ran when things got complicated.

That about summed it up.

She'd mapped it out from every angle, weighed the pros and cons, and finally come to the realization that she had only one option. She had to grovel.

Niko was right. She'd lived her entire life trying to protect herself from the pain of abandonment, and in doing so, she had been the one to walk away again and again. *The walking stops here*, she vowed. Today she would run.

She'd run to Niko's arms and beg for forgiveness.

And after she groveled and begged and threw herself on Niko's mercy, then she would find Mason, thank him for his kind offer, and turn him down. She'd known the moment she'd seen him on her porch that it was Nikolai Vulkov that she loved. There had been a time in her life when "safe" felt happy. But that time had passed, and she wanted more, so much more.

The June sun was warm on her face as it shown through her windshield. She pulled into the farm's driveway, praying that he hadn't packed up and left town last night. But a quick scan of the garage and barn showed the place was deserted. Niko's bike was missing, too.

Shit. Well, if she had to drive to New York to say her piece, she would.

Emma smacked herself in the forehead. Sunday. Farmers market day. "Please be there," she whispered as she turned around and sped out of the driveway, a cloud of dust kicking up behind her.

She kept chanting the whole way into town, not letting up until she parked on a side street and jumped out of the car. It was then that she realized she was still wearing blue plaid pajama pants. But that couldn't be helped now, and she wasn't turning around to go home and change.

Emma jogged the rest of the way to One Love Park where the farmers market was in full swing. The colorful canopies created a rainbow above homemade soaps and soups, hand woven socks, and fresh funnel cakes. The free-range petting zoo which consisted of farm animals milling about the park was, as anticipated, a wonderful disaster.

People called out greetings to her, but she was on a mission. He *had* to be here. She had to find him. It couldn't be too late.

Through her watery vision, Emma spotted him. And the relief cut through her like an axe. Her entire body sang. Niko was crouched down, taking pictures of Aurora who was cuddling a struggling chicken that looked like it wished it could return to its free-range life. Ellery, decked out in her Frankenstein shoes and glitter skull t-shirt, stood nearby gnawing on her black fingernails and checking her watch.

"Nikolai!" Emma waved.

He glanced up from the screen of the camera he held, a frown of concentration on his face. When he saw her, something that looked like hope lit his eyes before he carefully put it away, returning his beautiful face to the impassive mask.

She was running now, looking like a hysterical idiot in her pajamas. She knew someone would be live streaming her breakdown to the Blue Moon Facebook group and didn't care.

She was long overdue for putting herself out there, heart and humiliation be damned.

"I'm sorry. I'm so sorry," she gasped the words out. She gripped his forearms with her hands, determined to keep him here. She needed him to hear every terrifying word. "I was so wrong," she began, her voice breaking a little.

"Mama, what's happening?" Aurora hissed at Gia. Her sister held up a finger to her lips to shush the little girl.

"I spent my entire life trying to protect myself from hurt. I thought I wanted safe and stable and boring," she let out a short laugh. "But in protecting myself from hurt, I ended up locking myself away from life... and love."

Nikolai swallowed hard but said nothing.

"You saw me," she whispered. "*Really* saw me. And you loved me, not just for the role I played but for the woman I am underneath all my fears, all my needs. You saw that hot mess clinging futilely to control, and you still wanted me."

"So what are you saying?" he asked softly. She heard it, that slight hint of Russia woven into his words.

"I'm saying I love you, Nikolai. I want a life with you, whatever that may look like. I want to live a life of adventure with you. I want to be scared about losing you. I want to wake up sweating because you're draped over me every damn morning. I want to be late to work because we got carried away. I'll follow you anywhere as long as you promise to follow me, too."

Nikolai looked down at the camera in his hands. He pulled away from her grip, and Emma felt the first punch of fear. But he handed the camera to Aurora.

"Kid, I'm going to want some good pictures of this, okay?"

Aurora nodded solemnly when he looped the strap over her head. "That button right there. Got it?"

"Oh, God, please don't break that, Roar," Gia whispered under her breath.

Nikolai straightened and took Emma's hands. Her heart sang with hope, with love, with all of the feelings she'd ignored for so long.

"What made you change your mind?"

"Someone proposed to me and offered to let me make all the decisions in life from here on out."

"You're *engaged*?" There was fight in those beautiful dark eyes of his.

"Shit. Shit. Shit." Emma heard Ellery chanting softly as she swiped her hands over her pale face, dislodging her heart shaped sunglasses.

Emma shook her head and laughed. "No! He offered me everything I thought I wanted, except..."

Nikolai squeezed her hands. "Except what?" he demanded, his voice rough with emotion.

"Except you. He wasn't you. I can have everything I thought I wanted in life, and it won't be enough. It won't even scratch the surface because what I really want is you."

He was reeling her into him. His hands skimmed her hips, pulling her against him. "So you're not engaged?" he clarified.

She shook her head. "Nope."

Ellery bent from the waist and exhaled sharply. "Thank freaking God!"

Emma pointed at her. "I'm going to finish this first, but then you're going to tell me why you're watching this like a live-action soap opera."

Ellery flashed a guilty smile and gave a little curtsy. "Carry on."

Emma turned back to Nikolai and continued. "I don't want to be just friends. If you're interested in a full confession, I doubt I ever did. From day one, you've fascinated me, and I couldn't wait to spend time with you every single day."

"Then what *do* you want?" Nikolai asked, tracing his fingertips over her tear-stained cheek.

She closed her eyes and leaned into his touch. "I want to choose you every damn day. Even when it's hard. Even if one of us wants to give up. I want to fight and win and love you. I want to do this every day for the rest of my life." Emma brought her lips to his, sealing her words with a physical promise. His mouth heated under hers, stealing her breath and tasting the salt of her tears. She knew she was where she belonged.

He pulled back just the slightest bit, and she fought for her breath. "Say the words, Emma," he demanded.

She brought her hands to his impossibly beautiful face. "I love you, Nikolai. I love the havoc you're going to wreak on my life."

"*Our* life," he corrected.

"So, you still love me?" she worried her lower lip between her teeth. She needed the words from him.

"Emma, I have a confession to make." His voice was low, serious. "It might change how you feel."

She took a breath and then another one. She wasn't running. Not this time. "Okay. What is it?"

"I took one look at you yelling at a vendor on the phone and went into free-fall. I was never going to let you friend zone me, and I sure as hell wasn't going to let you run away from me."

"Sneaky bastard," Emma murmured. "I love your diabolical nature."

"And I love every damn thing about you, Emmaline."

"Even my crazy?"

"Even your crazy," he confirmed.

"Thanks for not giving up on me," she said, raising up on her tip toes for another kiss.

"Thanks for not making me regret this next thing."

"What next thing?" Emma asked, suddenly nervous again.

"Remember how you hate grand gestures that should have been joint decisions in the first place?"

"Oh, hell, Niko. What did you do?"

THE HOUSE that had teased at the back of her mind, the one she'd seen herself making breakfast in, spending lazy mornings in, had a bright red sold sticker slapped over the for sale sign.

First came the bitter tinge of disappointment that someone else had had the guts to go after her dream. Then came the dawning of realization.

"You *bought* it? But we just made up!"

Niko pulled a key ring from his pocket and handed it over.

"Keys?"

"These are yours. I told you I would fight for you."

"I broke up with you," Emma gawked at him. "What was your plan?"

"I witnessed something amazing yesterday afternoon, something that I want to be a part of, something that you're already a part of. So I decided that I'd buy your dream house here and torture you with my presence for the next year or so before I wore you down again. I'd show up at dinner every Saturday night, run into you at the gym, you know, the original plan."

"You really do love me."

"It's about time that starts to sink in."

She stared at the keys and back at the house. "I can't believe you'd do this for me. The things I said to you—"

"And the things I said to you. Let's just see if we can handle our disagreements a little more maturely in the future."

"You don't think they'll all be that bad, do you?"

"Us? No. Of course not," he said, giving her that devil's smile and pulling her into his arms.

"You're totally lying right now, aren't you?"

"Maybe."

"Probably."

"It'll be an adventure," he predicted.

"And not just in the bedroom," she said with a wink.

Niko scooped her up and she laughed. "Let's go check out our new home."

"You're supposed to do this to the bride," Emma said, looping her arms around his neck.

He bounded up the front steps of the porch. "Oh, we're getting married."

"Is that your idea of a proposal?"

"What? Are you expecting a puppy?"

"I was at least expecting the question!"

He slid the key in the lock and pushed open the front door. "Why? So you can agonize over it for weeks on end torturing both of us when you know there's only one answer? I think it's easier to just tell you we're getting married. Now, you can just get used to the idea."

Emma slapped his chest. "Nikolai, getting married is a big decision," she argued. "One that we both should be part of!"

The little yip of delight took her by surprise, and when she spotted the ball of yellow fur tumbling over giant feet toward them she gasped. "Oh, my God!"

"Yeah, well, so is getting a house and a dog," Niko shrugged.

EPILOGUE

"Surprise!"

The shout took Emma by surprise and had her sweeping Baxter up in her arms before he could pee excitedly all over the brewery floor.

There were people and balloons everywhere. Her team from the brewery, her family, the Pierces, it looked like half the town was here crowding around the bar.

"What is going on?" Emma asked, handing Baxter over to Niko.

"Happy anniversary," Julio announced with a debonair bow.

Cheryl looped her arm through Emma's. "One year ago today, you stepped up to lead our team. And look what's happened in that year." Cheryl held up Emma's left hand letting the emerald cut diamond catch the light.

The crowd hooted. Jax handed her a glass of champagne. Joey wielding a knife, stood guard over a sheet cake decorated like the brewery and its surrounding pastures. Emma's father was holding Lydia cozied up on a barstool with Phoebe, Gia, and Eva. Carter and Beckett stood side-by-side discussing the proper application of beard balm while Summer chased the twins.

"If I could have everyone's attention," Jax said. The crowd quieted. "Not so very long ago, my brothers and I were running ourselves ragged trying to get and keep the doors of John Pierce Brews open. And then along came Emma Merill, who replaced the three of us with style, with class, and with abilities that far outweighed our own. You saved us Emma, and we'll be eternally grateful to you. To Emma." He raised his glass.

"To Emma," the crowd echoed. Under Caleb's watchful eyes, Joey attacked the cake with a knife and a lot of enthusiasm.

She felt the tears threaten to spill and blinked them back. She'd already gotten into a screaming match with her lover at work once. She drew the line at crying in front of her team. "Did you know about this?" Emma demanded, poking Niko in the chest.

"Baby, there are no secrets in Blue Moon." The puppy wriggled around so he could lick Niko's chin, and Emma's heart exploded just a little bit.

She laughed, well aware that Niko was right. The public spectacle she'd made of herself last week at the farmers market was still the hot topic around town and had indeed been live-streamed in the Blue Moon gossip group on Facebook. The Beautification Committee had immediately claimed victory and offered Emma and Niko best wishes for their "long and happy life together."

Summer and Phoebe bustled up and grabbed her arms. "Girl talk," Summer said, winking at Niko. "Go find the boys and the beers," she suggested.

They dragged her to the bar where Gia, Eva, and Ellery waited.

"So now that you've had all of five seconds to settle into your new future," Summer began, "what have you two decided?"

Emma couldn't stop the smile if she wanted to. It was the kind of happiness she'd never known could come from just letting go. "Well, I spoke to your husbands, and they've agreed to let me work four days a week. So we'll be dividing our time between here and the city. Niko's planning to be more selective about his projects because he wants to free up more of his time to be here. So far, no definitive wedding plans, but we do know where we're going for our honeymoon."

"Where is that, dear?" Phoebe asked.

"Paris."

Joey walked up with cake in hand when Summer and Gia squealed. She rolled her eyes and walked away.

"Don't get yourselves all worked up. Nothing's written in stone. We're just going to enjoy ourselves for a while," Emma cautioned.

"Who are you, and what have you done with my sister?" Eva demanded.

"It's Blue Moon. There's something in the water here. You might start noticing it soon," Ellery said innocently.

"More like something in the Beautification Committee," Emma said, poking a finger in Ellery's shoulder. "Now can you explain how Mason showed up on my doorstep?" Emma demanded. "And why I think I saw him going into Righteous Subs yesterday?"

Ellery's grin was contagious. "A brilliant, if perhaps dangerous, ploy to get you to finally realize what you really wanted in life." She sighed with satisfaction. "It was my finest work yet."

"How, Ellery? How did you get my ex-boyfriend to fly cross-country and ask me to marry him?"

"Well, I knew you were going to be a problem what with all the abandonment issues and the long-term habit of running away. So first, we decided to make it sticky here."

"Sticky?"

"Yeah, make you love Blue Moon, love working and living here. Love being around your family. That was our subtle background work, which I'm guessing you didn't even notice since it's been going on the entire time you've lived here."

"You mean Gordon and Anthony shoving Bruce's real estate license down my throat was all part of the ploy?"

Ellery took a long sip of her diet soda through a pink curly straw. "It's like I always say, we can't keep pulling the same tricks. We have to evolve with the times. We saw the sparks flying between you two immediately and knew the hard part would be convincing both you and Niko separately that Blue Moon was the wonderful capital of the world. So we focused our efforts there."

"So you didn't think we were a terrible couple?" Emma pressed.

Ellery rolled her eyes. "Are you crazy? One look at you guys, and everyone knew!"

"Where does Mason fit in to all of this?" Gia asked in fascination and horror.

"Well, I knew we were still going to run into some old habit issues with you. So I started messaging Mason on Facebook. Super nice guy, by the way." A dimple appeared in Ellery's cheek.

"I know. I dated him."

"Anyway, once I discerned that he wasn't an insane person, we kept chatting, and I let him kinda sorta think that we were a dating service you'd hired."

"Oh, my God."

"Mason being the super nice, sweet guy that he is was

happy to help if it was necessary. So I kept him as an ace up my sleeve just in case you were extra tricky. Which you were!"

"Yeah, yeah. Extra tricky."

"When I witnessed your catastrophic fight with Niko at the brewery, I knew it was time for the ace. So I messaged Mason, and it turns out he was visiting family in Buffalo of all places."

"So you talked him into driving out here and proposing to me?"

"Like I said, super nice guy. He cares about your happiness, even though you dumped him. That says a lot about a man."

"I can't believe you convinced him to come here and take part in this ridiculous, over-the-top, insane scheme! No wonder why he looked so relieved when I told him no the next day. What would you have done if I had said yes?" Emma asked.

"Crapped my pants and then locked Mason in my basement, making his disappearance look like he abandoned you," Ellery said with a thoughtful frown.

Emma blinked slowly. "You're insane."

Ellery shook her head. "I'm committed to love. There's a huge difference."

"Okay, I can tell when an argument is going to go nowhere. So I'll just say thank you for whatever bizarre role you played in getting me out of my own way."

Ellery leaned in and surprised Emma with a kiss on her cheek. "You're very welcome. Now, about Mason. How big of a deal would it be if I asked him out?"

～

EMMA RESTED her head on Niko's bare chest, admiring the engagement ring he'd chosen for her. She stretched languidly.

"I don't know about you, but I think we keep getting better and better together."

Niko's soft laugh rumbled in his chest under her ear. "We have to dedicate ourselves to practice," he said, running his fingertips down her arm. "Hone our craft."

The bedroom door rattled against the frame, and Baxter let out a mournful whimper on the other side.

Niko sighed and climbed out of bed. Emma admired his fine naked form as he crossed to the door and scooped up the puppy.

Man and dog returned to the bed.

"Is it going to be a problem for you if my ex-boyfriend moves here to open an accounting practice and starts dating Ellery?" Emma asked, propping herself up on an elbow.

"Not if it won't be a problem for you if my Dad, Greta, and the rest of them come out for the weekend. Apparently, they're into this whole family thing and think they should come celebrate the engagement and new house and puppy."

Emma laughed. "I think that sounds great."

Niko dragged her over him. "I think so, too."

She traced a finger over his mouth. "You look happy, Niko."

"I don't have the words for how happy you've made me, Emmaline. But I think I can show you." His hands skimmed over her back to cup the curves of her ass.

"Niko," she sighed his name and took his lips. This was love. This was the foundation of something real and beautiful. This was the beginning of a lifetime.

AUTHOR'S NOTE TO THE READER

Dear Reader,

Well there you have Niko and Emma and the sneaky, manipulative, nosy Beautification Committee. The more Blue Moon books I write, the more clearly I see the town in my head and the more convinced I am that it exists somewhere. If you find it, please send me GPS directions.

I grew up in a small town and I love writing the dynamics of places that are one big extended family.

Favorite scene: Phoebe's bachelorette party. The bitchen. Also, the fight scene when Niko throws it out there that Emma is running away just like her mom did. Ouch! Oh, and the house/puppy proposal. Okay, basically the whole book.

I'm sure you can predict the next match up in Blue Moon. Emma's sister Eva just moved to town and Sheriff Cardona, when he's not handcuffing unfortunate strippers, has his eye on her. But there's a lot about Eva that no one knows.

If you enjoyed *Not Part of the Plan*, I'd love to hear about it. Drop me a line or leave a review! Sign up for my newsletter for bonus content and witty one-sided banter about new releases from me. If you'd like to stay in touch with me and feed me ideas for stories, visit me on Facebook and Instagram.

Thank you for reading!

Xoxo,
   Lucy

ABOUT THE AUTHOR

Lucy Score is a *Wall Street Journal* and #1 Amazon bestselling author. She grew up in a literary family who insisted that the dinner table was for reading and earned a degree in journalism. She writes full-time from the Pennsylvania home she and Mr. Lucy share with their obnoxious cat, Cleo. When not spending hours crafting heartbreaker heroes and kick-ass heroines, Lucy can be found on the couch, in the kitchen, or at the gym. She hopes to someday write from a sailboat, or oceanfront condo, or tropical island with reliable Wi-Fi.

Sign up for her newsletter and stay up on all the latest Lucy book news.
And follow her on:
Website: Lucyscore.com
Facebook at: lucyscorewrites
Instagram at: scorelucy
Readers Group at: Lucy Score's Binge Readers Anonymous

ACKNOWLEDGMENTS

Thank you to Dawn, Amanda, and Mr. Lucy for your pre-reader eyeballs.

Kari March Designs for the beautiful cover.

And a special shout out to Filthy Blue Cheese Olives and Dirty Sue Olive Juice for aiding my writing through truly excellent dirty martinis.

LUCY'S TITLES

Standalone Titles

Undercover Love

Pretend You're Mine

Finally Mine

Protecting What's Mine

Mr. Fixer Upper

The Christmas Fix

Heart of Hope

The Worst Best Man

Rock Bottom Girl

The Price of Scandal

By a Thread

Forever Never

Things We Never Got Over

Riley Thorn

Riley Thorn and the Dead Guy Next Door

Riley Thorn and the Corpse in the Closet

Riley Thorn and the Blast from the Past

The Blue Moon Small Town Romance Series

No More Secrets

Fall into Temptation

The Last Second Chance

Not Part of the Plan

Printed in the USA
CPSIA information can be obtained
at www.ICGtesting.com
LVHW042359131024
793725LV00024B/298

9 781728 282657